What didn't you do to bury me?
but you forgot that I was a seed

-Dinos Christianopoulos

ACES AND EIGHTS

ACES HIGH, JOKERS WILD BOOK 4

O. E. TEARMANN

ACES AND EIGHTS

Amphibian Press
P. O. Box 190
West Peterborough NH
03468

www. amphibianpress.online
www. aceshighjokerswild. com

Printed in the United States of America

ISBN: 978-1-949693-60-7

Reader Advisement

This book contains romantic and sexual scenes between people whose genders may not fit your expectations. If this offends you, consider yourself warned.

Everyone else, buckle up for the ride.

Event File 1
File Tag: Celebratory Occasion
Timestamp: 16:00-2-1-2157

"Hey birthday boy! Catch!"

The box sailed through the air. Kevin reached out to catch it reflexively as it sailed down the hall, and yelped as Blake smacked his rear. He should have known.

"Twenty one!" the finance officer exclaimed with relish. Kevin raised his eyes to heaven. "Blake," he began patiently, "you know I have a great deal of admiration for your skills; bear that in mind when I tell you that this 'birthday smacks' thing was a bloody *stupid* game when I was seventeen, and by the time I've hit twenty seven it's become more than a little egregious, not to mention utterly beneath my dignity and yours, and—ow!"

"Twenty two!" Sarah crowed behind him. Kevin sighed and, pointedly, put his back against the corridor wall.

"I hate you. Both. With a deep and abiding passion."

Sarah cocked her head, grinning. "Open your present and then say that."

Kevin eyed her as he undid the tape on the box. "If this is some indelicate gag gift, I'll have you know that I will not be amused, in fact I will be...oh...wow..."

With a grin, Kevin lifted out the t-shirt. The image printed on the fabric showed an ancient music distribution device, its magnetic tape spooling out artistically around the words 'Life is a Mix Tape'. Kevin laughed at the words. "A Rob Sheffield quote! Stupendous! Alright, maybe my hatred has been somewhat ameliorated." Stepping forward, he bowed his head and gave Sarah a peck on the brow. "Thanks, this rocks."

"Tell Aidan I made it to match," Sarah acknowledged with a grin.

"Hey! Don't squeal!" Tweak's high voice snapped as she opened the door of Aidan's office behind him. Kevin turned to give her a weary smile. "Thanks for the assist, Tweak, these plebes are—"

A sting across his rear was paired with Sarah's crow of, "twenty three!" Kevin sighed. "Sarah," he remarked in his best teacher-is-displeased tone, "I understand that you are proudly bisexual, but you do not, in fact, need to prove it by taking swipes at my ass. *You* may be bisexual, but I'm *not*, and I'm not impressed. Are we clear?"

"What are we doing that involves Kev's ass? Do I want to know?" Aidan asked, looking out into the hall with preoccupied eyes.

"Aidan, love, save me from the depredations of the mob!" Kevin threw out, putting on a vid-worthy show by pressing a hand to his heart. That got him a medley of chuckles from his boyfriend and his family. Aidan shook his head a little, lips quirked at the corners. "Okay guys, enough until dinner. I need Kev focused for talking through a mission plan. Go do your jobs."

"I *suppose* we'll let you have him for *now,*" Blake harrumphed, arms folded over his pot belly, "only *don't* be late for dinner, you hear me, you lovebirds? We're not letting Kevin duck out on a decent party *again* this year."

"Define 'decent'," Kevin countered. Tweak snickered as she sidestepped out of her commander's office. Crossing her arms, she looked up at Kevin. "My present. On your tab," she chirped. "Later. Not now. Take a 1-look. Try twenty three. Have fun!" Then she was off down the hall, her ridiculously oversized combat boots clattering on the prefab floor panels.

Kevin blinked, shaking his head as he stepped into Aidan's office. "You know, I've tried to requisition Tweak new boots three times this year. She won't give up those gun ships she's wearing. Any idea what that crack about a present references?" he asked, glancing dubiously over his shoulder as he took a seat. "Or do I want to know?"

Aidan shook his head, but he bit his lip in a gesture Kevin had come to know: the man was trying not to grin.

"No idea," his boyfriend managed, choking on a laugh, "though she did say she's got the bugs out of our systems. Eagle's pairing with Techo to send out a ton of virus shit aimed at Force systems."

"I heard," Kevin agreed absently, glancing back the way Tweak had gone. "The GreyNet's started getting restricted too, which is inconvenient on requisition runs. And that's not to mention the damn 'independent contractors' sniffing around our routes and our online communications, like the mangy scavengers they are." Turning, he eyed Aidan over the rims of his glasses. "Aidan, love. In all honesty, this present. Tell me I haven't just gotten pranked. Again."

"It's not a prank," Aidan protested, blue eyes twinkling. "Like she said; it's a birthday present. Though you should probably wait until we're done with work before you open it."

"If it's from her I shudder to think." Kevin replied as he took his seat. "I've already had twenty three 'happy birthday' slaps on the ass today. I'm truly beginning to despise birthdays. So what have we got on this?"

"It's another extraction, for the guys who're getting too much attention from that undercover job assigned to Base 1321. They need an out, ASAP," Aidan explained, pointing at the screen. "It should be simple, but we lost our contact in the garage that I thought we could use to get them into a vehicle under cover, and now I'm kind of staring at this and stuck."

Kevin leaned in. "Lost him, as in..."

"He transferred," Aidan replied. "He was pretty sure his supervisor was getting wise. He's helping out in a new Sector, but now we're screwed."

"Maybe not," Kevin mused as he studied the timetables on the screen, his mind flicking through possibilities. He moved the multicolored boxes of time slots around the screen experimentally. "If we try getting Hansen on this shift, he could walk over to the garage and...hm..."

It took another hour to sort out the difficulties and lay out an extraction plan to get the team from another base out of their undercover operation and off the Grid safely.

Kevin glanced at the clock as he leaned back, satisfied, and shot his boyfriend a sidelong smile. "Prepare yourself, the rampant mob is probably going to come banging on the door asking why we haven't come to the birthday dinner yet."

Aidan gave him one of his quiet, cockeyed smiles. "Guess I better give you this before they get in here."

Reaching under his desk, he tugged out a cardboard box, large enough that he had an awkward moment getting it into his hands. He laid it in Kevin's lap. "See what you think."

Kevin glanced down at it, brows quirking. "Now this is interesting. Where've you been hiding this, love?"

Aidan shrugged, deflecting the question. "This one's not just from me, but the guys decided I should give it to you. Open it?"

Carefully, Kevin unfolded the box's interleaved flaps. What he saw inside made his thoughts stall.

Stupefaction. That would be the right word for this feeling, he decided. Or possibly wonderment. An old word with Middle English and German antecedents, wonderment. It was a good candidate as descriptor for the joyful shock he was experiencing.

Sitting there, in his lap, was an analog music player, ranks of cassette tapes packed neatly all around it. The cassette player gleamed in the room lights, the colors in its petroleum-based plastic surfaces still bright. The stuff lasted so much longer than the agar-based plastics of the modern world. They'd probably be scrounging things from the days when it was used for another hundred years yet. The machine barely looked twenty years old. The chrome dials and trim were cloudy with innumerable small scratches, the patina of age and wear. Some of the brittle plastic cassette cases were spider-webbed with cracks, their plastic yellowing over the brilliant artwork and the fascinating titles.

He raised his eyes to Aidan's in amazement. His boyfriend was smiling like a little boy.

"Where...how...how did you find this?" Kevin managed, the words escaping in a breath of awe.

Aidan shrugged, his face alight. "I told the guys about all those songs that the Corps deleted off American servers after the Incorporation. The ones you talked about wanting to hear sometime? Tweak jumped the firewalls and got on some international collectors' forums under a fake handle, Jim went trading with Fringers. Janice called a buddy she knows. Yvonne ran and picked everything up when people got a lead on it. Topher fixed the player she found. He added new power conduits to it, replaced the old charge cord it had. All I did was give everybody clearance to go for it. So, what do you think?"

For a moment, Kevin was utterly lost for words. With reverent hands, he set the box aside. Then he leaned in and kissed his man long and deep, stroking his hair. "I think I love you," he murmured against Aidan's skin, feeling his amazement and his thankfulness like a cup running over in his chest.

"Later on I'll give you my present," Aidan replied, leaning into his touch.

Kevin laughed in thrilled bewilderment. "This isn't enough?"

"This isn't just from me," Aidan countered, returning the kiss. "Besides, after what you gave me that first birthday of mine we had together? I kind of owe you. So I got ahold of wine and something special."

"That wine sounds fairly special in its own right," Kevin murmured, "How—"

"Traded at Sector on my last trip up," Aidan murmured with another soft kiss. Kevin leaned into his touch.

"Mm. Do you know what the French say about wine?" he asked, tipping his head to breathe the words into Aidan's ear. He loved the little shiver that ran through his man as Aidan replied, "No? Tell me?"

"Quand le vin est tiré, il faut le boire," Kevin murmured, kissing Aidan's throat. "When the wine is drawn, one must drink it. And I think—"

"WHAAZZUUUUUP!"

The multipartite cacophony shattered the air. Kevin fell out of his chair. Scrambling to his knees, he glared up at the sound of laughter. In the doorway, five of their fellow Wildcards leaned against each other, laughing fit to burst.

"Perfect timing! Perfect!" Yvonne gasped out. Kevin sighed. "Yvonne," he remarked wearily, "remind me to hunt you down the next time you're snogging Sarah and make a fool of you, will you?"

"Oh sweetie, it's no fun to get after them, they do it on *any* flat surface." Blake snickered. "*You* two are the only ones who make such a fuss!" Behind him, Jim and Topher laughed like a pair of hyenas.

"You know, the last time I checked the regs, it was polite to knock on your commander's door when you wanted to talk," Aidan interjected mildly.

"Oh knock it off Aidan, workday's over," Sarah declared, leaning against Topher as she caught her breath. "Besides, we knew if the birthday boy wasn't working, he'd be with you somewhere." Stepping into the room, she offered her hand to help Kevin up. "C'mon, we want to celebrate!"

Kevin turned his eyes to the ceiling, mostly for show. "If that be my fate, then I shall resign myself to....oof!" he finished, as Henrietta wormed through the group to land on his chest, hugging him.

"Happy birthday!" The four-year-old giggled.

"Thanks," Kevin managed on a wheeze, "but you're a big girl now. You're too heavy for sitting on my ribs, sweetheart."

Aidan laughed as he reached down to gently lift Henrietta off, passing her back to her father as Sarah yanked Kevin to his feet. "Billie got her thing done, right?" He asked.

"Oh yeah." Jim agreed.

Aidan grinned, taking Kevin's hand. "Great. I don't see him on a sugar high near often enough."

"Sugar?" Kevin asked, bemused. "Oh dear, you lot didn't go about getting a cake together, did you? You know I'm not one for sweets."

"Too bad," Yvonne caroled as she led the parade down the hall, "it's your birthday, you get cake!"

"Blessed Redeemer give me patience," Kevin sighed, but he squeezed Aidan's hand and let the crew sweep him along.

The cake was surprisingly good; Billie hadn't tried to frost it, so it wasn't sickly sweet for once. The thing was the color of dust, but there was just enough cocoa powder in it to lend the flavor of chocolate. The movie that Sarah had dug up for a present wasn't bad either, though Kevin did have to take issue with some of its inaccuracies after the crew had finished their viewing.

"Aw Kev, can't you get off the history books and watch some stuff blow up for once? Come on, you liked it!" Sarah grumbled, shoving at his shoulder.

He shook his head. "I'm not saying it isn't a good movie, guys," he repeated as the credits rolled and his family booed his commentary, "In fact I'm really in love with the fierce conviction and the fortitude of most of the protagonists, and you have to give it this, it's both chillingly prescient and emotionally bolstering. And the roses were a beautiful symbol. It's an absolutely fitting addition to our collection."

"And that means you liked it?" Topher asked, blinking.

"Yes, that's what I said!" Kevin replied in amused exasperation. "That being said, I have to repeat, Guy Fawkes was *not* a freedom fighter. In fact, he was a religious terrorist in his own right. Forcing history to fit your narrative is a stylistic and cultural disservice."

"Aw Kev, you suck," Yvonne groaned.

Kevin smirked, though he felt himself blush as he spoke. "With great precision and consummate skill, yes, yes I do."

Topher covered his ears. Alice choked on her drink, giggling.

At his side, Aidan shared a look with his sister, the siblings giving each other very small smiles.

"Why's your boyfriend trying to take apart a pulp movie and analyze it like it's supposed to make sense?" Naomi asked patiently.

Aidan gave her a shrug. "Because he's my boyfriend," he quipped as he stood. "Okay guys, we have duty tomorrow. Lights out. I'm going to take the birthday boy to bed."

That, of course, got them a chorus of 'oohs'. Kevin flipped the general assembly the bird.

Finally, they made it down the hall and into their own room. Kevin glanced at his new analog music player where it sat on the dresser, grinned, then turned to run his hand over Aidan's soft hair. "So, you were saying something about wine earlier?"

"Mm-hm. Says it's Merlot. Bottle's in the top drawer," Aidan agreed, stepping in to lean against his boyfriend.

Kevin let his arms enfold the shorter man, lips running over Aidan's throat. "Lovely. Merlot isn't exactly a dessert wine, but I don't think I'll complain," he murmured teasingly.

"Sorry I couldn't find candles or anything," Aidan murmured with a gentle smile. "I know you like your sappy stuff."

"I think I've had my fill of sap for one day." Kevin replied, chuckling. "Birthdays ought to be marked, but why in God's name they have to mark my birthday by undermining my dignity I'll never know." Turning, he dug in Aidan's drawer and unearthed the bottle. "Ah, alcohol. Perfect balm for wounded pride."

Aidan laughed as he walked over and dug two plastic tumblers from their nest among his socks. "Got your pocket knife? I think we can get the bottle open that way."

Kevin slipped a hand into his pocket, pulled out the hand-decorated blade he'd kept on him since Aidan had made it as his Christmas present some years ago, and jammed the screwdriver attachment into the cork. With a few judicious wiggles, the cork popped. The scent of soft tannins and rich fruit wafted up.

Aidan held out the glasses with a crooked smile. "So my love isn't enough of a balm for you? I'm so hurt."

"Terribly thin skin you've got, then." Kevin rejoined with a small smile as he filled the glasses, handing Aidan one of them and taking the man's free hand. Sometimes, he had to make a wry joke when Aidan looked earnest like this, just to keep from repeating 'I love you' until he sounded like a fool.

He led his boyfriend to their bed and lay back once Aidan had taken a seat, shifting so that his head lay in Aidan's lap. With studied care, he took a sip of his wine, savoring the treat. "Now this is Merlot." he judged, swirling the dark liquid gently in the glass, before glancing up at Aidan. "Of course, your love might just be enough to ease my soul. Fancy giving me a demonstration of it tonight?"

"After the rest of your present," Aidan chuckled, leaning over for a soft, sweet kiss. His bright hair tickled Kevin's cheeks. "I told you I had something for you. And I thought you might like to read it before we get distracted."

"Mm, you thought wrong." Kevin murmured, raising his free hand to stroke the line of Aidan's jaw. "I've been reading all day. I'm ready to get *distracted*. Thoroughly distracted, in fact."

Aidan turned his head to kiss Kevin's fingers. "Five more minutes. Trust me; you'll like this."

"Make you a deal." Kevin murmured, fingers twining into Aidan's hair. "You read aloud. I'll keep myself amused."

"Sounds good," Aidan agreed. Kevin stroked his skin as the blonde man reached into his pocket, and grimaced. "Crap. My tab's back in my office."

"Use mine," Kevin offered, pulling it out and turning it on. "We can get yours in the...wait...where did this heart icon come from? I didn't put this on here."

Aidan gave a funny sort of laugh, sounding as if he was choking on the sound. Kevin glanced at him. Aidan was grinning shamefacedly. "That's Tweak's present," his boyfriend explained.

Kevin sighed. "Shall I open it or delete it?"

"We'll want to open it." Aidan leaned in, tapping the shortcut. The window popped into view, and Kevin blinked. Then his grey eyes opened wide. Cold panic and hot excitement shot through him. He swallowed, working to quell both. "Aidan...there's a whole lot of naked men on my tab. And I don't think that's anatomically possible..."

Aidan tried and failed to quell snorts of laughter. His voice was strangled with mirth. "She found something called the Kaleb Sutra, published in TechoCo territory out in the Eastern Seaboard Region. What's number twenty-three in there?"

With the terminal bewilderment of someone who'd been smacked between the eyes, Kevin found the page. Both of them stared at the animated illustration, watching two rather attractive young men do something that was probably physically impossible for the general population.

"Oh my..." Kevin murmured distantly. "Do you think that'd...no. Nobody has that kind of upper arm strength..."

Aidan laughed and leaned against his shoulder. "Looks like this will keep us busy for a long time, huh?"

"If only trying to figure out whose legs are whose...how the hell does a girl her age *know* this sort of stuff exists? *I* didn't know this existed," Kevin added in shock. He flipped to position twenty four, and swallowed. Now that would be fun. But how...

Aidan's chuckle in his ear derailed his train of thought. He glanced at his boyfriend out of the corner of his eye. "What?" Kevin asked, bewildered.

Aidan stroked his cheek. Kevin imagined he must be hot to the touch. He felt as if the pictures had lit matches under his skin. "You forget she lives on the Net?" The other man asked, cocking his head teasingly.

"Yes," Kevin agreed with preoccupied chagrin, "but why she's this well versed in sexual interaction when her main method of physical contact is breaking noses I don't...you're laughing."

"Yeah," Aidan agreed with a crooked grin as he leaned in for a kiss. "You're cute."

Kevin rolled his eyes, and tapped the screen. "We're taking *this* off my main tab and keeping it in our room."

"Fine by me," Aidan agreed, leaning in a little closer. Kevin shifted towards him, realizing that the bloody illustrations had done their work a little too well.

"Let's read what we got the tab out for," Aidan suggested. Kevin swallowed. "Er...actually, I...could we read later? That manual has had its intended effect, if you take my meaning..."

"Really?" Aidan ran the back of his hand down Kevin's body, brushing over his crotch. Kevin's pulse leaped. Aidan leaned back, looking him over with approval. "Guess it did. Want to put the wine down and get me my dick?"

Kevin shook his head with a smile, heat and wine pooling in his belly. "One day, love, I'm going to tie you to a chair and make you read Shakespeare and Sagan, to teach you how to use language. Of course, that scenario has its own distractions," he added, handing his wine over and lying on his belly to reach under the bed, pulling out the svelte black box. Setting it easily to hand, he retrieved his wine from Aidan, watching his beloved with a smile around the rim of the glass as he finished it off.

Aidan shook his head with a chuckle. "You know the oldy-worldy language isn't my thing. I prefer to listen to you use it."

"Philistine." Kevin teased. "Hence the involvement of a chair and rope."

"As long as you're the one reading it to me." Aidan finished his own glass of wine and set it aside, reaching for the slim box instead.

Kevin pulled off his glasses and set them on the bedside table. He slid forward, pushing Aidan down until he was lying over the other man. "What's the rush?" he murmured, kissing Aidan, feeling the warmth of his boyfriend's body beneath him. "Let's take our time, hmm?"

"Taking our time is what you want tonight?" Aidan asked softly.

Kevin kissed the angle of his jaw. "It is indeed."

"Okay, birthday boy. Taking our time. You got it," Aidan agreed, moving his hand from the box to Kevin's hip.

"Mm." Kevin agreed, relishing the words as he leaned into Aidan, fingers stroking his chest in slow circles, then dipping under the fabric of his shirt to stroke skin. He traced Aidan's collarbone with his lips, trying to peel off his winter jacket with one hand as he did. He failed fairly abysmally on the second task. "Damn thing..."

Aidan laughed and shifted, helping Kevin out of his jacket and shucking his own. "You got a lot on your desk? Maybe we'll take a lot of time tonight, sleep in tomorrow. Start duty a little late."

"That'd be at your discretion," Kevin replied, leaning on his elbows to smile down at Aidan. "Not mine."

They did take their time with one another, drawing out the evening and wrapping it around themselves like a blanket. By the time Aidan was done with him, Kevin felt as if his bones were made from warm gold, far too soft to allow him to move. For a long time after they'd finished their fun, they simply lay curled together.

Finally, Aidan kissed Kevin's throat, smiling gently. "How about wine and nude bedtime reading once we clean up, hunh?"

"Mm," Kevin agreed mildly. He lay still a little longer, basking, before Aidan moved. The sweet man cleaned him up with wipes from the bedside table, then saw to himself before pouring two more glasses of wine and fetching the tab. Settling back into bed, head on Kevin's shoulder, he slipped Kevin's glasses into his hand and pulled up a screen, setting the hologram hanging at their eye level. Kevin glanced at it once he'd gotten his glasses on, and sighed.

"Aidan, my best beloved, do we have to look at the Sector mission assignment roster *now?* To put it in direct and rather gauche terms, you just screwed my brains out."

Aidan turned and kissed him softly, grinning.

"I think you're going to want to see this. You've heard of seed banks, right?"

"Mm?" Kevin agreed muzzily, letting his eyes drift closed. Aidan had really wrung him out this time around.

Aidan's elbow nudged him gently. "Hey, don't fall asleep."

"Mmawake," Kevin murmured, though the afterglow, the wine and the low lights made that a somewhat dubious statement.

"Have you heard of the pre-dissolution seed banks?" Aidan repeated, words soft. Kevin nodded absently. "Mm. AgCo shut the public ones down in the US, but there are a number in the rest of the world. Why?"

"Because Regional put out an optional mission call for research and reconnaissance bases. They think there might still be a seed bank hidden up somewhere near Fort Collins."

Kevin's eyes shot open. He turned his head, meeting Aidan's deep blue eyes, then riveted his gaze on the screen.

Aidan was right: there was a mission call out marked 'Optional-Reconnaissance. Possible Resource Acquisition', followed by a short description of the assignment. With eager eyes, Kevin glanced at the 'Assigned Personnel' slot beside it, checking to see if anyone had snagged this gem.

He blinked. Then he turned to Aidan, slow joy welling up. "My name. My name's down there, and your approval for assignment."

Aidan nodded, smiling softly. "Thought you'd like it. National's decided that a couple of test farms like ours proved that bases can grow their own stuff without messing with their work, so they want to start putting more resources into getting us unpatented seeds. Get us independent food supplies. Fresh food makes a good bargaining chip too. I can cancel the mission assignment if you're too busy, I was going to ask first and then put in for it, but I wanted to snag it before—"

Kevin cut him off with a laughing kiss. "Busy? You got me an assignment hunting buried treasure! An actual seed bank! Aidan, this is phenomenally incredible. Thank you!" He pulled Aidan into a hug. Aidan chuckled and wrapped his arms around Kevin in turn.

"Happy birthday."

"Understatement," Kevin declared, giddy on the moment and the prospect of what he would be doing. Research. Discovery. And, if he was very lucky, bringing home the greatest of treasures. Dropping back against the pillow, he stared at the information window over his head, wide eyed. "Do you know what this could mean, Aidan?"

"We can be completely off the Grid, self-supportive. Grow our own food; *real* food, not the crap we're living on now." Aidan grinned and slid down the pillows to lay beside Kevin, his head pillowed on Kevin's shoulder. "We could actually make a difference, if we're not struggling just to get by."

"Exactly! And not stealing seed every damn year when the stock we've got loses viability...Aidan, we'd be self-sufficient! Practically free!" Kevin enthused, grinning like a kid. He kissed Aidan again, then disentangled himself and pushed the blankets back, bouncing to his feet.

"Let's see if there are any sources that we can start on, and—"

Aidan's hands pulled him back down into bed.

"Start with getting some sleep." Aidan chuckled in his ear.

Kevin laughed. "Fair enough, Aidan my love. And thank you for this. I don't think I can say it sincerely enough. This is..." Leaning in, he gave up on words and poured his gratitude into a kiss. "I'll start on it in the morning."

Kevin began his work with the full mission description. Regional had sent the results of their little test farm up the chain of command, along with the results garnered by a number of Rest and Retirement bases who'd used the 3D printing instructions the Wildcards base had disseminated and commercial seed to start their own small gardens. Using the information Kevin had stolen, they'd managed to remove the genes that kept the fruits small and ornamental for hobbyists, and some genius had figured out a gene splice to cut down on the water needs for soybeans and golden rice.

But the genes that made the second generation of all patented crops sterile were turning out to be fairly intractable, and the plants needed to be tough to survive on Duster bases. If the Force ever wanted to use the mobile gardens as more than a minor supplement to their diets, they needed unpatented seeds whose genes could be used as a baseline and a reservoir for desirable traits. With that in mind, the Regional Command Hub had approved putting resources into a small-scale reconnaissance project to source and recover seeds. It didn't approve much, but Kevin didn't need much to do this kind of work.

Kevin's mind flicked through possibilities as he read. If this seed bank turned out to be defunct, getting open-source seeds from other countries wasn't technically impossible. But it would be hellaciously difficult, and more than a little dangerous. If it still existed, the Fort Collins seed bank was a far better option.

Once he'd decided that he was using his time effectively, he dove into history. He read everything there was on the National Center for Genetic Resources that had been based in Fort Collins. It had been one of the world's largest gene banks, containing not only seeds but germplasm for over 8,000 species. If it still existed, it was truly a treasure trove of genetic material.

He started with research on the facility's original site on a National Banking training campus that had once been a state university, allowing himself to steep in his familiar bittersweet love for the works of the past. In the days when America had been a democratic country, the facility had been so well known and well respected that other countries had apparently sent their backup seed bank collections to Colorado for safekeeping. The region's University had been modestly famous; a gracious place of ancient trees, green lawns, beige buildings and red tile roofs. He allowed himself half an hour's indulgence, looking at the pictures of what the university had once been: a place where young people played on the lawns, slept on the library's couches between classes, and studied to become the people they'd wanted to be.

It had been a beautiful place.

He got down to serious work at eight-thirty on the dot. He dug up articles from the 2010s on the workings and the purpose of the Center, as well as its security measures. He reached out to a few above-board international contacts, asking them to get in touch with their networks and find out if anything was known on the seed collection that had once been housed in Fort Collins. Bringing up maps of the old university and the modern training campus, he superimposed the old map on the modern. There weren't many similarities. The building that had housed the seed collection was long gone. According to records, it hadn't been an underground storage facility, so a paved-over vault still in situ wasn't likely, thank God. Clearing a NatBank campus long enough to drill through asphalt would have been just about impossible.

So, the seed collection wasn't in its original site. But Fort Collins was surrounded by mountains. If the Democratic State Force could hide their Rest and Retirement bases up in the mountains, someone could most definitely hide an unmanned facility housing seeds in cold storage.

The operative word, of course, was 'cold'. If the facility did still exist—if—then it had certainly suffered a few power failures over the decades. People who had run such a facility would have known and planned for that. They would have looked for naturally cold environments.

Kevin brought up a heat map of Colorado terrain. And there were the Never Summer Mountains, just west of Fort Collins. He couldn't have gotten a better setup if he'd requisitioned it.

Now to find out if his suppositions were true.

Kevin turned on an energetic playlist full of songs from Poison, Huey Lewis and Billy Joel; a subtle hint that he didn't want to be disturbed. Or not so subtle, maybe.

Bringing up a new window and pulling out his system's biometric reading rig, he typed in three passwords, allowed the system to scan his retina and spat into the DNA reading tube. Then he entered the encrypted chat room.

He reached out to his godfather first, letting the plant geneticist know what he had found and asking for anything the older man might know. Then he touched base with his covert international contacts, asking for introductions and liaisons with anyone who might be able to help do research in the unrestricted democracies of Europe, India, Republic Sudamerica and Canada. He ran down the list of people who'd been in touch with his mom, adding them to his possible leads and finding contacts for them where he could.

"Have you eaten anything today?" Blake's voice scraped across his nerves, sharp and barbed.

Yanked out of his reverie, Kevin turned in his chair, blinking. "Ever heard of knocking?"

"Ever heard of blood sugar?" His mentor parried, "that brain works better when *yours* isn't in your *boots,* Red."

Blake had a point, Kevin had to admit.

"All right, I suppose I could use a break," he admitted, begrudging it only a little as he turned down his music, interlaced his fingers and stretched his arms over his head. His spine popped like a nutrient bar being stepped on.

"Ack," he grumbled as he stood, "some mornings, you know, I'm really starting to feel old."

Blake waved a hand to illustrate his dismissal of that thought. "Sweetheart, you're a *baby*. I *refuse* to let you be old. If you were classified as 'old', what would that make *me*, hm?"

"Do you actually want an answer to that?" Kevin asked with a smirk as he joined the older man in the hall. Blake batted at him. "Terrible boy! Teasing your elders, how *rude*."

Kevin rolled his eyes at his mentor's histrionics, grinning. Blake nudged him gently as they walked.

"Soooo, you were smiling when I walked in. How's the research going?"

"Surprisingly fruitful so far, pardon the pun," Kevin replied. "If I'm right, there's a viable site that could have housed a facility, there's some signs that AgCo never formally shut down or emptied the vaults of the seed bank, and…blessed Mary and Joseph, Blake. If this is real, do you know what that means?"

"Mm, we'll have the makings for decent bloody marys right here on base," the finance officer threw out with elaborate flippancy. Kevin snorted. "Drinks are the last thing on my mind. *Food*, Blake. Aside from the tangible aid it would be for the Force, I've got a personal stake here too. Decent fruit is what I really want. You know what I would give for decent strawberries? Oranges? I've missed oranges for years now."

"Mm, yes darling, we know *exactly* what you would give for seeds," Blake replied, eyeing him sidelong. "In fact, most people around here thought you were going to give your damn *life* for them, for a few days. Don't give as much as you did *last* time you went seed hunting, okay? *Nobody* will be happy with you if you come in here looking like you bottomed for an entire pro football team *again*. Least of all *me*." the older man drove his point home with one of his most sour expressions.

Kevin sighed, feeling a furious blush kindle in his cheeks. "Yes, thanks for reminding me in such vivid terms. Thanks very much."

"Just making sure it sticks in the mind," Blake replied airily, all mock-innocence.

They were in time for the tail end of lunch, and the cleaning up afterwards. Kevin was nearly done when a tap on his shoulder made him turn.

"Afternoon, Topher. What's up?"

Topher gave him a falsely bright smile. "Uh...hey man. Can we talk a second? In your office, maybe?"

"Sure," Kevin agreed, watching the younger man carefully.

He led his friend down to his office, closing the door behind them. Turning, he studied the boy he thought of as a younger brother. Topher was turning his favorite green fedora between his hands, fingers bending the poor thing's brim.

"Toph?" Kevin asked carefully, "Is something the matter?"

Topher raised eyes like a startled jackrabbit's "Hunh? Why d'you think something's wrong?"

"Well, you did ask for a private discussion. And you do happen to be mutilating your hat." He nodded at the hat in Topher's hands. The boy looked down, then gave a little 'oh!' of surprise and set the hat on the desk. He gave Kevin a sheepish smile and a shrug. "Nothing's all that bad. But I need some advice. Some dating advice."

Kevin quirked a brow. "Oh? Think you might be batting for my team?"

Topher shook his head, relaxing a little as he chuckled. "Nah man, not my thing. But...look, you had a lot of dates between Peter and Aidan..."

"I wouldn't quantify a night or two every six months as 'a lot', by general standards," Kevin rejoined dryly, "or 'a date', for that matter. But I did indeed have my share of bedmates."

"Yeah, well..." Topher dithered over the words as he spoke them. He raised pleading eyes to Kevin's. "You had this thing where you'd just walk up to a visiting tech, smile and chat for a couple minutes, and all the sudden he was going to your room for the night. You made it look easy," the younger man said, smiling hopefully. "I kind of want to pull something like that off, get the guts up to ask, you know? So I guess what I'm asking is...how d'you do that? How do you just chat somebody up, so they like you in five minutes?"

Kevin blinked. "Wait...back up. Who are you chatting up, exactly?"

Topher grinned, half abashed. "Uh...Billie. I've been hanging with her, and I really like her. But I don't want to freak her by getting this wrong, and she's shy, so...you gotta help me out here, man."

Kevin drew in a long breath. "Toph, let's take a seat."

Planting his elbows on his knees, he steepled his fingers, studying his younger basemate over them. *Only on this base,* he reflected silently, *and only in this eclectic little quilt bag of a family, would a gay Jesuit be asked to give a straight Muslim dating advice. I really, really hope I'm not about to make a hash of this...*

"All right. Let's start with this: the person you're approaching dictates everything about the way you approach. You need to be very clear on this, Toph: when I was inviting the men you saw, both I and the men in those encounters were looking for a physical outlet we needed with someone who was congenial. No strings attached. I wasn't serious about a relationship with any of them. I assume you'd like something more long term with Billie?"

Topher nodded slowly. "Yeah. I mean, I'd kinda like to date her."

"All right. Then you very much *do not* approach her the way I approached the men you saw me with occasionally. If I'm actually interested in a long term relationship, it's entirely different. Did you notice how I acted when I was getting to know Aidan?"

Topher grinned. "What, blushing a lot?"

"No," Kevin exclaimed, mildly exasperated, "well, yes, but no that wasn't what I meant. I was actually quite interested in Aidan, therefore I was circumspect with him."

"Circumwhat now?" Topher blinked. Kevin tried again. "I took it slow with him, because I had time. You have plenty of time with Billie. Therefore, acting suave is less important than acting genuine. Let her know that you're interested in spending time with her. Show her your games and invite her to play with you. Share some of those immersive holo-comics you read, I bet those would be a lovely afternoon's entertainment. Ask her what she'd like to do. After that, the ball's in her court. But you can make it clear that you'll be around if she's interested. And—" he held up a finger— "I hope this goes without saying, but you will also make it clear that you'll still be around *as a friend* if she's not. There's a lot of things I love about old movies," he finished, "but the 'nice guy who hangs on until he gets the girl' trope isn't one of them."

Topher looked mildly offended at that. "Man, I'm not an asshole."

Kevin laid a hand on the younger man's shoulder. "I know you're not, but you came in for dating advice; that's part of it. Most importantly, you need to *relax*. Let her set the pace. You can be honest; in fact, I recommend it. Hopefully you'll be better at it than I am. Feel free to outright say that you like her and want to spend time with her. But after that, patience and acceptance is key. All right?"

Topher blew out a long breath. "Okay, yeah, but...I mean...don't you have any tips for not looking like a dumbass and screwing it up? 'Just be yourself' doesn't feel like a lot of help."

Kevin squeezed the younger man's shoulder. "I know it doesn't. But if I'm being really honest? Being yourself really is the best thing you can be. To tell you the truth, I didn't really get anywhere with Aidan until I stopped being suave and spoke to him honestly. I was actually a bit of a fool. But the thing is, I *cared*. I was tongue tied because I actually cared. If you care, it's going to show. And it should."

Topher's face was full of hope and helplessness. "You sure I'm not going to look like an idiot?"

Kevin gave the younger man a reproving smile. "I'm sure you *are* going to look like an idiot, if it's real. And I'm sure that won't stop it from happening. Looking a little foolish comes with love. It's part of the package. So don't be afraid of it. Refusing to try because you're afraid of looking like an idiot? That would be the truly moronic thing to do."

Topher ducked his head, smiling at his hands. "I guess. Yeah."

Kevin smiled at the younger man. "Tell you what, I'll do you a favor. I'll make sure any planned Touchdown Party gets canceled, once you get the relationship going."

"Damn, I didn't even think about that," Topher looked horrified at the very thought. Kevin patted his shoulder. "It'll be fine. You've seen everybody else stumble around. We all survived. So will you. Just ask the girl if she'd like to sit down and play a game."

"Yeah," Topher agreed, "Thanks man. I...well yeah. Thanks."

"Any time," Kevin agreed with a nod. Lifting Topher's fedora, he dropped it back on the younger man's head. "After this point in a courtship, you probably don't want to take my advice, because I'd suggest reading her poetry in your lovely French-influenced Arabic and making her fall into your arms, overcome by your prose."

Topher snickered. "Yeah, you would, wouldn't you? Oh, hey. Printer needs more coloring agents for cloth. Can I get it on the list?"

"No problem, we'll do that run later this week."

"Thanks!" Topher was out of his seat and out of the room with a quick wave over his shoulder. Kevin smiled after him. That boy was growing up well. He had to laugh at himself for his parental attitude, but he really was proud of how Topher was turning out.

Turning, he flipped his system on. He blinked at the alert hanging in the air.

"Contact Regarding Seed Bank, Please Respond," he whispered, reading the words twice to make sure they were real. He couldn't quite believe it at first.

People. There were people contacting him, claiming to be the caretakers of the seed bank.

If this was true, he wasn't looking for an ancient time capsule. He was interacting with a functioning seed-storage facility. An actual, *staffed* facility.

He grinned. "Hell, yes."

"Tweak, I could use a hand. Got any spare time?"

"Yeah?" Tweak asked, turning in her coding chair and pushing her headphones off one ear. Kevin gave her a tired little smile.

"This contact has me jumping through ridiculous hoops to get in touch. Lend me a little expertise?"

Tweak glanced at her screen. She'd kicked the Corps hacker who'd been sniffing around Sector off the GreyNet and plugged his hole, her work for the base was done, and all she really had to do was a couple consults. Those could wait. She shrugged, pulled her headset off and stood. "Yeah, sure. What's up?"

"This contact's truly impressive level of paranoia," Kevin explained as they walked, staying close to the wall and leaving Tweak most of the room in the hallway. "Wait until you see this. I still can't believe the seed bank has a maintenance team, but that's who is driving me up the wall trying to touch base. Mainly I'd like help automating this sign-in so I can get to my specialty, which is actually talking to the contact."

Tweak dropped into his chair, studying his screen. The interwoven levels of security were a surprise. "Hunh." She blinked. "Wow."

"See what I mean?" Kevin asked.

Tweak nodded. "Yeah. These people are c-crazy worried 'bout s-staying hid. Already on a VPN, using the psiphon. S-scrambling their ISP's. And now they're b-bounce the c-c-communication through the mesh one m-more time before dec-crypting? Encryption's t-triple too. D-damn. Who *are* they?"

"People who appreciate privacy," Kevin replied with a shrug.

Tweak shot him a look. "Well yeah. Duh." She tipped her head, studying the screen. "G-good ideas. We should do s-some of this. All the b-bounties out on us right now." Those had been on her mind a lot lately. So many people wanted a piece of them. The cash offers out to bounty hunters contracting with EagleCorp were off the charts. Of course, the assholes didn't actually know who they were looking for: they were just told to find the base that had taken down the Viper Drones. Another set of bounties was out there for tracking the people who'd fucked over the Citizen Standing Scores, and there was one out on the people who'd put out the Supply Chain Vids, which was what the Grid had named the Folder they'd dropped a couple years back. The dumbasses couldn't even figure out that it was the same people doing all those things. Ninety percent of them couldn't figure their way out of a paper bag.

But the thought of the cash being offered still freaked her out. More security measures on their communications might help her sleep better.

Kevin sighed. "Could you get me a setup that will allow this conversation to happen in a reasonable amount of time? Please, Tweak. It's important."

Tweak tipped her head, eyeing him. He really looked like he meant it. He looked a little freaked, too. "Okay, yeah. Gimme…maybe an hour? Two, tops."

"Can I help at all, or would you prefer to work in peace?" Kevin asked.

Tweak waved a hand absently. "Leave. Call you when I'm d-done."

"Fair enough," Kevin agreed, turning away.

Tweak bit her lip, an idea blazing across her mind. "Hey, Kev. I do this. You t-trade me?"

"What are you looking to trade?" Kevin asked, turning back like he was wondering if she was going to ask for something crazy.

Tweak crossed her arms, nerving herself to get the words out. "Billie. Wants to d-date Topher. But she's s-scared. I s-s-suck at helping people feel b-better." She gave a quiet laugh. "Suck balls." Carefully, she raised her eyes, half expecting to get told off. "Help?"

Kevin gave her the kind of smile you give a doctor who's giving you a shot. He pulled his extra chair from its place against the wall, dropping into it. "Well, I'm happy to help if I can. Topher actually asked me for advice already. First off, you aren't going to get after him, are you? He is a gentleman, and quite considerate. You don't have to worry about Billie if she's dating him, and Dozer, Aidan and I will all have words with you if you break his nose again." Lowering his head, he looked at her over the rims of those weird old glasses. "Are we clear?"

Tweak snorted. "You're a fucker, CES."

"Only selectively," Kevin replied lightly.

Tweak rolled her eyes, but she couldn't help a little bit of a smile. He was such a dweeb, but his big brother act was sweet. "I'm n-not gonna touch T-topher," she promised. "But B-Billie's s-s-scared. R-real s-scared." She glanced down at her hands, not sure if she should rat Billie out on how much shit her fucking uncle had left her with. She still wished she'd been around when that was happening. Billie had just stabbed the fucker once, and that had landed her in jail. Tweak would have done a whole lot more to that fuck.

Then again, if the guys knew what Billie was going through, they could help. They were good at that.

"Older g-guy messed her up when she was a k-kid," she admitted. "Bad. Heads up."

"I'd guessed as much," Kevin agreed quietly. He leaned back in the chair, crossing his arms. "I imagine encouraging her to give it a try is a conversation you're really best suited to; after all, she trusts you." He sighed, pulling off his glasses and reaching for the little cloth he wiped them down with. "It's times like this that I really miss Andrea," the CES man murmured as he worked. "We could have sent Billie to her and seen her work her supportive magic. She was always so good at handling these sorts of situations."

"Billie liked her a l-lot," Tweak agreed quietly, feeling something tug inside her. She'd really liked Andrea too. She missed the friendly cook.

Kevin didn't say anything for a second. Then he raised his head, giving Tweak a small smile. "Well, we can try this: I'll send Topher some articles I've got on dating someone who's endured abuse. That will help them get off on the right foot. And we'll schedule a four-person game night to move things along. We can act as their mutual wingmen and relational training wheels. Once they relax, we can slip away and leave them to get on with it. How does that strike you?"

Tweak tipped her head first to one side, then the other, thinking it through. It was actually a pretty good plan. "Y-yeah. Sounds good. When?"

"After you've had a chat with Billie and gotten her feeling a little more confident?" Kevin suggested. Tweak pulled a face. She'd been so sure the guys would take over here.

"Yeah." She frowned, her fingers plucking at her bandages. "C-crap."

♠

She waited until after duty, when they were getting ready for bed. To keep her hands busy, she decided to make it a bandage changing night. Carefully, she unclipped the ends of each bandage where they were held in place along the backs of her hands, while Billie got into pajamas. She unwound the heavy swathes of white.

"Hey. Billie?" She asked as she worked

"Yeah?"

"You and Topher. You should do it. Date."

The last layer of bandage slid off her hand, displaying her caramel-colored scales. She slowly unwrapped the layers further up her arm, watching her snake-like scales shift color up from caramel to buff.

"Yeah?" Billie whispered. "You think?"

"He's cool," Tweak agreed as she pulled her dirty bandages off and dropped them in the laundry, "chill. So why you so freaked?" She unrolled a clean set.

Billie stared at her hands. Her words came out as whispers. "Tweak... I...I think I might be too broken for this..."

Tweak methodically clipped the new bandage on her right arm in place at the shoulder, giving Billie time to get herself together. When she raised her head, Billie was still staring at her hands, dark fingers picking at the blanket.

"Billie."

The taller girl raised her eyes. Tweak waited until her oldest friend was looking at her before she spoke. "That? That's bullshit. Nobody too broken. You looked around this dump?"

Billie sniffled, looking away. "M-maybe..."

"Maybe? Maybe?!" Tweak demanded, her voice rising into a squeak of irritation. "Maybe shit." Standing, Tweak sucked in a breath and touched Billie's shoulder. The sensation zinged up her arm as she spoke. "Billie. There. Are. Two Chicks. Fell in love on this base. There is. A guy. Born with no dick. Fell in love. With a guy. Who's CES. On this base. He. Runs. This. Base. There is a chick. Born with a dick. Calls the shots. On this base. They did good. On this base. So. Can. You."

Billie winced and shook her head, shrinking away from Tweak's touch. "I just...I can't...being with guys...you know what he did to me...I can't...I can't not see that...I'm scared I'll see that and freak if Topher and I do...y'know."

Tweak drew back, watching her friend, her annoyance cooling into a pang of guilt. "Shit. Thought you were j-just being chicken. D-didn't ...still?"

Billie nodded weakly, meeting Tweak's eyes for a second. Then she hid her face in her hands.

Tweak was still for a moment. Then she brushed her fingertips over Billie's fuzzy hair. "Hey. Billie. You can call me a s-shithead if you want."

Billie shook her head. "You were jus' tryin' t'help..." she mumbled between her fingers.

For a moment, Tweak sat still. "Yeah...but I kinda suck." She didn't know what else to say.

After a few minutes, Billie got herself together. Tweak watched as she raised her head.

"You like him? Topher?" She asked quietly.

Billie nodded, smiling weakly. "Yeah. He's funny. I don't get all tense with him. It's...nice."

Tweak nodded. "Okay then. Don't do the whole thing. Just s-start d-dating. First d-date. You. Me. Him. Kev. Games in the rec. Give me a s-signal. You w-want us to stay, you put your controller down on the c-couch. Y-ou want us to l-leave, you put your controller in your l-lap. Works?"

Billie stared at her for a moment, eyes wide and black and frightened. She swallowed. Then, tentatively, she nodded.

"That sounds good."

Tweak bobbed her head. "Kay. We're on."

♠

Two days later, the screen fizzled to life, the fantasy questing game swirling with color and music. 'Build your adventurers', the game's high-toned female prompter suggested as the avatar-build screen came up.

Tweak decided to be lazy, and selected one of her saved builds; a huge barbarian with a hammer. There was nothing like hitting things with a hammer to blow off steam.

Kevin had an elfin cleric who was even skinnier than he was; he added a ceremonial bell to the spellbook his character carried, and called it good.

Billie stared at the screen in bewilderment, then glanced at Tweak. She gave her friend a smile, then nodded in Topher's direction.

"T-topher. Wanna say how the different c-character types w-work?"

"Sure," Topher agreed with a quick grin. That was all Tweak had to do. After that, Topher geeked out all on his own. He walked Billie through all the character abilities and what made a character fun to play, showing Billie how to put her avatar together. She ended up with a naiad rogue who shot ice arrows, which was pretty damn cool in Tweak's book.

They started off a little stiff, but pretty soon the game had everybody laughing and goofing around, even Billie.

Kevin's character got eaten by a dragon after an hour, and he groaned. "I suppose I'll bow out gracefully. Where in God's name did that thing come from?"

"Maybe look up next time you try stealing dragon eggs," Topher chuckled. On the screen, his avatar grabbed another golden egg. Kevin clucked his tongue. "Yes, well, since the lizard's had her way I suppose I'll let you lot finish up. In fact, if Tweak steps out as well you two can take the side quest we unlocked."

Billie's eyes widened for a moment. She glanced at Tweak. There was fear in her face, but there was excitement too.

Tweak gave her a thumbs' up. Billie smiled a little as she set her controller down in her lap.

"Yeah. We can do that."

Tweak opened her mouth to say more, when Aidan stepped into the room. He was grinning like a lotto winner.

"Hey, Kev? You busy?"

"Not at the moment, in fact I'm recently deceased." The logistics officer stood and crossed the room, taking Aidan's hand. "What's—"

Aidan leaned in and muttered something, looking happy as a kid with a new toy. Now Kevin was grinning too, and now they were hugging. Tweak figured she got to call them on it when they started kissing.

"Hey. Guys. G-get a r-room."

Kevin flipped her off without breaking the kiss. Then Aidan was pulling him into the hall.

Topher blinked. "Hunh. Guess something's going right."

"Yep," Tweak agreed, standing. "Lots. Side quest. Have fun. Bye!"

Leaving the room, she realized she was smiling.

Kevin kicked the door of their quarters closed as he grabbed Aidan in another tight hug. Aidan was nearly dizzy with joy. He still couldn't believe the message scheduling his final surgery had shown up.

"The timing on this couldn't have been better," Kevin exclaimed, "Your implant-attachment surgery and my contact meeting will synchronize beautifully. We'll go in, we'll get you sorted out, and take two weeks for your recovery. That'll allow us to meet the contact who's in touch with the team caring for the seed bank in person, and then we'll get seeds and come home and..." he finished the statement with a giddy kiss. Aidan could almost hear the words he hadn't spoken: *and life will be so good.*

Aidan grinned at his boyfriend when they came up for air. "I'm still stuck on 'holy shit, this is going to happen'. Glad your planning brain's still running. I just...I can't believe...that I'll have the chance to...Kev, I..." He shook his head against Kevin's shoulder, not even sure what he was trying to say. Happiness lapped inside him like warm water.

A thought occurred to him, and he laughed. "We won't need the prosthetic any more, I guess."

Kevin chuckled as he ran a hand over Aidan's hair, long fingers gentle. "Good thing too. It wouldn't make it through security checks." For a moment, they stared at one another in a daze of joy. Then Kevin gave a little laugh. "I just got the most amusing image: an entire room full of confiscated sex toys somewhere in every EagleCorp PeaceKeeping office. Now we know what they do with their time off."

Aidan made a face somewhere between amusement and disgust. "Yeah, that's an image I really don't need."

"Fair point," Kevin quipped, leaning in for another kiss. "I'll get things scheduled and a route mapped, reach out to our contact. You already got your genome sent to the clinic so they can use it in growing the tissues, I assume. I'll work out a route and find us lodgings, send you a timeline so you can put in our paperwork for the leave and the mission tomorrow morning. How does that sound?"

"Sounds good," Aidan agreed quietly. "Sounds really good. And then we have to tell the crew what we're doing. For the plants, anyway."

Kevin gave a quiet groan. "Good God, that's right. It's going to be a circus too. You know Naomi will try to insist on going along to watch our backs. And Sarah. And everyone else will have a conniption over the fact that Liza will be in charge for three weeks."

Aidan shrugged. "They'll handle it okay."

Kevin gave him a thin smile, tapping the tip of his nose with one elegant finger. "So you say. But they'll grin and bear it once we explain what we're up to. Do you want to call a meeting now, or wait until breakfast?"

"It can wait," Aidan murmured, leaning into Kevin's warmth. He'd been grinning so long that his face hurt. "Kev...this is really going to happen, right?"

Kevin's arms wrapped him in warmth. "It's really going to happen, Aidan my love."

♠

The canteen was busy by the time they got in the next morning, people talking over one another and Janice arguing with Damian, who was trying to get her to move her work off the table. She gestured at the pieces spread across their oilcloth. "C'mon man, I'm halfway done with the piston an' I'm out of room in my space, give me five more fucking minutes! A little goddamn oil on the table isn't going to give anyone a fucking heart attack!"

Aidan gave the general bustle of the room a couple beats to settle. Then he cleared his throat. "Hey guys! I've got some news."

The canteen fell quiet, eyes turning to him. He drew a breath. "Okay. You know the crops we planted last year didn't give us any viable seed. We saved half of what Kevin brought us, and we were able to culture a lot of clones out of the tissues from those plants. We can probably get another crop for this year. But if we want a real fix for our food supply, we need to get ahold of unaltered seed and modify it to handle the conditions of the Dust. Well, Sector just approved us doing that. There's still an intact seed bank in the mountains around Fort Collins, containing seeds of crops that the Corporations never laid a finger on. The genetic material is perfect." He drew a breath. "And we got a contact who says that the seed bank still has personnel. A group of caretakers. I have approval to go on Grid and make an in-person contact. And I'm going to sign us up to take the assignment."

You could have heard a microtube drop in the quiet left by his words.

It was Janice who broke the stunned silence. "Well fuck me fore and aft." she remarked, grinning incredulously. "You're serious about this? It ain't April Fools' Day, is it?"

Aidan chuckled, shaking his head. "Nope. Kev and Tweak triple-checked the data, and it's legitimate. There's no telling what the contact we've made will have for us when we meet, but it's a chance I'm willing to take, if it means we can be self-sufficient."

"You think this contact is legit?" Damian asked carefully, chin in his hand as he watched the two men. Kevin cleared his throat. "The institutions were staffed by quite resourceful people with a true dedication to their work, so I'd lay odds on 'yes'. As long as the genomic material was maintained at the proper temperature, time shouldn't have done much damage. And if the facility has been staffed all these years, the chances of that are much higher than I had originally assumed. We just need to get there, make an agreement with the contact, and get our findings back here to—"

"Hell, I'm in." Janice cut in, waving her wrench. Dozer grinned, his blocky face practically splitting. "Same here." that set off a clamor of voices. As Aidan had expected, everybody wanted to go.

Aidan held up his hands for silence and waited until the excited voices died down again. "I'm honored that all of you are so eager. But for this, we need a small team. Kevin and I are going, since Kev knows how to get us around and I should be there with the authority to make deals with the contact we've reached, on behalf of the Force. I'm planning on leaving Liza in charge, until we get back." *Assuming we make it back*, his brain added silently. He told it to shut up and maintained his smile.

"I call bullshit." Naomi declared, pointing her fork at Aidan. "You two'd get killed alone, without any backup. Since when do we run missions with no backup?"

"Grid work." Kevin put in smoothly. "Best to keep things small and unobtrusive on the Grid. Backup gets you noticed."

Aidan gave Kevin a grateful nod. "And this trip is going to take us straight through Corps-heavy territory. Backup's more likely to get us killed than going in on our own, and the contact is requesting as much secrecy as possible. If we can, we'll keep in touch on the GreyNet, but that's only if it's safe."

"How long you going to be gone?" Yvonne asked quietly, reaching out to squeeze Sarah's hand nervously.

"If everything goes smoothly, three weeks." Aidan swept his gaze around the room full of his people. "If things go south…maybe longer."

The room went silent for a long moment. "Have you boys kept the bounties in mind?" Blake asked, his voice surprisingly quiet. "There's a lot of money on offer for your skins."

"Thank you, somebody says it," Naomi grumbled. "You guys need a gun at your backs at least."

Aidan gave himself a minute to breathe, before shaking his head. "No, I think we're better off running this alone. We don't know this contact, and they're paranoid. I don't want to spook them, and I don't want too many of us out there at once. Like you said, there's a bounty on our heads. All our heads. Kevin and I will take this. We'll leave next week. Liza, you'll hold down the fort while we're gone." He swept his eyes around the room with all the authority he could scratch together. "And the rest of you won't give her any trouble. We clear on this?"

A couple people shot one another smiles that promised a few shenanigans, but the crew gave general nods and noises of agreement. Liza threw a quick salute. "I'm on it...Aidan. I'll keep things steady."

"I know you will." Aidan agreed. "And I appreciate it, Liza. If anyone has any specific concerns for this period, I'll be in my office all afternoon."

"Can we get more on these seeds? I wanna know what I'm gonna be takin' care of. See if I can get in touch with anybody who can give me some advice." Janice added. That was all Kevin needed to go off on an enthusiastic, detailed explanation of every bit of research he'd found. Aidan relaxed in the general conversation, glad that it let him eat in peace. He gave Kevin's hand a squeeze once he'd finished his meal. His guy was still talking; he barely paused to give Aidan a smile. Putting his dishes into the washer, Aidan headed for his office and waited for the first person to come in and have their say.

He should have expected that it would be Naomi. She walked in, closed the door, and planted her fists on her hips. "Look. I know I said I'd take your orders. Yeah, you're in charge. But this isn't smart. The bounties out on our heads aren't pocket change, and all the Corps are gunning for us in particular. What are you doing besides what you told the crew in there?"

Aidan gave his sister a smile, his heart feeling like a balloon in his chest. "It's my last surgery, Omi. Sector got me a slot with somebody who can do my final surgery. They're growing the organ and the glands to implant, right now."

Naomi's eyes widened. "Wait, really?"

"Really," Aidan agreed, nodding. Naomi grinned, then stepped over, grabbed a chair, dropped down beside him and gave him a hug. Then, of course, she punched his shoulder.

"You should've told your crew the good news, dipshit. They'd be happy for you."

Aidan felt his smile go crooked with embarrassment as he looked away. "Yeah, I know. I'm still working on telling them that kind of stuff." He glanced up again. "I did want to talk to you though. The place we're using is a legitimate body-mod and implant clinic. If we sent them your genome right now, they could get an arm grown for you in time to fit with our schedule. Do you want that?"

Naomi gave him a cockeyed little grin, brushing her corn-silk hair back from her face. "Nah."

"You sure?" Aidan asked quietly. "We can make it work. We've got the funds."

Naomi shrugged. "You and me are wired different, Aidan, but I think I get you on this: I like the way people look at me these days. These scars? My off hand?" She tapped the case of her cybernetic hand with her flesh fingers. "These're my medals. They show off what I do. When people look at me these days they don't see a little girl. They see a badass. They see a fighter. I like it that way."

"You sure?" Aidan asked, watching his sister carefully. "I want to get you what you need, Omi. These days, I can do that, if you let me."

Naomi shrugged. "You're already getting me what I need. And I'm sure." Then she seemed to think of something, and pulled a face. "Shit. I just wrecked my chance to go in on this with you, didn't I?"

"Yeah," Aidan agreed. "You kind of did."

"Damn it." Naomi conceded ruefully. She eyed Aidan for a long moment, ice-blue eyes narrowed. Then she reached over and tugged him into a hug. "If I get told you're dead again, I will seriously bust your ass. You got that?"

"I got it," Aidan agreed softly, hugging his sister tight in turn. "I won't end up dead."

"Swear," Naomi's voice muttered against his shoulder.

"I swear," Aidan agreed softly.

A little more than a week later, Aidan followed Kevin's lead as they worked their way through the Grid crowds toward the hotel he'd chosen. Aidan had picked up a trick from his boyfriend that helped: if he kept his mind on a story or a piece of poetry while they walked, he took just enough focus away from his surroundings that he didn't jump when the pop-ups went off.

He still half-closed his eyes when he walked through somebody else's augmented reality holo. For some reason the woman had added dancing pixies and toadstools to her world, and Aidan had to resist the urge to swat at them.

"Watch it!" the woman shrilled.

"Sorry," Aidan mumbled, stepping out of her AR bubble. Kevin caught his eye, and he pulled a face. He really hated the Grid.

He stuck close to Kevin as the taller man navigated them onto a bus bound for a Zoncom neighborhood. The tech corporation's graceful white buildings soared up around them, billowing shade cloth leaving them in shadow below. The curving architecture gave Aidan the eerie sense that disinterested giants were standing over the street, watching the people scurry below like ants.

He was relieved when they reached their destination. The hotel Kevin had found them a room in was CSS class, clean and quiet.

"Down this way," his boyfriend put in quietly, turning down a long hall. He waved his falsified Citizen Card over the reader beside a room's door. "Redeeming reservation," Kevin stated. The door clicked open. Kevin caught Aidan's eye and ushered him ahead, stepping in behind him and softly closing the door. He carefully passed Aidan two sound boxes, pulling another two from his pockets. Aidan nodded and turned to set the two boxes in corners of the room, hiding them inside a bedside table and under a chair cushion.

"Clear," Kevin said from the other side of the room, "though I'd like to set a few more protections in place."

"What've you got?" Aidan asked with interest. Kevin pulled two round discs from one pocket and a vial from the other. "Hands-off arc for the door, and phage nanoids for the room. In case someone decides not to respect the 'do not disturb' sign."

Aidan nodded. "Good call. Want a hand?"

"If you'll spread the phage I'll see to the door," Kevin agreed easily, tossing Aidan the vial. He caught it, popping the lid and sprinkling the glittering dust into his hand. Carefully, he blew handfuls of it across furniture, over the floor and along the baseboards. He made sure to get it between the platform and the mattress of the bed, noticing as he did just how big the bed was and how good the sheets were.

"Nice in here," he remarked quietly, bringing up the phage app on his tab and activating the microscopic robots. The glittering dust faded seamlessly into the nooks and crannies of the room, patiently waiting to destroy all DNA-laden material that didn't have a heat source.

"Given what we're here for and how long we'll be staying, I reserved the best room I could," Kevin's voice filtered through the room. "You done with the phage?"

"Yeah," Aidan agreed. He smiled as Kevin's arms wrapped around him, and Kevin's lips pressed softly against his throat.

"You know Naomi used to get freaked as hell about phage when she was little?" Aidan murmured, leaning back into Kevin's warmth. "Some asswipe had shown her an article about phage nanoids that malfunctioned and started destroying more than just dead skin cells that aren't attached to heat sources. She had nightmares about phage nanoids crawling up your nose to eat your brains when she was nine."

"What'd you do for her?" Kevin asked softly. Aidan chuckled. "I said 'you wanna see something that really eats brains?' and showed her zombie flicks. The seriously campy ones. She watched the fake blood splatter and laughed her head off. There weren't any more nightmares after that."

"Nicely done," Kevin breathed against his skin, cradling him close. Aidan closed his eyes, feeling the tension of the day leaching out of his soul. "What time do we hit the clinic tomorrow?"

"Nine in the morning," Kevin murmured. Aidan nodded, feeling the strange, electric tension high in his chest; half fear and half excitement.

He turned in Kevin's arms, resting his head against Kevin's shoulder.

"Hey Kev?"

"Yes?"

"If things go sideways...get yourself out, okay?" He laid a kiss against Kevin's shoulder. "I want you safe."

Kevin gave a breath of laughter. "My beloved pessimist." His fingers ran over Aidan's hair. "Don't worry about me, love. I can take care of myself. And I'll always take care of you."

Aidan swallowed back his fear, working at a smile. "Thanks. But I'm serious. Be safe?"

"Always," Kevin whispered. Leaning back, he tipped Aidan's chin and brushed his lips over Aidan's. "We're here for something wonderful, you know. We should be celebrating."

"I'll celebrate after surgery," Aidan replied quietly. "Fate's a bitch. I don't want to tempt her."

Kevin sighed, resting his brow against Aidan's. "Fair enough, Aidan. Fair enough."

Aidan wasn't supposed to eat before surgery in the morning. That was fine with him; he didn't think he could have swallowed much more than the glass of water he took his mood meds with anyway. He watched the sink's water meter ring up the charge for the glass, his mind blank. His guts felt like they were full of static.

He got his meds down and returned to lay with his head resting on Kevin's thigh, doing his best to focus on paperwork he'd saved to his tab for the trip. Most of his morning work went into a more thorough report on the procedures they were using to cultivate their little mobile garden: documenting what had worked, and what had fallen flat on its face. Apparently Colorado soil was missing a few things that plants like blueberries needed; they'd found that out the hard way.

He also took a couple minutes to read the file on the clinic and the doctor he'd been working with, for what had to be the tenth time. Doctor Medevych was a Zoncom-contracted body modification surgeon, highly ranked in his field. He was also stuck in a very nice Zoncom cage on account of his specialty: he didn't have a lot of options for clinic work, and going into the wrong neighborhood in Denver without escort would probably get him killed. Only TechoCo was as permissive as ZonCom; the other Corporations ranged from distaste to homicidal hatred of body-modification work. In spite of that, Medevych had been working quietly with the Force for decades, and what had gone down in his record was impressive; everything from getting them medical supplies to saving lives of wounded Force members brought to his offices in the middle of the night, after missions went bad. He'd been replacing lost body parts, doing tricky surgeries like replacing spinal cords, and performing body modification for Force members for decades too. Aside from excitement about his own procedure, Aidan was looking forward to meeting such a solid ally.

Overhead, Kevin's screens flickered as he worked on coding some retro game and hummed quietly along with whatever was playing in his 'buds. Aidan couldn't help but glance at the clock on his tab as he read, willing it to move its digits. He wasn't sure if the hollow feeling in his gut was anticipation or hunger.

Finally, Kevin's leg shifted under him. "Time we were moving," his boyfriend murmured.

Glancing up, Aidan jerked his head in agreement.

They moved with care through the packed crowds of morning, blending in with the commuters. The sky hung heavy over them, grey with the promise of cold rain. They could use it, no question of that. Colorado always needed water. But in Aidan's experience, it only ever rained enough in February to make everyone miserable, not enough to do anything for the water table.

He was distracting himself with piddly things and he knew it, but he'd use what worked for now if it helped him control his heart rate.

The body modification clinic was housed in a spartan building of glass and unpainted concrete, soaring over their heads. Aidan was glad they were on ZonCom land. In this area, it was safe to reach over and take Kevin's hand as they stepped inside.

The cool, clinical air washed over them as the automatic door shushed closed behind. An attendant in mint-green scrubs checked her wall screen. Aidan saw his falsified credentials on there, read from the Citizen Card in his pocket when he walked in the door. The door wouldn't have opened if he hadn't been on the list, he guessed. This clinic was that kind of place.

The attendant minced over to them, smiling sweetly. "Good morning, Mr. Adler. The doctor's been informed that you've arrived. He'll be here to meet you shortly. Please, take a seat."

"Thanks," Aidan replied quietly, taking the seat he was ushered to. He squeezed Kevin's hand, using the connection to keep himself in the moment. He couldn't give any ground to the fears that threatened to swamp his mind.

Breathe, he told himself. *In for seven. Out for seven. Slow. This is going to work out.*

"Relax," Kevin whispered soothingly, squeezing his hand in return. "You'll be fine. Relax."

"Yeah." Aidan eked out. "I know. Just..."

"Mr. Adler?"

Aidan turned. A man was walking to stand beside him, his long white coat and his thatch of white hair shining in the clinic lights. His smile was gentle.

Aidan forced himself to release Kevin's hand as he stood. "Yessir."

The man held out his hand, shaking Aidan's. "Doctor Medevych. Why don't you and your partner follow me?"

The doctor led them to a handsome little office, bright and boasting a couple pieces of actual wood furniture. Doctor Medevych smiled once he was in his seat. "I hear good things about you, from our mutual friends."

"Same here, sir," Aidan replied, giving the doctor a nod. "I hear you're the best at what you do."

The doctor chuckled. "I appreciate the compliment. I'd like to go over today's procedure with you. Once we've discussed everything, we'll be giving you a sedative pill to begin the relaxation process, and you'll be prepped for surgery." The doctor tapped the surface of his desk, and a holo jumped into life, all clean lines and clear focus. The doctor gestured at it as he spoke. The images illustrated his words. "We'll be putting you under a full anesthetic and attaching the existing erectile tissue, nerves, blood vessels and urethra to this lab-grown penis, as well as implanting gonadal tissue that will produce testosterone and gonadotropins internally. We will also be attaching a vat-grown scrotum, though you do need to be aware that the testes aren't likely to be effective in terms of reproduction."

Aidan nodded. "No worries there." He shot Kevin a quick smile. Neither of them were going to be having a kid, that was for sure. Hell, they were helping to raise four kids already.

Doctor Medevych acknowledged Aidan's answer, going on with his quiet explanation. "Today's procedure will take about six hours. We'll also be implanting a short-duration nanoid conglomerate. After the procedure, the nanoids will block pain and ensure the attachment of all your nerves, as well as acting to monitor the integration of your tissues and the mast cells laid down by the auto pads. Your new organs should be functioning as part of your body within ten to fourteen days. For the first three postoperative days you'll need to wear a catheter and foley bag. You'll be a little stiff and will want to stay still much of the time. On day four, I'd like to see you getting up to take short walks around the room three times a day. You'll be released for recovery in five days. I'll see you again in ten days to check your progress. At that time, we'll check for integration of the grafts, the ability of the erectile tissues to function unassisted, and full sensory reaction. If everything is right, I can clear you for normal physical activity then."

The words 'normal physical activity' made Aidan's heart jolt in his chest.

"Do you have any questions?" The doctor asked. Aidan swallowed. He glanced at Kevin, who squeezed his hand gently and shrugged.

Aidan glanced back at the doctor. "Um..." he had to clear his throat to finish the sentence. "Just double checking; do I need to do anything different with my mood-stabilizing meds?"

Doctor Medevych smiled. "Your regimen won't be affected; I've checked the drugs, and there won't be any interactions. Anything else?"

Aidan swallowed. "Um...normal activity...does that include sex?"

The doctor nodded. Aidan glanced at Kevin, who was blushing like a tomato, and smiled. Then he turned back to the doctor. "Okay, that's all."

"Then we'll get started. If you'll step this way?" Standing, the doctor gestured at the door.

Aidan glanced back. Kevin stood, watching his boyfriend with an anxious smile.

"You going to wait around till I get done?" Aidan asked. Kevin took his hands. "Of course." Leaning in, he brushed his lips over Aidan's. "Godspeed."

Aidan let himself lean into Kevin's warmth for a heartbeat. Then he stepped away, and followed the doctor.

Kevin forced himself to stop glancing from the clock on his tab to the man sleeping in the bed beside him. The doctor had said anesthetic would take time to wear off. *Patience is a virtue,* he told himself sternly. He read with as much focus as he could force himself to maintain. In his free hand, his fingers fiddled with his rosary. The warm, dark beads clicked between his fingers. He'd felt a little silly pulling them from their safe place in his dresser and putting them in his pocket on this trip, but now he was glad that he had.

There was a proper, set form of prayers to use with the rosary. The decade. How had it gone again? He'd been praying on and off since Aidan went into surgery. He'd forgotten most of the Apostle's Creed, but he still knew the rest forward and back.

"Glory be to the Father, to the Son, and to the Holy Spirit," he whispered, holding the cross between his fingers. "As it was, as it is now, as it ever shall be. World without end. Amen."

The rustle of sheets whipped his head up. Aidan shifted in bed. "Kev?" His boyfriend's voice was a thin croak. Kevin's hand was holding Aidan's before he'd realized he was in motion. Aidan was still so pale, his eyes still closed. Kevin squeezed his hand gently. "Right here. I'm right here."

Aidan smiled drowsily, eyelids lifting a little. "Hi."

Kevin couldn't help but smile in return. He squeezed Aidan's hand. "Hi."

Reaching over, he pressed the room signal to let the doctor know Aidan had woken, then leaned in and smoothed Aidan's hair back from his face. "How do you feel?"

"Good," Aidan murmured in the tones of a happy drunk. "Really good..."

"Well that's good to hear," Kevin murmured, leaning down to brush his lips over the other man's

He heard the door open, and straightened as Doctor Medevych walked in. Aidan blinked groggily up at him.

"Hi...how'd it go?"

"The procedure was a perfect success," the doctor reassured, bringing up the bed readings and checking them. Kevin studied them discreetly himself, relieved at what he saw. Aidan was in fine shape. The doctor backed up the educated guess with a nod of satisfaction, turning back to Aidan with a smile. "Are you still feeling drowsy?"

"Unh-hunh." Aidan agreed. Doctor Medevych nodded. "That's not unexpected. In the morning we'll test your innervation and nervous response, but I did want to ask whether you can feel the implants at this time."

Aidan gave a tiny, rapturous grin. "Transplant, doc. I'm trans, so issa transplant, right?" His words fuzzed into one another.

Kevin chuckled, running his hand over Aidan's hair. "You're still quite high, my love."

"Mmhmmm." Aidan hummed, his head lolling. "Feels good." The drunken dreaminess in his voice charmed and unnerved Kevin in equal measure. Seeing Aidan this vulnerable always set his nerves on edge. This kind of helplessness in his beloved made him long to shut the door, lock it, and bar the world entry. He itched to walk the building perimeter, to check the security setup, to do *something* that would prevent the world from coming in and destroying this precious, fragile part of his life.

But right now there was no action to take. He simply needed to be present. And that was the most difficult task of all.

The doctor chuckled. Tapping the bed's screen, he input a bit of data. "He'll be hungry when he comes fully awake; feel free to call for food."

"Thank you. For everything." Kevin murmured. Doctor Medevych smiled, nodding at the bed. "Based on what I've heard about the projects he leads? It's an honor." With a last nod, he stepped out of the room.

Taking his seat again, Kevin watched his man drift in and out of consciousness, turning the rosary beads in his fingers.

He'd made a gigantic mistake in reading up on the history of this kind of surgery through some of Damian's resources. He'd been looking for reassurance. Instead he'd read a history full of reminders to be patient, caveats and caution. Thank God for the organ growing and grafting technology that had been perfected in the last century; in the old days Aidan would have needed a handful of surgeries, and scheduling those safely would have been nearly impossible. Today's affirmation surgery was so much faster.

The task of recalling his prayers helped him keep calm. It had been so long since he'd worked his way through the full sets of prayers his mother had recited in the mornings. He barely remembered the proper decade any longer. His mom hadn't used the strictly traditional one very often anyway; Hail Mary and Our Father were always part of it, but she'd usually skipped the Apostle's Creed and gone for something more contemporary, if he remembered right.

It was actually easier, in some ways, to cope when wounds were incurred during a bombing or a mission. Then there was a problem to address. Tasks that had to be done. Kevin didn't know what to do with himself in a safe hospital environment that expected him to simply sit and wait.

He brought his mind firmly back to recalling his prayers. He could have looked the words up on his tab, of course. A few keystrokes would bring him the lines. But somehow that never felt right. There was no logical explanation for the emotion, but he felt, somehow, that the prayers which had written themselves in his bones were the ones he needed to be speaking.

The beads were warm in his hand, soothing his nerves. Closing his eyes, he worked the worn wooden orbs through his fingers and called up one of his favorite prayers.

"Lord Jesus,

I give you my hands to do your work.

I give you my feet to go your way.

I give you my eyes to see as you do.

I give you my tongue to speak your words."

He worked a bead through his fingers for each line. Not exactly tradition, but this was what he needed in this time and place. Work for his hands, and words for his soul.

"I give you my mind that you may think in me.

I give you my spirit that you may pray in me.

Above all, I give you my heart

that you may love in me your Father

and all mankind."

"Kev?"

Kevin's eyes snapped open. Aidan was watching him, blue eyes clear and mild. "You need to finish the prayer?" he asked.

Kevin smiled, tucking his mother's rosary in his pocket. "I was just passing the time. The doctor said you'd need food. You hungry yet?"

"Starving," Aidan admitted. "But don't go yet...tell me how I look, first?"

Raising his head, Kevin met Aidan's eyes. Moving with care, he peeled the sheet back and looked over Aidan's body, eyes soft. Then he leaned in, and kissed Aidan. "You're breathtaking, Aidan my love."

Aidan's breath hitched as they kissed. Kevin drew back slowly, running a hand over Aidan's bright hair. "I'll bring you something. Won't be a moment."

There was reconstituted scrambled eggs, toast and yogurt on order for Aidan; soft, easily digestible food. Kevin sat the bed up and eased his boyfriend's hand around the spoon. "Think you got this?"

"Let's find out," Aidan suggested. He managed to scoop up some of the yogurt, but nearly dumped it down his front instead of getting it in his mouth. He gave Kevin an adorable, lopsided smile. "I guess not…"

With a soft laugh, Kevin lifted the spoon. "It's okay. We'll make it work."

Aidan smiled sheepishly. "Thanks, Kev. Love you."

"Love you too." Kevin murmured. "Now, eat."

Five days later, Kevin kept a supportive hand on Aidan's elbow as his man tottered across the hotel room on his routine walk of the day. "Steady now, don't rush it..."

"I'm fine," Aidan protested, attempting to lean on Kevin as little as possible.

"I know, but you're also recovering. You can afford to take it easy." Kevin reassured, maneuvering Aidan into a comfortable chair and pulling the other hotel-issue armchair up beside it. "Though I'll admit it's good to see you up." he added, gently carding his fingers through Aidan's hair. "I was running out of ways to keep you occupied in bed."

Aidan smiled up at his lover, a hint of mischief in his bright eyes. "Once I get the all-clear, you're going to have trouble getting me *out* of bed for a day or two."

"Five more days." Kevin admonished sternly, though he couldn't resist leaning down and cupping Aidan's cheek, kissing him.

Aidan returned the kiss eagerly. "Then you'd better stop teasing me. Ass."

Kevin smirked. "Ass again. Aren't you single minded."

"You do have a nice one," Aidan replied with a smirk of his own.

Kevin shook his head. "Down, boy. We'll get some work done, that'll keep you distracted. The contact's approved a date and time for our meeting; we're on for twelve days from now."

"Do we have a description on them?" Aidan asked, looking over the coordinates.

Kevin shook his head. "Not with this cagey bird. They didn't give us so much as 'I'll wear purple'. Or a gender. All I have now is a handle that I dearly hope is a screen name, which we're supposed to greet them with when they find us, as a code phrase. Bran ap Llyr, see?"

"Who the hell spells like that?" Aidan asked, blinking. Kevin laughed. "The Welsh, one of the European nationalities. Theirs is the only language I ever looked at and said 'no thank you'. But they're impressively stubborn about holding onto it. Anyway, since we can't do much planning about the contact themselves and we already went over the meeting site, I found the original list of species at the seed bank. If we decide beforehand what we're looking for, this will be a much more efficient mission," he added, getting out his tab and bringing up the list. "There's an awful lot, and the original compilers didn't make a distinction between ornamental and agricultural seeds, so the list's a mess. I mean, look at this. Nassarius ripens is right next to..." Bittersweet pain ran its blade through his heart. "Rosa rugosa var Rambling Robin." He touched the name, and a picture of a rambling rose species popped up, adorned with orange flowers rimmed in red.

Aidan stared at the list with his brows raised. "You realize I have no idea what any of these names mean, right? If it's not a carrot or a bean plant, I'm way out of my league."

"I know the names pretty well." Kevin murmured distantly, staring at the flowers on his screen.

"What's that look for?" Aidan asked, resting his head against Kevin's shoulder.

"My mom used to grow these." Kevin murmured. "These roses used to grow up our garden walls. They had such a scent..." He let out a soft laugh. "They were the perfume of summertime."

Aidan smiled and kissed Kevin's cheek. "Then we should bring some back."

Kevin gave an attempt at a smile for his boyfriend, but it didn't really work. "Perhaps we will."

Aidan's hand rested on his. "Wish I could've seen the garden. Sounds like your mom did a good job on it."

"More than good," Kevin agreed quietly. He glanced up from the screen, meeting Aidan's eyes. "I actually do have pics. Would you like to see?"

"Yeah," Aidan agreed. "I don't think I've ever seen pics of your parents, outside what you put up for the memorial table back in October."

A smile on his lips and a skewer through his heart, Kevin minimized the plant list and brought up an encrypted file, putting in his passwords and letting the tab read his retina. He'd heavily encrypted this precious folder and created several backups when he first arrived on base; a backpack full of books and trinkets, a change of clothes and a data stick acting as his emotional life preserver while his old existence sank behind him. He'd been fearful of what the Dusters would realize if they saw the images, at the time. He didn't open the folder often, but he made a mental note to take the heavy-duty security measures off. They weren't necessary any longer.

The image window rose from the tab, showing a lush walled garden and five people standing around a rose whose blooms were blue in the center, the petals tipped in bright red. Kevin's godparents stood on either side of the family, their earthy strength of build striking beside the tall, slim people in the center.

The red-haired woman was grinning, a strip of sunburn across her nose and her arms around a skinny boy in his early teens who was laughing with the same exuberance that shone in her face. A pale-skinned man with strawberry-blonde hair and a slightly heavier version of Kevin's own features stood with an arm around the woman's shoulders, smiling quietly.

Kevin managed a laugh. "Mom always got sunburned in the summer. She kept forgetting her hat somewhere or other; really should have been more careful. Dad and I were always reminding her. Naturally pale skin really isn't a survival trait in this part of the world." He pointed at the picture. "We were celebrating the blooming of her newest rose. Tio Berto still has the patent on it. This is Julia's Jubilee." He flicked the pictures. "This is Rambling Robin. And us fighting with it. This beast got everywhere, we were always pruning it. I kid you not, every time we worked with the rambler, we ended up looking like we'd been dancing with the Devil. Especially Mom."

The boy he'd been was younger in this picture; eleven, maybe. He was up a ladder and waving with shears in one hand, his mother on another ladder. His father was steadying the ladder Kevin was on and giving the camera a look that read 'yeah, I know, but he's having fun'. The climbing rose draped the old brick wall and tumbled over the spikes atop it, the blooms burning like red coals in the greenery. Below, beds of flowers blazed with color in the summer sun.

"The garden's gorgeous," Aidan murmured.

Kevin nodded. "It was. I loved working on it. We all did."

Aidan tipped his head, studying Kevin. He avoided his boyfriend's eyes by flicking pictures. Unfortunately, the next image wasn't nearly as pleasant. He frowned. "Damn. I should delete this one."

The image showed a garden party, guests beautifully dressed and enjoying themselves. In the foreground Kevin stood with his parents, his hair combed and lacquered into place, his white linen suit pristine. He'd been somewhere around fourteen. He'd hated that suit, but he had to admit, he had looked good in it.

Several prestigious guests stood around his parents. Most of them had been pricks in person. And the biggest prick of all was standing beside his father, smiling like a lizard.

"How come?" Aidan asked.

"Hm?" Tugged out of his reverie, Kevin glanced at him. "Oh. Sorry. Why should I delete the pic, you mean? Bloody Harrington's in it." He pointed at the pale man with that greased black hair forming a widow's peak. His father used to call the man 'the board room vampire'. The name suited.

"I feel like I know that name," Aidan said slowly, "Do you mean Harrington who owns—"

"The current CEO of Cavanaugh, yes." Kevin felt the old, banked anger rising in his chest as he spoke. If acid could be stored in deep freeze, this rage was the emotional equivalent. It lay under all his other feelings, biding its time as it aged and hardened. It put a bitter edge to his words as he spoke. "He was my father's vice-chair in my youth. Based on what I've been able to glean since, he's the one I'll kill one day if I want to balance the ledger on my parents' account. He was the one who started the conversation with the board along the lines of my family's 'removal'. And in that devil's bargain, he got my father's seat. But debts to the Devil will come due in time."

He realized that his hand had folded into a fist in his lap. He flicked to the next picture. But this one had fucking Harrington in it too.

He gave a mirthless laugh. "You know, the son of a bitch actually put his hand on my shoulder at my mother's funeral and tried to act like an uncle. He actually put on an act of being *sympathetic*. And I fucking *believed* him. That's how little I understood what my parents were dealing with."

He glanced up, taking in Aidan's slightly unnerved expression. He let out a long breath. "Sorry. That got a little darker than I expected."

"It's okay," Aidan replied after a moment. His hand rested on Kevin's leg. "I'd kind of like to hear about your parents. Not what they did; just who they were. If you want to talk about them."

Kevin flicked to a new picture: him and his dad in the car packed for the drive up to Vail, both wearing ACDC t-shirts. He was probably fifteen in the image. They were laughing, beckoning at the camera. Kevin had to smile at the sight, feeling his body relax. He'd loved those summer road trips.

He glanced at Aidan, and dredged up a smile. "Well. Mom. She was what they used to call an 'English rose.' She was always on the move. Fast-walking, speaking with her hands, full of energy. Quick to smile, quick to laugh." He smiled down at a pic of his mother with her circle of clinic aids. "Mom always acted like she had half her mind on something else; some new idea, a new plan. Bright red hair, like a wave of copper flowing to the small of her back. She had a sharp sort of humor that made her grin at graffiti and say things like, 'when you get knocked down, you're well positioned to nut the bastard in the fork.'"

He ran a hand over his own red hair. "I guess that's where I got it. And the way she'd speak, that beautiful British accent. She could make a grocery list sound like a poem." He swallowed. "And Dad. Dad. Always there, solid as a rock. He had a terrible workload, but he never let it stop us having a life as a family. He was always quiet, never raised his voice. He was always reasoning. Dad never let things cause him to act against his principles. He never yelled, never lashed out. He'd tell us honestly when he was tired, or brought low, or angry. I wish I'd learned to do that. I take after Mom too much." He flicked to another picture; himself and his father, asleep on the couch when Kevin was four.

His words came out rough around the edges. "He always gave the impression that there was something keeping him steady in his center, something nothing could touch. Dad called it his 'moral compass', corny as that was. He was the one to introduce me to old American movies, and I used to think Dad was just like John Wayne; big and tough and righteous, and kind." He glanced at Aidan, feeling the tears prick behind his eyes. "You know what he did when he figured out I was falling for a boy? He caught on before I did. He sat me down, put a hand on my shoulder and said 'we can make this work, okay? We just have to think it through.' Most Corporate fathers would have sent me to a psychologist, or a jail cell. But Dad set up layers of protection for Jake—my first boyfriend—and me. I don't think I can really make you understand how phenomenal that act of paternal love was, given Dad's position, his Corporation and his upbringing. He was...he was a man I hope I'll live up to, someday." He swallowed. "Lord, you'd think I'd be less maudlin with time. Sorry."

"Don't apologize for that, Kev," Aidan replied softly. "That kind of love and a decent way to grow up? I wish you hadn't lost it...but I'm glad you had it."

The anger that had been bubbling just under the surface of Kevin's soul seethed up, threatening to choke him. "I didn't 'lose' it, Aidan. I didn't 'lose' my parents. They were murdered." Hearing the rage in his words, he turned away from the man he loved before the emotion could boil over, letting it simmer inside his chest. Bad enough that Cavanaugh had destroyed his family, but they'd done worse. They'd killed his ideals, and his trust. He'd been ready to devote his life to making the Corporation into something better. When he'd read the letter his father left him and realized that the Corporation he loved was the reason his life had been gutted, he'd wanted to die on the spot. The Corporation had been his life, and they'd ripped him out of it and left him without anything to believe in, anything to depend on, or anything to hope for. They'd taken a Cavanaugh boy and ripped out the core of him. Kevin would never forgive them for what they'd made him into: a man with this *hate* burning in his soul. He'd never forgive them for what he'd nearly done on account of the bastards who killed his parents and his ideals.

Aidan shifted in his seat. "Kev? You went cold on me. You okay?"

Kevin set his tab aside. "Maybe this wasn't a great idea. It brings up...difficult memories."

"About your folks?" Aidan asked gently. Kevin shook his head. "Not exactly. About...well, what happened afterwards. I think I gave you the impression I turned Duster looking for a way to make the world better after I lost Dad. That's true today, but at the time... At sixteen, I didn't give a damn about the world. I wanted to make Cavanaugh bleed, and I went looking for a way to make it happen. I wanted to learn how to cause as much devastation as I could. I wanted to learn how to cause harm."

He sighed, staring at his hands. "I might have done it too, if it hadn't been for Commander Taylor. The Commander caught me the week I arrived on base with everything I needed: the command codes for a Cobra-class Drone-Jet, the coordinates for the Cavanaugh Creek subdivision where the members of the Board lived, the necessary command and navigation programs. I was waiting to drop a bomb when I thought members of the Board would be at home." He shook his head, smiling bleakly. "Taylor reamed me out like you can't imagine. 'We aren't killers!' he shouted in my face. He yelled so loud the words are imprinted on my brain: 'we're trying to make things better, not worse, and if you ever aim at the innocent again I'll put a bullet in your brain', that was what he said. And he was right. At the time all I could think about was the Board, and maybe they deserved to die. But their children, their families, their staff and neighbors didn't."

He raised his eyes to his boyfriend's, the old shame and rage churning inside him. "Bad enough they killed my parents. But the Corporation nearly cost me my soul as well, Aidan. I was on that precipice. I nearly fell. I almost became a murderer, because of what the Corporation did to me. And I'll *never* forgive them for that."

Aidan's eyes were wide. He sat frozen for entirely too long. Then he gave a tiny, nervous chuckle. "I guess I know why you got put down for logistics, if you pulled that off fresh from the Grid at sixteen."

Weakly, Kevin nodded. "You'd guess right. A week after that debacle, I was getting my first lecture off Blake." He glanced away. "I know I would have died anyway, if I'd stayed on the Grid. I knew too much, and I'd always be a thorn in the Board's collective side; heir to my parents' campaign, holder of their assets, my father's hereditary seat on the Board, and of course all their knowledge. I would have been an unacceptable danger if I'd been known to have survived." He glanced at Aidan, drawing a breath. The admission stung, but it needed to be made. "That anger kept me alive for a time, but it's...problematic. I'm not proud of it, but you need to know that there is still a streak of fire and ice in me. There's rage and there's viciousness in my nature. I hope to God you'll never really have to see it... but you need to know it's there. One day, you may need to help me control it. I hope you won't. But be aware that you might."

Aidan gave him a crooked smile. "Yeah, I think I figured out that it's there. And I know what gets you to aim it at somebody. I figure a good aiming mechanism makes for a good weapon."

Kevin sighed and glanced at the tab. It still showed the boy he'd been, asleep in his father's arms. His lips quirked. "Well. True enough. I suppose I'm a whole new kind of danger now. And we *are* going to take the sons of bitches down."

Aidan's hand reached over to squeeze his. "Yeah, Kev." Aidan agreed. "Yeah. We are."

Event File 6
Event Tag: Physical Activity Clearance
Timestamp: 13:25-2-27-2157/ 7:00-2-28-2157

The door of their hotel room closed quietly behind them. Aidan waited until he heard the lock click before taking hold of Kevin's lapels and pulling him into a hard kiss. "Come here, you," he laughed, pushing Kevin up against the wall. He'd spent all morning on tenterhooks as they waited to go to his final appointment, waited in the clinic, waited on the doctor's words. Hell, he'd spent years waiting to get here. Now it was over. His body was cleared for physical activity, and he was done waiting.

Kevin's fingers buried themselves in Aidan's hair as he gladly joined in the kiss. "Yes sir." he managed. The taller man caught his breath. "In a hurry?" he managed as Aidan lowered his head to kiss his throat, his fingers undoing Kevin's jacket buttons.

"'Course I'm in a hurry," Aidan agreed, his voice rough as he kissed down Kevin's throat and tugged at his shirt. "I've waited years for this. I'm *so* done with waiting."

"Hard to get much further if you won't let me get your pants off." Kevin whispered teasingly, trying to twist his hips under Aidan to get loose. The feel of him rubbing against Aidan sent a tingling thrill through his gut. "I can't get at them like this..." Kevin grumbled in his ear.

"Just stay still," Aidan ordered. High on the moment, he nipped at Kevin's collarbone as his hands wandered lower. "I got it."

"That command position getting to your head, is it?" Kevin teased, leaning in to nibble Aidan's earlobe, then grunting as he was shoved against the wall again. He gave a surprised laugh. "Woah..."

"Told you to stay still." Aidan stole a kiss before sliding down to unbutton Kevin's pants and yank them down, along with his boxers and his shoes. He got rid of Kevin's shirt as he stood, kissing him until they were both breathless. He stepped back to get his own jacket off, taking in the sight of Kevin bare and leaning back against the wall. A tight tension began to coil between his legs, a spring slowly being wound. He swallowed hard.

"Um...Kev? I want to try something."

"Oh?" Kevin crossed his arms, head tipping to one side. He looked like some old Greek god when he stood like that; one of the horny, trouble-making ones. "And what would this 'something' be?"

Aidan nodded at him, his breath coming fast. "I want to watch you touch yourself. See if I can get going just from watching. Can we do that?"

Kevin's lips quirked. "I do believe we can. Get stripped, sit on the bed, and I'll put on a show for you."

Aidan's pulse kicked up a notch. Grinning, he got himself undressed in record time, though he wasted a few moments looking down at himself. He was already a little hard from the kissing alone, and his body had never made him feel this good before.

Raising his eyes, he met Kevin's gaze across the room and dropped onto the bed.

Kevin gave him a wicked grin, trailing his fingers down his chest. He wasn't completely hard yet, but he was heading that way fast, and he traced the tip of his erection with two fingers, holding Aidan's eyes. Moving with seductive grace, he took his dick in his hand and began to stroke himself. His smoky silver eyes closed.

Aidan could hear his own heartbeat in his ears. His gut had gone tight, and the tension between his legs was intense now. Tingling heat began in his new organ and radiated through his groin.

Kevin kept his movements slow, his eyes closed, but he was hard now, his dick flushed pink. His head had tipped back in the way Aidan loved, the way that accentuated his long neck and made him look inhumanly perfect.

Aidan felt a strange, tight lurch in his gut, and looked down. Holy shit, his dick was hard as nails and twitching. That was new, and unbelievably hot.

Weirdly enough, he got even harder at the observation. The tense feeling in his dick was amazing, but it was starting to verge on painful.

He raised his eyes. Kevin's lips had parted, and he was breathing fast. Aidan's dick pulsed.

He grinned. *Okay, experiment's a success. I can definitely get hard from watching.*

Now it was time to do something with what he'd got.

Body twanging, Aidan stood. "Kev," he managed, hearing the heat in his own voice, "let up. Wait a sec."

It turned out that walking was a little bit uncomfortable when you were hard, but Aidan wasn't about to complain. Putting his head into the bathroom, he dug in their stuff and pulled out the can of lube they'd disguised as shaving cream. He crossed the room to press his body to Kevin's, their dicks pressed together. Heat rolled through Aidan's body. He stroked the hot silk of Kevin's dick, rubbing his own against it as he kissed the other man. He might be able to get off with this touch alone.

But he wanted more.

"You want to turn around?" He whispered against Kevin's cheek, "brace yourself against the wall?"

"I very much want to," Kevin's smoky voice whispered in reply. Kevin took his time with one more kiss. Then he turned so that his back was pressed to Aidan's chest, his ass against Aidan's dick.

Aidan grinned, leaning into Kevin. He indulged himself a little; he played with Kevin's hair, traced the planes of his shoulder blades. He ran his hand down Kevin's back slowly, letting Kevin's body and his own build on their sweet, shivering tension.

He stroked Kevin's ass with the flat of his hand, and Kevin pressed back against him.

Since it was so much fun to keep Kevin wanting more, Aidan trailed his fingers down Kevin's chest as well, stroking the head of his dick slowly. Kevin whimpered.

Aidan usually would have kept teasing him for a bit. But he felt as if he had a wild animal on a leash made of tissue paper. He'd *never* been this desperate for sex before.

"Kev? I really want to be inside you right now," he whispered the words against Kevin's throat.

Kevin pressed back against him. "Then be inside me, Aidan. That's where I want you."

The intensity of Aidan's joy was almost painful. He snagged the lube bottle and poured the gel into his hand. Reaching around, he stroked Kevin, slathering lube up to the base of him. Kevin's hips bucked, sending tiny shockwaves up Aidan's own shaft when skin brushed skin.

And then it was time to lube himself.

He thought he'd been ready, after all the play they'd had with the touch-sensitive prosthetic. He thought he'd known what to expect.

He was dead wrong. Stroking himself was like nothing he'd felt before. His dick jerked, sending hot tingling through his core. Aidan gasped for air. Shit, if this was just lubing up…

Leaning close again, he let his dick rest between Kevin's legs and kissed his shoulder blade, sliding well-lubed fingers inside him. He slid his other hand down to massage Kevin's balls. Kevin groaned, fingers scraping against the wall as his bracing hands folded into fists.

"Don't tease, love. I'm past that point..."

Aidan kissed Kevin's throat as he stretched his boyfriend, doing as he asked and simply focusing on the tight heat of Kevin's body, the pressure in his own.

"You ready?" The words came out rough.

"You have to ask?" Kevin's words were a pant. He leaned back hard against Aidan, hands pressed flat against the wall.

Aidan knew that invitation, and he took it. Positioning himself, he pressed inside the man he loved.

Every nerve in his body turned on. He gulped for air. The all-enveloping pressure, tight and hot and wet, was like nothing he'd felt when a device had routed signals to his body. This was beyond good. Sinking down inside Kevin, he felt as if he'd been cold all his life, and had suddenly found fire.

He pressed himself down and in, the heat of Kevin burning around him. For a breathless, motionless heartbeat, he held himself there and branded this moment into his mind. But he couldn't stay still. He needed to *move*.

His hips thrust, and his body took over. He and Kevin moved in perfect rhythm. Reaching down, Aidan added to the fun by taking Kevin in his hand and stroking him with every thrust.

Kevin's body convulsed around him, and Aidan gritted his teeth. The spring wound inside him would crack if the pressure didn't let up. Kevin was even closer to the edge, keening softly and shaking.

Aidan shifted, moving his hips so that his dick pressed over Kevin's prostate with every thrust. He loved the way doing that made Kevin arch his back and beg for release.

He wasn't disappointed. Kevin threw his head back. "Aidan please love, please, please now! All of you, all of you now!"

And Aidan gave his boyfriend all of himself, thrusting hard and fast. His nerves were on fire. Kevin gave the most amazing cry of joy, his whole body bucking as he came. His hole tightened around Aidan, his passage pulsing. Aidan's nerves went off like fireworks. The spring that had been winding up inside him released all its tension and its pleasure in one bone-shattering explosion. He knew he cried out, somewhere in there.

Then he was floating, and warm, and safe, and the world was somewhere else.

He rested himself against Kevin's support, working to catch his breath. "Holy...holy shit Kev...holy shit..."

"No argument here," Kevin panted back. "That...that was...stupendous? No...wrong connotation. Phenomenal? Tremendous? Mm...sensational. That was sensational. Yes. Truly sensational."

Aidan chuckled, nuzzling his face against Kevin's soft hair. "Okay. Sensational. We'll go with that. You want up?"

"What I want is that bed; my knees are weak," Kevin murmured.

Aidan discovered that now, afterglow included being a little dizzy. He gently pulled out of his boyfriend and helped him straighten up. Kevin pulled him into a tight hug, kissing the top of his head. "Worth the wait?" he asked softly.

Aidan hummed his agreement against Kevin's throat. "You...you're the best."

"The feeling's mutual." Kevin chuckled. "Though I may be walking funny today, I'll admit."

"Don't need to walk," Aidan replied with a chuckle. "We can just stay here all day."

"I can do that." Kevin agreed in a murmur. "And in half an hour or so, I'd like to take a closer look at your new features. A very...*detailed*...exploration."

Aidan grinned.

Kevin opened his eyes, studying him for a moment. Raising a hand, he stroked Aidan's cheek. "You're happy, right?"

Aidan laughed and kissed Kevin's palm. "I'm more than happy. I've never been this happy in my whole life. Why?"

Kevin smiled gently, and closed his eyes. "Just making sure. Let's clean up. Then lie down with me?"

Aidan did as Kevin suggested. He wrapped his arms around Kevin once he was back in bed, holding him close.

Kevin was still asleep when Aidan woke again. He slipped away carefully, stepping into the shower with Kevin's words in mind. *Detailed exploration.*

When he stepped out, Kevin was lying with his hands behind his head, watching him with half-closed eyes and a soft smile. "Who said you could get out of bed, hmm?"

"I figured, since you wanted a detailed exploration, it might be nice if I was clean," Aidan replied in a half-whisper as he climbed back onto the bed and kissed along Kevin's jaw.

"Mmm. That's why you're the commander, I suppose." Kevin murmured in his ear. "Forethought. On the other hand..." Twisting his hips, he coaxed Aidan onto his back. Lying beside him, he trailed white fingers down Aidan's length, over his stomach. "Once in a while, you need to quit thinking and relax. My job, I think."

"I thought your job was logistics," Aidan chuckled, running his fingers through Kevin's hair. "But I suppose making me relax is a good job, too."

"And a necessary one." Kevin kissed his lips gently, his fingers just barely touching Aidan's skin. "Now, love, this time it's your turn to stay still. Agreed?"

"If I have to," Aidan agreed, anticipation running through him. He grinned and folded his arms behind his head. "You'll have to tell me what you think after your *inspection.*"

"Ssh." Kevin slid his body against Aidan's, slipping up to kiss him slow. He stroked his long fingers along the insides of Aidan's thighs, touch feather light. He traced caressing circles, then softly, so softly, brushed fingertips over Aidan's balls. His fingers were gentle as a sigh, moving in spirals. Under his fingers, the flesh began to contract as Aidan's dick took notice. Aidan bit back a pleased gasp at the new sensation. He let his head drop back against the pillow.

"Kev…"

"We did it your way, love." Kevin murmured, fingers moving. "Now give me the chance to introduce you to the subtleties of this new anatomical feature of yours. There are much more refined sensations I can show you, if you can be patient…"

As he spoke, he stroked one finger up Aidan's shaft, tracing the head. The other hand continued tickling the insides of Aidan's thighs, tracing his balls, as Kevin kissed Aidan's throat, ran his tongue along the lobe of his ear.

Aidan inhaled sharply and bit down on his lip. "How do you cope?" he whispered, his voice strangled. These sensations were like tiny bolts of electricity, hot and cold by turns, and he didn't know what to do with them. The tension began to coil again. *That's my dick getting hard,* he realized. "Feels…feels so good."

"I've got practice." Kevin whispered, stroking the tip of Aidan until it twitched under his fingers. He smiled softly, then reached over, squeezing a little lube into his hand. Rubbing it between his fingers, he brushed his lips over Aidan's. "Don't worry. I'll give you plenty of chance to learn."

"You better," Aidan whispered, his voice hitching. He clutched at the pillow under his head to try and keep himself still.

Kevin kissed down his throat, soft red hair brushing his skin. His hand traced up Aidan's dick, trailing cool wetness, circled his head, and slipped down again, once, twice, setting a slow heartbeat rhythm. "Feel good?" he asked softly, watching Aidan's face.

"Mmm," Aidan moaned his agreement, head tilted back and eyes closed as he tried to keep breathing. They had played with the prosthetic like this once or twice, but the sensation hadn't been as direct, and it was driving him crazy already. He'd never been so aroused.

Kevin kept his touch light as he teased Aidan. Then his free hand squeezed Aidan's balls, and that was a whole new kind of thrill; a sudden, hard tug of heat and pleasure. Fingers caressing, Kevin chuckled. "That's just the start."

Aidan tried to respond, but it came out an incoherent groan instead. He shifted into Kevin's hand, relishing in every new feeling, every difference in the sensation.

Kevin teased, toyed, stroked every inch of Aidan. The coil of heat inside him was impossibly tight.

"Open your eyes, Aidan my love. Look at me."

Aidan snapped his eyes open, watching as Kevin smiled his slow, wicked grin and sat up, moving to straddle his hips. He rubbed their dicks together, holding Aidan's eyes and making him feel like he might just lose his mind. Then the pale man poured more lube into his palm. He reached behind himself with one hand and spread lube down Aidan's dick with the other, teasing the whole damn way.

"I see this meets with your approval?" he whispered teasingly.

Aidan whimpered and pressed himself further into Kevin's hand. "Cruel," he muttered breathlessly. His heart raced as Kevin continued to toy with him, driving him spiraling up and up and up.

"Only to be kind, love." Kevin whispered as he moved. Aidan's dick sank into Kevin's body. His lover's skin pressed against his balls. Pleasure arced over him.

"Let's see how long you can last, shall we?" Kevin's whisper was like smoke and chocolate.

"Probably not that long," Aidan gasped out. "This is fricking amazing..."

"You think that's good? I haven't done anything yet." Kevin murmured, leaning in for a slow, burning kiss. Then he leaned back, and took Aidan's entire length inside him.

Aidan was lucky he didn't bite through his tongue. Kevin was even tighter in this position, and holy crap he was hot, moving over Aidan. Just looking at him was making his heart pound, and the feelings in his body...

All of Kevin was gorgeous, but his dick standing proud as he rode Aidan made the whole thing impossible to look away from. Aidan reached out and put a hand around Kevin, stroking him fast. Kevin yelped in surprise, then in pleasure.

"Aidan," he panted in a tone that could have been a complaint if he wasn't so aroused, "I wanted this to last."

"It already has." Aidan whispered, speeding his hand. Then he tried something new. Moving his legs a little, he got some leverage and pressed up when Kevin came down.

Kevin's head dropped back, his eyes closed, and he rode Aidan faster. So that worked? Aidan grinned and kept it up, thrusting up in time with his boyfriend.

And Kevin came. A thrilled half-scream forced itself from his throat despite his best effort to keep quiet, as he tipped over the edge. He emptied himself over Aidan's belly, his passage wrapping Aidan in pulsing heat.

The sudden pressure made Aidan's hips buck as he lost control in one delicious rush, burning heat and joy going off like a laser show inside him.

When they'd rode out their orgasm, Kevin draped himself down over Aidan. A contented sigh tickled the skin along Aidan's throat. "Now that...was fun...."

Aidan laughed and kissed Kevin's temple. "That was fucking amazing."

Kevin gave a tiny snort. "Terrible pun, Aidan my love. Truly miserable."

Aidan had to smile at that.

They made love three more times that day, each time more slowly, more sensually, as they explored Aidan's body together. The sunset light caught in Kevin's hair, setting it alight as he sucked between Aidan's legs and set Aidan's body on fire. With a satiated sigh, he lay down beside Aidan a little while later.

"I'll get us tickets for tomorrow." He murmured as their breathing grew slow and easy. "Won't take us long to get to the rendezvous."

"Yeah," Aidan agreed dreamily. "Not long…"

They were out the door and on their way by seven the next morning. Kevin had gotten them done up as CSS level businessmen. He'd spent way too long messing with Aidan's hair. But it meant they could ride the high-speed train up to Fort Collins and deal with the Sector checks at each train station, which were a lot less of a pain than the highway.

Aidan pocketed his Citizen card as the Peacekeeper handed it back with a professional smile. The difference between what he got when he was passing as CSS and when he passed for lower Standing galled him, but he could use it today.

He followed Kevin to their seats on the train, resisting the urge to touch his hair. Not feeling it on his neck was weird, but the stuff Kevin had plastered it down with was even weirder. It felt like his hair had glue in it.

I still think I look like a dipshit,

He typed out on his tab once they'd settled down and the train had begun to roll.

Kevin glanced down when his tab pinged, and quirked his lips. He typed.

Oh, you do. But you look like a CSS dipshit, my love.
And that's what will make our day run smoothly.

He glanced up, winking.

I will say, you do clean up quite nicely.

Aidan rolled his eyes.

Twenty minutes later, they were going through the Fort Collins Sector check, and going to the garage where a Go car had been acquired for them. It was one of the finest models, and it had the ads muted.

"I'll take this car as a sign that Luck's on our side," Kevin remarked once he'd plugged the sound-wave modulation unit into the console to feed the car's systems innocent sounds and mask their actual discussions. He input their route, and the car shushed out of its parking spot and into the day.

Fort Collins was a little easier than Denver, with Siberian elm and honey locust trees growing up to shade the streets along with the shade-cloth. The ads here were mostly for leisure activities, a little less intense than the ones back south.

As they rode, Kevin glanced at Aidan and smiled. Pulling out his tab, he brought up a playlist. The first song was soft and hopeful, full of happy flute, guitar and words about being sent on your way.

Kevin reached out and took Aidan's hand, squeezing it tight. The excitement that had been bubbling through them both since Kevin's birthday fizzed in Aidan's chest. He shot his boyfriend a grin as the wide Fort Collins roads rolled out ahead, and the sun came through the clouds.

A new song started, bright and energizing as the spring sunlight. Kevin grinned and tapped his tab, projecting a window with the lyrics between them.

"I think you'll like this one, love."

Aidan read the words as the artist and Kevin sang. They were words of hope in the face of trouble, fierce and full of joyful resolve.

Kevin threw his head back, his red hair blazing in the sun as he sang,

"You broke the boy in me, but you won't break the man!"

Aidan grinned, loving the sight so much. Kevin caught his eye, and the world was full of wonder.

For the hell of it, Aidan raised his own rough voice, and sang with his boyfriend about Saint Elmo's fire burning and banners flying on a new horizon, while they rode towards a meeting that might just change their lives.

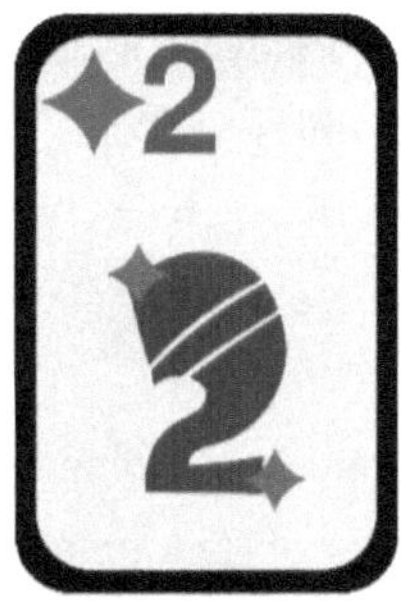

"What're you looking at?"

Tweak jumped a little at the sound of Naomi's voice behind her, but she got it under control.

"The g-guys. C-checking where they are. Trackers on their t-tabs."

Naomi leaned carefully over her shoulder, studying the maps on her screens. Sarah leaned in on her other side, too close. "Hunh, they're in FoCo already. Cool."

Tweak leaned away. Naomi glanced at her, pale eyes thoughtful. "You worried about them?"

Tweak shrugged. "Hunter chatter. G-got me thinking. Wanted to c-check. No big."

That was a load of bull, really. She was worried. The bounty hunters were getting way too good at their game, and there was half a billion on the table in Corps bounty and job offers. That was a lot of money.

Tweak tapped her screen, setting the AI pattern recognition bot she'd named Watchdog to work. It'd keep tabs on the guys' trackers and collate information from all kinds of sources in their area. Watchdog would give her an alert if anything was up.

That done, she turned in her chair. "Whatcha need?"

Naomi glanced at Sarah, who started to grin. Naomi's lips quirked.

"We've been thinking about doing some inter-divisional stuff. Munitions division keeps tons of intel on all the bases, but I got a look at the way most of the other bases secure their Munitions intel. And it's shit. So how'd you like to help out on some penetration testing?"

"Whatcha wanna do?" Tweak asked, watching the two women.

Sarah grinned. "Some dickwads off a couple bases told Naomi she was full of crap when she let them know their systems had holes. So we're going to give them shit and prove it. You know, all that 'red team' kind of stuff. You in?"

Tweak leaned back in her chair, fingers tapping on the arm rests. Sarah was grinning and Naomi was smiling. She studied their faces.

"This's a prank? You w-want me in? On pranks?"

"Well yeah," Sarah agreed, like that should be a no-brainer.

Tweak glanced down. They wanted her in on the pranks they pulled. They were asking her to get in on their favorite thing.

"You want in?" Sarah asked. Tweak raised her head. "Yeah. But Aidan said I'm not s-supposed to hack other D-dusters anymore. W-was in trouble l-last time. Big trouble. Write a pen-test m-mission proposal, but no red-teaming. C-clear it with Liza f-first. Okay?"

The two women looked at one another, their smiles smaller now. Tweak tipped her head, trying to get a read on what they were thinking. Then she gave up. "What? You guys l-looking at each other weird."

Sarah gave her a quick grin. "Nothing weird, Tweak. We're just proud of you."

Tweak clicked her tongue, rolling her eyes. "I'm not a kid."

"Yeah, you kind of are," Naomi put in quietly. "But hey, you're a whiz kid. That's something."

Tweak shot her a look, but she couldn't help but smile a little.

They wrote the proposal for penetration testing in an hour, and Tweak sent it over to Liza. She got a note back that read, 'Interesting. Sent to Sector.'

Leaning back in her seat, she stretched and checked Watchdog again while she waited for lunch. The guys were really moving; they were already halfway through the FoCo in a car.

Glancing at the clock, she realized that she was this close to missing lunch. That'd freak Billie out.

Putting her console in sleep mode, she headed down the hall.

"Hi Tweak!" Henrietta chirped as Tweak stepped into the canteen. The four-year-old clambered out of her seat and bounced over with a second-hand tab held out in front of her, a grin all over her face. Tweak grinned right back, squatting to get to the girl's eye level. "Hey Hen. Whatcha got?"

"We learned about plants today! Lookit, we drew how plants grow!" the little girl chortled, pointing at a circle of wobbly, bright sketches.

Tweak gave the little girl a grin. "Real cool!"

"Come see Tommy's!" The little girl enthused, reaching for her hand. Tweak braced herself, but the little girl froze, her eyes wide and thoughtful.

"Is today a touching day, or a no touching day?" Henrietta asked.

Tweak smiled, shaking her head. "N-no touching, Hen. G-good job. You asked. T-thanks."

"You're welcome!" the four year old trotted back to her seat, pointing at a spot. "Sit!"

"Hen," Jim put in, "it isn't nice ordering people. How do you say that better?"

Henrietta thought about it for a second, "Would you like to sit with us?" she asked. Tweak nodded. "Thanks."

Taking the offered seat, she turned to Tommy. "Hen says you drew s-some plants?"

"Unh-hunh," the twelve-year-old agreed. Pulling out his tab, he showed the careful drawing of a plant's life cycle, from a seed to a ripe tomato hanging on the vine. "Janice says if we learn this, we can help her and Alice plant the next crop."

Tweak studied the image, nodding. For twelve, the kid was really good at this kind of drawing.

"Wow. Cool."

"There you are." Liza's voice sent nerves zinging up Tweak's spine, but the woman was smiling when she turned to face her. Liza held out her tab, a message window open on it.

Message Handle: Sector40COM

Message: Penetration test approved. I authorize you to remind a few bases that they're getting sloppy. Tell Ms. Tweak not to do anything that causes long term harm. Enjoy.

"Magnum's answering our communications on priority these days," Liza added. "I guess he's pretty happy with what we're doing." She smiled anxiously. "Just one thing, Tweak. Have some fun, but don't make enemies, okay?"

Tweak bobbed her head. "No worries. N-naomi and Sarah're helping. They got ideas."

Liza's dark brows shot up. "Naomi, Sarah and you are pulling this together?"

Tweak grinned. "Yep!"

Liza let out a shaky breath. "Oooookay...just don't get somebody killed. Please. And make sure you eat lunch." Pocketing her tab, she gave Tweak a quick smile and a nod as she turned away.

Behind her back, Tweak rolled her eyes. Liza really didn't get it. If Tweak had wanted to do real damage to these idiots' systems, it would have been done already.

Turning, she started to head for the serving table, but Liza's voice pulled her up short.

"You guys, really? This is a food preparation area! Can't you make out somewhere else?"

Tweak wandered over and stuck her head into the storage closet, expecting to see Sarah and Yvonne. But it was Billie and Topher up against the racks of boxes and cans, looking ruffled and grinning shamefacedly. Tweak laughed.

"Nice, guys! Liza, you're lame."

She shot her note to Sarah and Naomi after lunch. They were in her office in minutes. She turned in her seat. "Kay. What base do we do?"

Naomi rested her hip against Tweak's desk. "The bitchy note I got was off 1399, so let's do their system."

"Cool," Tweak agreed, turning in her chair and picking up her 'buds. "Go do stuff. I'll m-message when I'm in."

Once she was alone, she got to work. Running through the GreyNet, she found the system for the base she wanted. Exploiting a system vulnerability that a two-year-old should have spotted, she slid in and used her favorite Remote Access Tool. The system opened up in front of her like an origami flower. She shot a note, and got on with running scans on their system.

"You were r-right," she stated when the two women stepped into the room, "this system's bull. All the m-munitions department records like this?"

"Enough of them are," Naomi remarked. "So how're we going to make our point without making enemies?"

Tweak tapped her fingers against the arm rest. "We can do anything r-right now. Your call."

The coding room was quiet for a moment. Then Sarah snapped her fingers. "Oh man, I've totally got it. Tweak. Take a screenshot of the desktop. Set that as the background. Then hide all the files and icons."

Tweak felt the excitement tingle in her fingertips. She grinned. "They're g-gonna freak! Totally."

Turning, she took the image, and collected the desktop shortcuts into a hidden folder. Once that was done, she set the image she'd taken as the desktop background. The window appeared exactly the way it had a moment ago, but now the icons were pointless pixels on the screen. Turning back, Tweak crossed her arms, grinning. "We'll wait till we hear them s-scream. Then we'll fix it and tell them how I got in. D-dead easy to fix."

Naomi chuckled. "Well that screaming fit will happen right about..." but whatever she'd been about to say died on her lips. She blinked.

"Tweak? What's the alert that just popped up?"

Tweak swiveled her seat, and felt her heart rate spike. On the screen, a snarling dog image was barking the word 'alert!'

"Fuck," Tweak hissed, and flicked away what she'd been playing with. Pulling up Watchdog, she typed queries.

"What's going on?" Naomi's voice had an edge to it. Tweak shook her head. "In a sec. Gotta work."

She zeroed in on the camera grids she'd fed Watchdog, homing in on the guys' trackers. There they were, seen through what looked like some business security system drone's feed.

There was Aidan, and Kevin, and some woman. Some guy was running their way from up the alley. And there was somebody with a rifle on the rooftop.

"Shit!" Tweak yelped. Naomi sucked in a breath. "Send them an alert, we—"

"I'll do b-better." Tweak snapped. Taking control of the drone, she grabbed a joystick and plugged it into her console with quaking fingers. Carefully, she used the stick to pilot the hacked drone. Now she just had to move fast and smooth enough.

The shooter barely looked up, until the drone was right over his head. By then it was too late. Tweak jammed the joystick forward, and the body of the drone clunked into the guy's skull at full speed.

Sarah whooped, and the sound sent Tweak's heart into overdrive. She whipped around, jabbing a finger at the door. "Get quiet or g-get out."

Snapping back into her focus, she fired off an alert to both men's tabs. The optical on her hacked drone was hazy, but she could see the three figures below looking up. She wobbled the drone in the air, then used it to hit the asshole with the gun again.

That done, she went looking for the next shooter. Hunters always worked in groups. She could feel the tension shivering under her skin.

"They g-gotta get out of there," she snapped, shooting off a new volley of tab alerts. "You shitheads, m-move!"

On the screen, the group broke and ran.

Event File 8
Event Tag: Proximity Warning
Timestamp: 13:22-2-28-2157

The car pulled into the lot in front of the run-down little museum. Kevin did his best to put on a cheerful face, though the site wasn't one that inspired much confidence.

"Well, these are the coordinates. The instructions are to walk through the exhibit, stop at the wheat shipping panorama and tap the glass, then step out the side exit."

"And we still don't know who our contact is, or what they look like." Aidan finished, resignation in his tone. Kevin nodded. "Afraid that's the shape of things. I've run a general perimeter scan, I'm not picking up any particularly worrisome signals. What do you say?"

Aidan considered the building for a moment, eyes narrowed. Then he drew a breath. "I guess we came this far. So let's go on in."

"Right," Kevin agreed, taking the sound-wave modulator off the dash.

The museum's interior was a dusty, stuffy little space that looked like it hadn't gotten funding since Incorporation. However, it was a free exhibit on the history of Denver, housed in an ArgusCorp area and showing forms of transport through the ages. They wandered past images of covered wagons, the steam powered train cars of three hundred years ago, and the grain silos beside the tracks. Kevin tapped the plastic of the display case around ancient photos of a manual semi-truck being filled with wheat from a silo. "Funny how heavy that tech looks, isn't it?"

"Yeah," Aidan agreed, "it's weird seeing windows on a semi. And there's all those sharp edges and corners on the thing."

"Definitely lacking in elegance," Kevin replied, meandering casually to the next exhibit. Internally, he kept a running clock. Half an hour seemed like a reasonable amount of time for men their age to see what there was on show at this little exhibit and lose interest. He caught Aidan's eye when he judged that they'd wasted enough time, and turned for the side door.

The door let them out onto a walkway opening onto the main sidewalk to the right, and an alley to the left. They made the left turn, and the cool shadows of the buildings enveloped them.

Kevin kept close to Aidan as they moved, eyes on the roofline overhead and the corners where concealment was easy. He didn't let his eyes focus at a natural level until they'd reached the blank wall waiting for them. Turning, he watched the mouth of the alley.

"I really hope we aren't about to end a wild goose chase," he remarked, for the sake of having something to say. Aidan gave him a cockeyed look. "What the...why would there be a goose here, Kev?"

Kevin tipped his head, giving his sweet, hopelessly under-educated boyfriend a smile. "It's a turn of phrase, love. It means wasting your time, from the fifteen-hundreds if I remember my etymology right. It was in the rewritten Romeo and Juliet we watched, remember?"

Aidan gave him one of his crooked smiles. "All I remember off that thing is Benvolio running across that roof with no pants. And that kiss scene at the end."

"You and your one-track mind. You really—" Catching movement out of the corner of his eye, Kevin turned. "Ah, here we are then."

At the mouth of the alley, a woman stood poised against the light. Not a particularly advantageous position, Kevin observed. One should never stand framed against the light when unfamiliar contacts were involved; it invited a blunt instrument to the head or a bullet to the gut if your guess about their motives was wrong.

But the young lady didn't seem to be thinking along such lines. Moving with confidence, she strode down the alley.

As she drew closer, Kevin took in the hair pulled back in a ponytail and the color of rich farm soil, curly as something from a movie. The face spattered with so many freckles that she appeared to have been stippled with a paint brush. The brilliantly blue eyes, accentuated by her blue coolant-lined jacket.

"Turning into a hot day," the young lady remarked.

Aidan nodded. "Looks like a storm's coming in too."

"Best if we get in out of the dust," Kevin added quietly.

The woman planted a hand on her hip, studying them. Her eyes narrowed for a beat. Then her lips quirked. Stepping forward, she stuck out a hand.

"Hi guys. Who've I been talking to?"

"That'd be me. Kevin, at your service." He stepped just in front of Aidan as they moved, subtly shielding him and glad that working with Yvonne had taught him to do it in a way that wasn't obvious. Kevin had learned how to camouflage the protective screening of those he cared about with greetings and good manners.

He shook the young lady's hand. "And this is my partner, Aidan. It's a pleasure to make your acquaintance in person, Ms. Bran ap Llyr."

"Go with Brandi," the young lady demurred with a flick-fingered gesture of easy dismissal. Her grip was surprisingly strong, the fingers calloused in his. She gave him a smile.

"Good to get in touch with you guys. I hear we have a lot to talk about. Cooling system parts for intel on seeds, that's the trade we've got in mind. You said you could get the materials for the types of cooling systems I specced?"

"What we can't print we can scrounge," Kevin agreed easily. "Though I have to say, I've never worked with a system this old before."

The young woman shrugged, smiling. "Not surprised."

Kevin slowly lowered the backpack from his shoulder. "May I put this down at your feet?" he asked.

Brandi nodded. Kevin set the bag down gently. "As a gesture of goodwill, the smaller pieces you've stipulated are inside."

Brandi blinked at the bag, then at them. "Hunh. Wow. That was fast." Dropping to one knee, she opened the bag, and blinked. She raised her head, eyes measuring. "How much is this going to run me?"

"No charge," Aidan replied with a small smile. "We wanted to start these negotiations in good faith."

Brandi gave a quick, bright laugh. "Okay, I'm impressed. That's some faith!"

"We act with as much honor as this rather battered world allows," Kevin remarked with a smile. Grinning, Brandi zipped the bag and slung it over her shoulder.

As she moved, something slipped from her pocket and clattered against the concrete. Brandi glanced down, and Kevin saw her shoulders tighten. Reaching down, she lifted what looked like a wooden coin, studying a mark in its center.

"Shit," she whispered. Standing, she scanned their surroundings with wide eyes.

"Something wrong?" Kevin asked, watching her move and feeling his body tense for action. His tab vibrated in his pocket, but he ignored the device in favor of watching their contact study their surroundings.

"Something, for sure..." Brandi agreed. "Not sure what yet, but something..."

Overhead, there was a whir and a hollow 'clonk!' Kevin whipped around. A small security drone wobbled in the air, looking for all the world as if it was waving at them. Then it plummeted like a diving falcon and cracked the skull of the man blearily hanging over the parapet. For the second time, Kevin realized. The sound that had alerted them meant the drone had already hit the man once.

The man, he noted, with a rather large gun.

"Brandi! Down!"

Kevin jumped at the sound of a voice he didn't recognize. The movement saved his life. Searing pain raced down his left arm as a bullet ripped a furrow along it. Another bullet pranged off the wall.

Kevin didn't need to think about his next move. Pushing Aidan behind him, he tugged a gun from the holo-holster on his belt, took aim and fired. The head on the rooftop across the alley ducked out of sight.

"Run!" he snapped. Covering their exit with a few more bullets, he suited words to actions. Brandi and the man who'd come running down the alley after her were making a beeline for the nearest bit of cover between the buildings, Aidan right behind them. Kevin overtook them in a few strides. They dodged into a warren of alleys between the buildings. Get distance, that was the key. Get distance between them and the shooters. The bastards might have friends, and they definitely had sensors in their gear that would alert their employers to the fact that they'd stopped moving.

But it wasn't just distance they needed; it was cover. Kevin's mind churned as they ran. They needed to get out of sight. Gunshots were an automatic alert for EagleCorp. An investigative drone would arrive within ten minutes to canvass the area and discern the issue. They didn't want to be running when that happened.

His tab buzzed in his pocket, but now definitely was not the time to answer it. His eyes scanned their surroundings, searching for something that would serve them as cover.

There. That'd do.

"Under here!"

They slid in tandem under a parked semi-trailer sitting on cinder blocks. Grit cut into Kevin's palms, counterpoint to the searing line down his arm.

The man with a mop of dark curls and the same blue eyes as their contact shot him a grin as he pressed his hands to the woman's shoulder blade, breathing hard. "Fuck this noise, hunh?"

"No arguments here," Kevin agreed, catching his breath. The young man gave him a nod. "Brendan. I'd shake hands, but Brandi's bleeding. Heads up, so're you."

"Kevin," he acknowledged with a tight smile, "and I'd noticed, but thanks for the tip."

"Bleeding?" Aidan exclaimed, turning on his knees. "Kev, what's the damage? Where are you—"

The bleat of their tabs cut off his words. Out of Aidan's pocket, a holo of Tweak at her desk projected.

"You s-s-s-shitheads!" The young technical officer snarled. "Answer your t-t-tabs!"

"What's our status, Tweak?" Aidan asked quietly, and Kevin heard him restraining his own fear for their techie's benefit.

"I t-t-took out two hunters with the d-d-drone," Tweak replied, eyes flicking away to fix on what Kevin imagined were several of her screens. Her fingers were typing as she spoke. Her words came in staccato bursts, fast as machine gun fire. "P-paired w-working team. Got them both. Knocked out. You're g-good for n-n-now, but I c-c-c-c-c..."

"Deep breath, Tweak," Aidan murmured. "You got this."

Tweak sat still for a heartbeat, sucking in a breath in the holographic image. She spoke a little more slowly as she began again. "I c-can't b-block all the s-security s-systems around you forever. Those g-guys were c-c-contractors. They've got m-motion sensors on them. Eagle will know they've s-stopped moving. You need to g-g-get out of there; EagleCorp is going to s-send people s-soon."

"I've got us a safehouse chosen," Kevin put in, nodding to their new acquaintances. "Care to accompany us for the duration?"

Brandi gave him a pained smile. "Thanks for the offer. I think I'm going to need some patching up."

"Same here," Kevin agreed with a rueful quirk of the lips. He glanced at Tweak's hologram. "By the way, beautiful work on the save with the kamikaze drone. I didn't know you could pilot them remotely too."

She gave him a quick, knife edged smirk. "Me? I can do l-lots. But I c-can't s-stop bullets. Don't get dead."

"Roger that," Aidan agreed with a smile. "We'll keep our tabs on us, Tweak. Track EagleCorp dispatch and reports, will you, and keep us in the loop."

"Kay," Tweak agreed, and touched something out of sight on her end. Her image vanished.

Aidan drew a slow breath beside him. "Okay, we're going to need to move. Triage first. How bad is Brandi hit?"

"Not bad, actually," Brendan replied cheerfully. "Just a big fat flesh wound. Brandi bleeds all over 'cause she's messy, is all."

"You're a jackhole, lil' brother," Brandi grumbled.

Brendan leaned his head against hers for a moment as he reached into his pocket and pulled out a roll of bandage. "Yeah, well, you're related to me."

"How about you, Kev?" Aidan asked. Kevin held up his left arm. "Just a scratch, I think, it's..." He stared as blood ran in a steady trickle out of his sleeve, a macabre little fountain.

Macabre was definitely the right word for it. It was a word coined in bloodshed; in the slaughter of the Maccabees when their rebellion failed so long ago. He watched with detached interest as his blood pooled by his feet, washing the concrete as the blood of the ancient rebels had washed the cobbles of Judea.

You, my friend, are going into shock, he calmly informed himself.

"Shit." Aidan whispered. Yanking Kevin's jacket off his shoulder, he dug in the pockets. Kevin was glad his man was up for it; the sight of his own blood coming out of the sleeve like rain out of a gutter wasn't leaving him in much of a state to see to it himself.

"You packed the nanoid foam, right?" Aidan murmured in his ear. Kevin nodded. "Inner lowermost pocket of my jacket, on the left."

Pulling the tube out, Aidan shook it and opened it over the long, freely bleeding gash in his arm. Pink foam poured down the wound, stinging like an invasion of fire ants until the numbing agent carried by the nanoids in the frothy matrix went to work. Kevin held his breath against the pain. It passed as quickly as it had come, taking the injury's burn with it. Kevin relaxed, watching as the nanoids formed a tight pink web over the gash, sealing it and beginning to treat the injury and shock.

Aidan squatted, watching him with worried blue eyes. "That'll hold for now. We'll put an autopad on it when we're safe."

"Sounds like a plan," Kevin replied quietly. He drew a breath. "Well, that was execrable. What was that about getting out of here?"

The room's door creaked on its hinges as Aidan levered it open. Kevin leaned against the wall once it was closed, feeling the weakness in his muscles.

"How are you?" Aidan asked, his hand on Kevin's shoulder.

Kevin gave him a smile of reassurance. "Mildly grazed, love. Nothing a little rest and an autopad won't sort out." He turned his eyes to their contact as she flopped on the bed. "Hope that goes for you as well?"

"Eh," Brandi agreed, "Nothing much."

Behind her, Brendan undid bandages and studied the injury as he peeled the backing from an autopad he'd pulled out of his bag. "Yep, just a graze. Probably a ricochet. You got lucky," he added to the woman who was apparently his sister.

"I got Hawthorn is what I got. Got a heads up." Brandi remarked over her shoulder, giving the man a smile. He whistled low. "You're getting good, holding your clarity in the middle of all this. Mom and Barley're going to be all over you when they hear."

Brandi shook her head, rolling her eyes as fond children did when talking about the quirks of parents. "Yeah, they will. Have I stopped bleeding, Bren?"

"Yep. Autopad's on," Brendan agreed, giving his sister a quick squeeze of the hand.

Kevin tipped his head. "So you two are actually siblings?" He asked as Aidan doctored him.

Brendan turned his frank, wide smile back on them. "Yep. She's five minutes older than me. Our sib's ten minutes younger. Lucky number three. So, you two are an actual couple?"

"Yeah, we are." Aidan agreed, though Kevin heard the slight twang of tension in his voice. He felt his own gut tighten. But Brendan only tipped his head. "Monogamous?" The young man asked, eyes alight and smile bright.

That definitely was not the response Kevin had been expecting. He blinked. "Ah...yes. Yes, definitely monogamous. Very."

The younger man snapped his fingers playfully.

His sister reached over and tapped the side of his head with two fingers. "Snake in his cage, little brother. We're working." Then she glanced back at them with a small, professional smile. "Appreciate the room assist."

"Not a problem," Aidan agreed, looking as poleaxed as Kevin felt. "Do you guys need to call in anybody else?"

"Nope, it's just us out here." Brendan quipped. "I navigate, she negotiates, Barley—that's our little sib—stays home and roots us. Just like our namesakes."

"Namesakes?" Kevin asked, feeling as if he ought to be making this connection. He must have lost a bit more blood than he thought. "Who's your...oh! Right! Saint Brendan the Navigator!" He glanced between the siblings with a smile. "Are you folks Catholic, by any chance? I don't meet many coreligionists."

The siblings shared a quiet smile. Looking up, Brandi shook her head. "Sorry friend, not Catholic. You guys just got a lot of good ideas off us."

She went on before he could put the pieces together on that. "So how'd we get tracked like that? We've been wiping our trail behind us, and we know how to do that. How about you guys?"

Kevin felt a blush of embarrassment ignite in his cheeks. Aidan rubbed the back of his neck. "Yeah, this one's probably on us. We're not leaving a trail, but our base has pulled some pretty hot stunts in the last few years, so the contractors are getting cash bonuses if they bring in Dusters. And it wouldn't be impossible to figure out that we're not from around here. Me, anyway. I'm not a grid kid." He shrugged. "They can't tell Dusters apart, but they can tell that we're Dusters. And the heat's on our people. Sorry about that."

Brandi and Brendan shared a worried look. The young man sighed. The young woman gave them an annoyed once-over. "A little warning would've been nice."

"Our mistake," Kevin put in, mentally kicking himself. He should have cased the area. Taken more precautions. He'd have to do that going forward, if they were really this hot of a commodity to the bloody hunters.

Brandi sat still for a moment, studying her fingernails. She let out a long sigh. "Okay. Let's try this conversation again. We hear you guys have the parts to retrofit and repair vintage large-space coolant systems. We need parts, you want genomes and samples of seeds. We're up to do that trade. You already showed us you're good for your part of it—" she gestured at the bag on the bed beside her, "—so we're good to talk to you about what you need."

"Crop seeds are the main focus for our organization," Aidan replied, glancing at Kevin. "Kevin has the list of species we're after. So once we work out a system for making this trade, I've got the authority to make deals. Do you have the authority to negotiate?"

"Yep," Brandi agreed, bobbing her head. "The Keepers have charged us to act as their voice in this trade, so what we agree to will be kept. You've got our word."

Aidan blinked, and Kevin read the surprise in his face. He sympathized; the wording was definitely strange. He really hoped these friendly siblings weren't going to turn out to be members of some deranged Fringe cult that had formed out in the middle of God-knew-where.

"Okay," Aidan agreed, "so how are we doing this? We can provide parts and skilled folks to install them for you, if we get your coordinates and work out an exchange plan that protects everybody."

"We've got the people," Brendan deflected with a winning smile and a shrug. "It's just the parts we need. No need for you folks to trek out into the woods. We're thinking a four-step trade: we do four swaps at four different places, and we trade a fourth of what we need each time."

Kevin leaned in. "I like your thinking. It ameliorates the threat of the entire delivery being seized. I take it you'd like to preserve your positional anonymity, which is understandable. In fact, I have to say I'm rather baffled at the fact that this seed bank has caretakers. If you hadn't reached out, we never would have guessed you existed. We were sure we were on the hunt for an unmanned storage facility, which is to say, a needle in a haystack."

He'd intended the words to be a joke and a compliment, but he knew the moment they hit the air that they'd been the wrong ones. Something subtle tightened inside both the siblings, closing their good humor away as effectively as slammed shutters. What was that about?

"Yeah, well. You take it right," Brandi replied, nodding. "If we're going to keep our vow, we need to stay hidden."

Kevin noted the word 'vow', wondering what significance it held for their odd new friends. They seemed conventional enough on the surface, but the more they spoke, the more hints they gave of something more beneath the facade. He filed the nuggets of information away for further examination as he spoke. "Fair enough. Here's the list we've begun. We're looking for anything with a high nutrient density and good heat tolerance, but this would get us started." Flicking on his tab, he pulled up the list he, Alice and Janice had meticulously built and vetted with experts from around the Region. The Latin names glowed on the window as he set the tab on the bed.

The siblings leaned in, dark heads nearly touching as they read. Brendan nodded. Brandi smiled.

"Hunh. You guys really did your homework."

"Indeed," Kevin acknowledged, watching their new contacts. "But turnabout is fair play. Now that we've proven our bona fides, we'd appreciate it if you'd do the same. I assume you've brought a sample of the seed?"

The siblings shared another slow glance. Kevin schooled his face into a calm mask as Brendan reached for his worn backpack. Unzipping it, he pulled out what looked like a vacuum-sealed travel meal. The young man set the plastic-wrapped tray between them on the bed. "In here."

Skepticism made a spirited bid to ruin the diplomatic mask Kevin had put in place, but he gave a polite smile and opened the tray. Frost crystallized on the plastic as the coolant gas dispersed in a puff of winter.

Inside, slices of cucumber, tomato and squash lay in rows. Elongated white and cream-colored seeds graced the vegetable tissues like pearls.

Kevin glanced up at Aidan, fighting down a grin. "These fruits are usually triploid in modern varieties. Seedless. Pass me the genome reader, will you?"

Eyes wary, Aidan passed him the genome reader they'd brought. Plucking out a cucumber seed, Kevin laid it on the plastic, set the genome reader to the proper species and passed it over the seed, watching the blue laser line caress the white surface.

The genome reader blipped, coming up with the gene code. Kevin pulled up a genome of a modern cucumber and hit 'compare'. The match came up negative.

Breath coming fast with hope, he pulled out his tab, sent the scanned genome to it, brought up his genome analysis app and hit 'Compare To Library'.

The black plastic pane churred in his hand. A loading bar fizzed into life above his main screen, the word 'processing' burning green in the air.

A heartbeat later, the results flicked on the screen. 'No Exact Match', the screen read. 'Closest Match: Cucumis sativus 'Beit Alpha', Cucumis sativus 'Spacemaster'.

"No exact match," Aidan read aloud. He turned, cobalt eyes full of concern. "Does that mean they're not—" He ended the sentence on an 'oof' as Kevin reached over and hugged him tight. It was an idiotic, unprofessional move and he knew it. But in that moment, he didn't give a damn.

"The seeds are real," he murmured against Aidan's throat, the words bubbling like champagne on his tongue. "They're viable. They're closely related to ancient varieties."

Aidan's hand squeezed his.

Brandi cleared her throat. "So I guess you guys like what you see?"

Kevin sat back with a laugh. "I'm absolutely in awe that what I'm seeing exists! These seeds exist! The Fort Collins seed bank actually exists!" He glanced between his contacts and his boyfriend, and smoothed a hand over his hair. The ache in his jostled arm pulled him back down to reality. "Erm...my apologies, I got a little carried away just there. Based on the parts you're asking for, I'd venture to say your group—it is a sizable group, I assume?— reached out only because your climate maintenance machinery has begun to malfunction. I'd just like to say, I'm honored that we're the ones you reached out to. Thank you. Thank you for showing us. And for trusting us."

"That's from all of us." Aidan put in, resting his hand on Kevin's knee. "We'll do everything we can to make this trade worth your time. So let's start making some plans for pulling this off."

Hours later, the shrill of a tab alarm in the dark nearly sent Kevin through the ceiling. If a man had to wake up in the middle of the night, the bleat of an alert was probably the worst way for it to happen. And if it had to happen, the tab being right beside a man's head made it that much worse.

Aidan sat up in bed as Kevin scrabbled for his tab. The blue and red blurred together in his eyes, and he hissed his annoyance between his teeth.

"Aidan, give me a hand; I can't see the screen."

Taking the device, Aidan read it and cursed. "Liza's calling us."

The tab's projection cut a swath of light into the room's darkness. Kevin finally found his glasses and fumbled them into place. In the projection, Liza and Janice peered at him. Liza was white-faced and worried. Janice looked grim.

Liza's eyes flicked to his, and her shoulders relaxed. "Kev. You're alive."

Janice let out a long sigh. "Thank fuckin' God you're okay."

"You've got a problem on your hands," Liza continued briskly, "we've picked up—"

"Gimme!" Tweak's high voice snapped, and fingers obscured the view for a moment. Then Tweak was glaring at them in the image, eyes narrowed into glittering slits. She looked furious.

"You. Guys. Are. Shit. Heads! Fucking. Stupid! F-f-fucking idiots! What the f-f-fuck—"

"Tweak!" Liza rapped out, "Give my tab back, right now."

"No!" Tweak snapped, the image wobbling as she gripped the tab on her end. "They're f-fucking s-s-stupid, I'm g-gonna—"

"Tweak, I said right now!"

"You can't yell at them if they're dead," Janice observed dryly from the side.

Tweak split her glare between the screen and Liza. Then she let out a classic teenager's sigh. "Fine. You tell them. Here."

"What's this about dead?" Kevin asked, glad he finally got the chance to get a word in. Liza's dark brows pinched together, her eyes on Aidan. "We have a serious issue, Commander. A mission-compromising issue."

Her manner rang every one of Kevin's alarm bells. If Liza was going textbook military on them, the situation was textbook Not Good.

"When EagleCorp came to pick up their people, they did a ten-block biological sweep," Liza explained tightly. "They found a pool of Kevin's blood, and ran the usual database check. But this time they didn't stop there. I don't know why, but they got high-level clearance and ran a Grid-wide full genome match."

Kevin's heart felt as if it had stopped. The involuntary gasp that came out of his throat was the sound of a kitten squeezed too hard.

"Are you saying—"

Eyes wide and dark, Liza nodded. "They tagged you, Kev. Cavanaugh knows you're alive."

Event File 9
Event Tag: Mission Compromised
Timestamp: 3:13-2-29-2157/ 10:30-2-29-2157 3:13-2-20-2157

Ice crystals seeded themselves in Kevin's chest. He jolted as a bleary voice muttered in the next bed. "Whatzit?" Brendan grumbled, "D'we gotta get up?"

"Who's that?" Liza asked.

"Our contact," Aidan replied, flapping a dismissive hand. "I need more details on this, Liza. What do they know?"

Liza swallowed hard. "They matched Kevin's blood with the file on his family: it's under fifteen years old, so it's still in the data banks. Cavanaugh has contracted six bounty-hunting teams to go after you; the hunters know they're looking for a CES-level Cavanaugh dissident. Tweak is tracking the chatter. You're going to have to move. Fast."

Kevin grew still, letting his panic settle into the crystalline calm suitable for performing the cold algebra of survival.

"Right then. Aidan, I'm going to need to split off from you lot and take the scenic road home; can't have our new friends paying for my sins. I'll get packed and slip out now, and—"

Four voices drowned his out.

"Kevin, you are not going out running the grid on your own!" Liza exclaimed, horrified and furious in equal measure. "Don't you dare, boy!" Janice growled. Tweak added "are you f-fucking n-n-nuts?" for emphasis, and Aidan's voice, sharp and hard as he made it when speaking in his official capacity, sealed the cacophony with, "hell no, Kevin. You're not going solo, you hear me?"

Feeling like a statue carved from ice, Kevin met the eyes of each of his team in turn.

"We need to be realistic at this point," he stated, his words toneless. "At the moment, I'm a liability. Better to have one person in danger than four."

He met Aidan's eyes last. They were wide and pained, hard to hold. But Kevin didn't look away.

"No sense in risking the team for one man," he stated.

"We aren't a team without you!" Liza cut in sharply. "You don't get to go all Catholic martyr on us, Kevin."

"Damn straight." Aidan agreed tightly, reaching over and grabbing Kevin's hand. "I'll make that an order if I have to."

"S-shithead," Tweak added irritably. Once again, she snatched the screen from Liza. "L-look. They know who you are, f-fine. I'll plant fake l-leads all over. You use s-synth. You got c-contacts. C-call somebody. G-get you picked up."

"I know a fella who runs a human transport rig, hides folks under produce," Janice put in. "We'll get you guys a ride. Cool your tits, Red. Don' go off 'fore you think about this."

The ice inside Kevin tightened its grip. He turned to Aidan, wishing body and soul that he could convey this in a way that would make his man *listen*. "You have no idea what Cavanaugh is capable of. Please. Don't...you're our Commander. We can't risk you."

I can't risk you, his mind whispered numbly. *I can't be the reason another person I love this much dies. I can't. It'll destroy me. Better to die in body than to see my soul ripped out again...*

"And you're the guy who keeps us fed and clothed. We can't risk you either." Aidan stated simply. Reaching up, he cupped Kevin's shoulder. "Besides, you think I'm any good when you aren't around? You know better."

Across the room, Brandi cleared her throat. Kevin jumped. He'd forgotten about the siblings again.

"Can we get a lead on what's going on?" The young woman asked, her curls a dark briar-bush around a face washed out by the tab's blue glow. In this light, her freckles looked like splatters of ink.

Kevin gave her a small smile, pulling his best cavalier act on like a slick poncho. "Sorry folks. I'm quite a hot commodity for Cavanaugh; my death was rather exaggerated some years ago, and they're going to be extremely interested in getting their hands on me now that they know I'm among the living. I doubt they'll care too much about who's damaged in the process. Therefore, it'd be wise if we went our separate ways and let this endeavor lie for a few months. Once things have settled down, we'll be back in touch. In the meantime, it'd be best if you headed home and kept your heads down."

Brandi bit her lip. She glanced at her brother. He ran a hand through his curls, leaving them standing straight up.

"Fuck." he whispered, "Do we gotta?"

"Think so," Brandi agreed, "shit. Yeah. Think so."

"Keepers're gonna skin us." Brendan sighed. He gave his sister a funny hand gesture, something like an archaic hang-ten signal, but not quite. Brandi returned the gesture. Then she turned back to them, her face pinched with the expectation of pain.

"Look. What you guessed earlier? You were right. We don't have months. Our cooling systems are running on spit and duct tape right now. Mostly spit. If we wait more than a month, we're SOL, and so are all the seeds. Everything." She gave a helpless shrug. "We're going to lose it all when the cooling systems quit."

Kevin hadn't realized his sense of hopeless dread could grow any deeper, until it did.

"And you waited until the very last possible second to reach out, why?"

Brandi gave him a cockeyed look. "Why? Well, because we've been the Keepers of the Vow since the Dissolution, that's why." Kevin could hear the capital letters in the words.

"The Keepers—" She cut herself off as Brendan squeezed her leg. Brandi drew a breath. "Look. There's stuff you aren't cleared to learn. But the only reason the seed bank still exists is because our people have kept the...we've stayed hidden. Radio silent. We've kept ourselves to ourselves. For generations." She drew a breath. "But our machines are falling apart. So we need help, okay? And we need it now."

The ice in Kevin's chest expanded, a glacier of numb fear. He sat still, staring at his hands. He stood as if he'd been told to, letting his feet move as his brain raced.

Alright. Fine. He had played this game for the past decade. If he couldn't play it for the highest stakes, he wasn't worth the position he held.

So.

Work out the problem.

Find the solutions.

Think.

He pulled off his glasses, polishing them as he paced.

"Right. Right. So, we have six bounty teams on our tail. We have heightened security issues. We need to formalize a set of exchanges that gets everyone what they need in the next three weeks. And we need a four-person covert transport. Right. Hand me the tab. Alright. Now, let's see..."

Fingers flying, Kevin reached for shipment rosters and brought up tables and patterns of surveillance around Fort Collins.

"Janice, you said you had someone? I need their contact handle. What are they, Zoncom on an AgCo contract?"

"Yeah. I'm sendin' his deets."

"Wonderful. I have someone on the AgCo side who can give us a hand. Thanks Janice. Liza, we need to sign off. I have a call to make."

On the screen, his friend nodded. "Be safe," Liza ordered.

"And stop bleeding." Tweak snapped. Kevin barked a laugh. "I'll try. Take care, all."

Signing out, he brought up a new contact. "Evening, Tio. Sorry about waking you."

Wary black eyes blinked at him on the other side of the screen. "Kevin? What's the call for?" His godfather asked. "You in trouble?"

"More than I'd expected," Kevin agreed ruefully. "I could use some Grapevine assistance."

The stout man crossed his arms. "Tell me. We'll see what we can do."

Once he settled into the rhythm, the planning flowed like water beneath Kevin's fingers. He spent the night collating, rearranging and planning. One by one, his companions slid back into sleep, leaving him to the deep quiet of night and the work he excelled in.

This time, he covered every eventuality. This time, the plans had to be perfect. The cost of failure was far too high to bear.

It was surprisingly easy to put the plan he'd worked out earlier into place, once he had the information he'd needed from his family. Step one: get their allies what they needed. Using information supplied by Tio Umberto, Kevin worked to pinpoint the places that manufactured or salvaged each of the sets of parts on the list Brandi had given him. He sent lot numbers and shipping schedules to Tweak for re-configuring, with instructions on the delivery coordinates for a set of four safe locations: a garage with a mechanic whose son was in the Grapevine. A machine shop where a Grid operative with the Force held a job as a manager. A chaotically-managed Zoncom truck loading depot where things regularly got lost or misplaced. And an easy exchange done at a salvage yard controlled by an ally. Fingers dancing, Kevin shot messages to the contacts in question. Two of them responded that night with agreements to make the exchanges. Kevin promised them a courier to pick up the packages they'd keep. The other two were probably asleep; he'd check for their answers in the morning.

Step two: keep the mission team safe and get them out. He wrote them the travel orders of employees being shipped between sectors to bolster the workforce for sugar-beet processing season, and recoded everyone's credentials for CPS level and AgCo affiliation. He'd wear his glasses to underline the appearance of poverty; a good thing, since he was going to run out of contacts if they were out here too long. He'd never admit it out loud, but Damian's point that Grid work would be easier with adjusted eyes was a good one.

Slipping out of the rooms, he rifled the donation bins at the We Care Inc. second hand center next door, under cover of predawn darkness. The security around the second-hand clothes center was a joke. He had to guess at sizes for Brandi and Brendan, but badly fitting clothes only added verisimilitude to their disguises.

Step three: get everyone up in an hour. Step four: hop the bus for agricultural workers headed East. The ID checks would be minimal.

Aidan woke as Kevin laid out clothes for them both at the foot of the bed, doing his best to hide the shaking in his fingers. He gave his boyfriend a small smile. "Morning. I've got us a connection at nine-thirty, a place to stay tonight, and a working extraction plan."

"Great," Aidan agreed muzzily, "and you got some sleep, right?"

"I will, when we're on our way," Kevin replied softly.

Aidan sighed. "Swear?" He asked. Kevin nodded.

Aidan watched him carefully. Eventually, he nodded. "That's an order, got it?"

Kevin breathed a laugh. "Yes sir." Now that the work was done, he could feel the adrenaline in his system ebbing. His mood would drop like a stone soon. But for now, he gave his boyfriend a bright smile. "Now, we'd best get our charming acquaintances up and moving. We have a ride to catch."

♠

It was in the back of the rattling bus, sitting still, that a night without sleep and his own failures began to catch up to him. The bus was nearly empty, only the ghosts of former riders lingering in the fingerprints on the windows and the odd bit of trash on the floor. Kevin gave it a full twenty minutes of riding before he pulled out his tab, found the bus's system IP, and ran the camouflage app that Tweak had perfected. The little program went to work looping the recorded footage and adding in a few subtle machine-generated changes to make sure it looked natural.

"The surveillance system's looped. We can relax." Kevin murmured. Brandi and Brendan gave him nearly identical tense smiles.

"You going to sleep now?" Aidan asked softly.

Kevin leaned his head back against the worn seat. His eyelids did feel like lead weights. "In a bit." Turning to the siblings, he held out his tab. "Here you are, folks. Your people will need to be at each of these coordinates on these dates to make the transfers. I've planned a secondary date for each venue, in case of issues. But if your people can make the first date, that would be better for all concerned. The code phrase your courier will need to give is 'I'm looking to plant a tree in the neighborhood, we need the shade'." He closed his eyes, hearing Brandi suck in a breath.

"Holy gods, you did this all in *one night?*"

Kevin cracked a smile. "It's what they keep me around for, or so they say. I still need to solidify Mario's date, but he thinks that will work. He'll check in with me as soon as he's talked to Tito about it. Other than that, these shipments should go off. Sagal will lend you a box truck from the salvage yard to move the bigger pieces of machinery; it's got unremarkable signatures and is manual-equipped. He's got it fitted out for covert use."

Brother and sister stared at him as if he'd performed a miracle. They were so impressed. But this had been easier than some requisitions he'd put together before. This little feat of planning and organizing was nothing to the mistakes he'd made.

Aidan's fingers stroked his hair. "Nice work, Mr. Rock Star. Now get some sleep. You look wrecked."

Kevin let his head drop back against the seat. "So does everything I've come in contact with on this trip."

Behind his eyes, his thoughts chased themselves. DNA matches were easy. Why hadn't he *thought* about that?!

Stupid. He'd been so damnably *stupid*.

The next safe house was in an ag sector; miles of monoculture crops, dotted with ramshackle towns. Ag workers weren't worth much; not enough for anything more than prefab housing. But to a pair of Dusters, the houses looked acceptable.

The door of the house they knocked on was opened by a child who couldn't have been more than three. She stared up at them with wide, solemn eyes.

Aidan smiled and crouched down to be on her level. "Hey, kiddo. Your ma home?"

The little girl stared at him. "Ma?" she asked, her voice high pitched. Kevin smiled. "Where's ma?"

Turning, the little girl pointed. "Sissy."

"Sissy will work, too," Aidan agreed encouragingly. "Will you go get her for us?"

A door slammed somewhere, and a dark haired girl of seventeen came trotting in, exasperation in every line of her body. "Maria! No abra la puerta a la gente! ¿Cuántas veces tengo que decirlo? No abra la puerta para la gente!" she swept the little girl into her arms, then stared up at the men. "Yes? What do you want?"

"Dust storm's coming," Aidan replied quietly, glancing over his shoulder as he straightened. "Thought we might be able to get out of the heat a bit."

The girl's eyes widened. "We'll get you something for a dry throat. Come in." she replied, parroting the pass phrase. When they were inside, she flicked a concealed white-noise emitter on the door, and turned to them curiously. "Is it now? Do we fight now? Revolution?"

Aidan shook his head. "We're still working. But we think we're on the trail of something that will give us an edge."

"Oh." The girl's face fell. "Okay. I'll go get Papa; he's out spraying the field."

"Thank you," Kevin added with a smile, though his heart ached for the girl. One day soon, they'd fulfill that promise of revolution and give her a better chance at life. He just hoped they'd all be around to see it.

Ten minutes later, a heavy-set, round faced man came in, dark eyes solemn. "You blown in by the storm?" he asked quietly, his accent the lilting sing-song of the Mexican refugee.

"Barely made it in before the wind picked up," Aidan replied, doing his best to smile.

The man's suspicion eased at that, and he smiled at the quartet. "Come in then, and we'll get something for you to eat, something for you to drink. Did you come a long way?"

Throughout the evening, Kevin said little, mostly finding a corner and focusing on a book he'd brought to read. He tended to say the wrong thing in gatherings like this. His speech, his vocabulary, even his accent gave him away as not one of their people. Better to stay quiet and be thought unlikable than to open his mouth and remove all doubt.

"Where's the next stop?" Aidan asked in a quiet murmur as the four of them settled into the barn to sleep that night. They were shielded by a white noise generator, but he kept his voice low. On the other side of the haystack, Brandi and Brendan murmured to one another.

"The next thing we take is a convoy truck. Under a load of this hay." Kevin murmured, distracted.

Aidan tipped his head down. "Kev? You still worrying?"

"Hmm?" Kevin asked, glancing up to meet Aidan's gaze in the low light.

"What's on your mind?" Aidan asked gently, reaching over to brush red hair off Kevin's brow. Kevin gave a weak half smile. "Just tired."

Aidan raised his brows, silently urging for the truth.

Kevin's smile grew cynical around the edges. "I guess...I thought I'd shed the past. Today proved me wrong. All this trouble was simply waiting for me to stumble back into it."

Aidan nodded, stroking his hair. "I hear you. Getting outed sucks. But we're okay. And you've got me to help, for what that's worth. I don't want to see you eating yourself alive about this." His fingers twined between Kevin's in the straw.

Kevin pulled his hand free. "No need to coddle me, Aidan. I fucked up. Let's be honest."

"It's not that bad," Aidan disagreed quietly. Kevin snorted. "I beg to differ. I was enthused. I was incautious. I left blood on the scene. Which put six teams on our trail. And that may well get us killed. I'm a danger. As long as you're with me, you're...you're in danger, my love. And I *despise* that fact."

Aidan was silent beside him. Then soft fingers tipped his chin up. "Kev? Look at me, okay?"

Wearily, Kevin opened his eyes. In the dim light, the worry lines between Aidan's brows had deepened. He held Kevin's eyes. "Don't do this to yourself."

Kevin looked away, closing his eyes. "I've got the alarm set. Let's talk in the morning."

"No," Aidan replied flatly, gently squeezing Kevin's chin. "I know that look. You *know* I know that look. You fucked up, so what? We're still here. And they're going to have a hell of a time if they're really that determined to try and find you—which I doubt. Odds are, they'll dismiss it as a system blip and increase security for a while."

"Aidan." The words stung as they left Kevin's tongue. "I'm a danger to the Cavanaugh Corporation, don't you see? What my parents knew, what I know, could hurt them if it got to their shareholders or the public. They'd want me dead for that alone. And on top of that I'm a traitor from a family of traitors. My family didn't stay loyal. Now they've realized I'm alive, they'll want my head."

"Why would they get anywhere near your head?" Aidan asked insistently. "We're a good team. We've got good contacts. You did solid work. They aren't going to find us."

Kevin shrugged. "Yes...maybe. But...." Finally, he raised his eyes. "Aidan...honestly, the enforcers they've got scare the shit out of me. It's why I had Damian install my kill switch. What they do to the people they capture..." He shook his head.

"I won't let them get to you," Aidan promised, his voice soft. "I know you're going to tell me not to make promises like that, but...I won't let them get anywhere near you." His fingers ran over Kevin's hair.

Kevin wished he could believe the words. But for now, he could believe in Aidan's touch. He rested his head on Aidan's shoulder. Gentle fingers stroked his hair.

"You going to quit bashing yourself?" Aidan murmured. For his sake, Kevin held up his free hand. "I surrender. No more self-recriminations, my word of honor. I was stupid, I screwed up, it's done. I just hope that's all that comes of it." He shrugged. "It just... brings up a lot, this situation." He turned to lay his head on Aidan's chest. "I'm sorry."

Aidan's fingers smoothed his hair. "Don't be." Aidan's lips brushed his brow, his arms enfolding Kevin. "We should get some sleep..."

Kevin nodded, but it was easier said than done. Sleep didn't come for a long time. When it finally arrived, it was haunted by memories of the past.

He dreamed of a noose around his throat. He dreamed of faceless men chasing him down endless Grid roads full of garbage tripping him up, smog that clogged his throat. He was running, running, bullets being shot off, running in the dry desert heat, and...

And then the dream changed.

The garden was in summer bloom, and there was a cold drink in his hand. He was sitting with his father. He was sixteen again, and they were sharing a beer. In the garden, his mother held up a rose and waved, grinning at him.

"So who's this Aidan?" his father asked with lazy good humor, and Kevin smiled. "He's a guy I met at work, I love him..."

As they watched, his mother spread her arms wide, and seeds dropped to earth and burst into bloom, into fruit and flower and a thousand shades of color. And Kevin laughed. He remembered no other dreams that night.

It was late in the morning when they helped load the last of the hay bales into the contracted truck, and shouldered their packs. Food made the bags heavier, food Kevin knew the family couldn't really spare, but he knew they wouldn't take it back. At the loading gate, the father of the family shook their hands solemnly. "Adios." He said it in a way that emphasized the original meaning: go with God. Kevin repeated the word, and meant it.

Turning, the four of them crawled into a concealed area in the chassis of the delivery rig.

It could have been worse. The space was wide enough and high enough to seat the four of them comfortably. It was even padded and lighted, a ventilation system running cool breezes over them.

There was a heart-thumping wait as the rig was inspected by the area foreman, going on his morning round. The relief between them was almost palpable when the slam of the rig door closing sounded. When the rig began to move, Kevin felt his heartbeat slow.

He stifled a leonine yawn. "Now, I'll get some proper sleep. This has got to be better than the hay..." Lying down, he rested his head in Aidan's lap. The rhythm of the truck lulled him, easing his body into a relaxation deeper than he'd felt in days. He had no idea how many hours of sleep he'd gotten the night before, what with the dreams, but it certainly hadn't been enough. Aidan's warm hand rested against the back of his neck, and the pocket of time nestled in around them; safe, and quiet, and easy.

Finally, Kevin fell asleep.

He wasn't sure how much time had passed when he woke again, sitting up and giving their companions a smile as he stretched. "You know, this may not be a bad trip after...."

BANG

A hole the size of Kevin's fist went through the wall of the undercarriage, cutting off his words. He had definitely spoken too soon.

Event File 10
Event Tag: Travel Reroute
Timestamp: 16:13-2-29-2157

"Holy *shit!*" Brandi yelped, grabbing Brendan and scrambling for the far end of their enclosure.

Aidan's brain stalled. A hole in the chassis. The size of his fist. What the hell could make a hole that big?

Kevin's fingers wrapped around Aidan's wrist and yanked, snapping him back into reality and pulling him along with a force that was definitely leaving bruises later. They pressed against the far side of their padded cubicle. Aidan's heart was going a mile a minute. He fumbled for his gun. But he'd put it away in the bag when they'd been loading. Damn it! What a goddamn awful time to have the thing wrapped up in his socks.

Another deafening bang and another hole in the side of the truck. Bike engines sizzled outside.

The truck swerved as gunfire ricocheted through the air. They must have hit the tires. Silence fell as the rig followed its damage protocol, pulling over. The engine died, leaving only the sound of moving bikes and the screech of brakes as the rig skidded to a stop.

Reaching into his pocket, Aidan flicked the GPS jammer he'd kept there just in case. It buzzed reassuringly in his pocket as it got to work sending out a signal that scrambled the ping from any tracker within a quarter of a mile. The semi and the assholes outside would look like they'd disappeared, and that was sure to set off some alarms somewhere. But it was better than being pinpointed immediately by the Corps.

"Jamming." He whispered in Kevin's direction. The taller man jerked his head in a nod. "Good. Here." The word was a hiss, and two hafts were shoved into Aidan's hands. "Taser on the right. Gun on the left," Kevin's voice breathed in his ear. Aidan could taste copper in his mouth. He nodded.

The bike wheels fell silent. Aidan did his best to keep his body loose and ready to fight. Tension twisted his gut into a knot.

"Easy as a whore!" A rough voice shouted outside. The door of their hiding place was ripped off. "Jackpot!" The man on the other side shouted, leaning in to grin at them. "We're gonna—"

And that was when Brandi pulled a black tube with a red lid from her pocket, and sprayed something reddish in the man's face. The man screamed, falling back. Aidan blinked.

"What the—"

"Good old fashioned pepper spray," Brandi replied with a quick, fierce grin. "Gives us a second. Get ready!"

The man outside was bellowing about his eyes and coughing up a storm between howls, but Aidan could still hear boots pounding outside. Feet slammed against the metal skin of the semi over their heads. Three sets, if Aidan was right.

Okay, he could do something about that.

Pushing the taser to its highest setting, he darted to the hole on the other side of their little cell and put his arm through. Pressing his taser to the metal of the rig's outer shell, he pulled the trigger. The blast sizzled the paint off the surface at the contact point, and electrified every metal surface on the semi. He smiled a battle-grin at the sound of two bodies thumping over their heads. The third hunter hit the dirt beside the semi and lay, shaking.

"Shock won't last," he rapped out, crawling back across the space on hands and knees. He threw his pack over his shoulder and grabbed Kevin's hand, jerking his head at the siblings. "Come on! Run!"

He stumbled as he hit the ground, one of his damn feet gone to sleep from Kevin lying on him. Of all the times. Kevin steadied him as they ran. Somewhere behind them, he heard gunshots.

"Cover," he panted in Kevin's direction, nodding at a stand of sickly trees to one side of the road.

Kevin gave him a quick, fierce grin. "Good, we—" the sentence ended in a whoosh of air as a body tackled Kevin, bringing him to his knees. His glasses skittered away into the roadside gravel.

Aidan skidded to his knees beside the tussling pair, reaching out and praying the taser had enough juice for one more jolt.

He never had the time to make the contact. The man straddling his boyfriend jerked as blood sprayed from the back of his head. The body on top of Kevin convulsed, and went limp. Kevin shoved him off with a gasp. He stared up at Aidan, blood that wasn't his spattered across his white face.

"Looked like you two needed a hand."

Aidan's heart kicked into overdrive at the unrecognized voice. He scrambled to his feet, gun ready in one hand and taser in the other.

A bronzed and black-haired man in riding gear stood watching him. A gun dangled from the guy's fingers like a toy. Aidan brought his own gun up. "Don't move!"

"Hold fire. I'm dropping my side-arm." the man called, carefully letting his pistol go. His voice rasped on the sharp air. "Ezra McLeod, reporting. My Commander said you guys had gotten hot. Sent me out to watch your backs."

The hammering of Aidan's pulse in his ears eased a little, but he kept his gun up. "Rank, personnel number, base, pass phrase."

"Ezra McLeod," the man replied, standing at parade rest. "Personnel number t-140stb, munitions specialist. Base 1347. We need to get under cover, before the storm comes in."

Breathing out, Aidan lowered his sidearm. "Okay. Thanks for the assist."

One eye on the guy, he knelt and picked up Kevin's glasses, handing them over.

"You okay?"

"Fine." Kevin murmured, wiping blood from his face and slipping his glasses on. Getting to his knees, he peered under the semi. "Ezra, is it? I count six bikes. How many have we—"

"I took out four," the bulky man confirmed. "Your friends flattened the other two. One guy's tied up, one's lying on the ground whining 'cause he's gone blind."

"Pepper spray will do that for you." Brandi added, wiping a smear of blood onto her pants as she walked up. Aidan gave her a nod. "You guys okay?"

"All good," Brandi agreed, "Brendan's over talking to the guy that we tackled. Trying to figure out how he caught up to us."

"Something I'd rather like to know myself," Kevin agreed, his voice taking on an icy precision as he stood. "I'll pin down their allegiance at least: see if this is Cavanaugh or simply Fate dealing her cards with a vengeance again." Aidan noted the rigid way the taller man moved, the way he was speaking: as if his syllables were chipped from ice. Shit, Kevin was right on the edge. He must assume it was Cavanaugh who had come after them.

He caught Brandi's eye, trying for a smile. "I'll catch up in a second."

"Roger," Kevin agreed tightly, turning. Brandi fell into line with him.

That left Aidan with the guy who'd given his name as Ezra, and a dead body. Trying not to look down, Aidan turned to the stranger. Process later. Get through the situation now.

"Official thanks for saving our asses," he managed, "I'll have to send your Commander a thank-you later."

Ezra gave a quick one-shouldered shrug, a flicker of a smile. His sunglasses reflected Aidan's own face back at him. "Not sure you'll get ahold of them; they're in the middle of a base relocation. But I appreciate it."

"Sure," Aidan acknowledged. "One thing though; I'm going to have to run the Paulson Procedure. Been a shit year for that kind of stuff."

Ezra shrugged. "Sure." He held out his hands.

Aidan pulled off his bag, digging in it for his DNA scanner. Finally unearthing the damn thing, he ran it over the man's hands. Ezra was human; his genome popped up without much fuss. The readout came up for a munitions specialist off Base 1347, his personnel number and info matching what he'd said. Aidan relaxed. Packing the reader away, he gave the taller man a smile. "Appreciate you being chill on procedure."

Ezra cracked a smile. "Hey, that's what you logistics guys are around for."

Aidan shook his head. "Command guy. I'm Commander Headly."

Ezra's brows drew together a fraction. "You're the commander? I thought that was the red-head."

Aidan shrugged. "That's my logistics guy. He's got the brains for Command, but he doesn't do the bullshit." He looked the man up and down. "Our profiles and descriptions weren't in your orders? They should've been."

Ezra snorted. "My Commander's on overload with twenty people trying to move a base, she just cussed at her tab and said 'Ez, our guys are at these coordinates I sent, go help. Take guns.' So yeah. Sorry, sir."

Aidan nodded. Giving orders on the fly while trying to do five other things at the same time, that was a situation he knew all about. He dredged up a smile. "Yeah, I feel for her on that. So what're your orders?"

"Act as an escort for you as you finish a recon mission and get off the Grid." Ezra explained. "Sounds like you got hot, sir."

"No shit," Aidan agreed ruefully. "Well, we can use the help. And the guns. We won't bother burying these bodies; they've got contractor-grade trackers on them. We're running jammers, but that won't last. The Corps don't care enough about contractors to send anything out here for a couple hours, but we don't want to hang around. Come on, let's see what the guy they got has to say."

They walked into what looked like a standoff. The man that Brandi and Brendan had taken down was sitting with his back to the rig, staring mockingly up. He was a big guy, the kind that looked like he might have been a football type when he was young. He wasn't young anymore; without the riding helmet the sun glared down on a creased, heavy face patched with scrubby beard. A mess of grizzled, dishwater-blonde hair was losing the fight to stay on top of his head. Slowly, he licked the blood from a split lip and spat it at Brandi's feet.

Kevin stepped in. "If I were you," he said in that tone that made the hairs stand up on the back of Aidan's neck, "I wouldn't irritate anyone right now."

"You ain't me," the bounty hunter grunted. "And if you were, you'd know how much your heads are worth right now. Fuckin' stupid, messing with me. Tracker on me, y'know."

"Oh, we know. And we're running a jammer. Of course, you could make this easy." Kevin replied, biting the ends off each syllable. "Voluntarily dismiss your report of a target acquired, and none of us need to go through this rigmarole. You can pass up a little money in exchange for getting out of this alive. A fair trade, I'd assume."

The dusty man laughed, a sound like gravel falling down a drainage ditch. "And if I like it hard?"

Kevin glanced at Aidan, his face as remote as a Greek statue. Then he pulled his pistol, and pressed it to the side of the man's head. "There's always this way of doing data removal, if you prefer."

"Hey, um—" Brendan muttered, but Kevin turned a look as cold as liquid nitrogen on him. The younger man fell silent.

"You won't," the sunburned hunter grunted, his lips drawn up in a smirk. "You wanted to kill me, you would've done it."

For a moment, Kevin stood absolutely still. Inhumanly still. Then the metallic clack of the gun being cocked shivered in the air.

The bounty hunter laughed.

Almost casually, Kevin moved his hand and let off a shot into the man's calf. The bounty hunter screamed; a high, feral sound that clawed at Aidan's ears.

Dropping to one knee beside him, Kevin stared into the man's eyes, his face terrifyingly blank. "You're right. I don't want to kill you," he agreed once the howl of pain had trailed off. "But I most definitely can make you wish I did." He slipped his gun away and pulled out an auto pad, holding it up questioningly. "So, will you cooperate? Or not?"

The man glowered, his face gone grey under the sunburn. His adam's apple bobbed as he swallowed. "Can't. Called in the pickup 'fore we started. Uploads to the 'net soon as it's recorded; encrypted and in Corps hands already."

"Well then," Kevin stated coolly, barely moving a muscle. "Furnish us with the name of the Corporation those hands belong to. When you were sent out. And what you were told to look for."

Aidan stole a look at the man's leg as his boyfriend spoke, feeling as if his bones were shivering. A neat crescent of bloody muscle gleamed through the fabric of the man's pants. Kevin had aimed with precision; the wound he'd inflicted wasn't much more than a gouge in the meat of the man's calf. But a bullet wound was still a bullet wound.

He'd shot the guy. Kevin had actually shot the guy.

Aidan had to swallow back bile. This shouldn't be a big deal. He'd had to use his gun before. Hell, he'd killed a man once, years back. Plenty of Dusters had.

But that was war. That was kill or be killed. Not cold-blooded cruelty to another human being.

Not this.

"No," their prisoner replied through gritted teeth. "Got too much at stake to go traitor with you."

Kevin stood, staring down at him. "Very well. Then I hope you like bleeding in the middle of nowhere." Turning, he nodded at the others. "We'll need to take a few of their bikes. All right with you, Aidan?"

"Yeah," Aidan managed. He was glad his voice didn't shake on the word.

He caught the eyes of Brandi and Brendan, both watching him appraisingly.

"Hey!" the man Brandi had blinded shouted, "Hey, what about me?"

Stopping in front of him, Kevin stared down in a way that made Aidan's whole body tense. "What about you?" He asked, and there was nothing of the man Aidan knew in his voice. Only ice and distant anger.

Then Kevin turned and walked around the side of the truck.

Brother and sister stared after him. Almost as one person, they turned a look on Aidan. Holding their eyes, he swallowed a lungful of air and gestured them forward.

"Keep an eye on these guys for a second, okay? I'll talk to Kevin."

The siblings shared a look. Then Brandi gave him a nod. "We'll do that."

"Thanks," Aidan acknowledged. Then he turned and traced his man's path around the rig.

Kevin was running a biometric lock-breaker he'd pulled from somewhere over the hand-pads of a bike, readying it to take a new genome as its code. Aidan stopped a few steps away, searching the mess inside his rattled head for the right words to say.

When he spoke, his voice grated in his own ears. "You going to tell me what the hell that was about?"

"He wouldn't give us the information. Now he has incentive to do so," Kevin replied without looking up. He sounded more like a recording than a living man; absolutely toneless.

"You shot him," Aidan stated woodenly.

"He wouldn't give us the information," Kevin repeated. "We'll give them a few minutes to sit and think over the permutations of possible outcomes. Their tongues will loosen once they've weighed their options, I imagine."

Aidan stepped in. "Kevin, stop. Look at me."

The eyes raised to his were blank and cold as silver coins. Aidan's hands began to shake. Stuffing them in his pockets, he held Kevin's gaze.

"You just shot a guy to make him take you seriously. You do realize that?"

"I do. Is this an issue?" Kevin asked, so still that he looked like a statue.

"You're goddamn right, it's an issue," Aidan stated, the words coming hot from his lips. "What's our overall objective? To be able to set up an internationally-recognized, democratic government one day, right? A legitimate government?"

Kevin blinked. "Well, yes, but—"

Aidan spoke over him. "Then we *don't* commit war crimes. We *don't* use torture on prisoners. That'd make us *terrorists*. What you just did was off the rails, and right out of our rule book examples of war crimes, Kevin. That's how the Corps fight. That is *not* how we fight. You told me not that long ago to help you control your vicious streak if I ever saw it? Remember that?" He stabbed a finger back the way they'd come. "Newsflash, I just saw it. And you are *going* to control it. Either you get your head on straight, or you stay the hell away from prisoners. Don't make me give that as an order. Because I will, if I have to."

He didn't know whether it was his tone or something in what he'd said that got through to Kevin, but something did. The other man looked away, his hands balled into fists. He bit his lip. When he spoke, his words rasped with mercilessly repressed emotion.

"They could have killed you."

"Yeah," Aidan agreed, "they could have. I'm a soldier. They're trying to kill enemy soldiers."

"You're a soldier," Kevin grated out, "but they are *not*. They are *scum. Jackals.* They have no morals. No *decency.*"

"Maybe they don't," Aidan agreed quietly. "But you do. And decent men don't use torture."

Kevin closed his eyes. When he spoke again, his words had lost their fire. "They could have killed you."

Aidan drew a slow breath. "Yeah. I know. But I'm still here." Carefully, he stepped in, resting his hand on Kevin's shoulder. "You got your head on straight?"

Kevin drew a shuddering breath. He shook himself like a man waking from a nightmare. "I think so. Think I do." Glancing at Aidan, he managed a weak twist of the lips. "Sorry."

"Just don't do anything you'll be more sorry for in the long run," Aidan stated softly. "You don't want to hate yourself later, okay?"

Kevin jerked his head in a nod. "Okay. Fair point. I suppose—"

"Hey!" the blinded man shouted on the other side of the rig, his words sounding like yelps. "Hey! Anybody! Don't leave me here! Take me somewhere that'll fix me up and I'll tell you whatever! Just don't leave me here! Hey! Hey, are you here?!"

"Fuckin' shut up, Earl!" The man Kevin had shot snarled. The panicking guy's response sounded the way a dog did when it was kicked. "Fuck you! I'm getting the fuck out of this alive! This's all your fault! You said it was clear, you said—"

"I said shut the fuck up, or I'll crawl over there and slit your fucking throat!"

Aidan sighed. "We better go break that up. So much for them being a team."

"I told you they were mangy scavengers," Kevin muttered bitterly, but he shoved his hands in his pockets and followed Aidan, staying quiet.

The guy was actually crying by the time Aidan crouched beside him, his face a splotchy mess of snot and tears. Or maybe that was the stuff that had been used on him. Aidan shot a look at Brandi. "What exactly is in that pepper spray?"

Brandi polished her nails. "Oh, the usual. It's mostly the concentration. EagleCorp's recipe, way better than the consumer stuff. Figure they can get a taste of their own medicine."

Aidan winced. "Man. Okay, so he's not dying."

Brandi shrugged, giving him a smile with too many teeth. "Nope. He wishes, but he's not."

Aidan made a mental note not to get on Brandi's bad side as he turned back to the suffering man. "You came out here to pick up a bounty. Who were you told to get?"

"Dusters. We were supposed to grab any Dusters," the man whimpered.

"Anybody in particular?" Aidan asked, carefully controlling his voice.

The man groaned. "Just Dusters. Eagle's sick of you shits. Called out a ton of bounties."

"You sure you weren't given anything more specific?" Aidan repeated. The man in front of him swallowed hard. "Look man, we just contracted in to grab Dusters. But there's this: we signed up to get a bonus if we grabbed a little CES Cavanaugh bastard who went with you," the bounty hunter's voice whined out like something from a broken instrument. "They picked up a DNA trail on him, posted the bounty and the genome to track on the Level 5 boards. We put in for it. Easy pickings, Duke said. We got it. Fuck, this was supposed to be easy pickings! Some stupid little rich kid on the run, that's all it was supposed to be!"

"Sorry to disappoint, but I haven't been a 'little rich kid' in a *very* long time." Kevin stated icily over Aidan's shoulder. The blinded man flinched at the sound of his voice.

Aidan turned to meet Kevin's narrowed eyes, and drew a finger across his throat. Kevin's jaw clenched, but he nodded.

"How many other teams put in for the bounty when you did?" Aidan asked, keeping his voice level. The man panted, his breath wheezing in his throat. He tried to wipe snot and tears from his face with one hand, groaning as he spoke.

"I don't know man! Seven, maybe eight. Couple of Level 4 teams contracted with Cavanaugh and some level 2 guy bid on the job first, but we got here first. We weren't looking at them, we were looking at the genome trail. Seeing where it went cold."

"And how did you choose this truck?" Aidan asked calmly. Further down the rig, the man who'd been shot raised his voice.

"Earl, you tell them and I'll skin you alive, you fucking—"

Wordlessly, Kevin stood, pulled something from his inner pocket and stalked down the rig. Aidan snapped his head to the side, watching, but Kevin only gagged the wounded man with a bandanna. He took a second to stare into the man's eyes, but he didn't do anything worse. Aidan breathed again.

"If you want to get you and your buddy out of this, you'll keep talking," he stated quietly.

The man's breath wheezed in the desert quiet. He gulped. "System tagged it as suspicious. Rig caretaker works with dissidents. Thought he might be doing smuggling on the side. It was on our list of rigs to check if it was outbound. We scanned it for heat signatures. Saw you. Your contact should've done heat sealing. We thought you were sitting ducks." His words trailed away into a wheezing moan.

On his right, Brendan spoke, and for the first time there was no laughter in the younger man's voice. "Tough shit, Gridlock. You thought wrong."

Moving with deliberate care, Aidan stood, dusting off his hands and thinking through his next move. "Okay, Earl. Tell me one more thing. Are those bikes yours, or are they rented?"

"Rented," Earl grunted. "Gonna pay for them with this haul. Still owe deposits. Fuck..."

Aidan almost echoed him. So, he had registered transport that was rented out. Somebody would have put trackers on those bikes to make sure they came back or got paid for. He had two injured enemies on his hands. He had a boyfriend who was this close to committing murder, and he had a hell of a long way to go before they were anywhere near safe. He had no chance of heading to any base, not when they were dragging this mess behind them.

He had a complete disaster on his hands.

For a moment he stood rooted to the spot, feeling the fear crawling up his throat. Standing quiet, he let it pass through.

Breathe.

In for seven.

Out for seven.

"Okay," he announced, "Guys, over here, other side of the rig. We've got some plans to make."

An hour later, the bikes were moving fast. They had a lot of ground to cover before the sun set. The cold was already starting to sting the tips of Aidan's fingers, and the shadows were growing long. It really wouldn't be a good idea to be out here when night fell. He was pretty sure they'd make shelter soon. Kevin had sent word to a vetted Fringe camp, once they'd gotten out of range of the hunters. They'd have a spot to flop. He hoped so, anyway. They deserved a little luck, after a day as epically shittastic as this.

For a moment, his mind flickered over the bounty hunters they'd left behind them, treated for their wounds and tied in the back of the truck. He wondered if EagleCorp had picked them up yet.

But he wasn't responsible for them. Only the people riding around him.

Night crept in around them like a black hunting cat. Aidan breathed a sigh of relief when he spotted the campfires ahead, brighter now than the tattered sunlight leaking out of the sky.

Pulling up his bike, Aidan nodded at his group. "Scope a camping spot; I'm going to go check in with the camp head."

"Roger," Brendan agreed. Pulling off his helmet, Kevin gave him a smile. "I'll see us settled."

Aidan nodded, more relieved than he really wanted to admit at seeing Kevin acting like himself again. Turning, he picked his way between the fires in the abandoned rail yard. They weren't the only squatters here by a long way; just the best provisioned ones.

A couple polite questions led him to a woman with salt-and-pepper hair and soft green eyes who greeted them with a smile, standing from the pan she'd been minding over her fire. The meat on it popped and sizzled.

"Been a while since we've seen anyone from your side," the older woman observed, adjusting the shawl around her shoulders. "I'm Rayna. You're the Wildcards boy, right? Good you made it in."

"Thank you," Aidan muttered, trying not to stare too hungrily at the meat on the makeshift pan in front of Rayna. "Sorry to intrude." he added politely, holding his hands out to the fire.

Rayna smiled. "No need to apologize. Got enough room for you all. And that'll be ready in a minute," she promised, glancing down at the meat and back at him with a wink.

Aidan grinned, relieved that he hadn't been taken for a greedy asshole. "How'd you get all this?" he added in gratified amazement.

Rayna reached forward to carefully flip the cuts of meat off the fire and onto a ragged metal plate. "We've got good hunters in our sector; good hunting, too, if you know where to look. My man hunts up something and we come down here every couple of weeks to look after the folks passing through."

Aidan nodded his thanks as he accepted the plate of sizzling... well, meat, anyway. He wasn't asking. Damn, it smelled good.

"Do you folks need anything?" he asked, raising his eyes from the treat. "We're geared up for a long trip, if you're running low on anything we've probably got it..." he added, hoping it was true.

Rayna hesitated a moment, glancing over her shoulder. Aidan realized that the nest of cloth wasn't baggage. There were two little kids cuddled up in the tattered blankets, their hair just peeking out to glimmer in the firelight.

Rayna turned back to him, reserve in the lines of her mouth and hope in her eyes. Finally, she leaned closer to mutter, "I know it's a big ask, but…do you got any medicine? My youngest got a cut a few days ago and I'm afraid it's getting infected. Couple other kids in camp need this and that."

Aidan nodded, his smile relieved. "Not a problem. Our compound's gotten lucky lately; we've got plenty to spare. And we owe you." he added, hating what he had to say next. His free hand rubbed the back of his neck. "We had a hunting team who came after us. We're pretty sure we shook the tail, but..." he shrugged uncomfortably. "Might want to keep an eye out."

Rayna bit her lip at that, the lines around her mouth deepening. But she nodded after a beat. "When the others get back, I'll set up a guard for the night. Thanks for the tip."

Aidan glanced down. "I'm sorry. We...it...the situation got out of hand."

"Happens." Rayna smiled, but even Aidan could tell it was a little forced. "With that in mind, gonna have to ask you to stay just the one night. We got kids here."

"We're gone tomorrow. We appreciate the night." Aidan agreed, more glad than he liked to admit not to hear an order to move on. Now that he was standing still, he realized how damn *tired* he was.

He pasted on a smile. "Where should we set up?"

Rayna gestured with two fingers. "That side's mostly empty. One thing, though. Need to see your hand. Too many mimics around these days; I gotta check genomes."

"Yeah?" Aidan asked, his heart jolting in his chest. Panic germinated like goat head seeds in his gut.

Rayna held his eyes, her warm gaze cooling a little. Shit, she'd seen his fear.

"That a problem?"

Aidan forced a smile. "Not unless you're on the Morality Code. Put it this way, you're going to get a look and think your reader's glitchy. It's not. I am." He held out his hand. "Hope that's not a problem."

Rayna watched him carefully as she pulled an abused genome reader from her coat pocket, running it over his hand. She studied the read, then his face. Reaching out, she put a hand on his shoulder.

"Aw honey, that's no glitch. And don't you worry. We're real democratic in this camp." She studied him with eyes that had warmed again, soft as green grass in her weathered face. "You okay with hugs?"

Aidan felt his lips crook in an awkward smile. "Um...not really? But thanks."

Rayna leaned in and kissed his brow. "Thanks for fighting, boy." She nodded at the plate. "Go feed your folks. Keep their strength up."

"I'll do that," Aidan agreed gratefully. Tired as he was, the warmth of her words felt like a blanket wrapped around him.

By the time Aidan had gotten back to his crew, Kevin rolled out the two sleeping bags, set five MRE's to warm up over the fire and had taken a seat, watching firelight bathe the faces of his companions with distant eyes. Brandi and Brendan had set up a neat little hemisphere tent that looked like it could fit them all if they wanted to squish together. Ezra was walking in the last of their stolen bikes, looking grim.

"Something wrong?" Aidan asked.

Ezra shot him a look. Aidan blinked. He hadn't seen the Duster without his glasses before; the guy had eye implants. He'd gone for the brass ball aesthetic, and the implants made him look like a bug. Man, what was with people getting the weird-colored eye implants? It never failed to freak him out.

Ezra flicked a sour smile in his direction. "Didn't realize I was going camping out here. I'm gonna be sore come morning, sleeping on rocks."

"You can borrow one of our bags," Aidan offered. "We can double up, right Kev?"

"Hm?" Kevin raised his head like a man waking up. "Oh, yes. Sure. We'll use mine, it's longer. Ezra, have at the other." Kevin sniffed, eyes widening. "And what've you got there, love?"

Aidan hefted the plate. "Actual meat, pass it around. Courtesy of the camp head lady. Watch out for the edges on the plate."

Brendan gave a quiet little whoop. "Nice! Thanks!" he exclaimed, forking a piece and passing the plate to his sister. She forked herself a slab and laid it over her MRE happily. "This's great."

"What is it?" Kevin asked carefully. Aidan elbowed him. "A gift. So be nice."

Kevin eyed the meat dubiously a moment, but he took a piece. "It does smell good," he admitted. Ezra almost grabbed the plate. "Hey, I'll take it if you don't want yours. Worst it's gonna be is rat. I like rat."

Kevin shuddered, closing his eyes. "Please don't say rat."

Ezra gave him a smirk. "Come on, don't be a little pussy."

Aidan felt Kevin's body go rigid beside him.

"Given that you've got a woman in this circle," the redhead snapped, "you may want to rethink your word choices."

Grease dripping from his chin, Ezra raised his brass eyes, eyebrows shooting nearly to his hairline.

Aidan reached over and squeezed his boyfriend's knee. "Kev. Chill."Raising his eyes, he held Ezra's implants. "My base doesn't use that kind of language, McLeod. If you're taking my orders, now you don't use it either. We clear?"

The man looked, for a moment, as if he was struggling to swallow something bitter. Then he ducked his head. "We're clear...sir."

"Good." Aidan stated with all the command he could shove into his voice. The very last thing they needed right now was a spat. "So, let's make plans. Brendan, you're sure all the trackers are out of the bikes?"

"Yep," the curly-haired man agreed between bites. "Gotten good at finding trackers these days. They're gone."

"Okay," Aidan agreed, "then this is the situation. None of us is going to be able to head straight home, not with the kind of heat that's on our tail. I used a bug written on my base to fake the registrations on these bikes, and they don't have trackers. We're set there. We'll stay in a safehouse tomorrow night, stock up on phage nanoids and Synth. Then we can split up and stay in three separate safe-houses the night after. That should get us clear to head home. Kev, you can work us up a solid route in the morning?"

"I can do that," Kevin agreed, "and in case anything does happen, I've already sent out orders to reliable people. Four delivery points are scheduled for this month. You'll get your deliveries, whatever happens to us," he finished, nodding at the twins.

Brandi smiled weakly. Reaching over, she clasped Kevin's shoulder for a moment. He gave her a warm smile.

Aidan let out a breath. "Then I guess we're all planned out."

For a few minutes, the group chewed their meat in silence.

"Think it's goat," Brandi put in eventually. "We cook it with carrots, tomato and wood sorrel at home."

"Yeah?" Aidan asked, hoping to lighten the mood, "love to get some recipes off you guys to go with the stuff we're going to grow, when we get out of this."

If, his brain interjected. *If we get out of this.* He told it to shut up.

Brandi flashed him a grin. "No problem. Between the tomatoes and the quinoa seeds, you guys are going to have some great stuff to cook. We'll give you some tips on storage too, so your harvest can stretch all year."

"And that's probably enough said about that," Kevin suggested quietly, glancing around the circle over the rims of his glasses. "Loose lips sink ships, you know."

Aidan blinked. "Kev, there isn't a reservoir you can sail a boat on for hundreds of...oh. Turn of phrase?"

Kevin gave him a quick, soft smile. "Turn of phrase, love. All the same..." he pressed a finger over his lips in a 'hush' gesture.

He had a point. Aidan glanced around reflexively. He didn't see anyone, but you never knew who was listening. He should have been thinking about that.

"Sounds like you have a whole little farm going," Ezra remarked. The siblings shared an easy smile. "Yeah," Brandi agreed wistfully, "back home."

"Nice setup," Ezra grunted between bites. "Where you getting the seed for veg?"

Aidan opened his mouth to cut the conversation short before it got dangerous, but Brandi and Brendan beat him to it. Sister and brother shrugged as if they were attached to the same wire. "Good stewardship," Brendan replied easily.

"And keeping the goats out of the garden," Brandi added with a sly smile. Brendan cracked a grin. "Oh gods above and around, Nellie Black, that bitch."

"Total bitch, and then her milk was awful!"

"Um...you left the rest of us behind." Aidan remarked. The fire popped.

Brandi giggled like a much younger girl. "Nellie Black's the head nanny in our goat flock. She got into the tomatoes and ate them down one year, almost killed them all. And then her milk was horrible for a week; sour as hell. It was such a waste!"

"And the bitch was smug about it too, I swear." Brendan added, chuckling.

Aidan had to smile as he watched the siblings grin, sharing the memory between them.

Ezra leaned in. "So, you've got tomatoes? What else you got?"

Brandi glanced his way, her smile fading into something less genuine and more social. "Sounds like you better eat dinner, you're daydreaming about food. Can't blame you; today was wild."

"You can say that again," Kevin agreed wearily. "I hope to God above we've gotten our quota of trouble filled at this point." He reached over and rapped his knuckles on a wooden rail-tie. "Knock on wood.'

The twins did likewise. For a moment, Aidan and Ezra shared a 'what the hell' look. Aidan was pretty sure he was never going to get all his boyfriend's little habits. But apparently these two did get whatever he'd just done. That was so many levels of weird. Cute. But weird.

Kevin reached out and squeezed Aidan's hand companionably, leaning his body against Aidan's as they ate. The fire popped and crackled in the silence. Aidan soaked in the quiet and the warmth as the meat filled his belly. God, he was tired.

Kevin's fingers stroked his hair gently. "Earth to Aidan."

"Hunh?"

"I said, don't fall asleep in your dinner."

Aidan shot his boyfriend a cockeyed quirk of the lips, sitting up a little straighter. Kevin gave him a soft smile. "Much better." Then he caught the look on Ezra's face, and schooled his own. "Got a problem?" he asked, quiet danger in his voice.

Ezra's brows rose over his false eyes. "Problem? Me? 'Course not. Just…weird to see someone treatin' their commander like a kid."

"We're not Corp drones, you see," Kevin parried coldly. "We actually talk to each other like human beings. My Commander is also my friend. Novel concept, I imagine."

The other man grunted, glancing down. The silence continued as they ate, until finally Ezra spoke. "Sir, may I speak freely?"

"Yeah," Aidan agreed wearily, too tired to think much before he responded.

"You and your guy, I'm figuring you're a couple. No offense, sir, but it's showing. Could get us all detained, actin' like that."

"We'll be sure to tell anyone who asks that you're an upright and moral citizen. I'm sure they'll be pleased to hear it," Kevin retorted, biting off every word.

Aidan winced. Shit, now Kevin was getting pissed all over again. This was so *not* what they needed right now; not when everyone was beat to hell and rattled from the day.

He'd need to say something, really get this under control.

The stranger spoke before he could figure out what would work.

"Better'n you, anyway." Ezra muttered under his breath.

Kevin stabbed at his meal with that sharp precision he took on when he was angry. "Ezra. Have you studied history?"

Ezra shrugged. "Not much for schooling, me."

"Well, here's an education then." Kevin picked at his food as he spoke, pushing the fake mashed potatoes into hillocks. "First, there was the Destabilization. Four presidents assassinated in fifteen years, gridlock, the democratic system breaking down. Then the Great Shutdown. Eleven months without a government. The Dissolution. The Corporations stepped in to protect their people and their profits over the next ten years. That was the Incorporation. Then the Morality Decisions started being handed down, along with the Eagle Eye acts and the Secure Liberty decrees. They started watching what we bought, what we said, what games we played, what we wrote and who we talked to, in order to weed out 'radical fringe elements' 'dissenting anarchists' 'morally unfit persons' and the all time favorite, 'terrorists.' Soon enough, there were the corporate morality trials. And today, the news is full of arrests and threat reports and trials. Have you noticed why?" he asked, voice unnervingly calm, like a teacher giving a lesson.

Ezra shrugged again, staring at his meal. "Don't particularly care, if I'm honest."

"Kev," Aidan began, but Kevin went right on, eyeing their companion coldly. "Most people don't. Because what does it matter compared to how you're going to eat tomorrow and when your rent is due?" he asked rhetorically. "But that's the problem. You see, they've given you an enemy to hate. They've given you something to fear and to fight; the perverse, the Other. Because what does it matter that there are no more civil rights, that shareholders and corporations run our lives, when there's threats out there? Threats like two girls in love or someone planting apple trees." he affected an expression of sarcastically exaggerated horror. "And of course, that's what you focus on, these horrible crimes that the media keeps telling you about. Because while you're fighting the terrorists and the immigrants and the 'fags', you're not thinking. And if you ever had the time to start thinking, you might wonder why it's illegal to collect rainwater, why groundwater has a twenty percent tax on it, why there's no such thing as upward mobility in the culture we've got and absolutely no way for us to make legitimate complaints. You might start noticing the bars on your cage, if you weren't given something 'better' to fret over."

"Kev, that's enough." Aidan stated, scraping the energy together to put some force into his voice. "We're all tired. We're all freaked. We all need to lay off each other until we've got some food and some decent sleep. Got it?"

Kevin glowered at his feet for a moment. Then he set his half-empty plate down. "It seems I'm not fit company this evening. So I'll get that sleep."

Aidan kept an eye on Kevin as he brushed his teeth, took off his glasses and crawled into their sleeping bag. He gave starting a decent conversation another try, but he was so damn tired and the whole situation pissed him off. Not long later, he crawled into the bag beside Kevin. He fell into sleep like a man falling off a ledge.

For the second time in the week, a blaring alarm brought him awake like a slap in the face. Kevin gasped beside him, jolting up in their sleeping bag. "What?"

Aidan rolled over and fumbled through his pack until he found the beeping tab. Reading the words, he was wide awake and cursing like Janice in seconds. "We're screwed. Tweak just sent an alert. We need to get out of here. *Now.*"

Kevin slipped free of the sleeping bag. "Who's on our tail?" he demanded, grabbing out a vial of phage nanoids.

"Eagle," Aidan whispered, fear cracking his voice. "It's personnel with drone air support, a fucking camp clearance!" He scrambled out of the warmth and into the night air, his heart beating like a snare drum. "They're half an hour out. If we don't move now, we're going to be obliterated."

Standing, he sprinted to the center of the camp and shouted with all the lung power he had.

"Everybody, Eagle's coming! Everybody up!"

"Oh holy fuck." Tweak scrolled frantically through data. "Fuck fuck f-f-fuck!"

She'd been afraid of this. She'd flagged all the systems she could get into, watching for data on Aidan and Kevin. And now it was up: a raid on the flop camp where one of the only decent guys she'd ever met—and, okay, another guy who she didn't hate— were sleeping. A personnel detachment out of Eagle, headed their way. Now that they were communicating outside their closed computer network, she could track the chatter between their devices. Orders given for their GPS coordinates. Orders to search for terrorists as they arrested the vagrants.

For a moment fear got her insides in a fist and squeezed. If Eagle caught the guys…

Tweak shook her head hard, slamming the spike of fear back down. *No. Fuck that. Not happening.*

Tweak hit a pre-coded series of keys, shooting an alert to both men's tabs with subroutines that turned the volumes on the devices to the max. She cursed until she stuttered, fingers flying over the keyboard, then slammed her fist into her chair.

Naomi shot up on the little cot she'd put in the coding room. "What? What's wrong?"

"They got tracked!" Tweak hissed. "The guys! They're in a c-camp Eagle's gonna c-clear! Fuck a duck!"

That got Naomi moving almost as fast as Tweak. She slammed the secondary console into action without another word. "Okay, I see their coordinates of their tabs...fuck that's a lot of EagleCorp goons. They're what, half an hour out? Fucking A..."

"Y-yeah..." Tweak agreed, biting her lip. For a moment, she sat paralyzed. She couldn't hack directly into the gear EagleCorp ops carried. Their codes were too good.

But she could do something else.

Yanking her keyboard to her, she started to type.

"What's up?" Naomi asked, watching.

"G-got an idea. Ssh." Tweak snapped out.

She knew TechoCo's parts. She knew how they read signals, and how to spoof them. Now she just had to see if she was that good and that fast.

Half an hour later, she sat back. "Okay," she managed, breathing fast, "Spoofed the GPS Eagle's using. They're g-gonna g-get off track. But they're g-gonna n-notice pretty f-f-fast. Buys people m-maybe an hour. Hour and a half. Tops."

Naomi shot her a quick smile. "An hour saves a lot of lives."

"Hope so." Tweak whispered, staring at the screen. Her heart was still beating too fast, and her skin was prickling.

Getting connected with her guys' HUDs, she ran an algorithm set that crunched the GPS information, the drone patterns, and the data available on security personnel movement to find them a secure route to the next safe-house. Sending it to their systems, she watched the dots acting as their avatars speed across the screen.

"Dammit! G-gonna get caught! N-never should've g-g-gone out there!"

"I hear that," Naomi agreed, sounding pissed. "I told Aidan this wasn't smart, but...anyway, no time for that. What do we do now?

"Fuck all," Tweak grumbled, wrapping her arms around herself and sinking into her console chair.

"And for people who don't speak cuss code that means..." Naomi asked, shoving her hair back from her eyes with her cybernetic hand.

Tweak sighed. "We w-w-watch the c-chatter. We t-track them, m-make sure they're okay. W-watch their v-vitals through their tabs, and—"

"Wait, does Aidan know you're tracking people's vitals through their tabs?" Naomi put in. Tweak gave her the look a stupid question like that deserved. "Tech. Officer. When they run m-missions, I run t-tech. *Genius.*"

She still loved saying the words 'tech officer'. Even in the middle of this mess, the term made her feel a little more on top of things. *She* was in charge of this.

Of course, if the guy who let her be in charge of something died, she knew she'd lose that. No way in hell anybody but Aidan would let somebody like her be an officer.

The fear squeezed again. Naomi hadn't said anything; she was just watching. Her eyes were hard to handle. They looked like they could open you right up.

Tweak looked back at her screen. "This s-sucks," she muttered, staring at the moving dots that showed her friends, and the fucking assholes after them. At least the guys were up and moving fast. Good. She drew a breath. "This all s-sucks. Sucks balls. Freaks me out. I'm a bitch when I'm freaked. S-sorry."

"Gonna say more than sorry?" Naomi asked. Tweak turned her head. "Hunh?"

Naomi was still staring. Her eyes sent a shiver over Tweak's skin. She looked away, listening to the other woman's voice instead of trying to meet her eyes.

"Gonna say you're gonna keep working on it? Try to fix it?"

Silence filled up the space in Tweak's brain that was usually full of work.

Taking a breath, she bobbed her head. "Yeah."

"Okay then," Naomi stated quietly. "So, does Aidan know you're tracking people's vitals?"

Tweak bobbed her head. "Asked me to. After Laz. Asked m-me to figure out how to t-track v-vitals and f-find a doc somewhere c-close if I s-saw things get hot. N-now I see things go s-sideways, I s-stick d-directions to the n-nearest safe docs on their t-tabs or their HUDs. N-no more people s-s-stranded." She smiled. "Aidan g-gave me c-call signs for the contacts and the new guy. I'm t-tracking all of the t-team. Things go bad, I can g-get them all out, no sweat. Force tried this once, years back. N-not secure enough. Got people c-caught by the Corps. My turn to try. We're t-testing this for a year. If it w-works, we're passing it to National C-command. Everybody use it, once I got the bugs out. M-make sure it's secure."

Out of the corner of her eye, she saw Naomi nod. "Nice idea," the other woman remarked.

"Yeah," Tweak agreed, "Hope so."

The dots moved. The EagleCorp icons disappeared off the bottom of her screen. Tweak split the screens so she could watch both her group and the enemy. The EagleCorp dots had stopped moving. Good.

"Those're Aidan's stats?" Naomi asked. Tweak nodded. "Yeah. These in green."

"He looks freaked," Naomi observed. Tweak barked a laugh. "No shit."

"So now we just watch the data for trouble?"

"Yeah," Tweak murmured. "Gonna get coffee. You want?"

Naomi nodded. "I'll take the coffee, you take the cot. Grab some shut-eye. I'll watch this and wake you if things hit the fan."

Standing, Tweak shook her head. "Don't need to sleep."

Naomi tipped her head. "I call bullshit. You've been awake for twenty hours with no stay-wake."

Tweak crossed her arms. "Gamma, remember?"

Naomi eyed her. "Yeah? Still human, though."

"You sure about that?" Tweak snapped, the words sharp as a little piece of glass on her tongue.

The blonde woman leaned easily back in her chair. "I'm sure your eyes are half open," she threw out with a smirk.

Tweak couldn't help but smile. "Hey! I'm Chinese. That's racist. Asshole."

Naomi snorted. "Anybody told you you're a brat?" she asked, laughter hiding in the back of her voice.

Tweak grinned. "Yeah. You."

She took a seat on the cot and pulled off her boots. "You need to w-wake me, s-say my n-name and flash a light in m-my eyes. Okay?"

"You got it." Naomi replied, dropping the blanket carefully over her. Tweak met her eyes. Naomi was smiling like...like a sister. Or a mom. "Now go to sleep; we need you fresh if this all goes to shit. The last thing we need is zombie code and brainless screw-up work."

"I don't screw up on work," Tweak grumbled, grabbing the pillow and curling around it.

Naomi sighed. "Sleep, Gurgi. Go there."

Weirdly enough, Tweak actually did.

She woke to the sound of Billie's quiet voice.

"Tweak? Oh Tweak, you don't gotta sleep in here."

"Gotta," she mumbled, blinking up at her best friend. "Gotta watch the feeds."

"I said I'd watch," Naomi added dryly from the console chair. "The guys're following your path with no problems, nice and steady. And I know for a fact if Aidan was here he'd send you to bed."

"What am I, six?" Tweak grumbled, drawing her knees up to her chest and nodding at the other side of the cot. Picking up the signal the way she always did, Billie took a seat beside her. Her short afro caught the light off the screens, giving her a bluish halo.

"How come you're up?" Tweak asked, studying her friend. Billie ducked her head. "I...Topher and I were having a game night, but he got called to drive Yvonne, they had to do a courier pickup. I stayed up to see him come home."

"Yeah?" Tweak asked, grinning. "You win before he left?"

Smiling, Billie shook her head. "Not that kind of game. I was playing with him, not against him."

"Niiiiiice." Tweak teased, and Billie ducked her head a little further down.

"Tweak, not like that...but I did kind of want to...ask you something?"

"Yeah? Want manuals on fourth b-base?"

"Tweak!" Billie groaned. "Not that, no. But...if I stayed in Topher's room some nights, will you...uh..." She shot a nervy glance at Naomi. The other woman held up her hands. "Don't mind me, I'm just doing my thing."

"Okay," Billie agreed, but Tweak knew that 'get me out of here' note in her voice.

Catching Billie's eye, she pulled her tab out of her pocket and handed it to the other girl. Billie gave her a grateful smile as she brought up a message window.

> **"If I stayed over in Topher's room some nights, do you think you'll be okay? You won't have nightmares, will you?"**

Tweak met her friend's eyes as she took the tab back, typing.

> **"I'll be fine, B. I got this. You go with Topher, okay? And if anybody says 'Touchdown', they are getting clown-porn vids auto-playing on their tabs till they die."**

Billie giggled as she read, covering her mouth to smother the laugh. She tapped the tab.

"You sure?"

Tweak grabbed a cached gif of two cartoon animals hugging.

"Sure. You aren't going to have nightmares, right?"

Billie glanced down, smiling. "Topher and me are trying just sleeping in the bed together a couple nights a week. If that feels okay...well, y'know. But yeah. I'm gonna be good."

Tweak grinned. Putting the blanket around herself, she gave her friend a hug. "You're g-gonna be great." Pulling back, she made a fist. "Tell Topher, he messes up, I rearrange his f-face again."

Billie gave a nervous giggle, shaking her head. "You're so bad."

"Me, I'm kick ass," Tweak replied with a grin a mile wide. "Now. Go snuggle. I got work."

"No you don't," Naomi threw lazily over her shoulder. "You gotta sleep. Lay down, Gurgi."

Billie made a little kicked puppy noise, eyes flicking from Tweak to Naomi and back. Tweak blinked at her. "What?"

"I thought you were gonna...aren't you mad?" Billie whispered. "She called you names..."

Tweak glanced at Naomi. The other woman gave her a long, slow smile. Tweak laughed. "Eh. I'll kill her later."

Billie had opened her mouth to say something, when Topher burst into the room. "Billie, you've got to see this! Come on, come down to Janice's, you've got to see this or you won't believe me. They're actually here! Tweak, Naomi, come on!"

Standing, Tweak crossed her arms. "I gotta watch the feeds. Can't leave."

Topher shook his head in dismissal. "It won't take long, come on!"

"Nope," Tweak shook her head. "It comes here or it waits."

Billie gave Topher a small smile. "I'll help you bring it in?"

They'd added to their group when they came back. Janice was carrying the big crate and quietly repeating herself. "They fuckin' did it. They actually fuckin' did it. I'll be fucked. They fuckin' pulled it off..."

Yvonne was repeating herself too, but she wasn't quiet. "Oh my god oh my god oh my god oh my god!" She sounded like a teenage girl in a bad vid about high school. Her ponytail bounced as she jiggled on the spot.

"What's this?" Tweak asked.

Topher grinned at her like it was Christmas. "Seeds. It's the first box of seeds we're getting in trade. They're real. The seed bank is real. They're really here."

Tweak gave them all unimpressed looks. *This* was what they were freaking out about? "I spend *hours* coding all these s-shipments and s-schedules, and you didn't believe it was real? If it wasn't *real*, I wouldn't c-*code* it."

"Let them have some fun, Captain Code-Monkey," Naomi remarked quietly. Tweak gave her a sidelong look, but she quieted down.

With reverent hands, Janice lifted the lid of the box. Inside, silver foil packages sat in orderly rows. Janice drew one out. A clear window in the front showed red-and-white beans, and a label that looked like somebody had actually written it by hand.

"Lemme see the docs," Janice murmured. Reaching for her tab, she scanned the box and brought up a list of its contents. Running her hand over it, she shook her head, laughing. "Gracias a Dios. Seeds. I can't believe this...now if they can just box us up an ag guy to help us grow it, we're all set." She laughed quietly, shaking her head. "Dunno how I'm gonna do this without—"

"Tweak!" Naomi snapped. Tweak jumped a foot. "What?!"

"The guys are running away from the safehouse! They're on the road, their vital signs are going through the roof and they're gunning their bikes at about a hundred! Come help me figure out what they're running from!"

Tweak scrambled out of her blankets and sprang into her coding chair, pulling up her systems. New sets of icons populated the screens, layering the area her friends raced through with information.

"Shit!" she squeaked, and Naomi clapped her hands to her ears.

"Goddamn, tone it down. What?!"

"Drones! After them! They're t-trying to outrun them! Shitheads." Tweak snarled, inputting furiously. "I'm g-giving them a route, and..." Her words locked in her throat as the screen flashed. She hated the tiny whimper that came out, but that was what terror sounded like.

"Tweak?" Naomi asked quietly. "Tweak? Hey. Hey. Come on Tweak. Talk to me. Tell me what's going on."

"K-Kevin's down. Hurt. Holes in his s-suit. B-bikes're s-s-stopped. Readouts say b-b—blood." Tweak whispered. Terror drew lines of ice under her skin. She gulped, the sound of everyone in the room loud in her ears. "N-not dead. Vitals good. B-b-b-but he needs a d-doc."

For a moment, she stared at the keys. She was frozen, shivering. Too many things to do. Not enough time. Kevin was down. Drones were coming.

They were going to die. The guys were going to die.

"Tweak?" Naomi's voice pulled at her attention, snapping it back like a rubber band.

She looked up, heart hammering in her chest. "I c-can't order them a c-car to get to the doc. They gotta get on the b-b-bikes and ride." She sat up a little straighter. "But you wanna see something cool? Watch this!"

She hit a key. On the screen, drone icons blossomed into light.

The bikes spat up gritty earth as they sped out of the small haven, and back into the world. Aidan watched in his HUD's rearguard camera as people scattered in all the right directions, shepherded by Rayna's voice and the routes he and Kevin had supplied. At least they had gotten people moving. With any luck, they'd get far enough to stay out of trouble.

On his HUD, the route Tweak had picked out for them drew a glowing green line down the road ahead. Aidan hung back, taking the rear guard as his team revved their bikes and shot into the night.

The safehouse they landed wasn't anybody's idea of a good time: it was a storage unit that somebody had incompletely rigged into a bunker. It had the absolute necessities, but it definitely didn't have anything else.

"Well, that was miserable," Kevin remarked as he dropped his bag. He was trying for cavalier, but Aidan could hear how thin the act was. Kevin sounded tired. Worse, he sounded rattled.

"Is this how it always is down here?" Brendan asked, running both hands through his hair to work the bike-helmet induced snarls out. "How do you guys not crack?"

Aidan had to laugh at that. "Who said we don't sometimes?"

Meeting Brendan's eyes, he realized that had been the absolute wrong thing to say. The younger man had been trying to hide behind a joke. He was just as freaked as the rest of them.

Drawing a breath, Aidan gave him a smile. "It's not usually this bad on Grid. You guys hit town when it's hot."

"Lucky us," Brandi grumbled, unrolling her sleeping bag and flopping onto it. She leaned her head on her brother's shoulder. "So what now?"

"Now we all get some sleep," Aidan stated, glad that his own voice sounded steady. "And we go on with our plans in the morning. Let's hit the sack; we all need to be fresh in the morning. Sleep in your gear and keep your stuff close at hand, in case we have to bug out."

He glanced at Kevin, who was studying his tab. "Anything from Tweak?"

Kevin shook his head. "Only our route to the next safe-house. We're clear, I think."

"Hope so," Brandi agreed wearily. Since she was closest, she reached over and turned out the single bulb lighting the room.

After a moment, she spoke. "Thanks for doing all this, for us."

"It's we who should thank you," Kevin murmured in the dark, and Aidan smiled at the familiar gentleness in his boyfriend's voice. "Because of you, something amazing still exists in this country. You've given us all an incredible gift. We're in a bit of a nightmare right now, but you've kept a dream alive for us all. We're grateful."

Brendan's voice chuckled in the blackness. "Man, you're a sweetheart. Sure you won't share, Aidan?"

Aidan laughed quietly, rolling to lay his arm over Kevin's chest. "If I said yeah, Kev would probably die from embarrassment. So I think I gotta turn you down."

Kevin's chest rose and fell as he heaved a sigh. "See if I say anything inspirational and heartfelt to you again, Brendan. Go to sleep, the both of you."

In spite of the words, Kevin's fingers found and twined with Aidan's, squeezing gently. He squeezed back, letting his eyes close.

It felt as if he'd been asleep two seconds when the crunch of a door being broken woke him.

This week officially sucks ass! He snarled inside his head as he scrambled to his feet, grabbed up his gun and took aim at the splintering door. Which exploded.

The next minutes stayed in his mind in snatches: quick flashes of image when the lights on a scope allowed him a glimpse. Brendan kneecapping an EagleCorp Peacekeeper with a short stick that had a big knob on the end he'd yanked out of his backpack. Kevin kicking one in the gut. Ezra body-blocking another. The noise in the room could make your ears bleed.

"Door!" Aidan hollered over the mess, ducking sideways around the Peacekeeper in front of him to shoot him point blank in the place along the side where two pieces of black body armor met, and the protection was weak. The man dropped like a stone, screaming.

Kevin reached the door first, and Aidan gratefully watched him lob three flashers outside, and one into the room. "Cover your ears! Close your eyes!" Kevin hissed.

The light bombs went off, hyper-flashing light diodes and supersonic sound emitters blaring outside. The noise was followed by a long series of retching and vomiting noises. Aidan turned back to his team. All still on their feet. Thank God.

He sucked in a hard breath. "Run!"

They raced for the bikes, kicking them into life and tearing ass down the highway.

It felt as if Aidan's brain was running even faster.

How the hell did they find us?! What gave it away?

Have we still got a tracker on us?

He watched the green light of the path to the next Force-vetted safe-house glowing on his helmet's face display. His pulse roared in his ears.

We can't go anywhere safe if we've got a tracker on us! Shit!

"Kev," he said into the mic, "We need to run checks on these bikes before we get anywhere important, make sure we're not riding trackers. They tracked us down way too fast."

"On it," Kevin agreed tightly. "Running a check through my tab. It'll send an alert to my display if anything comes up."

"Thanks," Aidan agreed.

"Sir?" Ezra added, "if I can take point, I got a place we can head. It's an old factory, down for demolition. Concrete blocks the signals, if we got a tracker on us."

Aidan thought about it for a second, then nodded. "Good idea. Thanks, Ezra. Take point."

The man's bike pulled ahead of his. He fell back in beside Kevin, blinking three times to bring drone patterns up on his HUD. Nothing on their tails. Maybe they didn't have a tracker on them after all.

Or maybe the Peacekeepers were just biding their time.

His heart was still beating too fast as they turned off the main roads and out onto an overpass.

"Better—" Kevin began, then yelped as a grav net slapped down into the road beside his bike. He gunned the engine, taking off. "Heads up everyone! Company!"

Aidan cursed under his breath and forced his bike to top speed. He swerved out of the way of another net. "They're firing off the rooftops! Get off the bridge!"

Gunfire snapped behind them, and Brendan yelled. Despite the man's best effort to keep his bike steady, it skewed to the left and toppled. He skidded across the concrete for what felt like hours in Aidan's rearview mirror.

"Bren!" Brandi yelped, nearly crashing her bike as she turned and pelted back to him.

"Fuck!" Aidan hissed. He spun his bike in a fishtailing circle, hearing Kevin snap the words "Laying down cover fire." in his ear. He nodded, pulling his own gun from his holster and aiming down into the rooftops where black-clad figures were hastily trying to rig a bullet-resistant covering. Some didn't bother, ducking under the body shields they carried.

Behind him, Kevin fired a rearguard action at the end of the bridge to give the younger man time to remount. Tracers fired through the street-light pierced gloom.

"Brandi?" Aidan demanded, hearing his heart pounding in his ears. "Is he okay? Can he ride?"

"I'll make it," Brendan managed as he clambered on behind his sister. "They hit my rear tire. I'll hurt in the morning, but I'm good."

Aidan let out a breath. "Great, then haul ass, we need off this bridge before—"

"Aidan! They're on the other side!" Kevin gasped in his ear, his voice brittle. Aidan shot a glance down the bridge.

"Fucking A!" He pulled his bike up short, eyes and brain skittering between the two sets of enemies on either side and the one below.

Nowhere to go.

Nowhere.

Or is there?

He stared down. *Crazy,* his mind whispered. *Crazy. We'll get killed.*

Then again, we're definitely going to get killed right here.

Okay then. Crazy it is.

"Onto the roofs!" he shouted, sending his bike off the highway and flying down onto the nearest flat rooftop.

The bike landed in a spray of gravel, but its gyroscopes pulled it up and back into balance. Behind him, Aidan heard the others land as he took off. In the distance he caught dismayed shouting, and grinned.

You think you can turn us in like a deliverable for a paycheck? Then you're earning every dollar, assholes.

"I used to ride canyons," he stated into his mic, eyes fixed as he jumped his bike across the next narrow alley and onto another flat rooftop, "I can get us a route. Stick close, stay behind me. Ezra, where's your factory?"

"Other side of the bridge we just jumped off," the man's voice grumbled in Aidan's ears. He hissed out a breath of frustration. "Shit. Okay, Kev, we need somewhere to hole up."

"On it, running an algorithm," Kevin agreed. "We need to lose the jackals first."

"I'm on that," Aidan acknowledged, racing the bike across the roof of a covered walkway. "Watch the tires; this part's slick."

Over their heads, the whine of drones picked up. Aidan's gut turned over. Just great. Exactly what they didn't need!

They dodged radio towers, jumping rooftops, the bike tires spitting up cinders.

Overhead, three drones closed in on a coordinated trajectory. Aidan watched them on his helmet display, stealing seconds from the real world to glance at the augmented one. Way too close.

"Ezra, Brandi, swerve randomly. Make yourselves difficult targets!" He barked into his mic.

"Roger!" Brandi replied. He just got a grunt from Ezra. And those drones were way, way too close.

Bullets punched into the rooftop ahead of his front wheel. Aidan swerved, heart running like an engine pushed too far into the red.

Then it stopped. Kevin's voice yelped in his mic, a cry of surprise and pain.

Aidan watched in the rearview as Kevin's front tire peeled away like the skin from a rotting fruit, his breath choked in his chest. Kevin managed the next jump, but lost control of his bike when it landed. He skidded, bike skewing sidelong as he tumbled over the handlebars.

Dizzy with fear, Aidan spun his bike in a tight donut, racing back. His bike sent up a plume of dust as he braked.

Leaping off, he waved the others on. "I'll take him. Go on, ride!"

He skidded to his knees beside Kevin. "Kev! Kev, talk to me!"

The taller man tried to force himself up, but only managed to push himself to his elbows before he collapsed again. A strangled cry tore out of him. Aidan stuck his hands under Kevin's back to help him up, and Kevin choked on a scream.

"What's up?" Aidan asked. Kevin shook his head. "Something's...in my back."

Peering over his boyfriend's shoulder, Aidan gulped. Kevin had come down on what looked like an old beer bottle, and the thing had splintered into jagged-edged shards. The plates of the riding jacket had protected his shoulders, but the glass had ripped in below them. Wicked chunks stuck out of his back like the thorns of a red rose, blood gleaming wetly along the points.

"Shit!" Aidan spat, looking from the man he loved to the drones closing in.

We are dead if we stay here. We are so dead.

But he can't move.

He's going to die.

Aidan's jaw clenched. A strange stillness came over him, the panic fading like water dried up by summer sun.

Okay. End of the line. Wasn't a bad ride.

He glanced down at Kevin. *Least I had him. I had something good. Least I get to die beside him.*

Watching the drones close in, he reached down and took Kevin's hands in his.

And then the drones went crazy. One whipped back around and took off the way they'd come, back towards the overpass. The other two slammed into each other in a yellow-white fireball.

Aidan's mouth dropped open. "What the..."

When he heard Tweak's high voice in his ears, he nearly jumped into the stratosphere.

"You guys hear me? You breathing?"

A cracked little laugh clawed its way out of Aidan's throat. "We're breathing, Tweak. Thanks for the drone assist. I'll get you a medal later, but I need a secure medical conta—"

A route flashed into place on his display, making him blink.

"Route to secure medical contact. Mostly underg-ground, hard to t-track. I put it on everybody's HUD."

"Ezra and the sibs, you got them all covered?" Aidan asked.

"Already said that," Tweak agreed distractedly. "G-got into the tech for the t-t-team on your tail, j-j-jamming. I c-c-c-can g-get into the freelance drones easy, g-got a back door into the P-peacek-k-keeper drones but that's harder. G-get moving n-now, b-before the P-peacekeepers are on your ass!" Tweak snapped. Aidan could hear her swallow in the mic.

"Hey. Kevin."

"Roger," Kevin managed, the word sounding like a groan.

"D-don't d-d-die. K-kay?"

Kevin laughed weakly. "I'll do my best to oblige. I've got a sliced open back and my head's...swimming a bit, but I think I'll make it."

"Good," Tweak stated shortly. "Signing off. Bye."

"Thanks Tweak," Aidan managed.

That said, he shoved his arms under Kevin's armpits. Kevin tried to protest as Aidan hauled him up. "I'll be all right. Ride, you're wasting time..." His voice sounded faint.

"Shut up, dumbass. And hold on." Aidan grunted, pushing his boyfriend onto the bike seat and climbing on in front of him. Grabbing both of Kevin's arms, he placed them around his waist, gunned the engine and raced on. Behind them, confusion reigned. A Peacekeeper drone slammed into the mess, adding to the destruction. Kevin's voice laughed in his ear. "Perfect."

"Hang on," Aidan replied tightly, making a last jump onto an underpass and revving the motor for all it was worth.

Half an hour later they pulled up inside a parking garage, deep underground. Aidan carefully helped Kevin off the back of his bike, spikes of fear filling his chest at the sight of blood matting the back of the other man's suit. He glanced at Brandi, who gave him a brave little smile as she supported her brother. Behind them, Ezra was looking over his shoulder. Good thing one of them had the bandwidth to watch their backs and check the perimeter.

"How's he doing?" Aidan asked. Brendan gave him a thumbs' up, but the gesture was slow and clumsy. Aidan drew a breath. "Have you fixed in no time. Come on, inside."

Supporting his boyfriend, Aidan hammered on the metal door set into the wall. "Doctor Kames! The storm's coming in, and it's a bad one! Doctor Coson sent us!"

The door opened a crack, one blue eye taking in the strangers on the doorstep. Then it opened the rest of the way, and Aidan breathed again.

Kevin gave a tight, pained smile as the motherly little woman in the doorway studied them. "Evening. Sorry for the inconvenience."

"We're in trouble," Aidan added.

"I've noticed." the shorter woman agreed blandly. "Okay, get him inside and on the table. Are you guys the reason for all the explosions?"

"Pretty good, wasn't it?" Kevin asked, with a laugh that sounded ragged around the edges.

The round-faced doctor looked him over patiently. "Which one are you, logistics or munitions?"

"Logistics." Aidan put in ruefully, propping Kevin up.

The doctor gave him a nod. "I'm going to need your man on an examination table now. Both of your men." she added, with a glance at Brendan. "In here."

She led them into an examination room fitted with two enamel-and-copper examination tables, padded with the kind of plastic cushioning that was easy to scrub blood off. Doctor Kames lowered the table. "Right, you first," she remarked, pointing at Kevin. "On your stomach on the table please. You're dripping blood on the floor. Miss, go ahead and lay the man you're helping on the other table please."

Together, Aidan and the doctor helped Kevin onto the table.

The doctor took in the situation with one careful look. "That glass is going to take some time to work on. Lie still for a second." Turning, she checked Brendan over. "You're not in bad shape. Lots of bruising, but your riding gear absorbed the road rash. Did your head come in contact with the blacktop?"

"Nope," Brendan replied, "but my shoulder did, and it hurts like hell."

"I'm not surprised," Doctor Kames agreed, checking the skin revealed by removing Brendan's riding jacket and his shirt. "You're going to have some really amazing bruises. But nothing's torn and nothing's bleeding, so give me some time with your friend, and then I'll get you something to help with the bruising."

Turning back, the doctor checked Kevin over quietly. She lifted an enamel bowl and a pair of forceps from a nearby table, and a spray can from another. "Alright, I'm applying a local anesthetic. Tell me when your back starts feeling cold."

"Roger." Kevin agreed weakly.

Watching the doctor peel Kevin out of his riding gear and pick glass out of his back was hell. Aidan tried to look at Kevin's hand instead of his back. His boyfriend's long fingers twitched in his, tightening in time with the occasional gasp. The sounds played counterpoint to the tinkle of glass falling in the bowl.

"Mm. Nice job, kiddo," Doctor Kames observed as she worked. "Concussion, abrasions, sliced back...well at least the bullet that hit your helmet didn't penetrate. You should keep that ricochet mark; it'll make a great story."

"How soon can he travel?" Aidan asked, his chest tight. The doctor clicked her tongue.

"Mmm...tonight if it's desperate, but I'd be happier if you stayed. I've got rooms for you. I can fix him up, but the autopads and the nanoids will take some time on this concussion and the ricochet wound. Do you want some pain meds?"

Kevin shook his head, and winced. "Rather keep myself sharp...Aidan. You keep moving. I'll catch up."

"Bull shit." Aidan retorted. "Anyway, they'll be looking now. Better that we lie low. Doctor, can we get those rooms?"

The doctor nodded, shooting a measuring look at Ezra. "Will you need three rooms, or four?"

"Three's fine," Aidan stated. "I'll room with Kevin. Brandi and Brendan will stay together. We don't want to take too much of your space."

Doctor Kames gave him a quick, smiling nod. Then she turned back to Kevin. "Well, hero, the nanoid conglomerate which will treat that concussion is injected, so you should be able to walk in about five minutes."

"Oh good," Kevin murmured. "May I sit up, then?"

"If you do it slowly," the round woman agreed. "Just take it easy."

"Roger." Kevin acknowledged. Biting his lip, he pushed himself up on his arms until he was able to awkwardly swing his legs around and sit up, breathing hard. He caught Aidan's eye.

"No worries, love. Remember the Black Knight? 'Tis but a scratch."

Aidan couldn't help but smile at his boyfriend's brave, totally failed attempt to act fine. He was hurting; it showed in the lines of his face. But he was still trying to put on a smile, and Aidan knew why. Kevin was trying not to scare him.

He squeezed Kevin's hand, faking a smile of his own. "You don't look as bad as that guy. But you're close."

In his seat, Ezra grunted. "If he's done, Doc, can I get a room?"

"Third door down the hall on the left," the doctor replied coolly. As Ezra left, the older woman caught Aidan's eye, raising a brow. He made a face, and shrugged. The doctor mirrored the gesture, turning back to Brendan and getting back to work.

As Brendan and the doctor chatted, Brandi sat with her eyes closed, her hand playing around inside her pocket with the little wooden coins she kept there. She pulled three out, studying them. Sucking in a breath, she glanced at her brother with worried eyes.

Poor kid, Aidan thought, *all fidgety and looking for something to do with her hands. I know how that feels. She's really worried about her brother.*

He watched as Brandi pulled another little wooden coin from her pocket. Raising her eyes, she caught his for a moment, lower lip between her teeth.

It took another half an hour to get everybody a bed. Kevin fell asleep almost at once, and Aidan was glad for that. All the same, it left him staring at the ceiling in the dark.

He was still awake when Kevin rolled in his sleep, and woke with a strangled yelp of pain. Sighing, the redhead flopped onto his stomach. "I hate back injuries," he groaned quietly. Aidan's lips quirked in a smile. If Kevin was complaining, he was doing okay. It was one of the funny things he'd learned about his guy: you could tell how bad he actually felt by how bad he said he felt. If he was openly complaining, he was okay. He never admitted it when he was really hurting.

But he could have been seriously hurt in that crash. Hell, he could have died. And Kevin's blood would be on Aidan's hands if his boyfriend did get killed on this crazy run.

The thought had been keeping him awake for hours. He'd approved this crazy mission. He'd given the okay. And it already could have gotten one—or both—of them killed, a couple times.

Doing his best to shake the thoughts, he rolled closer to Kevin, brushing his hand over Kevin's hair. "Don't roll over and it won't hurt."

"Tell that to my somnambulant brain," Kevin grumbled.

Aidan gave a snort of laughter. "Your what?"

Kevin chuckled. "Sleeping. I always roll over in my sleep. You know that."

"Yeah," Aidan agreed. "You always snuggle up too. Would it help to sleep in the med-bay until your back heals?"

Kevin grunted irritably. "No, it would not. I despise waking up in medical settings."

"Want to get back up and play cards? I think Ezra's still up; we could make it a hand of poker?" Aidan asked quietly.

Kevin sighed. "I'd rather not. I find Ezra a bit... rough-edged, for my   tastes."
Aidan chuckled. "Okay, Professor. He rubbed you the wrong way, I get it. But cut him some slack, okay? You're getting kind of close to being an asshole."

Kevin snorted. "I'm only returning what I receive in kind...but I'll try to keep it civil. Scout's honor."

"Good enough," Aidan agreed quietly. He laid his hand in Kevin's, skin warm against skin. Gently, Kevin squeezed his fingers."I'll drift off soon enough. Talk to me a minute, and I'll be out."

"I can do that," Aidan agreed, fingers stroking Kevin's hair. "I was thinking; what do you think the Vow is?"

"Hm?" Kevin murmured. "The...oh. What our mountain friends keep calling themselves, you mean. Keepers of the Vow? Sounds like some off-the-wall Fringe superstition to me."

Aidan had to smile a little at that. "Kev, Catholic boys probably shouldn't talk about anybody else's 'superstitions' the way you are. You kind of win the prize for Most Superstitions in a Religion."

Kevin blinked in the dimness. "Oh dear. Did that come out as dismissive?"

"Yeah," Aidan agreed, kissing his brow, "it kind of did."

"My mistake," Kevin murmured. "I'm really not sure what they mean. If they'd used the term 'covenant' I might extrapolate a Biblical reference, but the Vow? I've really no clue. Perhaps some sort of familial obligation? That's always popular."

"Yeah, maybe," Aidan agreed thoughtfully, "but they didn't say it like a family thing. There was something in their voices that made me think religious."

"Mm, you have a point," Kevin conceded. "But if it is, it's not in my purview...all the same, they are making good companions. And surprisingly efficient fighters. We should throw a recruitment offer to the younger cohort in their community, see if anyone wants to join up."

"If we can get them home," Aidan muttered. "Or us." The words seemed to tug everything he'd been thinking up and out with them. "I thought I could get everybody out of this," he admitted quietly, "but now you and Brendan are hurt, and we've still got a hell of a long way to go, and I didn't...God, Kev, I've fucked all this trip up. And now I got you hurt too. I'm such a fuckup."

For a moment, the room was still. When Kevin spoke, the note in his voice squeezed Aidan's heart. "Please don't, Aidan." Kevin's words cracked around the edges, small and tired. "If anyone fucked up, it was me. If I hadn't been reckless, we wouldn't have this heat on us. And I still feel like shit about the mess I've gotten us into, honestly. So please don't blame yourself. To put it bluntly, I'm holding on to you to get through this." For a beat, Kevin was silent. When he spoke, his words were whispered. "All of this is my fault."

Aidan swallowed hard. Forcing down his own emotions, he took Kevin's hand and squeezed. If it were him hurting in the dark, what would Kevin say to him?

He wet his lips, and came up with the best words he could find. "Okay. So we're both fuck-ups. And we're in a fucked over world. But if we hold on to each other, we'll do okay, right? You hold on to me, and I'll hold on to you. And we'll make this work."

Kevin sighed, and his fingers tightened around Aidan's. "Just don't let go."

Aidan rested his head against his boyfriend's, kissing his brow. "I won't. Go to sleep. I'm right here."

In the pale orange light from the hall, Aidan traced the outlines of the man he loved again and again, memorizing Kevin's face as he listened to the man's breathing fall into the slow rhythms of sleep.

In the strange quiet between one day and the next, a funny sort of calm grew inside him. The days ahead weren't going to be easy, but they didn't seem so impossible in the quiet. Moving carefully, he sat up. He knew he wasn't going to sleep, so he might as well put these hours to good use. He'd do some reaching out to local embedded Dusters and nearby bases, find them a secure place to stay for another couple nights. They'd let things die down. Then they'd split the team and get everybody headed home. It was going to take work, but if they stayed steady they could do this.

Quietly, he got up and pulled the covers back around Kevin. Stepping across the room, he slid his boots on.

He made sure Kevin was still out as he grabbed his tab and slid the door open, quiet as he could.

His footsteps seemed loud in the quiet halls. He poked his head into a couple rooms, looking for somewhere comfortable to curl up and work for a while. The first door he tried was a bathroom. He wasn't that desperate.

Next room down was the exam room. Not sitting in there.

Aidan casually poked his head into the third room down. Kitchen? Nah, the seats at the little table set in the wall looked like they'd be uncomfortable.

He was starting to give up on his plan and play with the idea of going back to bed, when something shifted behind him.

Crap, had he woken Kevin after all? His guy could move scary quiet when he wanted to. Or was it the sibs he'd woken up? He hadn't quite turned when something like a mosquito stuck his neck. And then the world faded to black.

When the world came back into focus, there was a light shining in his eyes. It hurt. Everything hurt. Why did his muscles hurt so much? What was the noise?

Why was it so damn hard to think? His brain felt like it was full of hot stuffing.

But the voice behind the light—flashlight, that was what it was, a flashlight— and yeah, he knew that voice.

"One terrorist, still warm. An' I got a bonus for you too," Ezra was saying over his head. Eyes stinging, Aidan just about made out another figure standing behind the light. Another gruff voice spoke.

"You better, after you fucked over two pickups."

"Hey, I landed the mark didn't I?"

"Yeah? I thought the mark had red hair."

"Long story, tell you later."

A grunt. "Noticed the mark's waking up?"

"Ah yeah. Fix that," Ezra's voice replied. There was a new sting. Blackness washed in again.

It was the cold that woke him the next time. He was freezing, shivering in a cold, black-tiled room. No wonder; he was stripped naked. Worse, he was strapped into some kind of metal scaffold, secured like a bug pinned in a case.

Not good. Not good at all.

Panic threatened to choke him, but he did his best to swallow it down. Whatever situation he was in now, losing his cool wouldn't help.

Head throbbing, he studied the room.

No Kevin. No Ezra. No Brandi or Brendan. Thank God, they were safe.

Then the scrambled egg he was using for a brain threw up a memory. Ezra behind a flashlight.

Son of a bitch, he growled inside his head, *the rat-fucking bastard sold us out!*

At least they didn't get Kev or the sibs.

Unless they're in another room...

Please don't let them be in another room...

A click somewhere behind him silenced his inner monologue. He heard a door behind him open, but he couldn't turn his head far enough to see it. Heart pounding in his ears, he wet his lips and listened as the crisp tap of footsteps drew close.

"Is it awake?" A light, feminine voice asked. Aidan strained to get a look at the speaker. Whoever it was, she sounded almost like a girl.

"It does appear so," a man's amused voice replied.

Aidan felt his chest tightening into a fist of panic as he tugged at the metal rods holding him splayed out. He couldn't move. Couldn't see. He could barely breathe.

A knife tip traced along the flesh of his back, barely more than a tickle. "We have some questions for you," the woman's voice added sweetly. "And I'd really suggest you answer. But to be honest..." The tip of the blade traced his cheek now, cold metal caressing. "I don't mind if you put off answering a little while. We like to have fun."

"Aidan Headly, Commander," he stated with all the calm he could scrape together.

"Tut tut. You aren't listening to the questions." The breath was hot in his ear. "It really isn't much, you know. A few names, a few locations. Or would you like help remembering?"

This time, the knife tip, ever so delicately, broke the skin along his cheekbone.

Aidan sucked in a breath at the sting. They'd talked about what to do in this situation, back at training. State your name, rank, and rights. One day there would be international human rights trials. If recordings of what happened survived, there would be as many Force members as possible speaking the rights they were being denied. He called up the words. "Aidan Headly. Commander," he repeated. "I invoke my rights as a citizen of this State under the International Bill of Human Rights."

"Wrong answer," the woman's voice giggled in his ear. The knife cut again.

Event File 15
Event Tag: Charlie Foxtrot
Timestamp: 04:31-3-1-2157

"Up! Get up! Incoming!"

Kevin shot up in bed. Then he nearly fell out of it as his back spasmed. Pain used his spine for a ladder as he pushed himself to his feet, meeting Brandi's panicked eyes.

"Where's your gun?" The freckled woman demanded.

Kevin grabbed the holster from under his pillow, hefting it as he slid his glasses on with the other hand. "Here. Where's Aidan, is he ahead of you?"

Brandi nodded, her hair a dark halo around her head. "Think so; some asshole's trying to break the door down. The doc's got an escape plan, so let's move!"

"Right," Kevin agreed quickly, grabbing up his gear and hissing between his teeth as he yanked on a shirt. The muscles under the autopad were definitely not happy with all the sudden movement, but he didn't have time to cater to them. He slung his gun belt around his hips and loped out the door after Brandi. "Lead the way."

Brandi headed down the hall. Ducking behind a cabinet, she put her shoulder against it. The cabinet squeaked forward on its wheels, and Brandi knocked on the wall panel behind it. It opened to show

Brendan's worried, pale face. Behind him, a tunnel that had probably once been part of a large sewer project stretched into darkness.

"Mind your head," Brandi warned, stepping in. "The doc said we're all supposed to break up into ones and twos, meet back up at the basketball court in the Five Points park. Pipe forks up ahead; you take the left, we'll take the right." She gave him a quick, worried glance. "You're moving okay, right?

If he was honest with himself, Kevin felt as if he was held together with autopads and chewing gum. But he'd felt worse. He nodded. "I'll manage."

Brendan gave him a wan smile. "Sometimes the Wheel really runs us over. Hang in there."

"See you on the other side," Brandi added with a nod as they reached the place where the pipes forked.

Kevin felt his way carefully through the darkness, the sewer dark swallowing up the sounds of his footsteps. The air wrapped him in a cool, moldering blanket that made him glad he'd grabbed his jacket. His pack tugged his arm down until he risked putting it carefully over one shoulder. God and all His Hosts, did he ever hate back injuries.

He smiled to himself as the turn of phrase Brendan had used came back to him. The wheel runs us over; wasn't that the truth. Though he'd said it with an odd gravitas; the Wheel. You could practically hear the capital letter.

What was that about?

He stepped around a trickle of nameless liquid running from a connecting pipe, and let the interesting little linguistic puzzle roll through his mind, idly amusing the front of his brain while the rest of it stayed alert for signs of danger. Until he had solid information to work with, it was best to keep himself calm and relaxed. Linguistic musings were useful for the purpose.

So, the Wheel. Inferences could be drawn. The Hindu religion had the Wheel of Dharma, there was that. Or was it Karma?

Of course, there had been Peter's Wheel of the Year too. Kevin still remembered the way Peter used to talk about the Wheel of the Year being off its axle when the winter snows failed to come, or when it hit a hundred and twenty outside. Peter had held to his Pagan view of eternal truth just as Kevin held to his Catholic perspective, but it was a damn sight harder to be a part of a religion that honored seasons in a world where the climate had changed such a lot, than it was to be a believer in a God who dispensed justice and redemption. Even in this broken society.

The Wheel of Fortune was another possibility, and a much more obvious one. Yes, the Wheel of Fortune made sense in context.

Too bad it wasn't a more intricate mystery. He could use a distraction from the smell down here.

Finally, there was a shaft going upwards. He went up the rungs of the ladder two at a time, but he took the time to check the collar of the hatch for a sensor, confirm that it wasn't wired, and open the manhole cover with care. Haste made waste, after all. And he wasn't about to waste his future on a careless bit of rushing.

The street was empty, quiet in the heart of the night. Sliding out, Kevin ran hush-footed into the safe embrace of the shadows.

He arrived at the forlorn little lot of concrete and shrubby bushes that glorified itself by the name of Five Points Park, ears pricked.

Under the basketball net, a shadow moved.

"Aidan?" Kevin breathed. "Brandi?"

"It's me," Dr. Kames' voice whispered in the shadows. Kevin nodded, slipping to the deeper shade beneath the abandoned pole.

"Get here all right?"

"Not much trouble," the chubby woman agreed with a tight smile. Kevin returned it, a rueful acknowledgment between equals. "I'm sorry about your place," he murmured, shifting his pack to a more comfortable position on his tender back as he waited. "You'll be alright? I can lend you a slick suit if you need."

The doctor shook her head. "You'll need it. I've done this before, don't worry. I've got a bolt hole and another clinic set up."

Kevin nodded. "Good to hear. Where's—"

"Hey," Brandi's voice hissed behind them. Glancing up, Kevin nodded at the twins, eyes searching the dark for shining golden hair.

Brendan checked his tab. "Hey doc, when did you send the other guys out?"

Doctor Kames glanced at him, her brows creasing. "...You two were getting everyone up while I disabled the protections on my back door. That *was* the plan we talked about."

A cold wire looped around Kevin's windpipe. He shook his head. "Somebody has to have sent Aidan and Ezra on; Aidan wasn't in bed when Brandi woke me. Doctor, didn't you send him and Ezra on?"

Dr. Kames shook her head, her eyes clouding. "I haven't seen him since you two went to bed. Or your friend."

Kevin turned on the siblings. "Brendan, you sent them on, right? You let them know we had a problem?"

Brendan's eyes were frightened as he shrugged. "I didn't see them. Either one. Maybe they heard and got moving?" he suggested weakly.

The wire in Kevin's throat pulled taut, making it hard to breathe. His heart constricted in a cage of ice. He shook his head. "Aidan would have woken me. This doesn't make sense. This doesn't make any sense."

Turning, he pulled out his tab and shot off a message.

Message Handle: KingOfHearts

Message: Aidan, where are you?

He stood frozen, waiting.

Waiting

Empty minutes crawled away like crushed insects.

"Kevin?" Brandi asked gently. "We can't stay here."

"I know, I know," Kevin muttered, fighting the panic rising inside him, "just give me a moment."

Bringing up his Force tracking program, he flicked his fingers to bring Aidan's tab tracker up. The cursor flickered. Then it spat up a statement.

Error 303: Device Is Not Responding.

"Oh no," Kevin whispered, hitting the search again and willing the error to be a lie. A mistake. A glitch. Anything but true.

"No. No, no, no, no," he whispered, shaking his head. He could hear the frantic note in his own voice.

"Kevin?" Brendan's warm hand rested on his shoulder. He shook off the distraction, stepping to the side and riveting his attention to the search on his tab. His mind churned over possibilities like a squirrel circling a cage.

Maybe the concrete of the tunnels had blocked the tracker in Aidan's tab. That had to be it. He'd appear in a moment.

Unless his tab had been taken from him and deactivated. Unless he was...

No. He wouldn't allow a world where Aidan wasn't coming to meet him here. It was unconscionable. He refused to consider it.

The cursor flickered.

Error 303: Device Is Not Responding.

Kevin's blood roared in his ears. He tried the search again.

Error 303: Device Is Not Responding.

The ice invaded Kevin's heart, weighted it down and sent it crashing into the pit of his gut. He closed his eyes. When he spoke, the voice that emerged didn't sound like his. He had to force each word out.

"I think my...my Commander has been taken."

My Aidan. My beloved, his thoughts whispered in the silence of his stalled brain.

He opened his eyes on a world with the gall to take his man from him. The world had no right to be so utterly, viciously, randomly wrong.

"We'll need to get under cover," he stated, his voice crisp. "and then I'm going to call my base. We're going to need to make some adjustments to the current plan."

"No shit," Brendan agreed quietly.

Twenty minutes later, they'd reached an abandoned auto-body shop that would serve as a bolthole for the night. The doctor left them at the door with a shake of the hand and a tight smile.

"Good luck in the storm."

"And you," Kevin replied, automatic pilot set to Good Manners, "Keep your head down when the wind blows."

Formalities seen to, he slipped inside, dropped his pack and spared a glance for the siblings. "Give me a few minutes. I need to inform my crew."

"Sure," Brandi agreed. The gentleness in her voice stung like salt in a wound.

Kevin found the most secluded corner he could, down in what had once been somebody's office. With the door closed, he tucked himself into the corner of the concrete box. The pain of the concrete against his healing back grounded him. He forced his numb fingers to bring up the messaging app of his tab.

He reached Liza on the fourth alert. She was bleary-eyed and pale, her hair down in the pony-tail she wore to bed.

"Kev?" She asked, blinking. "Honey, you look like shit. Are you okay?"

The sound of her voice shattered the composure he'd been working so hard to shore up. He closed his eyes, the words he had to say sticking like thorns in his throat. When his voice crept out into the room, it was nothing like his own. It sounded like the frantic, broken whisper of bomb-survivors and refugees he'd helped so many times. It sounded like the voice of a man who'd lost everything.

"Liza, they've...they've taken him. They've taken Aidan. They've taken him."

Liza shot upright, her dark eyes wide. "Oh no...oh shit...okay. Kev, honey, I know you're freaking, but try to stay calm and talk to me, okay? I need to know what happened."

Kevin shook his head, his throat tight. His chest was filled with broken glass.

"They took him from me, Liza. I can't lose him. I can't. I won't. I can't..." He had to swallow down the lump in his throat before he choked on the panic. "I can't lose him."

"I know Kev, honey," Liza murmured, "I know. And we're going to get him back. This is what we're going to do. You're going to tell me what happened. Then I'm going to get everybody up. We're going to put a team together. You're going to get some sleep. When you wake up, there'll be coordinates for a meeting place on your tab. We'll come and get you. Then we'll go get Aidan. Okay?"

Kevin felt as if he might suffocate on the fear in his chest. He nodded, tears burning behind his eyes.

"Okay, Kev?" Liza repeated quietly.

He sucked down a lungful of air. "Okay." Pulling off his glasses, he swiped at his eyes. "Sorry. Stupid of me, wasting time."

"It's not stupid," Liza demurred softly. "How's that plan sound? We get you in the morning, then we go get Aidan?"

Kevin nodded. "Yes. Yes, we'll do that." A strange alchemy was at work inside him, the panic changing its nature. Like steel in a forge, it was hardening as it cooled. Now it was a rage colder and harder than anything he'd felt in years. When he spoke again, he heard it in his voice. "And I will *kill* anyone who gets in our way."

Liza nodded, her face solemn. "Yeah Kev. You will. But right now I need info, okay?"

Kevin straightened his spine. All right. Fine. Fate had been a bitch once again. She'd dealt shit cards. Fine. Now he was going to play. And he was going to win this godforsaken hand. He had to.

He met his old friend's eyes. "Here's what I know."

Event File 16
Event Tag: Planning Session
Timestamp: 05:36-3-1-2157/ 24:00-3-1-2157

"Everybody *shut up!*" Liza yelled into the mosh pit that the canteen had become. Naomi leaned against the wall, watching as the Wildcards turned it down from 'freaking the fuck out' to 'really, really not liking any of this.'

She'd been about to yell herself when Liza did it for her. They didn't have *time* to throw fits like fucking kids. The Corps had her brother. They needed to get on the ball right this fucking second, not make a lot of pointless noise.

A new, louder voice cut the racket. "Hey, you drone-bait dipshits! You *heard* Liza. *Shut your traps!*"

In the wake of Janice's holler, the canteen was deathly still. Arms crossed, Janice cut her eyes around the room. She gave a jerk of the head. "That's better." Turning, she caught Liza's eye. "Go 'head, Liza."

"Thanks Janice," Liza acknowledged with a tight smile. Eyes narrowed, Naomi studied her body language. That girl was two seconds away from her own personal freak-out. She hid it pretty well, but she was definitely there. It was in her shoulders, and her eyes.

She pushed her hair out of her face with her off hand. She'd rolled out of bed when Liza had knocked on her door, and she hadn't bothered with a brush. Her brother was in trouble; she had bigger things to worry about. Goddamn, she should have gone with him when she had the chance. She'd had a bad feeling about this trip from the beginning. She should have been there to watch his back.

"Like I was saying," Liza stated, giving just about everyone in the room a dirty look, "Kevin says that Aidan disappeared in the middle of an evacuation, along with another Force member. We can't be completely sure, but it's a good bet that it was Cavanaugh who grabbed him. They've been hunting Kevin's gene signature across the Grid, and if it's them who took Aidan, we've got a hell of a lot of work ahead of us."

Liza drew a long breath. "I've sent a situation report to Sector. We need to wait for approval to plan a rescue. But as soon as we've got it..."

For a moment, the room was silent. Then Yvonne moved, and so did half a dozen others. Voices snapped like whips in the air.

"I'll get packed."

"Sarah, you got a spare gun?"

"Can we help?" Dilly's voice piped, and Damian's, "you two can go back to bed, that's how you help." came hard on its heels.

"Grab the slick suits, we'll need them," Sarah's voice called down the table. Jim almost talked over her.

"Still got that map of the area?"

"And who the hell said *anything* about going *anywhere*?" Blake demanded acidly. "All you little *kids* need to get ahold of yourselves and *quiet down*." He waited, staring down his nose, until the people who'd started moving were standing still again. Naomi watched him with interest. He wasn't one she would have pegged for getting in on controlling the situation. Maybe she'd read the guy wrong. He glowered right back at the crew as he spoke. "Look. I know you *all* want to help our boys. I do, too. But until we can get more intelligence, we *can't* run in. We'd be going in *blind,* and that, kids, is how you *die.* I'm not going to have the boys coming home to half or more of us in Corporation hands. So, simmer down, sit down, and let's talk about this like *adults.*"

"What if they don't come back?" Billie asked, voice wavering. With her hair still poofed out from bed, she looked like a hedgehog ready to roll into a ball.

Blake shook his head. "Like I *said*. We need more intel."

"Blake's right," Liza agreed quietly. "Tweak, do you want anyone with you on computers? Take your pick."

Across the room, the tiny girl tipped her head. "C-can I c-c-call off base if I n-need help?"

"Are you calling a Force contact?" Liza asked. Tweak bobbed her head. Liza relaxed fractionally. "Then yeah, sure. Alice? How's your apprenticeship going? You confident to handle trauma on your own?"

"I can do my best." Alice agreed, tipping her chin back.

Taking a step to the side, Damian put his hand on her shoulder. "That best is pretty good," he added. Alice shot him a quick smile.

Liza nodded. "Okay. Then this is what we need. Alice, Topher's going to be your escort. You're going out to the meet point with Kevin. Yvonne, you can pick up the seed shipment with Sarah. Topher, Alice, check Kevin over first, then get under cover and wait for further instructions. A three man team won't be hard to hide."

Naomi put up a hand. "Make that a four-man team."

Nearly the whole room turned to look at her. Any other day she might have smiled; they looked like puppies who'd just heard the kibble bag open.

"I'm going," she repeated, in case that hadn't gotten across yet.

Liza shook her head. "Naomi, I'm sorry but I can't authorize that. The base needs its Officers in times of leadership degradation, and—"

"And I'm going," Naomi stated, her voice calm as the pre-dawn desert. She ticked the points off on her fingers. "One, you don't know what this rescue's going to need. You're going to want the person with the widest tactical experience on hand. That's me. Two, you're probably going to need some demolition work at some point. Who knows how to do that? Me. And three," she added, holding Liza's eyes, "I already put blood and black marks on my record to protect *my big brother*. I really don't give a shit about putting more on there. At all. So, either you approve me going, or you don't approve me going and write me up for it later. More paperwork for you."

Liza held her eyes longer than she would have expected. But she wasn't winning this. Naomi had learned this game in childhood. Never look down. Never look away. Never let people think you can be cowed.

I used to stare down a guy who broke bones with his bare hands, honey. Give it up.

When Liza did look away, she bit her lip, glancing from Blake to Janice. Janice gave the stare-down a try next. She held Naomi's eyes steadily. Now there was somebody who'd been through the same school Naomi had. Hell, she was the professor. And Naomi respected that. But she wasn't backing down on this. She didn't so much as blink. Patiently, she let Janice look.

The older woman must have seen something she liked, because she nodded once, slow.

Blake cut his eyes between Naomi and Janice. Then he gave a huffy little sigh. "I don't know why we *bother* some days, Liza doll. But she was a grid operative, she *should* be all right." Blake stabbed a finger in Naomi's direction. "*Don't* get sloppy and make us come get you too, you *hear* me young lady?"

"I hear you, old man," Naomi replied dryly.

Blake snorted. "And *another* thing. Keep an eye on Kevin. Don't let him do anything *stupid*. Or worse, *heroic*." He made a face, as if the word 'heroic' tasted like vinegar. "He'll want to, with his boy in trouble. *Don't* let him."

"Roger that," Naomi agreed.

"We'll take care of him," Topher added.

Billie bit her lip. Then she leaned over, and kissed Topher right on the mouth. "Be safe, okay?" She murmured as she pulled away.

"Okay," Topher agreed, almost cross-eyed.

Blake gave a heavy sigh. "All right, *love birds*. Save the kissing for later." Glancing around the room, he waved his hands. "Well, what are you *waiting* for? *Don't* stand around here. Get these three kitted out and ready to go."

Anxiety in their eyes, the crew got to work.

At six that night, Topher pulled his bike to the side of the road, a line of gritty dust spooling up to hang in the air behind him. Pulling off his helmet under a pinyon like a green cloud, he dug one of their canteens out of the bike bag and took a quick, shallow sip before passing it to Alice. Naomi was glad to see them hydrating. She'd been thinking she'd have to remind them to take a break, but they were sensible. Good sign. It was easy to push when there was someone out there you cared about in trouble. Problem was, if you pushed too hard and too fast, you were useless to them when the real fight came. That wasn't how you won a fight. You saved your strength up like cash, collected it like water. Then you let it go at the right time, and you drowned the opposition.

Leaving her helmet on a minute longer, she checked her HUD. No drones for another two hours. Good. She pulled the helmet off in the pinyon's shade.

"You should drink more." Alice murmured. Topher shrugged, watching the road. "I'm okay."

"You need water after the ride," Alice admonished, taking her own long drink from the canteen. "The air recirculation in the helmets dries the air you were breathing out. And you're losing water in this heat."

Topher shook his head. "Got to save it. Kev should be here soon."

"Well, he's—" but Alice cut herself off, pointing. "There!"

The dust trail resolved into three bikes. A few minutes later, Kevin lined his bike up beside theirs, pulling off his helmet. Naomi heard Alice stifle a gasp. No wonder. The guy looked wrecked. The gentle, old-worldy sweetheart that she usually saw around their base was gone. This wasn't the professional guy with plans at his fingertips either, or even the happy brawler with a rebar sword she'd seen last year in the streets. The man in front of her had a face like a mask of white marble and two silver coins for eyes. The pair he'd been riding with were watching him like he might snap at any second as they pulled off their helmets.

Well, that wasn't good.

"Glad you made it." Kevin stated, and even his voice sounded strange; flat, every word clipped. "Thanks for coming."

"Kev," Topher exclaimed, "have you slept *at all*, man?"

"Yes." Kevin glanced up at the sun rising over the cloud banks. Behind his back, the curly-headed woman caught Naomi's eye, pointed at Kevin, and shook her head. Naomi nodded. She got the drift.

"We'll need to set up a shelter; drones in two hours," the red-head added. "I've got a slick-tarp tent in the pack."

Under the cool protection of the tent, Kevin took a seat, eyes a thousand miles away. Topher and Alice shot nervous glances at one another.

"What information did you bring? Do we have a location?" Kevin asked, glancing up. Naomi noted that his eyes never actually met hers, or anyone else's. He swept the tent like a searchlight, but there was about as much connection there as you'd get looking into a grocery-store scanner.

Naomi crossed her arms. Wonderful. Not only was her brother caught, she had to wait for the techs to figure out where he was. And while she waited, she had to babysit her brother's boyfriend, keep him from going off the rails, and help him deal with whatever the hell was going on in his head. And she was complete shit with other people's emotions.

"What we have is Tweak working on figuring out where he is," she stated. "In the meantime, we can start getting supplies together and start getting prepped for the run. But we know he's alive. We know it was either Cavanaugh or Eagle that got him; nobody else had a lead on you guys. And if either one of them was going to kill him, they'd publicize an execution like crazy."

Kevin closed his eyes, barking a sick little sound that pretended to be a laugh. At least he was showing an emotion. Even if it was pain and anger. That was better than nothing.

"Of course they would," The words came out of Kevin like a bad joke. "An immoral unnatural terrorist? They'd love publicizing that. It'd be a media frenzy."

The tent was silent for a heartbeat.

"So," Naomi repeated patiently, "media silence means he's alive. We know that. Tonight, we're going to get something to eat and some sleep. Tomorrow, Tweak will have leads for us, and we'll start making plans."

She met Kevin's eyes. *And you'll snap out of it and quit with cracks like that, bucko, or I'll slap you upside the head.*

She might as well have stared at the wall. He looked right through her.

Nobody had much to say once they'd eaten. The people Kevin had been traveling with introduced themselves in subdued voices.

Personally, Naomi liked a little quiet. But it wasn't right for this group. This wasn't a healthy peace; it was the kind of quiet you got before a lightning strike.

Maybe it was the edginess that woke her in the night, or maybe it was some tiny sound; she couldn't be sure. Sitting up slow in her sleeping bag, she checked the tent, and bit the inside of her cheek.

Goddamn it, Kevin you little shit. If you went off and got yourself shot I'll kick your ass.

Sliding past Kevin's empty sleeping bag, she slipped out of the tent. *I should've put myself in front of the door,* she grumbled silently to herself. *I seriously don't want to get Aidan back and then tell him his guy's gone. I really, seriously do not. He's totally head over heels for this guy. It'll break him.*

If those sons of bitches don't break him first, losing his guy will.

She stepped on that thought hard. *Nope. Not going there. He'll be fine. He has to.*

Outside, Kevin was using his slick poncho for a blanket, staring at the stars. He glanced up as she took a seat beside him.

"Evening," he murmured, his voice distant. "I came out to call Damian privately. Aidan...Aidan's not going to have access to his medication until we get to him. I wanted to check up on what symptoms we should expect. Didn't wake you, did I?"

"No, but you freaked me pretty good coming out here," Naomi replied quietly. "I heard about your back. Should you be lying on rock after that?" Kevin didn't answer.

Naomi glanced at the sky. "How are we on drones?"

"None for the next three hours," Kevin replied without really thinking about it. You could hear how little he cared in his voice.

At least he still cared enough to do basic safety. But damn, it was freaky to hear him so totally out of it. He sounded a little like Aidan on a really bad day, but he wasn't as honest about it as Aidan was.

"How bad's it going to be?" She asked. Kevin kept his eyes fixed on the sky. "Aside from whatever those soulless *sons of bitches* are doing to him, he'll be dealing with generalized muscle pain. Nausea. And he'll probably have a particularly bad depressive episode. Panic attacks, probably."

"Fuck." Naomi sighed.

Kevin closed his eyes. "Agreed."

For a moment, she watched him. The silence stretched.

She dropped back to lie beside him. "What're you looking at?"

"The moon," Kevin murmured. "Trying to see if I can spot any of the colony ships. They look like moving stars from here." He was silent for a moment. "I was up there once. When I was eleven. Dad and I were invited up by the pan-Asian cooperative who runs the medtec on ships."

"What's it like?" Naomi asked quietly.

Kevin sighed. "Breathtaking. If we live through this war, I'd like to take Aidan up there someday."

"That'd be cool," Naomi murmured. She heard the fabric rustle as Kevin nodded beside her. The cold wind whispered between them.

When Kevin spoke again, his voice husked with pain. "Naomi? I'm sorry." He swallowed as if it hurt. "If you came out here to punch me, feel free," he added with a firing-squad laugh.

Naomi turned her head. "Why would I punch you, now?"

"Because I should have seen this. I should have *seen* it," Kevin muttered, his voice pained. "I've been lying here since the call ended. I've been trying to figure it out. How we got tracked. How Aidan was taken. He was already out of bed when Brandi came to get us. No one saw him, and no one saw Ezra. I *knew* something was off about that man. I couldn't place it, but I *knew* it. I've been putting the pieces together. There were a number of bounty hunters after us. One was a level two operative. The best." He drew a slow breath. "Someone like that might figure out Synth and use it himself. Someone like that could figure out our basic patterns. The Corporations could have gifted a good dog like that with a genome from one of our captured people who hasn't been gone long; someone could miss being recorded as captured for up to three weeks, depending on their position. And if he was an operative using synth, he could have been leading us into a trap on that bridge." He drew a harsh breath. "Aidan gets up in the middle of the night. He's a light sleeper. It...I think it made him a target of opportunity. A chance for Ezra, if that's his name—which I doubt— to get someone in custody and send the heavies in behind him when he left." Kevin closed his eyes. "And it should have been *me*. They were after *me*. It's *my* head

Cavanaugh wants on a plate. They should have caught *me*. Instead...instead the man we love is paying for my sins. I wasn't careful, and it's Aidan who's paying the price. And I don't know if I can..." Kevin swallowed again, sounding like he was trying not to choke. "I'm sorry. I'm so sorry. This is all my fault. I should be there. Not him. I'd give anything to trade places, if I could."

Naomi gave that about fifteen seconds of silence. That felt about right. Then she reached over, and slapped Kevin right across the ear. It wasn't hard enough to do any damage, but it wasn't a love tap either. He yelped like a kicked cat, sitting up and rubbing his ear. "What the hell...!"

"Great. That gets through. Now you're listening." Naomi wrapped her arms around her knees, studying him in the moonlight. "Now hear this. You don't get to go back. You don't get to trade places. You don't get to change things behind you. Only things in front of you. And if you can't do anything about it, you freaking out about it is useless." She poked him in the arm. "You're wasting energy. Save that. You need it. We need what we've got if we're going to be any good when we get to Aidan." Kevin opened his mouth, but Naomi held up a hand. "Ah. Shut up. Listen. From now on, you cut this bull. You don't say 'I don't deserve this because it's my fault'. That doesn't help. You say 'everything I'm doing is to help him'. You need to sleep? You say 'I'm going to sleep so I'll be fresh to help my guy'. You don't want to eat? You say 'I'm going to get this down so I have the energy to help him'. That's how you make this better. Got it?"

For a couple seconds Kevin rubbed his ear and scowled at her. Then he sighed. "I take it you've given Aidan that talk before?"

Naomi shook her head. "Nope. He gave it to me."

Finally, Kevin actually looked interested in something. "Really? That's a surprise."

Naomi nodded. "Yeah. He said that was how he got through the really rough days. 'Cause I was around, and I was little, and he needed to take care of me." She glanced at the moon. "He told me that was what he was telling himself one time, when I said I was worried about him. He was saying it because he was promising me that he wouldn't leave or...y'know. Die."

Silence. The wind rustled the branches of the scrubby trees.

Kevin's slick poncho rustled. He rested a hand on her shoulder.

"We'll get him back. We *will*."

She shot him a sidelong look. "Well, I know that, pal. I only came out here to make sure you knew it too."

Staring at the moon, Kevin nodded. "I'm working on believing it. Thank you, Naomi."

Naomi got to her feet as she spoke. "Yep. Let's get some sleep. Need to be fresh tomorrow."

Crawling back into the tent, she kept an ear out for Kevin following behind. Listening, she heard him draw a deep breath outside the tent. She caught the murmured words he probably thought he'd whispered. "I'm coming, Aidan my love. Hold on."

"Fucking romantic," Naomi grumbled. "Get in here and get to sleep."

Event File 17
Event Tag: Enhanced Interrogation Practices
Timestamp: 11:10-3-2-2157

"Now?"

"Not just yet, dear. Give the drugs some time to work. We want it nicely tenderized before we start, don't we? No fun otherwise."

Aidan shivered. He'd been shivering for God knew how long; it was so cold in this fucking room, and colder in that over-lit coffin of a cell. They hadn't given him anything to wear. They hadn't turned down the lights either. He still wasn't sure if he'd gotten any actual sleep.

He tried to wet his lips, and sighed at the taste of blood. That hadn't been from these torturing pricks either; that had been from the damn guard last night.

It had probably been part of the treatment. Existential fear was a good way to break people. It could have been a way to make sure he knew anyone could start hurting him at any time, having the guard hit him in the mouth with no warning and laugh about it.

Yeah, well. He'd been getting the shit beat out of him by random assholes for years. What else was new?

Well, this fucking metal scaffold was. Being splayed out in this thing like a specimen really, truly sucked.

Another needle sank under his skin. He closed his eyes, forcing himself to breathe. Slow and deep. Stay calm. Sure. They could control his range of motion. They could hurt his body. But they couldn't screw with his head unless he let them.

God, his stomach hurt. He hadn't had anything to eat. Why did it hurt so bad?

No. Think clear. Think about the situation.

He could control the inside of his head. He'd been practicing that for years. He knew what to do with pain. He'd practiced that too. He had the scars to prove it.

Drugs. They were injecting drugs. That was something to worry about, depending on what they injected.

But he couldn't control that. He had to stick with what he could control, the inside of his head.

Sharp fingernails dug into the lobe of his ear.

"No falling asleep!" the woman's high voice sing-songed in his ear. He was pretty much ready to hate her on the grounds of that voice alone.

His heart was beating in his ears. Beating too fast. Shit, what had they given him?

Something that raised heart rate and paranoia. That was for sure.

Or was this something else?

God, he felt like shit. Not just the pain. He knew what to do with the pain. But this sickness in his gut. The shivers. The feeling that his bones weren't attached right. The weight in his chest.

Alright. Enough of that. Focus on breath. Focus. Breathe.

"Are you going to make me repeat myself? I asked you a question," the woman's voice chimed in his ear.

Don't say anything. That was the best move. If you gave assholes like this even a sign that you cared, they'd use that wedge to pry you open. Give them nothing but your name and your rights.

"Aidan Headly. Commander," he repeated for what felt like the millionth time, "I invoke my rights as a citizen of this State under the International Bill of Human Rights."

The skin on his naked back seared with another knife slice.

"Every time you say that, we're going to cut a little deeper," the guy hissed behind him.

Aidan said nothing.

The woman moved into his line of sight, staring at him with that creepy little smile of hers. Fucking bitch, if she wasn't actually having fun she sure was acting it pretty good.

Behind him, a door opened. Shoes clicked on the polished floor. Clicked, not clomped. That meant good shoes, not boots.

Aidan let his head hang, let his ears do the work.

"Christ!" a new voice groaned. Older, a man's voice. Frustrated, angry. Educated. "Who let you two have access to the prisoner?"

"Get out of our work space if you can't handle it, Jones," the guy who'd been using his back for tic-tac-toe replied, mockery in his words. The good shoes clicked against the floor as the man wearing them took a few steps.

"Consider yourself on report, Williams. You and your wife here. I've told you a million times, physical torture doesn't get us reliable information. Management has told you. A century of research should have told you. And now you've fucked over the most valuable information source we've had in a decade?" Walking around the damn scaffold, the man pointed at Aidan's legs. "Did you even notice that it's been through a procedure like this before? It's already inured."

"Who gave you permission to dictate to us?" The woman hissed.

"Supervisor Sims, since you two incompetents killed the last source of intelligence we had before we got much out of her," the man apparently named Jones shot back. He made a disgusted noise in the back of his throat. "Get the detainee out of that and into an interrogation room now. And give it some clothes."

Twenty minutes later, Aidan was still shivering. But at least he was clothed and sitting in a chair. You had to count small wins.

On the wall, an analog clock filled the silence with ticking. Across the table, Jones flipped slowly through a folder full of intel. He had it projected from his sleek black tab, so he obviously wanted Aidan to see that he had dirt and was going through it word by word.

That, or he really didn't care.

Focus on breathing. In for seven. Out for seven. Give this guy nothing to use in expression. In words. In body language. Give him nothing at all.

Pages flicked. The clock ticked.

Aidan didn't know how much time passed before the man shut down his tab with a purpose and stared across the table at him. After a second, he pushed the bottle of water by his hand across the table.

"You must be thirsty."

Aidan didn't react. He just faced forward and counted his breaths.

"I'm Internal Security Manager Jones," the man across the table offered next. "Can I get your name?"

"Aidan Headly. Democratic State Force Commander, Force Registration Number 133653-75," Aidan stated flatly. "I invoke my rights as a citizen of this State under the International Bill of Human Rights."

He did his best to stay still as the man eyed him. If he stayed still, his injuries didn't hurt so much. Damn, he was still shivering though. That couldn't be good.

"Unfortunately you don't qualify as a Cavanaugh Citizen. I can only enforce rights for Citizens who fall under, and abide by, the Corporate contract I'm hired to implement," the man across the table stated patiently, bringing up the file on his tab again. "And this discussion would be easier with an actual name to call you."

"Aidan Headly," he repeated, his face blank. Jones flicked his eyes from the screen to him and back. "I'm afraid that isn't good enough. According to this, you've made yourself physiologically divergent from your natural gender. You understand this is an offense under Cavanaugh mandate, and you're committing it by standing on Cavanaugh soil?"

Aidan sat still. Give this asshole nothing. Not a reaction. Not even an emotion. Let him have nothing to use. Anything he got, he'd turn into a weapon.

The man sighed. "Alright, Aidan then." Leaning forward, he interlaced his hands on the table. "I'm not trying to make this hard on you. If I was, I would have left you with the Williamses, wouldn't I? So don't make this hard on me."

Sorry, asshole, not buying it, Aidan retorted in the silence of his head. *Taking me away from a couple of sadistic pricks doesn't make you my friend. It makes you a complicit enemy instead of an active one.*

He wished the inside of his head was a little more silent. His mind felt like a transmission with a bad signal, staticky and full of intrusive broadcasts.

He went back to counting his breath.

The man gave an irritable little grunt, and flicked pages on his tab. "You know you're up against a lot of charges here. Terrorism, that'll get you thirty years at least. Unsanctioned Body Modification, that breaks the Perfection Mandate. You know that's a capital crime, right? That's the death sentence."

Breathe. In for seven. Out for seven. Yeah, so the idea of dying at Cavanaugh's hands was fucking terrifying. So what. He'd about died before. He'd been terrified before.

At least this way he'd go out a hero to his people.

All the same, what was it going to do to his base to lose another Commander they liked?

And Kevin. What was this going to do to his guy?

No, he snapped at himself, *that's what they want. They want your fear. Give them nothing.*

The man across the table leaned closer. He had salt-and-pepper hair balding on top. A clean-shaven face. Aidan studied details; a good way to keep the mind grounded in the here and now.

What the hell had they pumped into him? His heart was going a mile a minute in his chest. His bones felt like they were put together with rubber, loose and untrustworthy.

Not good. Not good at all. And this asshole was still talking at him. He caught the tail end of it.

"—could get the death sentence taken off the table if you were cooperative. Out of curiosity, did you know that your organization actually has a rogue member of one of our Corporation's managing families in its ranks? We believe you were traveling with him."

Aidan almost smiled at that. *Nice try, douche-bag.*

"It's him we really want, you know," Jones continued, sounding casual. "Funny that it's you in custody and not him. You really took the fall for him, didn't you?"

That almost made Aidan laugh. *Dude, you're so far off the bullseye that you're putting holes in the wall.*

Jones steepled his fingers. "I'm trying to help you here, Aidan. Fact is, we aren't interested in you. We want a traitor who's carrying proprietary genetic material and information. You? You're a little fish. You're some dust-rat from nowhere. Maybe you give orders to a handful of troublemakers, but you really think we care about that?

And now he wants to sting my pride and get me to boast. Yeah, I see what you're doing, Aidan thought sourly.

The guy took a sip out of the water he'd brought. "Sure you don't want some?"

Aidan said nothing. Gave the man nothing.

Jones tried a new tack now. Leaning in, he got earnest. "Look. All we're trying to do is take care of people here. Why is that something you want to fight against? We're improving the human race. We're working towards a world where nobody's sick. Where nobody's born in a body that makes them suffer. Where nobody's life is made more difficult by a few messed up genes. I mean, don't you think you'd be happier if your parents had gotten you a genome screening, and you hadn't been born wanting to do *that* to yourself?" He waved a hand. The way he said the words belied the act of empathy he was putting on. He sounded both freaked out, and a little angry.

Angry that anybody would choose to be what Aidan was. A freak.

For a moment, old shame nearly engulfed him. A freak. Fucked up. A genetic mistake, an—

NO!

Aidan closed his eyes for a moment, picturing all the intrusive thoughts as rats. He stuffed them in a cage.

This dickwad wants my shame. He wants my fear. He's not getting it. I won't give him anything. Remember what this son of a bitch is complicit in. Remember the vids.

Opening his eyes, he stared Jones down. *Your Corporation kills babies. I've seen it. You people sell newborn babies as dog meat. You think I'm a monster? I know you are.*

As he watched, Jones' earnest expression hardened. The suited man sat back, crossing his arms.

"So, you're a commander, that right?"

Aidan nodded. He forced his eyes to remain open. Crap, he could fall asleep right here.

"Then you know sometimes you have to enforce discipline on people. They may hate you for it, but you know it's for their own good. That's the reason for public executions of Unsanctioned Body Modification perpetrators, and other Mandate criminals. Have you seen an execution?"

Aidan blinked. The wounds along his back were beginning to burn from the pressure of the chair. But he refused to move. He refused to look away.

"We aren't animals like American AgCo," Jones continued. "We don't beat confessions out of prisoners. We don't put people in a pit and stone them to death for their offenses. But discipline has to be maintained. If you're convicted—and that's definite with you—you'll be covered by our news affiliate. Your crimes will be publicly read out. And then you'll be given a lethal injection on live stream. From what I understand it's very humane. Almost painless. We aren't interested in suffering. What we want is public order. Public safety. Discipline."

Aidan blinked. When he spoke, his voice was a flat monotone. "Tell that to Mr. and Mrs. Williams."

Jones sighed. Standing, he paced the room. Aidan watched him with half-closed eyes. Tired. He was so tired.

"You saw me reprimand them," Jones grumbled, "That kind of action isn't our general policy. Enhanced interrogation doesn't have good results. But some of my supervisors believe differently. Believe me, I'd fire the Williamses if I could. But my hands are tied here."

Sitting again, he held out his hand across the desk. "Look, work with me here and I can make sure they won't get near you again. Deal?"

Aidan stared at the hand, then at the man's eyes. This whole thing was starting to feel unreal, like something he was watching on a vid. But he knew a good-cop-bad-cop setup when he saw it. And he knew what actual good looked like.

He sat silent.

Jones ran a hand over his face. Then he stood, pushing a button on the wall.

"Take it back to its cell. I'm done for today."

When the guards tossed Aidan into his cell, they weren't gentle about it. He landed hard on a new injury, and couldn't hold back a yelp of pain. Wincing, he sat up and got himself curled into a corner, trying to conserve body heat.

God, he hurt. Everything hurt. His injuries stung. His joints felt like jelly. His bones were in the wrong places under his skin.

That part was familiar. It wasn't the not-rightness of dysphoria, thank God. But it was familiar. He'd had this before. When?

Fuck, it was so hard to think clearly.

Sleep. He needed sleep. He had to get some sleep.

He pulled his arm out of one sleeve of the smock they'd given him and used it to cover his eyes.

Sleep.

He could escape in sleep.

For now.

"Have you eaten today?"

"Busy."

"Stop for two seconds, Tweak. Eat something."

"Busy."

"I will pull the plug on your rig to make you take a break if I have to."

Tweak turned in her chair with a growl, glaring at Liza. "I'm t-t-trying to find Aidan!"

"And I'm trying to take care of everybody who's still here," Liza shot back. "That includes you, Tweak." The dark-haired woman crossed her arms, planted in the doorway. Reaching in her pocket, she pulled out a ration bar. "Eat this at least. If you pass out like you did last year, you'll be in bed for a day, and then you're helping nobody. Not us. Not yourself. And not Aidan."

The words stung Tweak straight up in her chair, ready with shade to throw right back in Liza's face. It was on the tip of her tongue, ready to jump loose, before she got ahold of it.

She wasn't angry at Liza, was she? No, not really. Liza was in front of her, so it felt like she was the one to yell at. But Tweak was angry at this entire clusterfuck of a situation, and yelling at Liza wasn't going to fix it.

She was a little bit proud of the way her brain caught on to that stuff these days; she was getting to the point where figuring out what she was actually mad at didn't take as much work. It made it easier to deal with people; they didn't always seem like they were causing her grief anymore.

She looked down at the ration bar in Liza's hand. Sighed. Reached out and took it.

"Thanks," she mumbled between bites.

Liza didn't say anything, but she pulled the spare seat out and moved it up beside Tweak's rig.

"Not going so great?" Her voice was so soft; she sounded like a mom talking to a kid who was crying. That was as nice as it was irritating.

"No," Tweak grumbled, snarfing down the bar.

"What're you trying?" Liza asked, staring up at the screens encircling the chair.

Tweak shrugged. It'd take longer to explain what she was doing to Liza than it would to actually do it. "You won't get it."

"You can still talk about it, if you want," Liza suggested.

Tweak shrugged. "D-don't. Waste of time."

Slowly, Liza got out of her chair. "You need to take a real break later, all right?"

"Yeah," Tweak agreed.

The footsteps pulled her out of her thoughts. She was supposed to say something. She glanced up. "L-liza? Thanks. For the eats, I mean. Thanks."

Caught in the door by the words, Liza smiled. "Not a problem. See you at dinner, right?"

Tweak bobbed her head instead of wasting energy talking. Once Liza was gone, she got back at it.

Back at banging her head against a wall.

The problem was using the information she had in time to do any good. Sure, she could get bots into every one of the Corporation systems, with a little work. She'd built back doors into most of the big Corporate installations already. She could look out through their cameras no problem. Her bot net stretched across most of the state.

And it did her no damn good at all, until she figured out how to get them to look for a specific face that none of their databases recognized in those cameras. She couldn't be everywhere, looking at everything. She could narrow it down to all the Cavanaugh centers and eyeball every cell manually, but that would take forever and left open the chance that they'd move a prisoner to EagleCorp facilities instead. No, she needed machine speed for this. She needed computers to sort the faces in the security camera input, and find the one they needed.

She knew there had to be an algorithm that'd work. Eaglecorp used something like this to track suspects across the country, didn't they?

But she didn't have an algorithm that a giant had poured cash into for a couple decades. The Dusters had nothing like that. She had what she'd been working on for the last two days, and it was garbage.

Sure, she could figure it given some time. Give her three months, six at most, and she'd get it.

But she didn't have six months. She had hours. And she really, really didn't want to lose a guy like Aidan because she was slow.

Pulling it close, she stared at the map of systems the Dusters had compromised, biting her lip. Her hands were fists on the keyboard.

"Shit, shit, shit," she whispered. Hissing out a long breath, she typed in the call sign, and waited. She *hated* doing this.

The message screen fizzled up, the man on the other end messing with his rig and muttering.

"Come on you piece of shit, work for once, you ancient piece of...oh! Hey Tweak."

Tweak gave the Wiigit Wings base coder a quick grin, glad the Alaskan had answered. "Hey D-d-den...d-d-d..." she swallowed hard. "S-s-sorry."

"'S'okay," the round-faced man on the other side of the screen replied. "You can call me Dan if that's easier. That's my anglo name."

Feeling like a dumbass, Tweak nodded. "S-s-sorry."

"No big. What's up?"

Tweak bit her lip, staring at her hands.

"I n-n-n..." She gulped in a breath. "I n-need help. The f-fuckers c-c-caught my c-c-commander."

Deniki blinked. "The Corps got your Commander?"

Tweak nodded. Deniki whistled low. "That's rough. Your chain of command replacing him?"

Tweak shook her head hard enough to make her hair swing. "We're f-f-finding him."

The man's black brows shot up. "Wait, you're going to try to get him back? From Corporate custody? Which Corporation?"

"C-c-cavanaugh," Tweak replied.

Deniki gave a little grunt of commiseration. "Your chain of command approved you going for him?"

"We're f-finding him," Tweak repeated quietly.

The man on the other end of the image stared at her for a minute. But, slowly, he nodded. "Okay. So, you need something?"

"Y-yeah." Bringing up what she had so far, she shared it. "T-trying to find where he's at. Want to run a facial r-recognition thing across the s-state. Got all in, bots are r-r-ready, but now I'm s-stuck."

"How many systems are we talking here?" Deniki asked. Tweak hit the command to share her bot-net map with him. He whistled. "Holy shit, you blanketed your state. That's a lot of CPU power to work with."

"Y-yeah, but I need an algorithm and I don't have t-t-time and I c-c-can't get the stuff to integration and I c-c-c-c..." the tightness in her throat made her cough. She sucked down oxygen desperately, one hand massaging her throat. Goddamn this stupid stutter!

"You okay?" Deniki asked cautiously. Tweak nodded and drew up her messaging app.

"Sorry, my throat's acting up. I'm freaking out a little here."

"Understandable," Deniki agreed quietly.

Tweak gave the big guy a smile. If she had to call somebody and admit she couldn't hack it, she was glad she'd gotten to know Deniki. He was good enough to keep up with her work-wise, and he wasn't a bag of dicks like most coding dudes. It was good to have somebody decent to talk code with.

"Okay if I type to talk?" Tweak tapped out.

The big Alaskan nodded. "Course."

"Thanks. So, I got nothing. I need an algorithm that'll look for a specific face in tons of camera feeds, and what I got now is shit. I tried ripping off the Social Stream for facial recognition, and it was a total wash. It's fine for photos, but it can't handle the real-time stuff. "

She shrugged, giving the man a quick glance before she typed again.

"What we have now is a way in to all the camera feeds, and a bunch of pics of the guy we're looking for, and I don't know how to get them to work together. I think I need two interacting algorithms; one to recognize faces in the camera feeds, and one to compare the faces to the pics of Aidan and send an alert when the right one gets found. I got no time either, and that's making this worse. I need this yesterday."

The man on the other side of the screen shoved his long hair back over his shoulder, studying the code she'd shared. "Yeah, I see that..." His black eyes narrowed as he studied the lines of code. "Okay...okay...so this didn't work at all, or did it stall out when it overloaded?"

"It froze solid,"

Tweak typed,

> "when it got too much data it just stalled out. Restarted it four times. Did it every time."

Deniki clucked his tongue. "Sucks."

"Sucks balls,"

Tweak agreed with a sigh.

The Haida man nodded. "Okay, so let's see…

It took seven hours. Finally, they settled on a Hidden Markov Model borrowed from an Alaskan animal-tracking setup, and tied that into a revamped version of the borrowed facial recognition code Tweak had stared at for so long.

On the other side of the screen, Deniki leaned back in his chair, working the coding kinks out of his muscles. "Oookay, all the alerts are keyed in. Now we let the bot-net run and wait for something to come up. Mind if I key this to alert me too? I want to see this when it works."

"Isn't your problem," Tweak offered.

The big Alaskan native shrugged one shoulder. "Eh. I like your Commander. Be nice to see if he's okay."

Tweak blinked. "Yeah? Sure. G-go for it, if you want."

"Roger that," Deniki gave a quick two-fingered salute and signed out.

Tweak sat back. She wasn't completely happy yet, but she was satisfied for now. There wasn't a lot she could do until the system sent out an alert.

She checked her personal tab to make double-sure the alert for the bot-net was set to high priority and pop-up notification, and winced. There were strings of messages from Billie and Liza both. She hadn't just missed lunch, she'd missed dinner too.

Billie's last message read:

> "There's food ready to reheat in the fridge unit. Middle shelf, covered plate. Please eat, Tweak."

With a sigh, she tapped out a quick response.

"Sorry Billie. Was working. Going to eat now. Thanks.

<(-_-) > ^ ^ ^ ^ ^/"

Cranky with impatience, she pulled the plate from the canteen fridge and stuck it in the heater. She wasn't hungry. Not that she was ever real hungry to begin with; the jitters that waiting brought on basically switched her guts off, it felt like. The food was even less interesting than usual. But she needed fuel.

She had just finished her meal when the bot-net set off an alert. Tweak took off out of her seat so fast that the canteen table rattled. She nearly lost her footing skidding around corners in the hall.

Deniki's call sign was already on one window when she made it to her rig, and the flashing 'Possible Match' alert on another. She tapped one with her right hand and one with her left. This time she didn't bother trying to talk to Deniki. Typing was faster.

"Hell yes! We got a match, maybe! You see it?"

"Yep, coming through on my end," Deniki agreed. "Good timing too, I was about to sack out. Bringing the feed online?"

"Going on now," Tweak agreed, pinpointing the bot that had sent back the alert and patching into the camera it indicated. This facility was a Cavanaugh thing somewhere out in Greeley.

In the camera feed, Aidan was being yanked out of a chair by three guards in some questioning room. He moved awkwardly, shuffling in their grip. Tweak wished he'd raise his head, but she got only the shortest glimpses of his face. Was he fighting the guards, was that why he was moving like that? Or was he having trouble walking?

Was he hurt?

Between them, the three men dragged him out through a door. "F-fuck," Tweak snapped, scrambling for the commands that would patch them into the hall cameras. She was about to execute the command, when Deniki waved a hand in his screen.

"Tweak, hold up! We can get intel here. See what they're saying about him. You got speaker access?"

Tweak blinked. She hadn't thought of that.

"Y-yeah. Here." She tapped the relevant command, and the sound flicked on. The balding guy in a suit who'd been standing behind Aidan was saying something to the last guard in the room when she tuned in.

"—you to make sure the Williamses don't touch it until I give permission, are we clear? I want it to stay in its cell until called for. It has pertinent information, and I don't want them killing it."

"Sir," the guard agreed, nodding as they pulled Aidan out with them.

Tweak bared her teeth at the screen and the brown-noser who was calling Aidan 'it' instead of 'him'. This fuck thought he wasn't even human.

The man took a seat. Across the table, two heavy guys with faces that got fed too often were staring at him with hard eyes. At the head of the table, a man with a lot more muscle and bronze eye implants sprawled in his chair instead of sitting. You could tell by the way he sat that he thought he was hot shit. Even had the smirk of somebody who thought he was on top.

The balding brown-noser shuffled his papers. "Gentlemen, now that you've seen the detainee, are you satisfied?"

The two men looked at one another for a moment. Then one of them leaned forward. When he spoke, an American AgCo drawl poured from his mouth like corn syrup.

"We appreciate the invitation to be involved, and the work you're willing to do with us. You're sure this sinner's got information on the genetic material we've been tracing?"

"I'm sure," the man with the copper eye implants stated. Tweak watched the suits dart glances between them. Baldy looked at Copper Eyes like he was a cockroach.

"Your proof, Mr. Fitch?"

"Using the synthetic skin and the terrorist genome I was given for this bounty-hunt, I acted as a member of their group," Copper Eyes explained. "I got the suspects talking, and discussions about a seed bank came out." The guy pulled out his tab, and hit a button. The sounds of Aidan, Kevin and a couple other people talking about seeds and gardens filtered into the room.

"Fuck!" Tweak snarled, slamming her fist against the arm of her chair. "L-liar! B-bastard!"

"Shush kid," Deniki murmured. "We gotta hear this."

Copper Eyes flicked his tab off. "If we can bring the rest of the team into custody, we can definitely get the coordinates out of the others. Two of them know the place for sure. The original target may know by now. All we have to do is use the detainee to lure them."

"I see," the fatter of the AgCo men drawled. He glanced at his partner. Then he tapped his tab. "We're authorized to pay this amount for the right to take custody of the detainee."

"I'm afraid we can't turn over control of it. It knows the location of a dissident who my Corporation has proprietary interest in acquiring," the Cavanaugh brown-noser replied smoothly. "But for…oh, three quarters of that amount, we're happy to expand our interrogation to explore these troubling issues. Illicit genetic material's definitely worth anyone's attention. If the coordinates of the material in question aren't something the detainee knows, will the successful capture of its conspirators be acceptable?"

"We can accept that," Mr. Fat said, speaking slow and easy. "However, if we're making a deal like this, we need a show of good faith."

"Speaking of good faith," Copper Eyes put in, "when do we hear about our bonuses? My team, that is."

"Bonuses?" Baldy gave a shocked little snort of laughter. "Mr. Fitch, as of today your group has lost their corporate contract with Cavanaugh. Another specialist team will take care of picking up the terrorist you failed to bring in."

"WHAT?!" Copper Eyes snarled, bolting out of his easy seat.

Baldy smirked incredulously. "You really thought you'd get a bonus? You botched your attack, missed the deadline, failed at two capture attempts and shot employees contracted to another Corporation. You made it necessary for us to pay remunerations to a trucking firm. And you couldn't so much as manage to bring the original target in. You screwed up, Mr. Fitch. Cavanaugh Corporation hires only the best. When we contract with a Level Two acquisitions team, we expect the best. You've proved that you no longer *are* the best. Your dismissal papers will be in your inbox."

"About those poor folks that died," Mr. Big added, "you know we're bound to a cooperation contract with EagleCorp, and they're not happy about their contractors being gunned down by your contractors. Real unhappy, in fact. If we're going to trust you to take good money and bring us good information, we'd like something in return. Your man's a criminal in our sights." He nodded at Copper Eyes.

Baldy glanced the same way. He looked at Copper Eyes as if the man was something stuck to his shoe. "Yes, I can understand your feelings, given the situation. I'll call a security team to escort him into your custody."

Copper Eyes' hands balled into fists. "You two-timing sister-fucker."

From their pockets, all three Corporate types pulled variations on electrical weapons. Baldy had a slim little taser-pistol. Mr. Fat had something that could have been used on cows.

"You're done talking," Baldy told Copper Eyes, saying the words like he was giving a command to a dog.

Tweak glanced away, meeting Deniki's eyes in their call screen. "What the f-fuck?"

The Alaskan snorted. "That's Corps for you, loyalty of a seagull. Okay, switch to...oop, wait up. Something's going on."

Copper Eyes had been still for a couple seconds. But now he was moving, taking off out the door and down the hall.

Tweak switched cameras as fast as her fingers could move, following the guy. She watched him dash up a set of stairs, blaze through an office worker's area, skid up more stairs and book it out a reception area, onto the street.

"Shit," she muttered in awe.

"No kidding," Deniki agreed.

Tweak stared at the screen a minute more, taking in the last few seconds. Then she gave her head a shake. She wasn't here for some bounty-hunter. She was here for her brother.

Her brother. Because that was what he was, wasn't it? She'd never said it before, not to herself even. But Aidan was her big brother as much as Billie was her little sister. She'd bleed for him any time, because he'd do it for her.

Her fingers flew over the rig's touch pads and keys. "I n-narrowed it d-down, so we'll get a look in...yeah! Here. Here he is, he's...oh s-s-shit..." her words died on her tongue.

In a bright-lit room, Aidan was lying on his side, his eyes covered with a sleeve. The jumper he wore was spotted with splotches of blood, stained with sweat.

Fingers fumbling, she tried to get the camera to zoom in.

Aidan was a mess. It seemed like there was blood all over him. Blood crusted the cheek she could see. Aidan was crying, and the tears were tracking lines in the sticky redness across his face. He was shivering too. And then she realized why he had been walking funny.

The man's feet were bare, and covered in wide purple bands of bruising. Every one of his toes looked broken.

Tweak covered her face with both hands, feeling like she was going to throw up. Her breath hitched in her chest.

"Sadistic motherfucking sons of bitches," Deniki growled. "Tweak? Stay with me. I've got the site coordinates. Stay on the line, okay?"

Sickness and panic were threatening to lock up Tweak's muscles, even her breathing. But she got herself to nod.

"K-k-kay," she managed.

"I'm sending all this to your crew. Everything we seen. Coordinates. The whole shebang. Now you know where he is, you can go get him," Deniki murmured. For a big man, he could have a really soft voice when he wanted.

Tweak took a few slow, counted breaths. She pictured her panic as water boiling in a pot. In her head, she turned the heat off.

When she was ready, she took her hands away from her face, staring at the image of her commander—her brother—in that white-lit cage.

"Yeah," she whispered. "We're g-gonna g-get him."

<u>Event File 19</u>
<u>Event Tag: Double Agent</u>
<u>Timestamp: 06:10-3-8-2157</u>

In the dawn light, Kevin repressed a snarl. "Our signal's spotty again. Bloody *hell*."

"We getting anything?" Naomi asked.

Kevin shook his head. "Nothing yet. They must be going after the GreyNet bandwidth again."

"Bastards," Topher grumbled, holding his hands out to the little cookfire they'd rigged under a slicktarp awning. Preoccupied, Kevin nodded as he tapped his tab. He had to check in. Tweak should have called by now. He *needed* to know if the base had found out anything about Aidan. Had he missed Tweak's call with these bloody signal outages?

"What's that?" Brandi asked, sitting up from her absorbed watch over the cooking breakfast.

Kevin raised his head, squinting. He shaded his eyes against the rising sun. "Dust cloud."

Beside him, Topher pulled out their only pair of infrared goggles and looked through them. "Biker. Shit."

Kevin glanced up sharply, then got to his feet, preparing a taser. "Just the one?" he asked quietly.

Topher nodded. "Just one. Looks like he saw us, too; heading our way, off-road."

Kevin nodded, eyes fixed on the approaching dot. Now was no time to act rashly. This could be a number of things, friend and foe alike. Time would tell.

The bike pulled up slowly, the driver holding up their arms in surrender. Kevin wasn't completely sure yet, but at a guess he'd have to say it was a man, with that build.

"Don't shoot!" the rider shouted. "I'm gonna take off my helmet. I ain't a problem. Don't shoot."

That voice. Kevin was nearly sure he knew it, but…

And then the helmet came off.

In the time it took Ezra to step off his bike, Kevin had dropped the tazer, grabbed his pistol and let three shots off into the dust at Ezra's feet. The traitor yelped, dancing in place.

"Jesus Christ!"

"Give me one good reason not to put the next bullet in your head." Kevin stated, every word a shard of ice on his tongue.

Breathing hard, Ezra met Kevin's gaze. "I know where your man's being kept and the security weaknesses that'll get you in. Pass codes. Any data you got from the 'net? It's bull. Decoy stuff. They know you want him, and they want you walking into a trap."

"Kev?" Topher asked warily. Kevin didn't let his attention waver.

"Stay out of range, Toph."

"Uh, what the hell?" Naomi put in, casual as ever. You'd think someone had gotten in front of her in the line for breakfast.

Kevin kept his eye on the enemy and his rage on its leash. He'd let those shots off into the dirt because he *needed* to see this man afraid. That said, killing him wouldn't do much good.

"Or maybe *you* are the trap," he stated quietly. "We fell for it once, after all. That'd be a nice 'pay day' for you. After all, you only care about what you can get, don't you? And what can starving Dusters give you?"

"Look," the bounty hunter replied flatly, "I've got nowhere else to go. You think I'd do this shit if I had another choice? My gang's ignoring me, the Cavanaugh was gonna trade me like a fucking poker chip, and I sure as hell don't want to die. You want my intel? I help you get your man back, you and your hackers get me a new ID. That simple."

"You're the—" Alice gasped, her face contorting into a mask of rage Kevin had never seen her wear before. "The hunter! The hunter who got Aidan! You fucking bastard! How *dare* you come to us, you son of a two-dollar hooker!"

Kevin glanced to the side, noting Naomi at his shoulder.

"That right?" She asked quietly. "This the guy who turned Aidan in?"

"Yes," Kevin agreed.

Naomi nodded. "Great. Thanks for the heads up." Then she stepped forward, and crashed her cybernetic fist across the turn-coat's jaw.

"Wake up." Kevin slapped Ezra's face hard enough to make his head rock.

On his other side, Brandi shot a censorious look at Naomi. "What'd you punch him for?"

"Didn't have a knife," Naomi replied casually, shrugging. Brandi rolled her eyes. "He can't talk if you broke his jaw. We need him talking."

"Eh," Naomi replied easily. "I pulled the punch."

Kevin administered another brisk slap. While he sympathized with Naomi, he wished she'd waited for a more apropos time.

Ezra woke with a jolt, snarling. He strained against the restraints the team had improvised around his arms and legs in the five minutes he'd spent unconscious. "You fuckers!"

"If you want another slap, keep talking." Kevin growled. "Otherwise, shut up. *Now*."

Ezra glowered as best he could, but his mouth snapped shut.

"Good." Kevin stepped a little closer. "Now, tell me who has my Commander."

"Your fuck buddy?" Ezra sneered. "Cavanaugh's working him over, getting paid by AgCo to get stuff about those little gardens out of him. He looked like shit the last time I saw him, just about dead. Either you get deets out of me or you're out of luck, you sick faggot."

This time, it was a proper punch rather than a slap that Kevin delivered, fast and sharp as a snakebite. "If he's dead, so are you. So I suggest you come up with a more satisfactory answer, or you're going to be of little use to me. And right now, I'd suggest that you make yourself valuable, because I'd very much like to put a bullet in your brain. Are we clear?"

"You're not a killer," Ezra replied with as much of a smirk as he could manage, "You already proved that. So I guess you need a better threat."

Kevin's body burned with rage as he spoke. "I haven't been a killer yet, but you're the reason that someone I love isn't here. You'd be amazed how far that can push a man." The gun clicked as he chambered a round.

Ezra snorted. "Killing me ain't going to get you what you want, and you know it. Your threats suck, kid. Here, I'll send you a how-to guide for next time. Where's your tab?"

That threw Kevin off balance. He blinked. "What?"

"You suck at threatening people?" Ezra repeated quizzically, staring up. He rolled his head. "What, you think I was actually going to send you a how-to guide on threats? You're dumber than I thought."

Kevin bit his lip until he tasted blood. His fingers ached with the strain of stillness. Oh, how he wanted to pull the trigger. Perhaps a killing wound wasn't the answer, but a kneecapping shot might just—

A gentle hand rested on his, and he looked up into Brendan's face.

"It won't help," the younger man murmured. "He'll get his. Just not now."

With an effort, Kevin nodded. Putting the safety back on his gun, he dropped the thing into Brendan's hand and stepped away, breathing deeply, head bowed as he tried to get himself under control.

"Why should we trust your intel?" Brandi asked. In the tense quiet, her words hung in the air. "Or you?"

Ezra groaned. "Maybe because I'm coming to you and fucking groveling? Look, I ain't slept. I been running all night. Cavanaugh was ready to sell me to some AgCo goons who wanted to be on EagleCorp's good side. They want to string me up for shooting a couple of their guys on the job. And by the way, I *saved* your lives when I did that."

"Sorry, but you saved your investment," Brandi deflected, voice flat. "You wanted to bring in a live bounty. That's all."

Kevin felt as if the words were a lash, cutting across his soul. A live bounty. An investment. That was him.

Aidan was in hell, because of him.

The man he had been calling Ezra had just opened his mouth, when Kevin and Naomi's tabs sent out shrill call-incoming alerts.

"I've got it," Kevin stated, nodding at their prisoner. "Watch him."

When the image screen fizzed up, it gave Kevin a perfect view of a furious Tweak.

"The f-fuck don't you answer your calls?!" The little coder snapped, looking every inch the spitting kitten. "I been c-calling since last n-night, twat-waffle!"

"I see you've been taking lessons from Janice again. Lovely," Kevin replied numbly. "The GreyNet's been recalcitrant out here. We didn't get your calls. Tell me there's something, Tweak."

Tweak huffed, crossing her arms. "Stupid t-tabs. Need to b-boost them. Better signal r-reception. I g-got Aidan!"

Kevin drew a deep breath. "How is he?"

Tweak winced. "Not s-so g-good. In trouble. In G-greely. I got the building. Got the schematics. You're g-gonna have trouble g-getting in."

"Understatement," the man he'd known as Ezra grumbled. "You're dead on your own."

"Whozat?" Tweak asked, turning her head as if she was trying to peer out of the screen. Kevin waved a dismissive hand, turning his back on the hunter and walking to a more private corner of the slick tarp's cramped protection. "Not important. Tweak, what condition is he in? Will he be able to fight if we have to?"

Tweak's eyes grew wide, making her look much younger and so much more fragile than she would ever let on. She shook her head.

"He's h-hurt. B-broken feet. B-blood. L-looks sick."

A fist squeezed Kevin's guts. He closed his eyes. "Damn it all."

He started at a hand on his shoulder. On the screen, Tweak waved a hand. "Hey Alice."

"Hey Tweak," the medic remarked, giving a quick wave. "Mind if I sit in? I want to hear more about what I'm going to be treating."

"Feel free," Kevin tried for his normal courtesy, but his voice was hollow.

"So, what'd you see, Tweak?" Alice asked.

Step by step, the little coder laid out what she'd seen in terms of building specifications, security measures, and Aidan's condition. Every word felt like a ball of lead weighing Kevin down.

When Tweak finished, she glanced between them. "You guys g-got it, r-right? Want me to c-call somebody else?"

"We can't call for anybody else, hon," Alice replied quietly. "We don't want to risk anyone else."

"Oh," Tweak replied, her voice tiny, "yeah. That."

Kevin forced himself to focus. He had work to do. "You've done beautifully, Tweak. We're heading that way as soon as we've worked out the plans on our end. Keep us informed, will you?"

Tweak bobbed her head. "I'll try some tricks for the signal stuff. See if I can get you a b-better c-connection. B-bye."

The screen fizzled away on the air.

"Let's get food," Alice murmured, "we'll think better then."

Eyes closed, Kevin nodded. "You have a point."

Ten minutes later, food and water were carefully set down in front of the hunter, his hands unbound.

"Talk," Kevin stated when the man was finished wolfing down his food.

Ezra eyed him like a feral dog. "You're heading for the Greeley Cavanaugh Center, right?"

"What do you know about getting in?" Naomi asked, voice empty of emotion.

"I've got security scans and blueprints," Ezra replied carefully. "But you'll need to get thumb-print replicators and shit. And you don't get my intel 'till I get a promise I've got a new ID after."

"Honor among thieves." Kevin replied quietly. "That's understood. A new identity and a way out of the country in exchange for Aidan's life."

Ezra held out his hand, a silent demand on his face.

Quietly, Kevin took the hand and shook, but he held on a moment longer. "Betray us this time, and you. Will. *Die*. I want to make that absolutely clear."

The augmented copper eyes held his, unable to blink. "Never been clearer," Ezra replied, nearly matching his tone.

Kevin nodded slowly. "Then let's get to work."

Event File 20
Event Tag: Coercive Force
Timestamp: 11:30-3-8-2157

Aidan couldn't move. He knew he should want to. But moving took effort. Moving meant pain.

Easier to lie here. Easier to be still.

If he lay still enough, long enough, all of this might just stop. Everything would stop. Breathing. Heartbeat. Pain.

All he had to do was lie still. Be patient. It would happen.

Footsteps. The door was opening. He knew he ought to feel something. Fear, at least.

But he had nothing left. Not even fear. Dying wasn't frightening. Dying would mean all this would stop.

A booted foot nudged him in the ribs.

"Well, it's no good to us like that." Mrs. Williams grumbled irritably.

"They do this sometimes," Mr. Williams replied soothingly. "We just have to find something that will pull her out of her shell..."

Aidan noted the misgendering with distant irritation. Was getting called 'her' worse than getting called 'it', or better?

Was either one really better than the other, when they were both insults?

When Mr. Williams spoke again, he sounded almost jaunty. "I think I've got an idea. Will you get the guards to get her ready, dear?"

Aidan closed his eyes.

Ten minutes later, a needle burrowed under his skin. "Not too much adrenaline, dear. We don't want heart attacks."

"Oh, I was careful. And a little dopamine too. Should get things started. Time to wake up." The voice was a singsong. "Wakey wakey, missy." Mrs. Williams tutted like an irritated kindergarten teacher. "You've been a very naughty young lady. I mean, look at what you've done to your nice young body. All these nasty things."

Here we go again, Aidan thought wearily. Same metal scaffold. Same cold. And the pain. That was always around these days.

He closed his eyes, and waited for it to be over. It was always the same questions. Where was Kevin. Where were the seeds. Where was his base. Where was the Sector base. At this point he couldn't answer two of those if he wanted to. And he'd die before he'd answer the other two.

Pretty soon, probably.

"Very nasty." Mr. Williams' voice agreed.

"Such a lot of nasty things. *Dirty* things. Are you paying attention, miss?"

Aidan let his head hang. He really didn't care what they were chattering about.

A slap stung his cheek. "Open your eyes."

The pain brought him back to the moment. He raised his head, glaring half-heartedly at the woman in front of him.

Bitch.

Delicate as a surgeon, the woman picked up a scalpel. "Today we're going to clean up the mess you made of yourself. You'll be a nice young lady again. Won't that be nice?"

Aidan's breath caught, the fear cutting through the numbness. He had spent so much time and energy, worked so *hard* to make himself look the way he felt. His stomach knotted.

"No," he breathed when he could finally make sound. "No, don't...."

He never should have spoken. The words brought a glint to the Willamses' eyes as the blade lowered.

They both jerked as the door was opened. "You two. Leave it alone. I need it."

"What?" Mr. Williams demanded. "The supervisor said we could extract the information at our discretion!"

"And you aren't doing any good." Jones retorted. "We've got a more efficient method. I said leave it alone."

The knife trembled in Mrs. Willams' hand. "But—"

Striding across the room, Jones slapped the blade out of her hand. "This was supposed to get information, not entertain you two," Jones snarled in her face.

Aidan closed his eyes, trying to control his breathing. He didn't want to know what the 'more efficient method' was, but it wasn't that knife. He'd cope.

Being forced to walk was hell. His feet felt like they'd been stuck full of nails and broken glass.

Again the interrogation room, but this time there was a medical technician in his white coat standing against one wall. "That about ready?" Jones asked. The technician nodded mutely.

"Do me a favor, Harvey." Jones remarked, easing himself into a chair. "Explain to the prisoner what you're calibrating."

With an expression that said he wished he wasn't there, the young man wet his lips, never looking Aidan in the eye. "It's a carrier fluid for two types of nanobots. One set will...will stimulate the Broca's area and main memory centers of the brain. The other stimulates the reward centers and releases large amounts of dopamine and oxytocin." the young man trailed off, shoulders hunched.

Aidan swallowed hard, his heartbeat drumming in his ears. Nanobots in his brain. They were going to try to strip his free will from him. That kind of thing usually killed its victims, but it worked.

And if it worked...

If it worked, they could rifle his mind and take all the people he treasured. Naomi. Kevin. His crew. The people he was entrusted to protect.

He let his head hang, let himself sit as if he was bowed by the weight of the realization. And he got ready.

"Sir? Do we need more restraints?" the weedy little tech asked. Jones snorted. "The detainee isn't going anywhere, Harvey. Get on with it."

Wait for it, Aidan told himself, *wait for it...*

The tech's hands touched his skin.

Now.

He bucked his head up and to the side, right into the tech's face. He felt the man's nose give way beneath his skull. The tech gave a strangled little scream as blood fountained down his front. He dropped the syringe, and Aidan pushed his chair back, broken feet screaming as he put his weight on them. He shifted the chair a little, and brought the chair leg down on the syringe. It shattered.

"Guards!" Jones hollered. And then there were running boots, and a fist in Aidan's gut. He vomited yellow bile on one guard's legs, and the part of him that was still thinking anything at all cracked a grin at the yell of disgust. The rest of him curled up and waited out the beating.

Maybe this time, they'd finish the job.

He called out a couple slurs and insults. The fists came harder.

Good. Get it over with.

Jones was shouting something.

"Hold, are you deaf?! *Stop?!*"

Breathing hard, the guards drew back. Aidan blinked away blood. Jones was glaring at the guards.

"I'm going to take this call. You two stand still, and do not touch the detainee. You hear me? *Do not* touch it. I'm stepping out."

And then he was looking at a bare wall, and the whimpering tech, and the machine. One of the guards gave him a last smack across the back of the head. One of them told the tech to get out and call somebody else.

For a little while there, Aidan had felt himself sharp and present. But the unreality was drifting back in now. The room, the blood and bile in his mouth. The pain. None of it felt real. It felt like a bad AR simulation, one your brain spotted mistakes in. Nothing felt connected.

The way Jones sauntered back into the room seemed even less real. The man took a seat, smiling like a weasel. "Your friends came looking for you, Commander. So, unless you decide to cooperate, we're going to give them something to find."

Raising his head as much as he could manage, Aidan snorted. "Liar." His voice was a broken wheeze.

Jones' lips curled up just a little more. "You must be good, to get such loyalty. Shame it's going to get your people killed. Why don't we watch?"

Jones waved a hand, and the screen fizzed to life. In it, Kevin, Brandi, and Naomi were following that stinking son of a bitch Ezra down the hall, moving in battle formation. Brendan and Brandi were bringing up the rear, Alice between them with her medical bag on her back.

The sight turned his heart to water. "No," Aidan whispered, shaking his pounding head. He wanted to shout at the screen, demand they go back before it was too late, but he knew they wouldn't hear them.

Damn it! He wanted to grab his sister and shake her, grab his guy and remind him that they had protocol for these sorts of things! If he hadn't taught them that no one man was worth risking the entire base, what sort of commander was he?

"If these people are worth anything to you, maybe now you'd like to cooperate?" This time, Jones' voice had a new tone to it. This time, he was smug.

In that moment, Aidan loathed himself. He was just about worth taking a couple orders from, on a good day. But his life wasn't worth half of any one of theirs. His life wasn't a fair trade for his kickass sister's, or his amazing guy's. They needed to be alive; he didn't. If they died for him it would be a complete waste.

But the fucking Corps weren't giving him a choice between his life or theirs. They were making him choose between their lives and the rest of the base, the rest of the Force. Either he watched as the Corps slaughtered his man and his friends, or he gave up the compound and everyone else that depended on him. He stared blankly at the surveillance feed, his mind chasing itself in circles and hating every single turn.

In the corridor, Kevin watched Ezra carefully, wary of any false move. "How much further?"

"About twenty feet," Ezra replied in a whisper. "Should be on the left." Kevin nodded, following close.

Stopping at a heavy door, Ezra pressed the device that falsified a thumbprint over the reader, and input a code. The door clunked.

He input a second code. "That tells the security drones we're permitted," he explained tersely over his shoulder. "They're off. Let's go."

The corridor beyond was a line of blank doors, grey-painted and metal-plated. Ezra tapped the door of a cell. "Here. I never got this code."

"Got it," Naomi murmured. Stepping in, she pulled two pieces of putty from a small box in her pocket. Embedding two wires in them, she stuck them to the door and stepped back, spooling the wires with her and tapping at the small box they were attached to.

"Pick up the pace," Kevin murmured, checking his tab. "We've been here five minutes. Odds are we'll have a human guard on us in the next three; I'm amazed we haven't seen one yet."

"Kevin. Seriously. When I'm holding explosives, don't rush me," Naomi replied patiently. She looked from the door to the box in her hands, nodded, and tapped.

There was an understated 'whump', and the door rattled out of its lintel. Kevin's heart leaped.

"I'll take point. Cover me."

Stepping forward, he shot a glance up and down the hall, then pulled the door open.

On an empty cell.

Kevin's heart turned to lead.

Behind him, there was the clatter of ceiling tiles, and the harshly digitized voice of a security drone.

"You will be detained for questioning on the grounds of trespass on Cavanaugh Corporation property and property damage. Turn and face the security unit. Raise your hands. Failure to comply will result in the use of deadly force. Please comply."

Cold dread slithered down Kevin's backbone, crawled into his belly and sank into his blood.

Moving on wooden feet, he faced the drone. A gun barrel was staring him in the face. He saw Ezra snarling at another. Brandi and Brendan looked like wild animals caught in a hunter's scope. Naomi had gone stone-faced, her eyes empty.

Kevin's heart was a bird in the cage of his ribs, desperate for escape.

"Security officers have been called," the unit stated flatly. "Do not move."

The moment was hyper-real. Kevin smelled the tang of metal on the air, heard his blood coursing in his own ears.

So. This was it. This was the last move in the game. They'd lost.

But he still had one ace up his sleeve. He'd sworn that he'd never give these sons of bitches the satisfaction of destroying him on their terms. He knew exactly what they would do with someone like him, a traitor to their Corporation and their codes. He would not submit to their breaking. He would not be used by Cavanaugh to make an example, meant to cow both his people and theirs. If he had to take his exit today, he'd take it on his own terms.

He glanced at Naomi, and gave her a nod. He gave Alice a smile. Leaving them behind was a wrench, but they'd be better off if he wasn't around to coerce. Making friends watch each other die slowly was a favorite tactic. He could spare them that.

He raised his eyes to the drone's camera. Time for his exit. It would have to be now, before he was silenced. Before the neurotoxin emitter implanted in his brainstem was deactivated. If he wanted to play his last card, it had to be now.

He had only a handful of words to speak. Only a handful of words: the first stanza of the most oddly hopeful poem he'd ever read. Emily Dickenson had been an odd bird, hadn't she just.

He raised his voice. "Because I could not stop for Death, he kindly stopped for—"

The lights in the hallway died with a clunk.

"*Fuck*!" Tweak snarled miles away. *Stupid.* Her people were going to lose, and they were going to die. Because of one *stupid* mistake. And they might even take the rest of the Dusters down with them; most people weren't as strong as Aidan. Under that kind of treatment, they'd break.

For a moment, Tweak stared at the screen. Then she swallowed hard. "I'm gonna hafta d-do it. N-n-not sure it'll w-work, but I think it's g-gonna."

"Do what?" Billie squeaked, wringing her hands.

Tweak's hands flew as she spoke. "Everything connected to everything. Corps think makes 'em strong. Makes 'em weak too, you know the systems. Virus in the right places, bingo! I checked, double checked. Gotta avoid all the basic systems, gotta avoid water, sewer, emergency. But everything else, done. Gone. Wipeout! Won't break anything; just nothing talking to anything else. For months, if I'm right."

Tweak's fingers hovered over the keys that would complete the commands. She swallowed in a throat that was tightening, making it hard to breathe.

On screen, her friends were in trouble. But she'd already gotten so much heat on them with her last few attacks. If she did this... The terror burned in her muscles. She pushed back from her rig, trying to pace through the panic. She wrapped her arms around herself, trying to breathe steady.

"Tweak?" Billie's soft voice stopped her feet. Her best friend, her sister, was watching her with wide eyes. "Tweak, what's up?"

Tweak swallowed hard, massaging her throat to ease it up before she spoke. She tapped one foot to burn off some of the energy as she put the words together. "B-billie, I do this, we c-c-can't hide ever ag-gain. N-no more b-being s-s-something they can ignore. The C-c-corps will come after us for real if I do this. Hard. Not j-just D-d-dusters. They'll c-c-come after m-me. They'll hunt the c-coder who pulls this. I know it. I seen Techo's p-protocols. Seen their threat p-priority l-list. This? This is the thing that f-freaks them out worst. They'll p-put all they got behind g-going for m-me, I d-do this. That's why I n-never did it b-before. We do this—I d-do this—and we g-get ready for w-war."

"But we'll have the guys back?" Billie asked, nodding at the screen.

Tweak gulped. "Think so."

Billie bit her lip. "You think...Tweak, you think maybe we can fight a war if we've got everybody behind us? I kind of think we can. I think...I think maybe we don't need to hide, if we've got the guys."

Tweak's nervously tapping foot was loud in the silence. Closing her eyes, she willed herself to be still. "Y-you think so?"

Billie smiled; the expression was small and frightened, and so damn brave. It was the smile she'd given Tweak when they'd decided to break out of detention. It was the smile she'd given when they'd decided to trust Jazz, and when they'd decided to join the Wildcards. "If I've got you and...and Topher, I can do this. If you got me, and we got the Wildcards, we can do this. And we do. So... let's do it."

Tweak drew a breath deep into her lungs. Then she nodded. "Kay." Taking a seat at her console, she began to type. "I'm gonna do one extra thing, fix these Corps bastards. Got the building all picked out, no problem."

She glanced at Billie, and grinned. "Watch this."

She pressed a button. For a radius of three states in every direction, the connections between every Corporate-affiliated device on the Grid went down.

In a building in Greeley, Jones nodded, satisfied. "Perfect way to pin your team down, letting them walk up and open your cell. They may be just a little too loyal."

"Let them go," Aidan pleaded, his voice cracking. "Please…you've got me. Just let them go." Useless words, and he knew it. But he had to say *something*.

With a clunk, the lights went out. For a long moment, no one moved.

"What the..." Jones peered at his tab.

Aidan stared at the eerily lit face beside him, tears stinging the cuts on his face. The power was down. It was common out in Duster bases, but it never happened on the Grid. That gave his people an advantage. And the walls weren't soundproofed—the white noise filter would have gone down with the power—so maybe if he screamed…well, what did he have to lose? Without giving the guards time to react, he shouted Kevin's name at the top of his lungs and wrenched against the cuffs.

"Shut it up," Jones growled, holding his tab closer to his face. "I need to—" When it exploded, it took most of his face off.

Aidan yelped as the tab exploded. The guns and tabs on the guards' belts went off too, dropping both of them to the ground. Out in the hall, a series of bangs from God knew what were going off. He couldn't see anything now that the pad's light was gone, but he screamed his lover's name again, begging any God out there to let someone hear him.

"Do you hear that?" Alice asked in a wavering whisper.

Kevin raised his eyes from the crumpled drone, unable to take it in. His mind felt tangled, pulled in too many directions. Apparently it wasn't easy to wrap your mind around the idea that you weren't going to die after all. Then he yelped at the voice that cut the air. "Hey guys! Somebody p-pull out a tab!"

Fumbling in his pocket with stiff fingers, Kevin yanked out his tab. "Tweak?! What—"

"Can it, stupid! I cut power. Cut s-signals too," Tweak stated as she typed. "I overl-loaded the w-w-wireless c-charge c-c-conduits. Blew p-power packs on everybody's d-devices. Guards are down. All d-down. Go get Aidan! I f-found him. I'll g-guide you. G-go!"

Far away down the hall, the shout came again. Kevin took off running, heedless of dead and dying enemies, heedless of his friends shouting behind him and the darkness ahead of him. His tab projected a map ahead of his feet, creating a line of blue arrows in the blackness.

Drawing a breath, he shouted Aidan's name. "I'm coming!"

"Nutcase," Tweak's voice muttered as the tab overlay she was managing guided him.

Kevin was rewarded, finally, with Aidan's pale face in the beam of his flash. Skidding inside the small room, he nearly lost his footing on a pool of blood. He dropped to his knees beside the chair Aidan was cuffed to. The room reeked of blood and vomit, and his beloved looked like death warmed over. The beam of the flashlight Kevin had put down beside the chair underlined the bruises, the slices in his flesh, and the haggard look of Aidan's face was made no better by the blue-white light coloring it from below. But he wasn't dead. Right now, Kevin didn't care about anything else.

"You're alive. You're alive." his hand stroked Aidan's hair back from his face as he repeated the words, giddy with relief. He laughed, and realized he was crying too, tears wet on his cheeks. "God...Aidan..." he drew a shuddering breath. "Let's get you out of here. Do you think you can walk? Oh God above, of course you can't. Your feet. Those filthy, craven...okay, don't try to walk."

Aidan pulled weakly at the cuffs holding him in his seat. "Get me loose?" His voice was a creaking wheeze.

Kevin pawed at the pockets of the dead around them, found the lock fob, then let out a wumph of air as his shoulder took the weight of Aidan's body. "Oh damn, love, you're a mess...God I'm sorry Aidan. I...hold on, the others will be here soon, we'll get you out of here." he murmured, shifting so that he could cradle Aidan as best he could, given the situation. "It's okay. We'll get you out of here." he murmured, stroking Aidan's head as it rested on his shoulder. "I've got you. It's okay." Stupid words, but the most soothing he could think of.

Hot wetness soaked through his shirt, and Aidan shuddered with a sob. "Shouldn't have come," he whispered through the tears. "Could've died..."

"I'm here." Kevin whispered. "I've got you. I'm right here. I'm not going anywhere. Just hang on to me." He raised his eyes at the sound of footsteps, catching the eyes of his friends. "He can't walk." he murmured, arms wrapped tight around Aidan. "We're going to have to hotwire a truck or something."

Brandi let out an inarticulate little noise. "Oh great gods..."

"We can strap him to one of the bikes," Naomi muttered, skidding to her knees beside her brother. "We can rig something. But we have to go."

"Right," Kevin agreed. "Right. Of course. Let's move." Kevin agreed, glancing at Alice. "Can you do anything for him?"

"Here? In the dark?" Alice's voice was a squeak. "No, not in the dark, I need light and supplies and..." she trailed off, swallowed hard. "I got some stuff that'd knock him out for the trip, dull the pain..."

"No," Aidan gasped, shaking his head weakly against Kevin's shoulder. "No drugs. No more drugs."

"You can handle the pain for the trip?" Kevin asked gently, "You sure?"

Aidan shook his head again. He was shivering, and his teeth chattered as he eked out the words, "No more drugs. Please."

Kevin nodded, stroking Aidan's hair with his free hand. "Okay. No drugs. Just lean on Naomi and me, try not to...no that'll never work with your feet like that. All right, we'll carry you as a group."

For a moment, his eyes caught Ezra's. The urge to shoot the piece of shit was almost overwhelming, but the feeling passed. He had more important things to do.

"We need to get home and—" Alice began, but Kevin caught her off with a shake of the head. "No, too dangerous. We'll find a bolthole with a supportive medical professional and get Aidan seen to."

Taking a breath to compose herself, Alice nodded. "He's going to need a lot of medical help. Let me see..." Carefully, she checked Aidan over, asking him what hurt. Apparently everything did.

Kevin wanted badly to *kill* whoever was responsible for this. But, based on the room, they were probably dead already.

"Looks like minor internal bleeding. Could get bad if we don't take care of it soon," Alice murmured.

Aidan shook his head drowsily and tried to move closer to Kevin. "I'll be fine. Just keep...keep going."

Kevin hitched Aidan's arm so that their bodies were as close as they could be, eyes distant as he tried to think. "Alright. I think I've got an idea, if we can pull it off fast enough..."

They got Aidan out of that nightmare room and settled him as gently as they could in the hall, using their tabs and flashlights as illumination. Kevin winced at the expression on his beloved's face. He was in so much pain.

He tapped up the call on his tab. "Tweak, you still on the line?"

"Kevin?" Liza's voice sounded tinny and strained through the tab's speakers. "You idiot; you're supposed to be running, not wasting time!"

"Yes, well, we're a little hampered in the running department. We need a hand," Kevin replied a touch acerbically. "Is Tweak there?"

"Oh, she's here all right," Liza agreed irritably. A bandaged hand waved in one corner. "She's gloating," Liza added.

Kevin blinked. "Over what?" He asked, wondering whether he was going to appreciate the answer.

"I took the Grid down!" Tweak singsonged, popping into the tab's screen like a kitten playing. She looked ecstatic. "I pulled it off! I knocked the grid out! For three states! Three states!"

Kevin's jaw dropped. "You what?"

"She did," Liza confirmed, watching Tweak do a little victory dance around her coding room, bouncing on the balls of her feet. "She also sent a command that messed with the wireless charging systems and overloaded the battery packs of anything with a Corporate signature in that building. She made everything into bombs. How'd that work out?"

"Impressively. It looks like an abattoir in here," Kevin replied quietly.

Liza sighed, looking down for a moment. Then she rallied. "Look, the Grid's down, which means all the vehicles that aren't affiliated with a fire station or a hospital will have switched off or gone to manual. Tweak left the emergency and essential systems alone, but everything else is down. The Peacekeeper force will be down to barricading roads, and they'll be doing it blind. That's good for you guys. How's Aidan?"

"A mess," Kevin admitted, "but he's breathing. He can't walk. Any chance you guys can hack an ambulance from there and send it to where we are? Quickly? Try for...oh, a number one or number five, no Corporation man will pull one of those over; they cater to the CES exclusively. If Peacekeepers see one of those coming, they'll automatically get the hell out of the way. And it will have cutting edge supplies. Pardon the pun."

Liza cracked a grin. Tweak gave a machine-gun chatter of laughter. "Awesome! On it. G-go to the l-loading bay, I'll s-send it there."

"Be careful," Liza added.

"Trying. Thanks Liza." Kevin finished the call, and knelt, squeezing Aidan's hand. "Okay, all we have to do is get to the loading bay, and then we'll be out of here. Sorry Topher, we're going to have to leave the bikes." He met Aidan's eyes. "Ready?"

Aidan nodded weakly. He tried to stand up before either Kevin or Naomi could help, but they both swooped in and caught him before he fell.

Kevin gritted his teeth against Aidan's pained whimper and lifted his love as best he could. "Let's move. Naomi, I've got his shoulders. Get his legs."

It was hell finding their way through the dark, relying on the occasional emergency sign to guide them. But they finally pushed the door of the loading bay open, and Kevin's gut relaxed. "I'll get Tweak a year's supply of coffee for this," he murmured, admiring the gleaming Number One Emergency Vehicle. "Come on. Alice, can you take care of Aidan in the back?"

"If I can't, Damian will bawl me out." Alice quipped ruefully, jogging ahead to pop open the doors.

It took a lot of work getting through the mess that the roads had become. Undirected Go cars bumbled into one another like concussed juggernauts. People ran panicked through streets with no ads. There was already the sound of screams and sirens in the air, and Kevin knew it'd get worse. It was only a blessing that ambulances had backup manual controls.

"This is when I wish I was on a bike," Topher lamented quietly as he worked their way through the mess.

In the back of the ambulance, Alice bit her lip as she began to work on Aidan's deepest injuries. Everyone did their best to lean out of her way as she worked, but given that they had about as much space as protein patties in a wrapper, they couldn't do much to help her.

"Commander, please let me give you a local anesthetic at least," Alice asked the fourth time Aidan gave a little cry of agony. "What I have to do...the pain could put you into shock..."

Kevin turned in his seat, helpless dread clawing at his innards as he watched. Aidan was barely aware of anything, flickering in and out of consciousness. He shook his head weakly against the stretcher, staining it with his blood. "No more...just...need some sleep..."

"Alice," Kevin called back. "Give him a full sedative."

Alice glanced up with the eyes of a trapped animal. "But he said—"

"I know what he said," Kevin cut in quietly. "But right now, he's incoherent, and he's in pain. And he's my...and I've got the right to speak for him about things like this, don't you think?" Turning in his seat, he caught Naomi's eyes. "What do you say?"

Naomi, stone-faced, nodded. "He'll thank us later." Turning in her seat, she looked at Alice. "I'm his sister. And I'm giving you permission to do anything you need to do to make sure he's healthy, until he's thinking straight enough to make decisions. Okay?"

Alice managed a weak smile. "Okay." Quietly, she prepared the deep sedative, and set the micro-injector against Aidan's skin. "He won't even feel it."

Kevin nodded, and forced himself to turn back to the road.

It took five incredibly claustrophobic hours to get out of the city and into the outskirts, and it wouldn't have happened but for the vehicle's special clearances. Once they were far out on empty roads, they pulled off. The ambulance bumped and rattled on tires never designed to go off-road.

They pulled up beneath a stand of gnarled Russian Olive trees. Topher and Kevin worked together to toss a slick tarp over the vehicle, just in case. After that, there was nothing else to do but stretch cramped muscles and think.

Topher made a small fire just inside the slick tarp, enough to give them a bit of warmth and cook the last of their supplies for supper. Kevin paced. He was strung out on exhaustion, but he couldn't sit still. Alice was still working, and he didn't know what else to do with himself.

"We might get lucky and catch some prairie dogs out here." Brendan remarked, trying to sound cheerful.

"We'll help if you'll teach us?" Kevin replied, pausing in his paces to give the other man a smile. He needed to talk about something, anything, to fill the gnawing silence. Silence had been easy when he'd been trying to find Aidan. He'd had a purpose driving him then. But now, sitting helpless, he found himself desperate for something to say, something to do. He realized he was tearing a withered blade of grass into confetti, and stopped himself.

"We've got enough for tonight," Topher replied thoughtfully. "But we might as well try it in the morning. Or we can go back to some town and loot a store? That'll give us enough to get to the next base."

Ezra snorted. "From what I saw, there'll be nothing left by the time any of us got back in."

Kevin nodded ruefully, then glanced up as Alice came to take a seat beside them, peeling off her bloodstained gloves. They burned blue when she tossed them into the fire.

"How is he?" Kevin asked tightly.

"He's a mess." Alice replied in a sigh. "But he'll live."

"Can I—" Kevin began. Alice shook her head, pulling off her scrub cap. Her braids came tumbling down to frame her face. "He's asleep. Sedated. There's no point in sitting with him."

For a long time, no one said anything. Alice stared into the fire, the light dancing in her dark eyes. When she did speak, her voice was no louder than a whisper of wind through the grass. "How many people did we kill today?"

"Don't do that to yourself, Alice," Topher muttered, staring into the fire. "Just don't."

"How many?" Alice repeated.

"Enough." Kevin stated quietly. "People who've done worse. And deserved worse."

Alice stared at her hands. "Some of them were just doing their jobs. Guards. Janitors. People like that."

Kevin glanced away. "You worked on Aidan. You can't really say that anyone who can support *that* is just 'doing a job', can you?" The conversational tone in his voice sounded brittle. "And if they were there, they were supporting it. You can't say 'I just took orders'. You can't say

'I was just doing a job.' When you support a group that tortures and robs and murders, and you know it, you are complicit. Period."

"How many of them didn't know?" Alice asked quietly. "How many of them were just brainwashed folk going about their everyday lives? Not everyone knows what we know."

Topher scrubbed his fingers through his hair. "I told you, Alice. You're going to make yourself feel like shit. Stop it. We did what we had to. Like we always do."

After a moment, Alice dropped her head into her hands, her braids falling to curtain her face. "Why does the world have to be so fucked up?" She whispered.

No one had an answer for her.

Topher sighed and wrapped his arm around her shoulders, pulling her in for a friendly hug. The fire crackled quietly in the silence.

Dinner was hard to choke down, but Kevin managed it. Pushing the remains aside, he glanced up at Alice. "Can I go sit with him?"

"He's not going to wake up for hours yet," Alice replied carefully. "But…as long as you don't wake him."

Kevin nodded his acknowledgment, standing. "Thanks."

The back of the ambulance smelled of blood and antiseptic. Aidan looked only a little better asleep than he had awake. Very gently, Kevin took a seat, taking Aidan's limp right hand in his. His fingers were cold.

He could see the bulges where Alice had applied auto-pads and gauze, bandages and an IV drip. There were other, subtler lumps; bruising so deep it looked like it went to the bone.

Why the hell did humans do this to one another?

Hate. Fear. Money. And maybe evil.

Kevin watched Aidan's chest rise and fall. Eventually, he very carefully laid down beside the wounded man, his head pillowed so that it just touched Aidan's shoulder. For now, it was the only thing he could do. He could be there.

Aidan came slowly back to consciousness, and regretted it. Couldn't he have just stayed forever in the painless, floating place? He shifted and groaned. *Fuck,* he hurt.

What had happened? The last he remembered, he had been in the cold room and they'd been preparing nanobots to strip away his sense of self. Where was he now? Who was lying beside him? He tried to turn his head to look, but everything hurt.

"Hi." The word was a whisper in his ear, and gentle fingers stroked his hair back from his face.

Aidan flinched away from the touch. It took him several drowsy moments to recognize the voice. "Kev…?"

"Right here. I'm right here." Kevin murmured. "You probably ought to remain still, by the way. You're in rather poor shape, if you hadn't noticed."

"You shouldn't have come," Aidan muttered back, his voice soft and slurred. "Protocol…put everyone in danger. Not worth it."

"Fuck protocol." Kevin replied simply, squeezing his hand. "Besides, we were in more danger if they broke you, so if you need to rationalize it, that's your reason."

Aidan squeezed back as much as he could. "Wasn't gonna break. Kill myself 'fore I broke. Keep you safe."

"You and me both. So don't scold. How do you feel?" Kevin asked gently. "Stupid question, I know, but…"

"Pretty sure I died back there," Aidan muttered. "Just…pretty sure I'm dead and you're takin' me to heaven, or wherever the hell I'm goin'."

"Afraid not. Remember, I told you I couldn't handle seeing you die. Therefore, I've revoked your right to do so." Kevin had put on his best teachery tone for the comment.

Aidan smiled weakly. "Who died and made you God?"

"I don't aspire that high, but I'll kick Saint Peter out of his chair for the day on your account." Kevin laid his head down again, closing his eyes. "You can sleep. We're safe here. Middle of nowhere, well hidden." Gently, one hand cupped Aidan's jaw. "You're safe, love. I'm making sure of it."

Aidan sighed and closed his eyes again. He didn't feel safe. Nowhere felt safe. "The Cavanaugh guys...are they on our tail?"

"They're dead," Kevin murmured. "We took care of everything. When you're really awake, I'll tell you everything. For now, trust me when I say we're safer than we've been in years, okay?"

"Okay," Aidan replied drowsily. The pain and the need for sleep tugged his eyes closed.

"How is he?" Naomi asked quietly as Kevin took a seat beside her. He gave her the best smile he could manage. "Sleeping. You did wonderful work; he looks much better," he added, nodding at Alice. The lie came off his tongue badly. He glanced back at the fire. "We should probably move soon."

Topher nodded. "We can pack up in five minutes. Just give us the word."

Kevin sighed, pulling off his glasses and polishing them on his shirt. He'd lost his handkerchief somewhere. "I guess...maybe we'll sleep one more night here? I'm not sure...I'll need to plan us a route too..."

"Give me coordinates and I'll get you there," Topher promised. "I've got stay-wakes and enough energy to drive another twelve hours, at least. Just tell me where to go."

Kevin glanced up, smiling bleakly. "Toph, the kind of route I've got in mind is going to take days. Given what's going to be on our tail after the stunts we've pulled, we need to fly so low under the radar that we're knocking the heads off the dandelions, if you take my meaning.

And frankly...I don't know where to start heading for. Not yet..." He ran a hand through his hair. "I guess...look, let's all get some sleep, and we'll find the nearest safe-house in the morning. We'll plot a route from there, I guess."

Topher hesitated a moment before nodding.

Alice studied him with gentle eyes. "I've got sleep tablets if you need them."

"I'm alright." Kevin murmured. "I'll bed down in a bit. You guys get some sleep, okay?"

Kevin rolled his sleeping bag out in the cramped space afforded by the ambulance. It was a tight fit, but he wasn't leaving Aidan alone tonight.

He glanced up as Naomi stuck her head in. She gave him a small smile. "If you're taking that spot, I'm taking the cab. Sound good?"

He gave her a small, tired smile. "Sounds good. I'll wake you if he needs us."

Naomi nodded, closing the door. A moment later, he heard the cab door open and close, and the rustle of Naomi getting comfortable. He fell asleep to the sound of Aidan's breathing, so glad to hear it again.

Aidan woke near dawn with a scream. He tried to sit up, and nearly fell off the narrow bed. Chest heaving, he looked around, eyes wild and unfocused.

The noise brought Kevin awake with a gasp, and he scrambled to his knees beside the bed, the world dark and fuzzed around him. He grabbed Aidan's hand in both of his. It was slick with cold sweat. "Hey, hey. It's okay. Take a couple deep breaths for me."

Aidan ripped his hand away with a whimper that cinched Kevin's heart in a vice. Wild-eyed, he stared uncomprehendingly. "Kev...? What the...what the fuck happened?"

Kevin managed a smile. "Well, we made a stellar rescue, for one thing. And the grid's down for a radius of three states in every direction. And we're going home. Those are the highlights. You want to hear the whole story this early in the morning, or wait until breakfast?"

In the ambulance cab, Naomi sat up from her improvised bed. "Aidan? You okay?"

Aidan stared for a long moment. Finally, he blinked several times. "Omi? I...the grid's down for...what? That's not possible."

"Thank Tweak. Or blame her, possibly." Kevin ran a hand over Aidan's brow, eyes anxious. "You're cold. Do you want more blankets?"

"I'm fine," Aidan lied, shaking his head. His body was shivering under Kevin's hand, slick with sweat. "Where are we?"

"Out in the badlands between Greeley and the state border." Naomi replied. Leaning over, she pushed Aidan's hair out of his face. "We're under a slick tarp and every drone's down. We're safe. You're seriously fucked up, big brother."

Aidan smiled weakly. "Yeah, well. What else is new?"

"You want to go back to sleep?" Kevin asked gently. "Or I can tell you the rest..."

"Tell me," Aidan insisted quietly.

So Kevin sat on the edge of the ambulance bed, Naomi leaned over the seat, and they told Aidan everything. They explained how Ezra had turned back up, how they'd decided on a course of action. They told him about the empty cell. Kevin explained how Tweak had pulled off her biggest stunt yet and saved their asses. He tried, weakly, to put into words how he'd felt there in the dark, searching for Aidan, knowing he was alive and terrified that he was in danger. He explained about the ambulance ride. By the time they were done, Kevin was lying beside Aidan on the narrow bed under two blankets, their hands twined together as he tried to warm Aidan without hurting him. Naomi kept her hand on her brother's shoulder, gently reminding him of her presence.

For a long time, Aidan lay silent, staring at the ceiling of the ambulance. Kevin could almost read the thoughts on his face. They hadn't just pulled a stunt this time. They'd hit the Corps right where it hurt, in their security and their connectivity. And that meant all hell was going to break loose soon.

The wounded man sighed, and closed his eyes. "If they'd caught you guys, too, I…that's why we have the protocols in place. One man…they wouldn't have gotten anything out of me on my own, but if I had to see you guys go through that, I…you could have screwed the entire Force, you know that?"

"And if we didn't, we would have lost you. Given the odds, I was willing to gamble." Kevin murmured, squeezing Aidan's hand. "Protocol only goes so far."

"But you're not above it," Aidan protested weakly. "I know you guys love me, but…we can't throw away the cause for one man, no matter who it is."

"Deal. You don't get yourself in trouble, and we won't rescue you," Naomi replied quietly.

"If it helps, Commander Magnum's signature is on this mission," Kevin added quietly. "It's not just us you matter to."

Aidan blinked muzzily. "Wait…seriously? He…he told you guys to come get me?"

Naomi gently chucked him under the chin with one finger. "What, you thought we broke orders and every rule in the book to come get you? That's kind of…actually, yeah that sounds like me. And you," she added with a nod at Kevin. "But we followed orders this time. So relax."

Aidan sighed the ghost of a laugh. "Okay. Yeah. Good news. But we need to move." Carefully, he pulled his hand away from Kevin's and tried to sit up, only to gasp in pain and fall back to the narrow bed. "Fuck."

"I'll go get Alice." Kevin said quickly, sitting up. "Maybe you shouldn't move…"

"Don't want to be an invalid," Aidan grumbled.

"You don't want to screw up the healing process either." Kevin retorted. "Then you'll be in bed for a longer time. Good God, Aidan, it's been less than twelve hours since you were nearly killed. They had you for a goddamn week; anyone deserves some down time after that."

Aidan shook his head against the hard pillow. "I'm a commander and we have things to do. While the grid's down, we could—"

"You're not doing anything," Alice stated as she climbed into the back of the ambulance and studied both of them. She sighed. "The alert on the bed said you tried to get up. Don't do that, sir. Let me take a look."

Aidan pulled a face, but he didn't protest.

"I'll get us moving." Kevin said over Alice's shoulder. "You okay with us heading to the nearest safe house, Aidan?"

Aidan nodded. "As long as we're not getting tracked. I'm not going to screw anyone else, if I can help it."

"Roger that," Kevin agreed.

The ambulance jolted into life not long later. Sitting in the back like a sardine in a can, Kevin did what he could to help. Alice bit her lip as Aidan winced with the vehicle's movement. "It's not far." she murmured, checking the injuries and clicking her tongue as she got to work changing the dressings; some of them had bled through the autopads. Her murmured apologies as she stepped on people's toes or jostled them while she worked became a counterpoint to the sound of tires on grit.

They parked the ambulance in an abandoned warehouse that had once housed heavy machinery. A few pieces still sat around here and there; the bucket of a backhoe, gigantic tires, an engine. Kevin studied the surroundings through the ambulance window, satisfied. It was a good place to take cover.

Aidan tried to sit up. Alice put a hand on his chest. "Sir, you really do need to stay down. The mast cells in the autopads won't form new skin right if you don't hold still. Please. Damian told me that...look, I've got a medical officer's authority, so right now, please do what I ask.

You'll rip the injuries open again if you start moving around a lot this soon, and you've got to stay off your feet. Please?"

"I'm not going to stay in here while everyone else is out there," Aidan replied, though his voice was more tired than stern. "We need to plan."

Alice nodded. "Okay, fine."

Five minutes later, everyone but Ezra had found awkward seats in the confines of the ambulance, forming something like a ring around Aidan

"You told the asshole to sit outside?" Naomi asked. Kevin nodded, and held up his tab, where an image of the bounty hunter sitting by the truck wheel showed. "And I put Topher's tab on one of the ambulance struts for a camera." Nodding, Naomi reached across the cramped space and took the device. It still amazed Kevin that they could fit everyone in the thing, though it did not make traveling in it fun for anyone.

Aidan glowered halfheartedly at Alice. "This is not what I meant."

"Yeah, well, we're not the ones half beat to death," Topher replied with as much of his normal humor as he could manage.

"You did get what you asked for." Kevin added with a trace of amusement. "Just not what you meant. Can he have some breakfast, Alice?"

"Yes, if it's soft and easy to digest," the medic agreed. "Have we got any egg and sausage MRE's?"

Everyone in the vehicle save Aidan made a face. That was worrisome. He had to be feeling awful, if he wasn't even up to complaining about the food.

"We've got one," Topher replied. "But we've got to go hunting for something, and see if we can find some water."

The made Aidan sit up a little straighter, scowling. "We don't have water? Shit. Someone give me a tab."

Kevin rolled his eyes in frustration, but passed over his tab. At least that involved holding still.

Aidan set about tapping on the pad as best he could, though it looked awkward. Finally, he cursed quietly.

"Tab's not getting a signal."

"Bloody hell, again?" Kevin took the tab. "Here, I'll patch us into one of my TechoCo identities, I've got a reroute that will let us piggyback off their ISP without giving away our position."

He opened and ran the algorithm, then blinked. "That's...odd. TechoCo's net is down. Here..." He tried the ISP that was leased to ZonCom, under another assumed identity. It was down as well. This time, a window popped up.

"Dear User," it read, "There is currently dangerous unrest occurring in seven Western states. For your security, the Net has been disabled until the threat is contained. Thank you for your patience during the inconvenience."

Kevin blinked, poleaxed. "But...they can't. They can't do that."

"They did." Alice said in quiet shock, reading over his shoulder. Kevin shook his head. "No. No way. Nobody's that crazy. The Corps would lose billions if the Net was shut down across a state, even for a day. And cutting people off...everyone's lives are online. People won't stand for it. The Corps have got to be insane to pull something like this. They wouldn't dare..."

"They dared," Naomi stated woodenly.

Frantically, Kevin hit keys. "I can't get through to the base at all. Even the GPS is down."

"What's that mean for us?" Topher asked, fear in his voice.

Kevin swallowed hard. "It means...we're blind, aren't we? We're in the badlands, and we're running blind."

"So," Naomi stated into the quiet. "We've got no GPS, they've got no drone capabilities. We can't call home. They can't find us."

"And we're low on food and water," Kevin added. The words seemed to have a physical weight. They crushed the moment in on itself, weighted it with anxiety and a numb sort of dread.

"Plus the medical situation," Alice added. "If there's anything I'm not trained to deal with..." She shook her head helplessly.

"And we don't know where the next safe house or the next base is." Kevin added numbly, the reality beginning to unfold inside him like a poisonous flower. He ran a hand over his hair. "Shit...I can't believe this. The Corps are suicidal..." he glanced up. "We've still got some options. I have a couple coordinates saved. Does anyone have a compass app?"

"Yep," Topher agreed. Kevin nodded. "All right. Then we'll play Underground Railroad. At each stop, we'll ask for directions to the next destination. We'll get home within two weeks, three at the outside. I imagine."

Aidan turned as best he could to watch him. "But we don't know where it is, and we don't really know where we are. We've lost any kind of GPS. We can't afford to go wandering off in the middle of nowhere, not knowing the location of safe-houses, water, anything else. And we're supposed to get stuff to Brandi and Brendan's people. Soon. "

Kevin tried for a smile, pained by Aidan's confusion and his fear. "Aidan, love, we took care of the seed deliveries. Think back; that's taken care of."

Aidan stared at him for a moment. "Oh...shit, sorry. Yeah. But we're still out here. And lost."

Kevin laid his hand over Aidan's. "We'll figure it out. In the short term, we'll plan to hit a few stores on the way; we certainly won't be the only looters."

Brendan cleared his throat. "Brandi and I know how to find water out here, and food. We can take care of you guys until we're in cities."

Kevin shot the siblings a grateful smile. "Thanks."

Brandi shrugged. "No problem. Topher, Naomi, c'mon and we'll teach you how to find water."

"We should all probably leave," Alice added, eyeing Kevin as everyone else clambered out of the ambulance. "I want Aidan to get some sleep."

"I'm okay," Aidan managed.

"Don't be an ass, love." Kevin murmured, lips quirking in a weak smile. "You look like a man who was hit by a truck. That subsequently backed up, I may add." Reaching out, he squeezed Aidan's hand. "If it helps, think about this; the Corps have really slit their own throats this time. Cutting people off from the Net and all communication after a breakdown of order is beyond the pale, even for them. People may not remember it often, but somewhere deep down, they're still Americans, and this is beyond Corporate stupidity and corruption. They've crossed the line into dictatorship now, and people won't stand for it. They will put up with a mountain of shit, but this is too much. And I have a feeling that it may just be enough to wake people up. Think about that."

Aidan snorted weakly, his eyes closing. "I hope you're right,"

Kevin studied his face. "Are you sure you won't take something for pain?"

"I'm fine," Aidan repeated wearily.

"You're not." Kevin murmured, "but—" and then something heavy hit the side of the ambulance. Kevin's head whipped round, and he was on his feet in an instant, grabbing his gun from its holster.

Outside, Alice was shouting ineffectually, and Topher was doing his level best to beat the daylights out of Ezra. Kevin might be tall, but he wasn't a big man by any means, and it was practically impossible for him to wrench two men who really wanted to fight apart. But Naomi jumped in beside him, and between them they got the two apart.

"What the hell do you think you're doing?!" he spat, glaring at them both. "Are you two both mentally deficient or something?!"

Topher glowered at Ezra, wiping blood from a split lip. "He wanted to go back and turn you over in exchange for getting the Net back on."

"I wasn't actually going to turn him in, fucktard!" Ezra snarled back. "I was going to steal a mimic, fake them out, get the 'net back on so we're not totally fucked!"

Kevin shot a calculating look at the hunter. "Topher," he stated quietly, "Settle. You're smarter than this."

"He said a lot of other stuff, too." Alice added, brown eyes hot. "About this all being Aidan's fault and yours. Prick."

"Yes, well, I've heard worse." Kevin replied, "And brawling isn't going to help with—shiiiiit." his sentence ended in a growl. He let go of both men to stride back to the door of the ambulance, where Aidan was standing shakily, barely upright and clutching at a gun. "You self-destructive imbecile. Sit down before you fall down."

"Now look what you've done, fucking asshole. We should have left you for the Corps," he heard Alice snarl in Ezra's direction. Then she was at his side, helping him steady Aidan.

"I'm fine," Aidan hissed through clenched teeth. The lie was so blatant that his pants ought to have caught fire. He was pale and shaking, his skin beaded with cold sweat. He sucked in a breath. "This needs fixing, and I'm the commander. The hell is going on?"

"Ezra just started a brawl, that's it." Kevin demurred.

Alice nodded, backing him up. "He said shit until Topher lost it and punched him."

"What kind of shit?" Aidan asked. Kevin watched the weapon in his hands warily.

"He was saying he wanted to turn Kevin in and blame everything that happened on him, to get the Net turned back on," Alice muttered.

"Fucking hell, I said we'd make an offer! Not that we'd do it," Ezra sneered. "You people. They want you, and we don't want to die out here in the middle of fuck-all. So we offer something, we get something, and then we pull a double cross. This is not that hard to understand, you dipshits."

Aidan swayed on his feet, closing his eyes a moment. Then he opened them, and raised the gun. The barrel wavered in Ezra's direction. "I'm done with you. Get the fuck out."

"But I helped you people!" Ezra protested irritably. "I helped them get you out and they promised I'd get—"

"Don't care," Aidan interrupted. "You talk about my people like bargaining chips, you leave. Get out."

Kevin watched as the hunter's face flushed with dark blood. Stepping in, he made a grab for the weapon, but Kevin had already brought up his gun to back up Aidan's. "Don't even think about it."

The click of Topher's weapon behind the hunter and Naomi's gun on his left completed the hemisphere of firepower. That, Kevin thought, ought to be enough to make anyone back down. Hopefully.

Ezra slowly moved his hand away from Aidan's weapon and shook his head. "Fuck you. I want to survive."

He pulled out a tab, bringing up an Emergency Peacekeeper app.

Before he'd hit the button, his head jerked back. Blood trickled down from the bullet wound in his forehead as he sagged to the ground.

Naomi lowered her gun. She met Kevin's eyes across the corpse, her face blank.

"Needed to happen," she stated. He nodded.

Then he had bigger things to worry about; Aidan collapsed against him, the weapon he'd clutched clattering across the concrete.

Kevin caught him with a gasp. "Guys, help!"

Naomi jumped over the body of the man she'd shot to help her brother. Alice cursed under her breath as she surged forward to help her patient. "Get him back in the truck. He's bleeding again!"

It was a tense half hour as they worked, supporting Alice as she patched injuries. Finally, Kevin took a seat against the ambulance's tire. He raked his fingers through his hair, then realized he'd probably tracked blood across his temples; his fingers were red. "Blast it all..." he growled, walking to a water jug and using precious drops to moisten a rag he was using for a handkerchief, cleaning his hands. Glancing up, he gave Naomi a nod where she stood sentinel.

"What did they do with the body?" He asked, feeling the weariness in his bones.

"Covered it in phage and threw it down into a dry wash," Naomi replied quietly. Kevin nodded. That seemed fitting. A man who lived like a scavenger deserved to be buried like one. Raising his eyes, he met Naomi's. "Well done."

"Eh." The blonde woman shrugged. That was all that needed to be said.

After a while, Alice came out to take a seat beside the vehicle's tires. Quietly, Kevin sat beside her, passing her the rag. Alice gave him a weak, grateful smile and washed her hands and arms. For a long time, no one said anything.

"The next time he says he's fine," Kevin remarked conversationally, "I'll personally throttle him." He'd hoped to break the tension in the air, and it worked, at least a little; a smirk out of Alice and a small snort of amusement from Naomi was about the most he'd expected, and more than he'd hoped for.

"Wish the 'net was up," Naomi replied after a moment. "Then we could record it and send it home. I bet Tweak would get a kick out of it."

"If wishes were horses." Kevin replied with a bleak smile.

Alice raised a quizzical brow. "What?"

"Something I learned from my mom," Kevin murmured. "If our wishes were horses, my how peasants would ride." He leaned his head back against the metal of the vehicle.

"Horses'd die out here," Naomi muttered. "No food for 'em. Barely any for us. Brandi and Bren are hunting for dinner. They took Topher along."

Kevin nodded. "Good plan. With any luck, they'll find something." He glanced back at the ambulance. "Alice, may I—"

"He needs to sleep, Kev," the medic admonished quietly. "Don't go in there."

"Fair enough," Kevin agreed, closing his eyes.

The crunch of feet on gritty soil announced the foraging team's return an hour later. To Kevin's surprise, they'd found quite a lot: three prairie dogs, a rabbit, and a number of dirt-encrusted roots tied up in Brendan's jacket, along with a handful of wizened berries.

"We'll use a hubcap to cook all this up," Brendan announced cheerfully, splaying a rabbit on the floor and cutting it open with a knife. The sight was mildly disgusting, if Kevin was honest with himself. "Found a patch of snow behind the building too, so we've got water! Topher's going to go and fill a couple jugs with it; we'll keep it in here where it can melt." Brendan continued cheerfully. "I'll wash the meat and the roots out there, and then we can roast this all up."

"I'll get us started," Brandi added, building a little pile of something fluffy and laying sticks over it. She flicked a lighter in the mix, and it ignited on the concrete with a wumph. Ducking back towards the door, Brandi grabbed handfuls of sticks and laid them over the little fire, until it was crackling merrily. She was adding branches a moment later.

Beside him, Naomi voiced the question that had been running through his own mind for some time. "How do you guys know all this?"

Brendan glanced up with a quick smile. "Eh. We're mountain kids."

"Speaking of that," Brandi added, "Me and Bren have been talking. If we can head back towards the mountains around Fort Collins, we can guide you guys to somebody who can help. There's a vet in the Poudre Canyon who will work on the human animal now and again, if you get me. We could rest there. It's safer than anything else around."

Kevin raised his head, glancing at the siblings. Brother and sister watched him with calm blue eyes.

"You're sure you can find your way without GPS?" Kevin asked. "We can't afford to get lost, with Aidan in this shape."

Brendan's sunny smile flashed. "Hey, I'm named for the Navigator."

In spite of everything, Kevin's lips twitched at the corners. "Fair enough."

<u>Event File 24</u>
<u>Event Tag: Medical Aid</u>
<u>Timestamp: 05:45-3-10-2157</u>

In the morning, Aidan was cold to the touch. Kevin felt his forehead, and glanced anxiously at Alice. They'd been taking turns watching him through the night, and Alice still had the heavy-eyed look of waking in the pre-dawn light.

"His body temperature is awfully low..." Kevin murmured. Frowning, the medic checked the bed's biometric readings of her patient.

"How bad is it?" Naomi asked from her makeshift bed at the foot of the ambulance cot.

"Not good." Alice muttered. "I'll get him some heat pads. Give me some room, guys."

Once he was out of the ambulance, Kevin allowed himself the luxury of squeezing his eyes closed for a moment, feeling the constriction in his chest.

He glanced up as a hand touched his arm, and tried to smile at Topher. The younger man clasped his shoulder. "Hey. Kev. He'll be okay."

"Of course he will," Kevin agreed. "Sorry, Toph, I'm just tired. Now, let's get ready. We've got a long road ahead of us."

It was not a fun drive for any of them. Kevin tried to keep his attention on the road in his seat beside Topher, eyes scanning. He had read about the ways people had navigated before satellite tech; by stars and sextant, by sun and moon and charts, by handheld maps and compass. But who had ever believed the GPS could ever be cut off in this day and age? Who had physical maps anymore? No one.

In the back, Aidan gave little groans that clawed at his heart when they hit particularly egregious potholes.

Against all reason, Brendan did seem to know all the old navigational tricks. He guided them along back roads that were barely tracks, past the ruins of pre-Dissolution settlements and across the rutted skeletons of former highways. It took four hours, but slowly, they climbed into the canyon that the Poudre River had carved over the centuries.

"Topher, stop. We're here." Brendan remarked after one more hair-raising mountain pass had been navigated.

Topher squinted through the dirty windshield. "Are you sure? I can't see anything."

"There between the rocks. There's a road," Brandi pointed out.

Kevin blinked. "That, my friend, is not a road. That's barely a footpath."

Brandi shot him a pitying smile. "It's good enough for a road in the mountains, Gridlock." She turned to catch Topher's eye. "We can drive it for you, if you want."

"I got it," Topher replied quietly, gunning the engine. The ambulance groaned, going up an incline its designers had never intended it to face.

Their reward for reaching the top of the path was a neat, white-painted and picket-fenced building with a grey roof and a hanging sign: Vision Valley. Veterinary Services. Horse Rental. All Are Welcome.

Gesturing for everyone else to stay inside, Kevin got out of the ambulance. Carefully, he took in the area.

"There's no one here," Topher muttered, poking his head out the window and frowning through his infrared goggles. "No heat signatures, no slick tarp, nothing."

"No TV or concierge service, either," a cracked voice wheezed behind them. Kevin spun to stare at a raw-boned old man leaning on a shotgun. The man grinned, showing gaps in his teeth. "You boys look lost."

"There's a storm coming in," Kevin replied carefully, trying to hide the surprise in his voice. "We were looking for a place to bed down for the night."

"You sure this's good enough for you sophisticated types? You sounded awful disappointed there." the man's dark eyes glittered when he smiled.

"You still scaring the Gridlocks, Wally?" Brandi called, hopping out of the ambulance. The old man's eyes lit up as he saw her. "Ya-ta-hey, Brandi. How's the Wheel turning for you?"

"Ya-ta-hey, Uncle. It's a little wobbly," Brandi replied, drawing level. "Kevin, Topher, this is Wally Yellow Horse, born to the Bitter Water people, born for the One Who Walks Around clan; he's Vision Valley's farrier and equine guy. Wally, these are the Wildcards, Duster folks, coming to help us keep the Vow. One of their guys got banged up pretty bad on the way. He needs to see Doctor Molly."

The old man nodded once, slowly. "You two picking up strays again, I see," he observed with the patience of the old.

"Only the cute ones," Brendan quipped as he hopped out behind his sister. Kevin worked hard to maintain his pleasant smile, impatience bubbling in his gut. They shouldn't be standing here. They should be taking care of Aidan. But being the ill-mannered guest wouldn't do him any good now.

There was a sound like a few rocks rubbing together as the old man chuckled, looking him disconcertingly straight in the eye. "I'm just giving you shit, Duster. Come on inside." he added, waving one knobbly hand as he walked towards the house. Behind him, Kevin and Topher shared a dubious look.

Brandi caught their eyes. "Well? Get Aidan and come on, Doctor Molly will do good things for you guys."

It was surprisingly pleasant in the little house; white and clean as a good hospital should be, but on a much smaller scale than the usual facility. Pictures of animals graced the walls all around. Brendan held the door open as Kevin and Topher got Aidan through it on the ambulance stretcher. In the corner, Wally looked up from his conversation with the woman behind the counter. "Your man don't look so good." he murmured, watching the little group.

"It's been a long few days," Brandi replied with a tired half-smile.

In the stretcher, Aidan shifted and groaned as he woke from another fitful doze. "What the...hell?" Shifting, he started to move and whimpered, kicking reflexively.

Kevin ignored that conversation happening to one side. "Brendan, hold this end please." Handing off the handles of the stretcher, he stepped over to take Aidan's hand and run a hand over his brow. "Hey love, hey, it's okay. It's Kevin, okay? Relax, it's just me. We're getting you some help. Shhh...don't give him any tranquilizers." he added in an undertone as the woman behind the desk came out with a bottle. "Right now that won't help...Aidan, take a breath, love. Open your eyes..."

Aidan stopped thrashing at the touch, but his brow was still furrowed, his breathing erratic. Leaning down, Kevin pressed his lips to Aidan's brow. "It's me, Aidan. It's just me. Shh, it's alright. It's okay. I'm right here, and you're just fine. You just need to take a couple breaths?" he murmured, stroking Aidan's sweat-damp hair. "Come on love. Couple deep breaths."

"Kay," Aidan murmured weakly, eyes closing again.

Warily, several more people came out of the hall and into the vestibule as Kevin stood. In the back of the crowd, a woman pulled off her cowboy hat and nodded at Brandi. "Good Turnings, Brandi. What the hell did you bring in here?"

"Good Turnings, Doctor Molly," Brandi murmured. "These folks came to help us keep the Vow. And one of them ended up paying in blood for that. Can you help? He's pretty messed up."

"I can see that, sugar," the old veterinarian muttered, stepping past her helpers to look down at Aidan. "You awake, boy? Open your eyes if you're awake."

Aidan's eyelids flickered, but his eyes never properly opened. "Aidan Headly, Commander..." he mumbled. The old woman's lips pursed. "Okay, kids, let's get him in the exam room. Davy, Rachel, you're with me. Arthur, Andi, Wally, you keep up on our usual work. Move, kids."

The doctor directed them down a hall and into a room, iron-grey braid swinging behind her. "Table should be long enough; it fits Great Danes and ponies." She looked Aidan over once he was laid down, then shot a searching look at the Wildcards clustered around. "Who's been taking care of him?"

"Me," Alice put in, flashing a quick wave. "Medic Poblotskie, Base 1407."

"All right medic, give me the details," the veterinarian replied, studying Aidan as she spoke.

"Shock, withdrawal symptoms due to withholding of mood stabilizing medication he was prescribed, multiple bladed-instrument injuries. Contusions, deep bruising and small bone breakage. Indicative of torture," Alice rattled off. "Severe exhaustion, malnutrition, and dehydration. The sons of bitches broke all his toes. I suspect some blunt-force trauma to internal organs; no protein in the urine, though. Plus whatever drugs they were pumping into him. And that's not including whatever mental and emotional damage they inflicted; I don't have much psychology training, so I can't diagnose that very well. Heart rate and breathing elevated, white blood count high. Temperature at ninety-four eight since four this morning. Sweating, nausea and lack of coherence."

The litany sounded like a dirge in Kevin's ears. Naomi hissed a breath between her teeth.

On the table, Aidan shifted. "Can...can I get a blanket? I'm cold..."

The vet clucked her tongue. "Rachel baby, get the table warmer turned on. Dave, blanket. We'll need saline. Surgical autopads. Internal nanoid conglomerates. Let's move, kids."

As her helpers moved around her, Doctor Molly turned to look their rag-tag team up and down, pouring antiseptic foam from the wall dispenser into her hands and rubbing them together as she did. "Bren, Bran, you kids scoot; we need room in here. The rest of you; how are you related to the patient?"

"We're his family. Sister, boyfriend, base mates," Naomi stated, gesturing at the people in question as she did.

Doctor Molly nodded, skin pulled taut along her cheekbones as she pursed her mouth. "Okay. I'll keep you informed. We don't have much for you folks, but you can sleep in the bunk room; our seasonal hires aren't in for the year yet, and all the tourists who rent our horses won't arrive for a couple months. If you want to stay busy we can use help around the place. You don't need to worry about the locals; plenty of folks up here have come to me instead of a Cavanaugh doctor. They won't fault anyone else for doing the same. Now, shoo. I've got work."

The man glanced up from spreading a blanket over Aidan, and nodded at the door. "Go get that vehicle into one of the garages; it's a little showy where it is."

"Roger," Topher agreed, turning and jogging out.

The bunk room provided a comfortable set of bunk beds and a basic amenities station. There was even a cramped shower space, though an advisory hung on the door reminded users to draw a bucket of water and soap down rather than turning on the overhead spigot.

Quite suddenly, there was nothing else to do. They were safe, for now. Aidan was cared for. Nothing was required of Kevin. Which meant that everything he'd shoved down would have time to boil back up. Today was going to be hell.

"Alice, you want a wash?" Kevin called, peering inside the shower stall in a vain effort to distract himself.

"I want to sleep. For a week," Alice called back longingly. "And then I want to knit and watch your stupid movies."

The little spark of normalcy in this mess made him smile. He did his best to keep it alive. "Yes, well, you see if I expose any more cinema classics to your name-calling."

"You will," Topher yawned, kicking off his boots and flopping onto a bunk.

Stepping out, he watched Naomi stand at the window, staring. She wasn't so much like her brother that he could read her easily, but they did share that look in common. The look that said too much was going on inside.

Quietly, he stepped to her side. "How are you holding up?"

Naomi gave him a sidelong glance, her lips turned up in the barest hint of a smile. "You always look for somebody to take care of in times like this?"

"Generally, yes. It means I don't have to deal with anything going on in my own head," Kevin replied with a gallows smile. "Or so they tell me."

Naomi's smile widened a little. Reaching over, she gave him a gentle shove in the shoulder.

"I'm good, Captain America. And you're wrecked. Go lay down."

Kevin gave a quiet laugh. "Easier said than done."

"Try," Naomi suggested.

Eventually, he did.

He woke to someone shaking his shoulder. "Kev, we need you in the house," Alice whispered. "Here's your glasses, come on."

He sat up in bed, his chest constricting. "Aidan?"

Alice nodded. "We can't get him to calm down; he's screaming. The doctor wants you to try talking to him."

"Shit." Kevin scrambled out of the bunk and took off running.

Aidan had been moved to a hospital bed in another room. He was whimpering by the time Kevin made it there, still thrashing, with four people trying to hold him down.

"How do I help?" Kevin called, his guts knotting as he watched his boyfriend claw at the hands clamped around him.

Doctor Molly looked up, breathless. "You know him better than we do; you keep him calm and remind him of where he is. You got through before; see if you can do it again."

"No," Aidan whimpered, shaking his head desperately as the medics worked to keep him from yanking out the IVs he needed. Kevin didn't know what to do. All he could think to do was to kneel beside the bed and run his hands over Aidan's brow, whispering soft words in his ear. "Love, it's me. Nothing's going to happen, you've got my word. We're at a safe house, we ran here, they're trying to help but you have to hold still or you're going to wreck their work."

When that had no effect, he desperately searched his memory for something, some memory that would pull Aidan out of this state.

"Hey love, remember your birthday a few years ago? Remember I said I didn't want to sleep without you, wanted you to stay with me? Well, I meant it. I'm staying with you. It's okay. But you have to stay with me. Just stay with me, okay? Stay with me."

Aidan's breath hitched. He turned his head toward Kevin's voice. Kevin's heart leapt as his eyes opened, but they were bleary and wild. "Kev...? Kev, you're here...?"

"Yes love. I'm here." Kevin whispered, gently brushing his lips over Aidan's. "You're just a little out of it. We're getting you some medical help, understand? They're trying to get you fixed up, you're a mess, but you will be stubborn and put up a fuss, won't you? How about I stay here, and you relax and try to let the medics get you patched up, okay? I'll be right here. Just relax," he repeated, brushing Aidan's mussed wheaten hair back from his eyes. "Hold my hand and relax, okay?"

"Don't let them get you," Aidan pleaded, his fingers tightening around Kevin's. "Don't let them…don't…"

Kevin glanced up at the medics, fear in his eyes, but he lowered his lips to Aidan's brow. At least he understood this touch. "I'll be fine. We'll both be fine. I'll take care of you, trust me. You rest, and I'll make sure we're safe, okay? I'll always be here. I'll always make sure you're safe."

Aidan gave the barest hint of a smile. "Yeah. Guess so." Slowly, his body relaxed.

When he was sure Aidan was asleep, Kevin very gently set Aidan's hand down on his chest, standing. He raised his eyes to study Doctor Molly at work. "Did he do too much damage?"

"Well it's not good. But it's not that bad either," the veterinarian replied wearily. Kevin nodded. "Doctor, if it's all right, I've got a sleeping bag with me. I'd like to sleep here in the medical bay, if that's feasible." he murmured, nodding deferentially. "In case he wakes up like that again. I'd rather be here. Please."

Looking up, the wiry woman nodded. "We've got someone here at all hours if he does wake up on you again. But having you in here'd be good. We'll get you a cot."

Aidan woke up twice more that night, screaming, before the sedatives he'd been given put him into a sleep that even terror couldn't interrupt.

Kevin woke late in the morning, and lay for what felt like ages, watching Aidan breathe. He was just considering getting up, when Aidan's eyes flickered. He sat up, gently taking Aidan's hand and squeezing it. "Hey love."

"Hey," Aidan whispered back. He smiled weakly. "You eaten?"

"Not yet, I'll eat breakfast with you," Kevin replied with a smile.

The young lady medic had been cleaning something not far away. She moved over the bedside. "You're in no shape to eat right now, sir; I'll get you a protein shake."

Aidan pulled a face.

"Yes, you really are that bad off." Kevin murmured. "Sorry. But if you're a good boy I'll make sure it's strawberry flavored." It was a stupid, supercilious joke, but anything was better than this knot in his throat, the way Aidan looked making him want to...do something, anything. Joking distracted, at least a little. It was stupid and he knew it, but it was better than nothing.

Aidan wrinkled his nose again. "I'd rather it was you-flavored. Then it might at least be not disgusting."

The medic squeaked in surprise and blushed bright red.

"You're scaring the normal people, love." Kevin murmured, smiling down at him. Aidan was still trying to make jokes and lighten the mood, even when he was lying here looking like grim death. It was enough to break his heart, but Kevin played along, leaning in and brushing his lips over Aidan's brow. "Better hush, or I'll have to hush you up."

"Oh, hush me up," Aidan replied with something that was almost a laugh. "Please."

"When you're better." Kevin murmured, but he gave them both the indulgence of a soft kiss, fingers twined in Aidan's hair. "Now drink your breakfast, okay?"

Aidan searched Kevin's face for a long moment, ignoring the medic returning with the shake. With a wince, he lifted his bandaged hand to cup Kevin's cheek. "I thought I'd never see you again...it about killed me."

"Well, here I am." Kevin murmured. "I'm not going anywhere."

When the medic had taken her seat in the other room again, Kevin gently kissed Aidan's palm. "I have to admit, I'm rather frightened of how glad I am that Tweak blew the bastards who mishandled you all to Kingdom Come, after what they did." He glanced up, meeting Aidan's eyes. "If you want to talk about it, I'm listening."

Aidan smiled crookedly, sipping at his breakfast. "What's there to talk about? They fucked me up, and you got me out. Could have put the Corps on all our friends in the process, but…you got me out. And I love you. You know that, right?"

"I know that. And you know I do," Kevin agreed softly. "So please, don't shut me out. Don't keep it to yourself. When you're panicking, if I touch you, you pull away. I want to know how to reassure you. If I touch you like they…if I do anything that reminds you of them, stop me, okay? And tell me what you need."

"I don't know what I need," Aidan admitted, his voice cracking. He swallowed hard and squeezed his eyes closed. "When I wake up, I just…I can't stop it. I don't know how, Kev…I don't know what…I don't know."

"I know." Kevin murmured, squeezing Aidan's knee. "It's okay. I know. You don't have to talk. Just finish your breakfast, close your eyes, get some sleep. Your body's still cleaning house after all the garbage they put in; it needs its rest to do that."

"I don't want to sleep," Aidan muttered, finishing his breakfast. "I keep having nightmares."

"I know." Kevin murmured. "That's the brain cleaning house. But when you have one, just put out your hand, and I'll be right here, okay?"

"But I can't remember." Aidan tried to state it as a fact, but it came out as a whisper. He wiped tears off his cheeks with his bandaged hand. "When I'm having them, I can't…I can't remember it's not real."

Kevin didn't know what to say to that. So he only leaned over, and laid his head on Aidan's shoulder. "It'll be alright."

Aidan leaned his head against Kevin's. Slowly, his breathing eased, and Kevin listened to him fall back into sleep. He took the half-finished nutrient shake out of Aidan's slack hand.

Sitting up and pressing the button to lay Aidan's bed back down, he smiled groggily at the medic on shift when she held out a cup of coffee. "Oh you're an angel...I never got your name. Sorry, I'm afraid my manners are a little sub-par at the moment."

"Understandable," the medic replied with a patient smile. "It's not easy watching someone you love go through PTSD. I'm Rachel, Molly's youngest. Wish I could do more for you two, but...you know how it goes. We've got only so much, and even the Corps haven't managed a way to fix something like this without time."

Kevin nodded. "I know. I've seen it once or twice; drugs help but they're no cure. I take it you've seen this before too?" he asked. Beside them, Aidan slept deeply, dead to the world for now.

Rachel smiled sadly. "Yeah. Watched a good guy go through it, couple years ago. There's no easy way to deal with it, but...he's got a good rock in you. That's something."

"Thanks. And my apologies to you by the way." Kevin smiled awkwardly. "I'm afraid you're going to have to hear a lot of disgustingly sappy pillow talk until he's over this. I *swear* we're not usually like this."

"It's cute," Rachel replied sheepishly, "And if it helps him, I'm in no position to complain. My duty is to my patient."

"Well, you're a ministering angel, and you perform your duty with grace and charm. If I had a hat I'd tip it to you." Kevin raised his glass of bitter dregs. "To angels and healing hands." He drained his cup. "When should I come back?"

"We're putting him in his long-term casts around ten, if you want to be here for that," Rachel suggested. He nodded. "See you at ten, then."

Kevin was bleary-eyed when he joined his friends around the little bunk-room table and the impressive breakfast they'd been given. He gulped coffee like ambrosia and hoped it'd act as such.

"How's Aidan?" Topher asked instantly.

"Healing." Kevin replied quietly. "Kind of out of it." he admitted after a moment. "The sort of thing you'd expect when some sons of bitches push a man to the limit. Where are the dynamic duo?"

"They said they were going to help with the animals," Naomi replied as she popped a couple strawberries in her mouth. On the far bunk, Alice lay snoring quietly.

Kevin nodded, staring into his coffee. Black plastic fingers rested on his shoulder. He glanced up at Naomi.

"I'm taking tomorrow night," the blonde woman stated quietly. It wasn't a question. Smiling wryly, Kevin nodded. It was a wrench to give in, but she was right. He tended to forget there were two people who could reach Aidan in his dark moments, now. They'd both be in better shape if they shouldered the burden together.

Topher watched him with anxious eyes. "If there's anything I can do, Kev…I mean, I know I'm not a medic or anything, but if there's anything."

Kevin smiled. "I know, Toph. Besides, you already helped me save him; you've done a lot. We owe you, you know. You didn't have to come."

Topher shrugged. "You're lucky you didn't get everybody. He's all our commander. You're not the only one who loves him, you know. Just not in that way." He took a roll from the plate they'd been given, biting into it.

Kevin smirked. "I should hope not. Our bed's barely big enough for the two of us, and even then it creaks."

Topher eyed him, chewing slowly. "I'm not fourteen anymore, Kev. You don't have to make jokes and tell me everything's okay."

Kevin paused for a moment, surprised by the younger man. Then he nodded, smiling bleakly. "Thanks for the reminder. Sorry if it came off that way."

"Nobody's perfect," Topher replied around another bite of his breakfast.

Kevin downed one more cup of coffee, before grabbing his tab. He flicked its screen to life, and sighed. "Still no Net?"

"Nada," Naomi agreed irritably. "I've got an alert set on mine; it'll tell me as soon as we got something. So far we're out of luck. It's starting to piss me off."

Kevin nodded ruefully. "You're telling me."

He nibbled disinterestedly on a bit of breakfast, before he gave it up and stood. "Well, at ten Aidan's getting proper casts put on, so until then I think I'm going to find out if I'm any good with animals. See you in a bit."

It was best if he stayed moving.

He found Brandi and Brendan in the horse barn, cleaning a stall with Wally chatting to them over the partition as he brushed a horse.

"Need another pair of hands?" Kevin called. Wally glanced up, giving him a once over. "You need sleep."

"I'll get some tonight; had a bit too much coffee to pull it off at the moment," Kevin acknowledged wryly.

Brendan nodded, holding out a pitchfork and nodding down the row of stalls. "We're about done mucking out, but an extra hand spreading the hay would be good."

Kevin nodded, taking the pitchfork. It was pleasant to set his hands to work that didn't require his mind. Forking the sweet-smelling hay out of its bales, he spread it in each horse stall with the help of the others. Wally led one horse out and brought another in.

"Hey Kevin?" Brandi asked eventually. He glanced up. "Yes?"

"You're a Catholic, right?"

"Jesuit, yes," Kevin agreed as he forked hay. "Any reason?"

"Is Aidan one too?" The young woman asked. Kevin barked a laugh. "Oh, good God, no. Aidan thinks my religion is essentially witch-doctoring, I think. But he tolerates it. Why?"

He glanced up, and realized that both siblings were watching him.

"And how's he feel about witch doctors?" Brendan asked, voice studied in its neutrality.

Kevin blinked. "Er...I don't catch your drift."

"I was going to ask if I could do some spell work for him," Brandi remarked tartly, "but I guess I forgot the bone through my nose and bongo drums."

That was when the penny dropped for Kevin, and he wanted to kick himself. He stuck his fork in the hay and turned to talk properly to the siblings who'd been good friends on this nightmare of a mission.

"I'm sorry, Brandi. Brendan. I spoke out of turn. If Aidan doesn't mind Alice or me saying a prayer at his bedside, he won't mind you doing spellwork. I'll ask him, if you want. Once I've extracted my foot from my mouth."

Brother and sister studied him for a moment. Then Brendan elbowed Brandi, cracking a smile. "See? Told you. And you the big greenwalker who gets the hints."

Brandi rolled her eyes. "Jackhole."

Kevin smiled, getting back to work. "Given how much Catholicisim borrowed from European Paganism over the years, I'd be a hypocrite not to respect your works."

Another penny dropped then. "Wait! You said that when we met! You said I borrowed...I can't believe I didn't catch that."

"Now he gets it," Brandi chuckled. Kevin laughed. "I was a bit distracted. I dated a Pagan at one time too; you'd think I would have picked up the reference. He teased me about it more than once."

"We kind of can't resist teasing Christians, get that in the cradle," Brandi quipped. "You should hear our elders. 'The Christians' is a cuss word for them."

"Hey kids?" Wally called as he led the next horse into the stall, "You about done?"

"Yeah, Wally," Brandi called over her shoulder. "You want a hand with morning feeds?"

"What I want is a hand keeping eyes out," the old man muttered as he came within speaking distance. "I know Molly says we're good, but some of the coyotes around here walk on two legs, you get me?"

The siblings shared a slow look. Brendan nodded. "We get you, Uncle." Brandi agreed, turning back to the older man. "We're on it. Kevin, you're supposed to check on your guy when?"

"Ten," Kevin replied quietly. Brandi glanced at the clock—an actual analog clock, of all things—on the wall. "About that time."

Kevin studied the device, and realized with a jolt that she was right.

"I'll walk you over," Wally suggested. "C'mon, boy."

The mountain air was surprisingly cold when they stepped out into it, carding through Kevin's hair like a comb of ice. He pulled his coat tighter about himself as they walked.

"Drugs aren't going to help your friend," the man beside him remarked, apropos of nothing. "He's dying. Killing himself inside, I think."

For a moment, terror ran a knife of ice through Kevin's chest. But he would not let it be true. He raised his head, glaring at the man speaking words on things he had no concept of. But he managed to bite back the rage, as he'd forced down the fear. He was, after all, a guest. "I'm sure he'll be fine under the doctor's care."

The old man shook his head. "Nope."

"Are you a medic now?" Kevin asked, his voice tight.

The old man shrugged. "Nope, but I know what I'm looking at. He's got a dark wind inside him. The kids can do more with that than the doctor." the old man added quietly. "Their folks'll do better than them."

Kevin raised his eyes, half way between perplexity and irritation. "What?"

The old man watched Kevin patiently as they walked. "Sometimes, we see too much evil. Too much disharmony. There's a blackness in some human beings; you folks call it evil. Well, some of them, they can take some of what's in them and put it in you." the old man's voice had a soft, cracked singsong quality to it, strangely comforting. "When war gets inside you, when evil gets into you, it is a dark wind around your soul. Soul's like a candle; too much wind can blow it out."

Kevin glanced down. He bit his lip, fighting to control his fear. He pushed open the medical office door without another word.

"Everything okay?" Alice asked, stepping out into the hall as they entered.

Framed in the door, Wally studied Kevin for a moment, cowboy hat casting a shadow over his face. In it, his black eyes seemed to glitter.

"Ask how soon the boy can move when you're in there. In case."

The words, or perhaps the man, sent a shiver up Kevin's spine. He nodded all the same. "I'll do that."

"What was that?" Alice asked as he joined her.

"Just Fringer nonsense." Kevin muttered as he pulled off his jacket and hung it up, doing his best to dismiss the words that had sent cold shivers up his backbone. After all, plenty of Fringers were off the wall. Dusters were fighting the system; Fringers just got off it. Some of them were simply free spirits getting loose from the Corporate bullshit, but some of them were completely 'round the bend.

"Kev, you're being a jerk," Alice remarked distractedly as she washed her hands.

Kevin gestured at the door, irritation flaring to burn away the fear. "But he—"

"Doesn't matter what he did," Alice cut in, eyeing him levelly. "*You're* being a jerk."

Kevin sighed as he stepped after her. "Alright. Alright. Thanks for the reminder. Did the doctor approve something for the pain?" he asked as they entered the examination room proper. By the time he got into the room, the doctor and her assistants had already taken the temporary splints off and slid empty lattice sleeves around Aidan's feet. Doctor Molly and Rachel were in the process of filling them with liquid silicone. On the table that Aidan wasn't sitting on, Dave was checking over a dog who looked at him with reproachful eyes.

"How's he looking?" Kevin asked, leaning against the wall. The dog wagged their tail, and Kevin smiled. "May I pet them?"

"Sure, this is Mandy," Dave agreed. Moving quietly, Kevin reached over and fondled Mandy's soft ears. Aidan glanced at him with a half-smile as the flat sleeves on his limbs filled, becoming supportive trellises of tough silicone.

"Not that bad, actually. Bone and muscle wise, at least," the doctor remarked as she worked, her grey braid swinging over her shoulder. "Autopads taking care of these slices and abrasions no problem. Nanoids have taken care of the internal stuff I was worried about, and they're working on the bruising. Baby, how's his temp?"

"Ninety-five two, Mom." Rachel replied, her auburn braid swinging almost in counterpoint to her mother's. Doctor Molly clicked her tongue. "I don't like that. Aidan, you feel hot? Cold? Shaky?"

"Shaky," Aidan shook his head. "Still cold. And still kind of freaked out."

"Not surprised," the veterinarian muttered. "We got your blood work done; looks like they dosed you with L-DOPA and adrenaline, probably a couple times. Had you breathing carbogen at night, if my guess and your elevated blood carbon-dio rates are right. Makes sense, given the dreams you've been having. We got you back on your anti-depressants, but aside from a little propanol and something to get you some sleep, I don't think we want to add much more to the load on your system. We'll get you some melatonin and oxytocin precursor in the evenings with a sedative, try and get your system to settle back down so you can rest."

"Any chance we have a timeline for when the effects will fade?" Kevin asked. The veterinarian tipped her head for a moment, then shrugged. "Fraid not. Everybody's different."

That really wasn't the answer Kevin had been hoping for, but he nodded. "How much longer do you recommend that we stay, to ensure his healing?"

"Any reason?" Dave asked, setting his patient into a carrying crate. Kevin nodded at the door. "Your friend Wally mentioned two-legged coyotes sniffing around. I tend to prefer the term 'jackals', but I took his meaning. You've been lifesavers, and we don't want to bring trouble down on your heads."

Doctor Molly bit her lip. Then she sighed. "Let's give it a week and see if the Net comes back up. After that...we'll see."

Hard as it was to sleep, it was harder to wake up. Aidan felt like he was trying to claw through black mud to get back to consciousness.

"Hey Big A," his sister's voice murmured. The old nickname made him almost want to smile.

"Hey Omi,"

"How you feeling?" Naomi asked softly.

Aidan forced his eyes open, working to smile for her. "Like hot garbage," he croaked. She'd always been the person he could be honest with.

She gave him a lopsided smile. "Yeah, you look like it."

Aidan nodded, swallowing in a mouth dry as sand. "You look tired. I keep you up?"

"Yeah," Naomi agreed, "you had some pretty wild nightmares. You remember them?"

Aidan sighed. Oh, he remembered them alright. "Yeah."

"Want to talk about them?" Naomi asked quietly. Aidan squeezed his eyes closed. "No."

"I can get your tab, get your shrink app up and head out for a bit if that'd be better." Naomi murmured eventually. Aidan shook his head. "They took my tab, remember?"

"Shit. Yeah. Didn't think about that," his little sister replied softly. For a moment, her eyes darted around. "You still cold? You want another blanket?"

"All I need right now's company, Omi." Aidan replied quietly. "You're doing good with that."

For a moment, his sister looked a little freaked. Then she covered it over with a smile.

"Okay." Naomi's flesh hand lay itself across his. For a little while, he just lay like that, letting his sister be close and the pain be far away.

But he had a job to do. He needed to protect her. He needed to protect his people, and his allies. He tapped the control window beside his hand and sat the bed up a little, looking around the space. Walls full of shelves and covered gear, a dusty little window. A couple comfy chairs beside his bed. This wasn't the room off the vet's operating theater. When had he gotten moved in here? He searched his fuzzy memory, but it was like walking a minefield in a blizzard. He gave up and asked.

"Omi, I don't want to be useless, but...I can't think straight. Where are we? How many days have we been here?"

"We're still at the vet's office. Been here three days," his little sister replied quietly.

He winced, trying to sit up. "Shit. We need to get moving; we stay here much longer and these people will start getting noticed. We—"

"We're fine. And you're not ready to move," Naomi murmured, a hand on his shoulder. "They moved your bed into a storage room off the bunk-house, so their office looks normal now. They filled up the cabinet behind you with stuff for you; blankets, medicines, all that kind of stuff. Remember them talking to us about it?"

Aidan tried to think back, and gave up again. "Don't think so. My head's kind of a wreck."

Naomi's smile faded a bit. "Yeah. Guess it is." She sat up a little straighter on the edge of his bed, bracing herself the way she always had when trouble came their way. "If anyone asks, nobody's seen you and the rest of us are hired hands. We're good. Relax."

Aidan shook his head. "We aren't good until we're home. Is the net back up?"

Naomi made a face. "No such luck." She glanced down at the bed monitor, then reached up and touched his brow. "You're still running under normal body temp."

"Must be why I'm cold," he murmured. He could've told her that all his dreams were full of freezing cells. But he wasn't putting that on her.

"Where's everybody?" he asked into the quiet. Naomi shrugged. "Helping out. We're acting like hired hands. Kevin got bit by a horse."

"What was he doing with it?" Aidan asked. Naomi snorted. "Trying to pet it like he was ten years old. He's about melting into a puddle with all these fluffy animals around. You got a winner there, bro."

In spite of the sense that there was a lead weight pulling him away from the conversation, he managed to smile. "Yeah. I know."

"You want a nutrient shake?" Naomi asked.

Aidan shook his head. "Eugh, no. Am I still on that shit?"

"Well, yeah, technically, but I could sneak you something," Naomi suggested. "They got real eggs here. From chicken's butts and everything."

Aidan chuckled, surprised at the sound. "Gee, thanks. Now I *really* want to eat them."

Naomi smirked. "I'll go get some then."

Without her in the room, Aidan found his eyes drifting closed again. It was so hard to stay awake.

Something shifted in the corner and his heart rate shot up. He turned his head with a gasp. Nothing there.

He groaned, closing his eyes. He was really starting to hate the way his brain was overreacting since those bastards had...

No. Don't think about that. If he started thinking about that, he knew he wouldn't be able to stop.

God, he could fall asleep right now. Hadn't he just been asleep? Why was he so tired?

"Eggs," Naomi announced. "And toast. And then I'm sacking out. One of the guys will check in on you around lunch. Sound good?"

It was so hard to open his eyes. His sister was watching him with worry when he managed it. He hated making her look like that.

"Sounds good," he agreed, working to smile.

The food looked good, but he felt as if every bite was fighting to come back up. He only managed half the plate.

"You need the rest of that," Naomi prompted.

He shook his head. "Gonna have to wait; my guts are acting up. Sorry, Omi."

Naomi studied him for a moment. Then her lips tipped up. "I got a better idea. Be back in a sec."

A few minutes later, she was back with a steaming mug. She pressed it into his hands, and the smell of lemon peel and honey filled the room. Wrapping a blanket around her shoulders, Naomi plopped down beside him. Her movement jarred some of the lines of pain running through his body, but he wasn't going to complain about a little physical ache. He had his sister here, doing what she'd always done for him: offering the quiet comfort that she was so good at giving.

His little sister rested her head on his shoulder as he sipped the hot lemonade she'd made him. The warmth seeped into his bones, almost banishing the shivering cold.

"Thanks, Omi," he breathed into the quiet, reaching out with an arm heavy as lead to rest around her shoulders. In that moment, they could have been kids again, curled up in the fort of blankets and hot lemonade they put up to protect each other from the world.

"No big," his little sister whispered.

Her presence eased him into sleep again.

The next time he woke, it was the middle of the night, and there was a gun in his face.

Still groggy with the drugs that were supposed to keep him asleep, Aidan stared at the gun. He should have been afraid. Mostly, he was just fucking exhausted.

The man holding it was shaking, wide-eyed and terrified. "What's your name?" he demanded, his voice shrill.

Aidan kept his eyes focused on the gun barrel. The only thought his brain came up with was: *you have got to be kidding.*

"Aidan Headly," he stated quietly. Out of the corner of his eye, movement flickered. He stalled for time by clearing his throat. "Aidan Headly. Democratic State Force Commander, Force Registration Number 133653-75."The ratty man's face cracked into a smile.

In that moment, Kevin stepped up beside him on cat-silent feet. Pressing his long-barreled pistol against the man's temple, he pulled the trigger. The man folded up without a sound, the neat bullet hole in the side of his head bloodless. For a moment, Kevin stood like a statue, cold and white as the moon. Then he was in motion and human again, almost tripping over his feet as he crossed the room and dropped to his knees beside Aidan's bed. He stroked Aidan's hair, wide eyes searching his face."Did he touch you? Did he hurt you?"

Sucking in a long breath, Aidan shook his head. "You got here about two seconds after he did. Thanks."

Kevin bit his lip. Leaning in, he pulled Aidan into a bone-creaking hug. Then he drew back, and Aidan watched his mask of calm slide back into place.

"Well, that was interesting. There were six of these plebes. They set one of the storage sheds on fire to keep us distracted. I told Naomi to try to keep one alive if she could, and—" there was the thud to the side of the building that rattled the window, and Kevin smiled bitterly. "She said she'd see what she could do." Leaning in, Kevin kissed his brow. "Rest, love. We've got this."

Aidan wanted to stay awake, wanted to ask what the hell was going on. But the dark reached out and tugged him back down.

When he fought his way into the waking world again, there was sunlight in the windows, and it was Brandi and Brendan in the room with Kevin and Naomi now. The dead body was gone.

"—need to move, but we're not sure where the next base is at this moment," Kevin was saying to the siblings when he tuned in. "We were discussing it."

"What do we know about the assholes from last night?" Aidan asked. God, his voice sounded awful. He sounded like he had the flu.

Everyone's head shot up. Kevin was at his side in a heartbeat, and Naomi too.

"Hunting team," Naomi explained without much ceremony, "Cavanaugh contract. Huge bounty went out to every hunter, with a warning that the Net was going down, before the Corps shut things off. The Backwoods Bros from last night are locals; they got the word that strangers had come here, so they tried their luck."

"What was on fire?" Aidan muttered, trying to remember the events of the night before. "Something was on fire, right? Is everybody okay?"

"All of us are fine. All of Molly's folk are fine," Kevin stated quietly. Aidan thought about asking what had happened to the bounty team. Then he decided he didn't want to know. He sat up carefully. "Okay...so we're not secure. We got a route to somewhere new?" The room went deathly still. Glancing down, Topher shuffled his feet.

"We don't have coordinates," Kevin admitted eventually.

"I still say we stay," Topher put in. "The local team's toast, and nobody else can track us here with nothing to go on."

Kevin shot him an irritated look. "Topher, we had this talk. We aren't endangering these people."

Against the wall, Brendan cleared his throat. "We...might be able to help."

Brandi's head shot around so fast that she looked like she'd given herself whiplash. She stared at her brother.

"Bren."

Brendan held her eyes. Brother and sister shared a long, slow look.

"Bran?" Brendan murmured. Brandi bit her lip. She wrapped her arms around herself.

"What do you think?" Brendan pressed gently. Brandi sighed. "Bren...I don't know...I mean..."

"Wally said it was a good idea," Brendan suggested. "And the last time turned out pretty good, right?"

"Yeah, but..." Brandi trailed off, fear in her eyes.

"Ask, maybe?" Brendan murmured.

Naomi tipped her head. "Ask what now?"

Brendan gave her a noncommittal smile. "Just give us a second, 'kay? Go on Bran. Ask."

Carefully, Brandi took a seat in the corner, crossing her legs and reaching into her pockets. Naomi shot Kevin a look. Kevin shrugged.

Slowly, the young woman churned her fingers inside her pockets. She breathed like a sleeping woman as she moved.

Carefully, she drew out three of those little wooden toggles she carried, studying them.

"What'd you get?" Brendan asked quietly. His sister shifted like someone waking up. Glancing up, she gave her brother a smile, and laid the toggles in front of her. They were something like coins, marked with odd little glyphs.

"Ash, and Alder," Brandi murmured, "and Broom."

Another coin tumbled out of her pocket as she shifted, and the siblings blinked. Leaning down, they both studied it.

"Rowan," they whispered, and something about the blending of their voices sent a shiver up Aidan's spine.

Brandi took a breath. Then she nodded. "Okay." Pocketing her wooden coins, she stood.

Brendan met her eyes. "So it's the right thing. The Trees said."

Biting her lip, Brandi nodded.

Aidan felt as if he'd been caught in a web of things he didn't understand. But this solemn pair were staring at him now, and something in their eyes left him feeling...not at ease, maybe. But less anxious than his common sense told him he ought to be.

"Okay you guys," Brendan announced, "Pack, we've got a two-hour drive."

"To where?" Kevin asked, eyes intent. Brendan turned to hold his gaze.

"We're going to take you home," Brendan murmured. "We'll take you to Coomb Olwen."

Aidan fell into a doze almost as soon as they strapped him into the truck, breathing too fast. Kevin stroked his hair gently, watching Alice as she ran scans. Naomi sat beside the cot, watching them all and feeling useless.

Alice shook her head, worry showing in her eyes. "There's no infection, and the toxins are cleaned out, but he's getting colder."

"Can you do anything?" Kevin asked, and Naomi heard the fear in his voice. Alice nodded. "I'll put the bed heater on and get him more blankets, but I don't dare give him any more sedatives. Honestly...it's like his body's in a tailspin. I don't know what to do, Kev."

"This is stupid, Kevin," Topher muttered, arms folded over his chest. He glanced at his usual place in the driver's seat, which had been taken by Brendan. "We should have stayed there and—"

"And brought enemies down on those folks while we watch Aidan get worse?" Kevin retorted sharply. "It's true, Topher. He can't sleep through the night without dangerous drugs, he can barely eat, and the doctor was worried about the levels of narcotics she had to give him. Both he and I are priority fugitives at the moment, we've already cost our hosts one arson attempt, and we'll bring hell down on those people if we stay long enough to be tracked to their door. So you give me a better option. Got one? No? Then stop talking."

Topher bit his lip and looked away. Naomi blinked. She'd never seen the red-head go off on the kid before.

She watched Kevin as he sighed, raking his hand through his hair. "That came out badly. I haven't slept much either. Sorry."

"S'okay," the boy muttered, but he didn't raise his eyes.

Kevin glanced down at Aidan, his brows knitted. Naomi couldn't blame him. Aidan looked pretty bad. In fact, he looked worse than he had when they'd first gotten him to Vision Valley. How long could a man live on almost no sleep, with his body running on adrenaline?

Not long.

On the long drive, Naomi did the most sensible thing she could think of: she took a nap. She needed to be sharp when they got there.

She woke with a jerk when the truck stopped. Aidan gasped awake, and Kevin caught his hand. "Hey, we're here. You think you can handle walking?"

"Where's 'here'?" Aidan asked weakly, even as he struggled to push himself up.

"Coomb Olwen," Brendan announced cheerfully from the driver's seat as he pushed the door open. "And we got some good news, there's folks here who can get you back up to scratch."

Turning her head, Naomi looked out the window. There were radiating lines of small, domed houses sunk in the land and roofed in sod outside the ambulance door, all the doors facing east; facing them. Here and there, people poked their heads out of the doorways, eyes impassively watching. After a minute, or maybe a decade, someone stepped out. A heavy-set young man hefted a short stick with a knob at the end. Naomi had seen Brendan fight with one of those. They could do some serious damage, when you used them right.

"Who are..." the man in front of them began. Then he caught sight of the man stepping out of the driver's seat, and his bearded face changed completely. He gave a happy shout. "Brendan!"

"Mickey!" Brendan laughed, darting across the brown grass to run up and tug the other man into an enthusiastic kiss. There was a whoop, and another young man and a woman ran out of one of the houses, embracing and kissing Brendan in a laughing four-person lover's tangle. Out of another home, someone shouted Brandi's name. Brandi hopped out of the ambulance with a laugh. "Barley!"

Striding across the wiry grass, she grabbed someone who had to be the sibling she'd talked about, bear hugging them and being hugged in turn by a curvy little person with a shock of dark curls that matched hers.

The greetings seemed to open some sort of flood gate. All around the ambulance, people of all ages came out of the houses. The siblings were drowned in greetings; hugs and whoops, slaps on the back and, in Brendan's case, an awful lot of kissing. One arm around Brandi and the other around his sibling Barley, Brendan raised his voice. "Everyone! Is Mother Marta around? I need to talk to Mother Marta and the Keepers! And can somebody find Silver?"

"You've got me," a tall person called, sliding with easy grace through the crowd. Naomi watched the way they moved, and decided not to make any decisions about their gender for now; at first glance they looked like a man with long white hair, but something in the way they stood, the set of their shoulders and the flowing red skirt they wore made her question that guess. Better to ask if it came up.

Brandi gave the older person a quick hug, then stood on tiptoe to speak into their ear. They nodded, straightening, and shot a look at the ambulance. The eyes were a startlingly pale blue-grey in their nut-brown face, almost colorless. Those eyes gave the impression that they might just be able to see through you.

Naomi stepped out of the ambulance. She ignored the ring of silence that formed around her. These people were none of her business. Aidan was. "Brandi. Brendan. You're getting Aidan a bed, right? He needs to get settled."

"Of course," Brandi agreed quickly. Turning, she raised her voice. "Folks, these friends are the ones who've given us the tools to keep the Vow. They shed blood for us, so let's make welcome for them. One of them's hurt; he's going to need a good warm bed. Anybody got a room?"

There was a moment's silence. Then a voice like fresh bread and butter filled the circle.

"We've always got room for our friends, don't we, folks?"

One of the proudest, most eye-grabbing women Naomi had ever seen strode into the circle. A mass of white braids falling to gleam against her dark skin, she practically shone in the loose yellow dress she wore. What she did wasn't just a smile; she beamed.

"Mother Marta," Brandi said, bowing her head. The older woman walked over and embraced her. "It's good to have you home, child."

Then she looked over the little team that had climbed out of the ambulance. Looking at them and trying to see them through this woman's eyes, Naomi couldn't help but feel her heart sink a bit. They looked like bums; all road-frazzled and sleep-deprived.

Stepping forward, the woman took Naomi by her off hand, holding the black plastic palm in both of hers. "You are welcome in this place," she stated, and the realness of the words made Naomi blink. Not many people said something like that like they meant every word.

The woman did the same thing all the way down the line, and every time, the words sounded true.

While she did her thing, eight older folks stepped out of the crowd behind her. All of them had a little grey in their hair somewhere. One lady looked like she'd fall over the next time the wind blew. But all of them had that calm, open thing going for them that the lady in yellow did.

When the lady had shaken her last hand, she stepped back, and the line of old folks was nine. Something about the way they stood was familiar, but Naomi couldn't place it for a second. Then it hit her. They stood like Commanders. Not the swaggering kind, but the really good ones who ran bases because they knew how.

"We are the Council of Keepers," the woman who had to be Mother Marta announced, "And we welcome you, warriors."

Of course, it was Kevin who stepped forward and, of all the crazy shit he could have pulled, he bowed like someone off one of his oldest vids.

"And we are grateful for the welcome. More than we can say."

Mother Marta nodded, her big brown eyes soft. "The healers will get your wounded man settled. Why don't the rest of you come and sit with the Keepers? We need to talk."

Twenty minutes later, they were sitting inside one of the small dome houses, and nine elder statesmen of their community were looking at Kevin and his team with benevolent eyes, leaned against pillows on the warmly rug-strewn floor. Light from above and the heated floor warmed the room, making it cozy. The décor put Kevin in mind of art nouveau, if that aesthetic had been plumped out and softened with nubbly fabrics and pillows.

His emotions ran like mice in the cage of his head, demanding that he go to Aidan, watch over him, be with him. But for now, he did his best to master himself behind his mask of good manners.

In front of them, Brandi and Brendan were having some sort of blessing done by two elders; aromatic smoke from a burning censer was passed over them by one, and water from a clay bowl was flicked over them by the other. Then Barley stepped forward and pulled two charms on woven thongs from under their shirt, grinning at their brother and sister as they slipped the two necklaces over their head. They slipped the green pendant over Brandi's head, and the blue one over Brendan's. The yellow pendant around their own throat gleamed like glass.

"Blood calls blood. You come safe home to me." Barley stated, and their brother and sister joined them in saying the next words. "Round and round, three times three," the siblings said in a harmony that was almost eerie in its perfection, "our Triad is whole, and forever shall be."

Barley gave their siblings a quick hug. Then the three of them sat down with the Dusters.

Kevin caught Alice's eye for a moment, seeing the bewilderment in them. He gave her what he hoped was a reassuring smile.

"So you're the Dusters who got us the parts to save our seed bank," Mother Marta said after a beat. "We're glad to meet you. Three of the four exchanges have been made, and we've started work on the coolant systems. We're only waiting on a few small parts at this point. Because of you, the seeds of the future will be saved. Protecting those seeds is the Vow everyone in this valley is sworn to, and we are blessed that the Wheel brought people like you to us when we needed you."

Kevin smiled. He glanced at his friends, but it appeared that they were letting him act as spokesman. He sat up a bit straighter against the cushioned bench that ran around the wall. "I believe we left a few parts off the list, because we'd brought them with us to offer to your scouts. We've got them with us, and we're glad to be able to give them to you. Working with your community has been an honor."

He cleared his throat. "But I'm afraid we have an issue. Our Commander was badly wounded in resisting demands to give your location away. Under ordinary circumstances, we'd take him home for treatment, but since we're without GPS and threat tracking capability due to the Net shutdown, we aren't sure how to reach our base safely from here. May we ask to stay and get him some medical aid until the Net comes back on? We'll leave as soon as it does. We have no intention of bringing trouble down on you."

Sure, he had no intention of it. But fear of it? Oh hell yes. He almost wished Brandi and Brendan hadn't made the offer. If Cavanaugh tracked them here…

He shoved that thought aside.

The elders listened quietly. Kevin felt as if his words were dropping into a pool.

Eventually, the man on the far end spoke. "It's been our creed since we took the Vow to keep out of things going on out on the Grid. Taking in strangers is always a risk."

"But a wanderer shouldn't be turned from the door," a frail woman on the other side of the line suggested. "That truth is older than the Vow, older than this country. And these wanderers have secured our future. What would we be if we turned away allies that would pay in blood to help us?"

Heads nodded all along the line. A heavy-set woman shrugged. "My take is, they're here already, so whether the Vow is kept or not is a moot point. Somebody's here, and he's hurt, and he doesn't want to hurt us. Under those conditions, I'd take in a squirrel."

"Yeah, we know," another elder remarked with the first levity Kevin had seen, "You did that two winters ago, and the thing's still hanging around."

A gentle chuckle rippled up and down the line of people.

"We've taken in deserving wanderers before," a man dressed in cream and brown robes added, "we'd be some hypocrites if we turned this group away on this day."

"Hands up for granting the request?" Mother Marta asked. Seven hands went up. After a few moments, an eighth rose a bit more slowly. Mother Marta nodded. "Alright. You folks are welcome here, on conditions. You don't give our location to anyone, by intent or by inaction. You threaten nobody here. And you don't draw your weapons unless your life is in danger and you have no choice. Do you agree?"

"We agree," Kevin replied without missing a beat. None of those conditions went against their own ethos; he could agree without a qualm.

Mother Marta favored him with another one of her all-encompassing smiles. "Then welcome to Coomb Olwen, folks. We'll get you rooms in some of the homes."

"Could I ask for one more thing?" Kevin put in, deferential. "I'm the partner of our commander, and this is his sister. He knows us, and we've been calming him down when he has nightmares. Could we have room to sleep near him?"

The elders gave him looks in which he read a number of things; compassion, curiosity, reserve. And, mixed in there somewhere, pity.

"Of course you can," Mother Marta agreed warmly. "We'll call someone to come and lead you to the healing hall."

Following their guide between the rounded homes in the early dusk of the mountains, Kevin watched children run in and out of doorways. Round windows were coming softly alight all around as the chilly spring night came slinking in to lengthen the shadows and put a snap of cold in the air. Around them, people went about a life that was shocking in its sheer contentment.

They reached the long hillock of a building without too much fuss. Inside a room pleasantly rounded in contour and warmly whitewashed, Aidan lay dozing in a bed with a heated blanket wrapped around him. The room was a strange cross between a medical ward and a cozy bedroom. Kevin took it in as he crossed the space to sit at his boyfriend's side, his environmental perception training working away in the back of his mind. He noted that a printed station holding all the necessities for medical care was set into the wall just there, but cushioned chairs and warm hand-worked furniture gave a homey sense to the space. A candle that smelled of honey and lavender burned beside the sick man's bed. It made for an oddly pleasant setting.

Aidan was deeply asleep, his breathing more even than Kevin had seen it all day. He looked almost peaceful, like a saint who'd passed through his sufferings and earned his reward.

Kevin ran a hand gently over Aidan's brow. The man's skin was chill and clammy to the touch. His heart sank.

"Lyra," Mother Marta called, "When you got a second, we need two cots in the wanderer's room!"

"Course, Marta!" a voice called down another hall.

The comfortably padded woman gave Kevin another one of her wide smiles. "Lyra will help you two out tonight, and your friends have a room down the hall. You can rest here without fear."

"Thank you." Kevin murmured, giving another bow that he'd recalled from his Japanese lessons. It seemed to fit the manner of this community.

The gesture got him one last wide smile as the older woman left.

Looking over, he watched Naomi press the back of her flesh hand to Aidan's cheek. Her face was blank, but her shoulders drooped.

Kevin took a gamble. Standing, he laid a hand on her shoulder. "Naomi? He's strong. He'll fight this."

Swallowing hard, Naomi nodded. "He better. I told him I'd kick his ass if he died again."

Kevin smiled, squeezing her shoulder gently as a sprightly little woman with a shock of tawny curls came bustling in.

"Here's those cots, folks!"

There weren't only cots, but blankets, pillows, and loose robes to wear as night gear. The things were incredibly cozy. After the month he'd had, Kevin felt practically indulgent. Sleep came like a blessing.

Deep in the night, Aidan's screams woke them both. Kevin scrabbled in the dark for Aidan, and got an arm in the gut when Aidan thrashed that winded him. "Naomi, get the light on!" he yelped. In the dark, there was a thunk and another cry from Aidan as he hit...what? The table? The wall?

This attack was one of the worst, Aidan thrashing like a man in a fit. When the light did flicker on, it showed a body arched and shaking, straining against something terrible happening inside. He thrashed again, and this time Kevin could see enough to catch his hands and hold him, doing what he'd done over and over, trying to settle Aidan down. But nothing worked.

"What's going on?" the voice of Lyra exclaimed through Aidan's yelps and whimpers.

"He's not calming down!" he called over his shoulder as Aidan bucked under his hands. "Help!"

"Wake him up!" Naomi demanded.

"I'm trying!" Kevin replied in panic, then lowered his voice. "Aidan, please, please, it's just us, you're okay, come on now, wake up, it's just us..."

The medic soaked a rag in a little water from the medical sink and ran it over Aidan's brow. If anything, the wet rag on Aidan's skin made his muscles stiffen even more. "Both of you, help me hold him!" She demanded. Naomi grabbed her brother's legs, stopping him from damaging his healing feet. Between them, they managed to keep him in the bed.

After what felt like an eon, the muscles under Kevin's hands relaxed. Kevin sat back, wiping his sweating face as he stared down at Aidan. His chest hurt. His gut hurt. And Aidan looked like the living dead.

He raised pleading eyes to the medic on duty. "Can you do anything?"

The little woman stared down at Aidan, her brow furrowed. "I can try, but…well, I can try. Let me see..."

In spite of himself, Kevin drifted off again as the medic worked. Fear tainted his sleep.

For the next few days, Aidan drifted between the waking world and the world of nightmares. In his dreams, the past and the present blended together. Sometimes it was his father cutting him open with a knife while he lay helpless. Sometimes it was his first boyfriend drowning him in icy, black water. Sometimes Sam was the one in a guard's uniform, beating the crap out of him. Sometimes it was his dad.

Just as often, it was the Cavanaugh bastards who'd actually done it; that couple of evil clowns the Williamses with their blades, that fucker Jones with black pits for eyes and chains in his hands that reached out to wrap around Aidan's throat. And the cold. The cold was endless.

He lost track of the number of times he woke up screaming, covered in sweat and breathing like a drowning man. Sometimes it was Naomi who he woke up to, sometimes it was Kevin. Their voices and their touch brought him back to reality, but he never got a good grip on the real world. Every time, the nightmares would put out their tentacles and yank him back down into the dark again.

He'd lost track of the days and the nights. Even the nightmares started to blur into each other. It made the lucid moments feel like islands in a black ocean.

Deep in some night, he woke up with the sick assurance that he was tied down, chained, handcuffed. He clawed at the restraints. Soft hands held his, and Kevin's warm body rolled him so that they were spooned together. "Aidan, wake up, please. It's a dream, you're okay," his soft voice whispered fervently.

Aidan lay panting in Kevin's embrace. Slowly, painfully, he rolled over and curled against his lover's warmth. He realized that he was whimpering, and hated the sound of his own weakness.

Kevin kissed the top of his head, holding him tight. "Ssh love, ssh....just a dream, it was just a dream, you're safe here with me. It's okay..."

Aidan shivered in Kevin's embrace until the worst of the panic passed. He gasped for air, but found his throat tightening. Hot tears came spilling down his cheeks. Why the hell was he crying?! He gulped, trying to steady his breathing. It didn't do any good.

Kevin rocked him softly, whispering gentle things in his ear. "Hush love, hush. It's all right."

"No it's not," Aidan choked out. "It's all...it's all fucked up. Everything's all...I can't..."

"Yes you can," Kevin whispered into his hair. "Just hang onto me. I'm right here. Hold on to me, and you'll be alright."

Shame washed through Aidan's chest. No, he wouldn't be alright. He'd never been alright, and now it was worse. Now he was a burden on the people he loved.

Kevin's fingers stroked his hair. "Close your eyes, love. Close your eyes, I'll sing you to sleep."

Aidan let his heavy eyes close, hot tears stinging his cheeks. Kevin gently wiped them away with a corner of the blanket.

"Live in my house, and I'll be your castle, just pay me back with one thousand kisses..." the soft voice breathed. Aidan almost felt like smiling. Classic Kevin, sappy as anything. They'd watched *RENT* so often that Kevin knew the words of every song by heart. They'd watched it whenever they were down, and it had always cheered them up.

The soft words in his ears, he slid back into the dark.

An eternity later, Aidan's eyes flickered open to daylight.

"You awake?" Kevin asked gently, stroking his hair.

"You look like hell," Aidan muttered in reply, studying his boyfriend's haggard face. "It's my fault, isn't it? I'm sorry...I'm so sorry, Kev..."

"Shush." Kevin whispered. "None of that." Softly, he kissed Aidan's cheek.

Aidan remembered moments like that. But everything else melted into one long blur.

The doctor and her assistants checked him sometimes. His nightmares and night terrors had strained his physical injuries, they said. He needed to lay still, they said. He caught snatches of words.

"...doses above this level can cause dependency, but he's not responding to..."

"...worried about that temp..."

"...will be alright, won't he?"

Those words were said by Kevin, and they made his heart turn over. There was so much fear in his guy's voice. But he couldn't do anything about it. He felt fucking *useless*.

Somewhere in some evening, Aidan woke to singing and warmth. Brandi and Brendan were standing on either side of his bed, their hands on his chest, and a third person was standing at the foot. They were singing something in a language he didn't know. There was some kind of plant stuff in one set of their joined hands, and an actual burning candle in the other. The three voices mingled; haunting, slow and strangely beautiful. Not sure if this was a dream or not, he let himself slip away into the dark again.

On the fifth morning of their stay Kevin woke with a start, feeling as if someone had tied knots in his muscles and glued his eyelids together. Daylight was streaming down from overhead, and something was sitting at the foot of the bed. For a moment, Kevin's blurred eyesight gave the impression that a snake was curled there, and he reached carefully for his glasses, his heart hammering. The corrective lenses showed him something much less uncomfortable. The...man? Person, better go with that for now, who'd been introduced as Silver was sitting quietly in a chair. They gave a gesture of acknowledgment with the cup in their hand as Kevin sat up. "You drink tea?"

"I'll drink anything with caffeine right now," Kevin agreed, "and I'll be grateful for it. Thank you, er...would you prefer ma'am, sir, or elder?"

"Elder will do. I'm twixt," Silver replied, smiling around the rim of their mug. "Good of you to ask. We don't usually expect good manners from Gridlocked folk."

"I do my best," Kevin replied politely, wishing like hell he wasn't in a silly robe with this stranger staring at him. But since the person was in something a bit like a kimono with their hair braided in a few pieces of amber and silver jewelry, he wasn't completely out of place.

Silver nodded at the bed. "The healers asked me to come and check in. Said this is more of my line of work than theirs."

"Psychologist?" Kevin asked hopefully.

Silver see-sawed one hand in a more-or-less gesture. "Close. How's your guy?"

"He's had better nights," Naomi mumbled as she sat up. "Better months too. You supposed to be in here?"

The older person nodded. "I help out with the healing."

Naomi gave the elder a slow once-over. "Kind of fancied up for a doctor."

Kevin rolled his eyes heavenward. "Naomi..."

Silver chuckled. "No worries, little fighting sister. I'm not the flesh and blood doctor; I do more of the heart and soul stuff."

Naomi grunted. "Shrink. Okay, he can use one. I gotta pee." With a nod for Kevin and a quick, "eyes up, okay?" she was out of the room. Kevin gave the older person a sheepish smile. "Sorry. Naomi's a bit...direct."

"Noticed," Silver agreed, pouring Kevin a cup of tea and handing it across.

"If you don't mind me asking, how do you get tea here?" Kevin asked, covering his other concerns with professional curiosity. Silver shrugged. "Oh, we grow it. Got a grow operation that takes pretty good care of us. We'll show you, if you've got time. Council's cleared you to be treated as allies; only right. You can see where all your work and those parts got to." They sipped their tea. "After we get your fella fixed up, of course. How much is he to you?"

The quiet directness of the question poleaxed Kevin for a moment. "Everything," he answered before he could think of a better reply. He could have kicked himself for that. He sounded like a lovesick puppy.

The answer seemed to satisfy Silver. They nodded, taking another sip of their tea. "Drink that before it gets cold," they suggested comfortably. Kevin took a sip. The tea was delicious; warm, full-bodied and hinting at dark chocolate.

He nearly spilled it down his front when he heard Aidan's voice. "Kev?"

Kevin scrambled to set the mug down and kneel beside the bed. "Right here, love. How do you feel?"

Aidan gave a parody of a laugh. "Like crap."

Kevin worked to pull off a smile. "Well, good news, there's someone here who can help you get up to scratch. Their name is Silver, and they're a psychologist."

Aidan sighed, brows furrowed as he closed his eyes. "'S too early to poke at my brain..."

"Says you, son. It's nearly ten," Silver replied with a quiet laugh. Pulling their chair closer, they leaned forward to stare into Aidan's face. After a moment, they leaned back, brows raised. "Just one trouble piled on top of another inside of there, isn't it? Got the wrong soul stuck in the wrong body to begin with. That sure didn't help."

The little room went silent. Kevin felt his body stiffen.

Aidan straightened up, his face unreadable. "How the hell did you know that? You don't have a genome scanner. Did the medics tell you?"

Crow's feet appeared around the older person's eyes as they smiled. "You worry about gadgets too much, you don't see anything. Besides, seems you fixed that part of it. This new problem though..." they shook their head thoughtfully, shining braid swinging. Then they rested their chin on one gnarled fist. "They really did a number on you, your enemies. What happened?"

Aidan looked away again. His hands balled into tight fists against his blankets. When he spoke, his voice was tight and low. "Corps captured me and tortured me for intel. I didn't give them anything, so they kept going."

"That isn't an explanation, that's a news bulletin." the elder murmured.

Aidan shook his head. "What is there to say? They tortured me, end of story. Torture is torture."

Silver gave Aidan the look a teacher gives a student who's playing stupid. "Now, you know that's shit."

"I don't want to relive it every time someone asks what happened," Aidan snapped, "I don't want to go through it all again."

"Fraid you're already doing that." the elder murmured, holding Aidan's eyes. "Dreams at night, right? Flashbacks? Panic? Your brain says you're done, but your spirit's still living with the darkness. Man lets that go on too long, maybe he goes crazy. Maybe he gets mean, or drunk, just to try to feel something that isn't the darkness. And maybe he goes looking to die to get away from it. Still doesn't fix the problem, but it feels like it will. Being sick's better than being scared, some bodies think. Some spirits."

Aidan lowered his head like a defeated man. Kevin glanced at the stranger, repressing irritation "Couldn't this wait until after he's eaten some—"

Silver held up a hand, cutting him off. "You hungry, son?"

Aidan shook his head, staring at his hands.

"You want to be? You want to get better? Or do you want to pretend everything's fine until you give up one of these days, and blow your brains out? That's up to you, but you need to decide."

"Wouldn't blow my brains out. I'd OD on sleep meds; easier to clean up," Aidan replied quietly. He glanced up as if he was surprised that the words had come out of his mouth as every muscle in Kevin's body contracted. Aidan winced, glanced Kevin's way like a child who'd said a curse word in front of the teacher, and closed his eyes. Kevin's heart cinched in on itself. Those words. So calm. So collected. Aidan had it all planned. Bloody hell, he'd planned how to kill himself, hadn't he? In detail, probably.

Silver tipped their head again, watching Aidan. "I hear you're a leader. That right?"

Aidan snorted dismissively. "I've got the title, but I suck at it. Only reason my base is doing so well is the folk under me."

Kevin gave him a sidelong glare. He loathed it when Aidan denigrated himself. The elder caught his eye, and gave him a sly smile. What the hell was that about?

"So I imagine you seen a lot of fights?" the older person continued, "Gotten your people through a lot of crap? It's what you're used to?"

Aidan shrugged, eyes on his hands. "Have to fight to survive out here."

"Got that right." After a moment, the person held out a hand. "My name is Silvertongue. Spinner. And I think this can get sorted out, man who fights. You have to want it, though. Do you want to heal?"

Aidan hesitated a long moment, frowning at the extended hand. He glanced up at Kevin, his eyes filled with fear, and pain, and so much love. Kevin didn't know what the man he loved was looking for, but he held Aidan's eyes, reaching out to gently stroke his hand. Aidan smiled, and the expression nearly broke his heart.

Finally, Aidan turned back and carefully shook the elder's hand. "Aidan Headly, Commander, Base 1407." he replied quietly. "And I...I want to get better."

Silver nodded slowly, twice. "Then it's a good thing you know how to fight, 'cause what you got to do is get in and get your soul a brighter story to tell, before this dark one you're stuck with kills you. We've got a lot to talk about." Silver turned to pin Kevin with those strange eyes. "Spitfire. You and Little Sister, go get some breakfast. Go relax. Aidan and I are going to have a talk."

Kevin glanced down at his boyfriend, so vulnerable in his weakened state. He didn't even have his sidearm to hand. When he glanced up, Silver was giving him a smile that said they knew exactly what he'd been thinking.

"I don't bite, Spitfire. And you folk helped mine. The least I can do is return the favor. We pay our debts in Coomb Olwen."

Kevin held their eyes. "Understand this, Elder. He's...he's not just everything to me. He's the heart of us."

"Oh dammit, Kev..." Aidan groaned, but Kevin ignored him.

"He's the tie that binds my family. You need to know that."

Silver's bright eyes seemed to flicker for a moment. Then they nodded. "Now I know."

Kevin drew a slow breath. Then he nodded. "Right." He reached over and gave Aidan's hand a squeeze, brushing a kiss across his lips. "I'll check in after breakfast, alright?"

"Roger," Aidan agreed quietly, his smile crooked.

Finally, Kevin forced himself up and out of the room. He caught Naomi in the hall. "The psychologist wants some time with Aidan. Let's get back into our own clothes and get something to eat."

Naomi gave him a cockeyed look. "You sure about this?"

Kevin shrugged. "Not completely. But beggars can't be choosers. Come on."

Together, they walked down to the room where clothes were washed, retrieved their own things and dressed, before heading back to the entrance. Kevin tuned in on a conversation as they entered the vestibule, his ear caught by his base name.

"Somebody said the Commander of the Wildcards is in here? When did he get in? Is he okay?" a man in a hooded coat was asking the lead doctor of the facility. The doctor nodded in Kevin's direction, and the man turned.

Kevin's breath caught in his chest. He felt as if his heart had stopped.

Mastering himself with difficulty, he managed a single, strangled word.

"Peter?"

"Kev? Oh my bright gods, Kev!" In three quick strides, Peter had closed the distance between them and grabbed Kevin in a rib-creaking hug. He kissed Kevin's cheek, his eyes alight. "I can't believe you're the ones who got us the gear for the seed bank! I can't believe you're here! I...but somebody said the Commander of the Wildcards was really sick. Is that right? Is Taylor okay? What happened? Can I see him?"

Kevin's brain felt like a bricked tab. For a moment, all he could do was stare at Peter, his mouth working.

"Who's this guy?" Naomi asked, menace drifting like a shark under the calm surface of her voice.

Kevin gently disentangled himself from the man he'd loved so much, years ago. "Naomi, this is Peter, a former Wildcard. Peter, this is Naomi Henderson-Adler. Our Munitions Officer. And her brother is our Commander these days. Aidan. Aidan Headly."

He felt like a bot running an automated script as he made polite introductions, and Peter stuck out his hand to shake. "Pleasure, Officer. Did Lazarus finally get demoted?" he asked, glancing at Kevin.

Kevin smiled bleakly. "He died. Last year."

Peter's dark eyes went wide. "Oh no...and Taylor? He retired, right? Please tell me he retired."

Kevin shook his head. "Died a few years back. Cancer."

Peter bit his lip, the old pain of loss in his eyes. It was a look that had made Kevin pull him in for a hug more than a few times.

"Damn it." Peter whispered, lowering his head. He drew a steadying breath. "I'll light a candle for them."

With a quick shake of his black-curled head, he raised his eyes. "So who else is here? And what's wrong with your guy? And how are you?"

"Alice and Topher are with us," Kevin explained, staring at the face he'd known so well once. *Peter.* Peter was actually here, and barely changed. He was still boyish and black-haired, with his coffee-and-cream skin and his beautiful lithe build. He was still sweet and fragile, and sad-eyed.

Kevin swallowed. "As for what's wrong, they had my man in Cavanaugh detention. Interrogation. He's not in great shape." Stuffing his hands in his pockets, he shrugged. "Neither am I, honestly."

"Take it you guys are old buddies?" Naomi asked.

Kevin gave her a lopsided smile. "Old boyfriends."

Naomi glanced between them carefully, eyeing Peter up. "Oh. Yeah, he's your type." Any other day, Kevin would have asked her what *that* was supposed to mean.

"Your man?" Peter asked, glancing between them. "You said your man, Kev. Is...is it like that?"

Holding Peter's eyes, Kevin nodded. "Yes."

Peter stared at him for a moment with those liquid black eyes. Then he sighed, crossing his arms as if he was protecting himself.

"Oh boy..." After a beat, he raised his eyes. "I know this is hella awkward, but I'd love to see everybody. Can I show you guys around and hang out?"

Kevin glanced at Naomi, gauging her reaction. She seemed unfazed, so he turned back with a smile.

"Of course. They'll be delighted; it'll be the only pleasant thing that's happened this month."

Outside light snow was falling through the biting air, and Peter hurried them between the lit dome-houses to a structure slightly larger than the others. Inside, the sod-house was one gigantic kitchen and eating area, and what had to be a quarter of the community was happily gathered to eat and chat. Children ran around the room in little knots of noise and excitement.

For a moment, Kevin's fear rose like a wave. The idea of bringing what chased them down on this lovely place...

"There they are!" Peter exclaimed, grabbing Kevin's hand and yanking him through the hubbub. Alice glanced up, and dropped her fork.

"Peter?! *Peter!*" Jumping to her feet, she enveloped him in a bear hug. "Holy shit, what are you doing here?! I thought you were getting out of the U.S.? How are you here?" She exclaimed, running her hands over his shoulders before tugging him in for another hug.

"I was going to try," Peter laughed, dropping down in a seat to get his hug from Topher as well, "but a friend of a friend put in a word, said a Pagan group needed a good program writer to help with something big. So now I monitor the programs that control the water and nutrients to the grow systems here, and keep an eye on the environmental controls for the seed bank. I finally talked the Council into letting me and the Walkers reach out when the big coolant motors conked out for the third time. I swore I'd secure the messaging so Brandi'd have a safe chat line." Ebullient as he'd ever been, he grabbed flatbread from the serving plate in the center of the table, spread it with honey and butter, and bit down

"Walkers?" Topher asked, blinking.

"Mm," Peter agreed, chewing, "That's Brandi and Brendan. And a couple other folks here. Walkers are part of a Triad; basically three people that care a lot about each other right? Siblings, lovers, close friends. It's a charm we do; one person stays here when their Triad heads out. The bond calls them home. Those three are the strongest Triad; triplets, and a Perfect Triad too."

"And you've lost us," Kevin remarked, smiling in spite of himself. It was so much like the old conversations they'd had, Peter always so far ahead of everyone else. The other man laughed. "Sorry, sorry. Lots of new vocab for you guys, I took a bit learning it too. Okay, so they're triplets, right? And Brandi's a girl, Brendan's a guy, and Barley's twixt. Non-binary, see? So they're three states of gender as well as triplets. They make a perfect triad. It's seen as really strong magic." He took another bite, eyeing them. "Don't give me that look, guys. You believe weird shit too, if you think about it objectively. Magic's just code written to get the world to do stuff, that's all."

"Yeah, you always said that," Topher agreed with a smile. "Good to see you, man."

"Good seeing you too, kiddo," Peter teased, reaching over and ruffling up Topher's hair, which made the younger man grumble.

"Man, I'm not a kid! Why do you always do that?"

"Because you always look so cute," Peter replied with an easy laugh. It really was like old times.

But the times had changed. Kevin watched Peter and Topher horse around, uneasily nibbling at something. He needed to keep his energy up. But half his mind was watching for the flash of white hair, hoping to see Silver and know that the interview was done with. He hated sitting here. He didn't belong here. He ought to be checking for dangers. He ought to be with Aidan.

"I could show you guys the growing operation if you want?" Peter was saying, when he managed to wrench his attention back to the moment. "Or the seed bank? You guys are cleared as allies, so I can take you in and give you the tour."

Kevin smiled softly. "It sounds lovely, Peter, but I should stay near Aidan until he's feeling better. Once he's out of the woods, I'd love a tour."

Some of the merriment drained out of Peter's eyes, leaving them with that soulful look that had always tugged at Kevin's heart. But he put on a quick smile, and nodded.

"Oh, yeah, of course. We can do that. Do you know who's looking after him?"

"Silver," Naomi muttered at her meal, sounding just a bit like her brother did when dealing with the Sector Quartermaster on a bad day.

Peter brightened up. "Silver? That's awesome, they're great. They helped me get straightened out when I first got here." He ducked his head like an embarrassed child. "I was kind of a wreck those days."

So you were a wreck? An insidious little worm of anger whispered inside Kevin's head. *Funny, you weren't the one who was abandoned as if he'd never mattered at all.*

He did his level best to shove the unworthy thought back into the dark where it belonged. Peter had done what he had to do for his sanity in those terrible days after the failed raid and the dead friends they'd seen. And he *had* asked Kevin to go with him. Hell, he'd begged.

But Kevin had stayed. And Peter had left.

Peter caught his eye, grinning. "Okay, so you guys got to tell me about Kevin's man! How bad was their getting together, hunh? How long did it take for Kevin to switch over from James Bond to Big Sweet Goofus?

Topher gave a laughing groan. "Oh Alhamdulilah, it took *months,* man! It was *awful,* they were both dancing around it and pretending it wasn't happening!"

"It was rom-com level bad," Alice chimed in teasingly. "Kev trying to be all low-key and suave, and all the time looking at Aidan like he wanted to roll over for a tummy rub."

"Or a something rub," Topher put in with a snort of laughter.

Peter tipped his head back and laughed. "Dear gods alive, of course. So Aidan didn't get sick of it and make a move?"

"Aidan's not a horndog like you, Peter." Alice laughed, poking their former basemate in the chest.

Kevin let them have their fun. Eventually, they settled down to chuckling and eating.

Kevin gathered his courage, and cleared his throat. "So...how are you here? Are you doing better than...than before?"

Peter's depthless eyes met his again, and he felt the hint of the tug he'd once had to sink into them. The gorgeous man gave him a smile, warm and open. "I'm a lot better. A hell of a lot. Leaving you—losing all you guys—about killed me, but this is where they need me." Peter turned to hold Kevin's eyes. "I love...all you guys, but I'm whole here. And I'm doing good work."

Kevin fought down the words that nearly escaped his throat. *You were doing good work at home. And we needed you. And you abandoned us. You left us. You left me.*

His throat felt tight, but he smiled at the man he'd once loved. "It's good to see you so happy, Peter. And I can see why; this is a beautiful place. How do you keep so well hidden?"

"Like we said, Gridlock. Skills!"

Kevin turned as Brandi and Brendan grabbed chairs, Barley right behind them with a plate of rolls and a pitcher of what turned out to be goat milk. "You spilling the beans, Peter?"

"Barley, the only one around here who spills things is you," Peter replied with a teasing grin. Brendan and Brandi both chuckled, and Barley smiled sheepishly. "Yeah, yeah, I'm a klutz, I know." Turning, their round face lost a little of its humor. "We heard your guy still isn't doing so great."

"He's with Silver right now," Kevin replied quietly. "We're hoping the psychologist can help with what the doctors haven't."

"But Silver's not a—" Barley started to say. Peter put an arm around their shoulders. "Pagan equivalent, Barley darlin'. You say potato."

"So your entire community is Pagan? That's fascinating," Kevin remarked, gladly distracting himself by glancing about the room. Peter had mentioned Pagan communities in the mountains in those terrible days before he left their base, but Kevin hadn't been sure if it was a reality or a daydream. He still couldn't believe a place like this was *real.*

Brandi smiled as she poured herself tea and added goats' milk. "Yeah. That's how we got started, really. Our elders a couple generations back were the Pagan Student Alliance down at the old public university in Fort Collins. A couple worked at the seed bank, some were mountain kids, some were just getting by. The usual thing. So when the Dissolution Riots started getting crazy, they were at a meeting putting a protection circle together, and somebody said 'my professor's crying in her office because she thinks the seed bank is gonna burn.' Somebody else said 'man, that'd suck, that's so much work down the drain'.

"Story goes," Brendan continued, "somebody in the gang piped up and said 'my uncle has some land up in the Never Summer, there's a cabin, we could stay up there.' And somebody else worked for a moving company, so he knew where to borrow a box truck."

"Anyway, one thing led to another," Barley chimed in as they dropped a knob of butter on their oatmeal, "And the whole PSA and their kin hiked it up there to wait for everything to get better."

"Course, it didn't," Brendan followed off, their tri-part story sounding like a performance. How many times had the triplets heard this story? The way they bounced it between them, it had to be a community touchstone.

"And so we all settled in Coomb Olwen, and planted our seeds, and grew our roots, and bore the fruit of three generations, keeping our Vow and walking our Path." Barley finished dreamily.

Brandi burst out laughing. "Gods above and around, you sound so much like Silver it's scary! Your mentor been drilling you on sounding all ancient, Barley?"

The shorter person stuck their tongue out, grinning, and took a bite of their breakfast Kevin watched the siblings with a smile as they ate. What he wouldn't give to have been born in a place as easy and free of care as this. He'd been born into a fortunate place, true enough. But he'd learned too early that the garden of his life contained a snake.

With very little prodding by the Wildcards, Peter launched into a discussion of all the tools and techniques that he and his community used to keep Coomb Olwen safe; everything from signal dampeners to the shape of their homes was designed to hide them from threats and keep them from notice. Kevin let the conversation wash over him, let his body relax and his eyes wander over the people in the wide room. The sense of warmth was almost tangible, the vibrant contentment of the gathering hanging in the air like sunlight.

A flash of brightness caught his eye, and Kevin turned to see Silver in the doorway. The possible psychologist came wandering over as if they had all the time in the world, stopping several times to chat with this person and that before they reached the table.

They nodded. "Mind if I grab a seat? Like to talk to you folks."

"Of course," Kevin agreed faster than he should have. He scrambled out of his seat, offering it to the elder. "How's Aidan?"

"Well, I've seen worse. But then I've seen better," Silver stated quietly. Their eyes moved slowly around the table. "It's not just his body that's wounded. It's his soul. One of my responsibilities is to lead people through a set of ceremonies that can help someone heal those wounds. But you need to be there for him if he decides to go through it. He'll need all of you, one way and another."

"What does he have to do?" Naomi asked, wary as a coyote in the brush.

Silver picked up a muffin, cracking it open in their fingers. "A couple things. A purification. A dedication to the path he walks. His willpower, of course. He'll have to do the ceremony alone. You can't face that for him. But then there's what he'll get on the other side of it. He'll need you to be there for him then; he'll be on the way to healing, but that's a long road. I'll need you to be there to see him on it. You people ready to help him?"

"Yes," Kevin said instantly, and heard Naomi match and mirror his words. "Of course!" Alice exclaimed, and Topher finished their chorus with "what do you need us to do?"

Silver smiled at the table. "What I need you to do, as a group, is get comfortable with the idea of healing as a thing that people travel through. And get comfortable seeing it done in a way that you're not used to. Talk about it with each other. Talk about it with him. But we do need to do this soon; the way I see things, until his soul starts healing, his body can't." Silver stood. "Talk it over, see what you think."

With a quiet smile, they walked away.

For a moment, the table was silent in the bustle of the communal kitchen. Peter looked between them. "Guys? Silver's good. They saved my life, if I'm honest. If they want to do something, then Aidan should do it. It's—"

"You aren't seriously going to go through with a bunch of voodoo bullshit, are you, guys?" Alice managed to cut down on the vitriol in her voice, but the comment was still pretty acidic when she spat it out. A few people shot uncomfortable glances their way.

Peter glanced up at her for a moment, before returning his gaze to his bowl. "Stand down, Alice. It isn't bullshit."

"But—" Alice began.

Kevin carefully cleared his throat. "Alice, have you ever done any research on psychosomatic disorders?"

"What?" Alice asked, perplexed. Kevin shrugged. "The biochemical interactions of the brain are complex; we don't understand them all, but we do know that psychological or neurological imbalances can cause catastrophic repercussions in the body. Is it really such a stretch to believe that indigenous peoples around the world intuited the fact, and learned to address it in a symbolic and narrative way? After all, isn't that what modern therapy does, essentially?"

Alice blinked. "I'd answer that if I understood more than half of what you just said, Mr. Dictionary."

Almost relieved by the old joke, Kevin tipped his head back theatrically. "Why me?"

"Because you're a history nerd," Peter replied, light and cocky as his literary namesake.

"Philistines, the lot of you." Kevin grumbled, glad to see something like a smile cross Alice's face. He glanced at Naomi. "What do you think?"

Naomi shrugged. "I think a shrink's always done Aidan good. I say give it a shot. I don't care if he—gah—if *they* use a couple candles and a poem. Long as it works. You?"

Kevin let out a slow breath. "I know that prayer can work, in the right person. And stories have power. I see this through the same lens. I'm still...well, I'm worried. Of course I am. But if Aidan wants to..." He sighed, running a hand over his hair. "I'm worried about him," he admitted.

Alice gave a quiet grunt of commiseration. "Same here. Felt like nothing I did was any good for him after the bleeding stopped, so I guess..."

Kevin pulled off his glasses, polishing them as he let his mind settle. Eventually, he put them back on. "I'll go have a word with him at lunch. See what he thinks. How he's feeling. If he wants to try this...well. It can't hurt."

By the time Kevin had walked with the kitchen staff to the healing hall through the blustery spring morning and slipped into Aidan's room with a bowl of soup, his boyfriend had fallen asleep again. But at least he seemed peaceful this time. Kevin took his place in one of the comfortable chairs beside the bed and chewed at a roll, playing a game of Go on his tab as he waited. Eventually, Aidan shifted in his bed.

"Hey," he remarked, his voice thin.

Kevin raised his eyes, nearly choked for a moment by the sheer frailty of this man he loved so dearly. Standing, he took a seat on the edge of the bed and brushed Aidan's hair back. "Hey. How are you?"

"I'm alright," Aidan whispered, pressing his cheek into Kevin's fingers.

Kevin bit his lip against the sudden flare of impotent anger in his gut.

"You know," he managed conversationally, "I'm really starting to hate the words 'I'm alright' and its synonyms. A man who's obviously thought through his own suicide is not all right, Aidan. I hate it when you lie to me, you know that."

Aidan winced, his brow furrowing. He closed his eyes. "I'm not...Kev, I...I'm *trying* to be alright. I know you worry, and you hate yourself for not being able to do anything for me, and I...I don't want to keep adding to that. I can't keep adding to that. I don't want to drag you down with me, so I...I hope that if I tell myself I'm alright enough, it'll be true. Please...please don't be angry with me."

The words were like razor blades in Kevin's chest, slicing him open. Had he really been letting the anger show that much? He'd frightened himself when he'd snapped at Topher, a boy who was scared and stressed. He hadn't meant to do it. But if he was frightening his gentle, brave boyfriend, it had gone beyond too far. He *had* to do something about that going forward. Right now, he needed to find some way to ease the fear and pain in those blue eyes.

Shifting, he lay down beside Aidan, wary of his wounds. He stroked Aidan's hair. "Oh my love, I'm not angry *at* you. But...I can't help but be a little upset when I find out the man I love thinks about dying that much." Softly, he kissed Aidan's brow. "I fought for you. I'd *die* for you. But I can't fight off what's going on inside you and....and God damn it, that does make me angry. Not *at* you, but...angry, all the same. I can't help it; comes with the red hair." He kissed Aidan's cheek gently, wishing he could do more and mindful of the damn injuries. "And it comes with being terrified of...look, if you don't want me upset, don't make me wonder if I'm going to lose you. Please. Because...well, I love you." He added a kiss to Aidan's throat, nuzzling softly against his beloved, his words a touch broken.

"You're not going to lose me," Aidan promised in a hoarse whisper. His arm wrapped around Kevin's shoulders. After a moment, he spoke again, haltingly. "I...you're the reason I haven't...I only said yes to all this because of you. Because I...I don't want to lose you, either. I don't want to hurt you. But that's all I feel like I'm doing nowadays." His breath hitched as he tried to swallow a sob.

Heart aching, Kevin brushed his lips across Aidan's. "Don't think like that. I...Aidan, I'd gladly hurt like this in order to be as happy as I am with you." Gently, he kissed his beloved again, and again. Aidan's tears flavored the kisses.

For a long time they simply lay together, soothing one another with their presence. Eventually, Kevin gently disentangled himself and sat up. "Your lunch is going to be cold, I'm afraid."

Aidan gave him a lovely, lopsided smile, his face tear stained. "I'll live."

The soup was cold, but it was still good. They talked as they ate; Kevin told Aidan about meeting Peter, and about the community they had found themselves in. Bit by bit, he worked his way back to Silver.

"Do you think you want to take him up on his offer?" he asked.

Aidan looked up, meeting his eyes with a level gaze. "Them, Kev."

"Damn, my mistake," Kevin acknowledged ruefully. "But what do you think?"

Aidan watched him for a moment, mulling his words over. "If I said yeah, would that bother you? I know it's not your religion."

"Neither is Christmas or Easter, historically speaking," Kevin replied easily. "I'm of the school that God, in his wisdom, created nothing He didn't wish to see in existence for some purpose. Evil happens only when the purpose is thwarted, you see. So if there are different names and different faces He—or She or They—can be seen by, well, so much the better. More people will be led to Him. The terminology is somewhat immaterial."

Aidan actually smiled at that. He mimed an 'over my head' gesture with one hand. Kevin chuckled.

"I asked Silver if you could be there for this healing thing," Aidan murmured when he'd finished what he could stomach of the soup. "They said I have to do it myself; it's going to take three days. After that, if I'm not having these fucking nightmares, let's get a bed together again."

"Agreed," Kevin murmured, cupping his cheek. "I miss you."

Tears welled in Aidan's eyes once more. "I'm sorry, Kev. I've been so much of a fucking pain, and—"

Kevin cut him off with a kiss. "Stop that. Got it?"

Aidan swallowed weakly. "Got it." He drew a shuddering breath. "Okay. Ceremony thing. After breakfast tomorrow."

"Alright then," Kevin agreed. "I'll stay tonight. Ceremony in the morning. After breakfast."

They ate quietly in the morning. Eventually, Silver came wandering in as if they were dropping by for tea.

"Morning, boys. Aidan? You ready?"

"Yes si...yes, elder." Aidan agreed, tripping a little over the title. Silver nodded. "Alright. Kevin? Go ahead and go for a walk. Always something to do around here. Go help out."

"Right," Kevin agreed, standing. But he froze in the doorway, caught by the fear in Aidan's eyes.

How can I leave him alone like this?

Swallowing, he turned to the elder. "Please...isn't there *anything* I can do to help?"

"You want to help?" Silver asked, eyeing him levelly. "Alright. Here's what you do. Go find Peter. Ask him to show you the Shrine

Wood. Find a shrine. Take an offering. Make your prayers. The one who listens to you will hear." Silver cocked their head, eyeing him like a craftsman eyeing a piece of machinery. "And if you really want to be a help in the future, you could work on draining some of that poison in you. Your soul's full of it. That anger. Good fuel, sure, but it burns awful hot. Burns anybody who stands too close. Maybe you've noticed."

Kevin drew a breath, body tensed into defense by the words. But he forced himself to relax. After all, the elder had a point. His rage had been so near the surface lately. He'd snapped at Topher, the boy who he'd wanted to protect since the day he'd first seen him wrapped in a recovery blanket, all scared-kid eyes and trying-to-be-brave posture. He'd frightened Aidan, who'd seen far too much rage in his life. It was one thing to go after an enemy. Anger was good for that. But if his rage began to hurt his friends…it didn't bear thinking about.

"Fair point." He straightened his shoulders. To give himself a little breathing room, he allowed himself to indulge his curiosity. "What god do you call on?"

The ageless-seeming person smiled. "You've read enough to know that. Think about it. My title is Silver Tongue for a reason." They nodded at the door. "Go on. See you in a couple days." Gently, they shut the door in Kevin's face.

Peter was playing checkers with Topher when Kevin found them. Peter bounced up. "Oh hey! Want the next game?"

"Actually, I'd like a little help finding the Shrine Wood?" Kevin asked. "Once your game is done, of course."

"No worries," Peter agreed, taking his hand. "Come on, it's kind of a hike but it's pretty. You dressed warm enough?"

"Enough," Kevin agreed, reclaiming his hand and pulling gloves out of one pocket. "I'm not worried."

"Great," Peter agreed, pulling the hood of his jacket up. "Come on, Shrine Wood's up this way."

Together, they walked through the town. All around, people were working at various tasks; weaving baskets, working a small 3-d printer in a house with the door open, feeding goats in a pen attached to a small barn hidden under a slick-tarp. All the house doors seemed to be standing open, and people walked in and out somewhat randomly. Children ran around everywhere, until a man stepped out of a long sod-house and rang a bell. Then all the children funneled inside.

"School?" Kevin guessed.

Peter nodded. "Yep. We raise our kids a lot like Dusters do; everybody gets raised by all of us. I've got twelve kids I'm teaching code and programming. It's fun, and they come up with some great ideas sometimes. Nobody's told them what you can't do yet," he added with a chuckle. "It's kind of amazing to watch them go at it."

"You're telling me; you should see our kids these days," Kevin agreed. "Dilly and Donny have become prodigies, and Tommy is going to be some sort of officer by eighteen, he's so responsible."

"Yeah, how are they all? And how's Dozer? How's Mally over at 1425?" Peter asked. They passed the walk in easy chat as the circles of homes gave way to gardens protected by slick tarps on poles. To one side, a group of people were working at what looked like the entrance to a bunker sunk into a rocky hillside, packing up boxes. Peter grabbed his hand. "Check this out!" Trotting over, he raised his voice. "Is that the last box for the trade?"

"It is," a man called back with a smile, "and we already shut the doors and made sure we ran a system update to keep the counts on the seed stores current. Relax, Keeper!"

"Thanks for that," Peter laughed, "but I came over here to show one of our friends the seeds his people are going to get. Kevin, take a look."

With a flourish, he lifted off the lid of the nearest box and fanned three foil packets out between his fingers.

Kevin touched one gently, reading the name. "Amaranth. That's going to be beautiful when we've got it growing."

"You bet!" A woman helping out agreed, "We grow it again every two years to keep the seed and mycorrhizae stock fresh, it's gorgeous."

"You're sure you can find the way with the GPS down?" Kevin asked, glancing up. The idea of someone being lost with this treasure was too much to bear.

Everyone in the group gave him some variation on a dismissive smile.

"The Walkers know how to get around without so much tech, Kev," Peter put in gently. "Relax."

Kevin tried for a smile. "Sorry, I've never been in a connection outage this long. The idea of being unable to reach anyone is playing merry Hell with my sangfroid."

Peter rolled his eyes, grinning.

"You want to stick a note in the box?" the youngest woman in the group—a girl, really—asked. She dug a notebook and a pen out of her pockets. "You know how to write analog, right?"

"I do, thanks," Kevin agreed, "It'll be good to let our people know we're still at it."

Sitting down, he stared at the paper for a moment. How did one wrap up everything that had happened in the last few weeks?

"About that special request we made," he asked, "did it make it into this box?"

"The coffee beans?" one of the helpers asked. "Oh, yeah, we stuck it in, along with some of the soil beasties it needs to thrive. We'll trade you if you get it growing; it doesn't like this elevation no matter what genes we change. Good luck!"

"Thanks, I appreciate it," Kevin replied with a smile, glancing down at the paper. After a beat, he jotted down a few paragraphs. Tearing out the pages, he folded them neatly and laid them on top of the seeds with a smile for the group. "Thanks."

"Welcome," the auburn-haired matron of the group replied, giving him a smile.

"Want to head up?" Peter asked, nodding at the trail leading out of the village. Kevin glanced back at the seeds in their grey box, then at the closed door beyond them. He'd love to wander through that door and into that precious seed vault…

But not today. That wasn't what he was here to do today.

The fields and grasses gave way to scrub as they walked, then to trees. Soon they were hiking up into the mountain proper, and the altitude hit Kevin a bit. Just as he felt his lungs start to tighten, something like a pleasant ballooning happened in his chest, and the taste of mint peppered the back of his throat: his nanites at work, boosting his oxygen uptake. He'd have to eat something when he got back and give them some fuel, but for now it was a blessing.

Peter didn't have nanites as far as he knew, but the shorter man also didn't seem to react. Granted, he'd lived here for some time now.

"I miss everybody, you know," Peter remarked, breaking the silence of the mountain forest. "But you especially. It's so great to see you."

"Good to see you too," Kevin agreed with a smile. "I really am glad to see you happy, my dear Pan."

Damn, there he went, slipping into pet names. That wasn't fair to either of them.

Peter paused for a moment, reaching out to clasp Kevin's shoulder. "Kev? Stop a second."

Kevin suppressed a wince. "Sorry, I spoke out of turn."

"No you didn't," Peter replied gently. "You still think of me that way. That's fine. Same here. That's why I wanted to say…look. You could be happy here too. You could stay here. You don't have to go back."

Kevin stepped away, crossing his arms to lock out the touch he'd craved so much, once upon a time. "Peter, please don't. I did love you. With all my heart, I did. But you left me alone. Aidan came to me." He swallowed, fighting the tightness in his throat. "I fight beside him. I belong beside him. If that's a problem, I'll go the rest of the way alone."

"Kev, don't get like that," Peter pleaded, stepping in. Softly, he touched Kevin's crossed arms, his eyes wide and liquid-dark. "It doesn't have to be him or me. It isn't like that. You could both stay. We could build a house. Make a triad, the three of us."

For the skin of a second, Kevin was tempted. Terribly tempted. To have both the men he loved as deeply as this safe in the same home, growing old in peace together...it was a dream come true.

But it was also an illusion. Slowly, he let out a breath, and shook his head.

"We need people like you to protect the seeds of the future, Peter," he murmured, "but those of us who have the capacity to be on the front lines have the duty."

"Do you have the capacity, babe?" Peter asked gently. "Because I've been watching you. You're this close to snapping. It's hurting you, and it hurts me to see you that way. It's eating you up inside, always being so *angry*."

Kevin looked away. "I...I know. A lot of things..." he drew a calming breath. "A lot of things have been stirred up lately. And I've let them get to me..." He shook off the thoughts, straightening to look Peter in the eye. "Until the Corporations are beaten, all safety is an illusion. What you offer is beautiful. But I can't accept. I can't bring what will come hunting me to this place. Cavanaugh found out..."

With a jolt, he realized that he'd never told Peter his truth. He had loved this man, but he'd never been brave enough to tell him the truth about himself and his parentage. Peter had joined the Wildcards seven years before, and he doubted that anyone else had filled him in during his time. And now the time to do it was gone. The realization was a wistful one, full of a vague sort of aching that left him feeling hollow.

Setting emotion aside, Kevin cleared his throat. "The things we had to do to save Aidan have marked us as priority targets for several Corporations. I won't bring the dogs at our heels to this place, Peter. I'm not done with my part of this war. Not yet." He drew in a lungful of air. "Someday we'll rest. But not yet."

"Someday?" Peter asked, and Kevin heard the soft sound of impending tears in his voice. He smiled weakly and leaned in, brushing his lips over his former lover's brow. "Someday. In the meantime, find another farmer to work beside and bed down in Midsummer's Eve grass, will you? Be happy. You were right, you belong here. And...and I want that for you."

"I want it for you, too," Peter murmured. "You're holding so much inside, Kev. You're wrecking yourself, inside. Maybe it won't be here with me, but you have to do something about that. I mean it."

Kevin swallowed. "I know. I know. And...and I'm going to start. This trip's been an unpleasant slap in the face, personal mental-health wise. A rude reminder that I'm...well, that I'm not nearly as together as I thought I was." He fought for a smile. "I guess I needed it."

Peter smiled gently, reaching out to cup his shoulder in one hand. "When the Gods send a message, sometimes they aren't real subtle. Come on, the Shrine Wood is up this way."

They hiked for another fifteen minutes in silence, before they reached something truly amazing. Wide boles of ancient trees, wickerwork frames, and hollowed slabs of stone stood on a wide hemisphere, each framing some piece of art. At the center was the abstract, flowing carving of a woman holding a child, but around the circle were all sorts of things. At the entrance, a flickering flame and a bowl of water stood guard in their own pillars of stone.

Kevin's eyes ran over the circle in wonder. He could see something like an Aztec-inspired skeleton with maize at its feet here, what he was fairly sure was the Green Man of Europe there, great antlers coming out of his head and carved vines sprouting all around him. There was a great golden sun disc in another shrine. Another cloche sheltered what looked like a pair of snakes woven around each other in a sort of contorted S. Over there was a man with two ravens on his shoulders. Further down was something he swore he'd read about somewhere; an African woman carved with waters gushing at her feet, brightly painted. That was Oshun, wasn't it? Some of the others baffled him completely.

"There's so many," he murmured. Peter nodded. "And these are just a few of the Gods. Just the ones the folk here call to." He gave Kevin a sidelong smile. "Sorry, babe. There's no cross."

"I didn't expect one," Kevin replied with a pat for Peter's back. Tentative as a child alone in a cathedral, he walked round the circle of shrines, studying the deities who were represented in their dozens.

He came back again and again to the abstract woman holding a child. She looked like a simpler, less human version of the Virgin Mother he'd always known.

He glanced back at Peter, standing at the gateway to the Shrine Wood. "The only name I know Her by is Mary," he whispered. "Would it be an insult to use that here?"

Peter shook his head. "She knows that name too."

Kevin looked down at the statue's feet. Wilted flowers, bright bits of weaving, polished bits of stone and wood, even food sat at the feet of the stone, among many candles. Some were still burning.

Feeling like a child who'd gotten himself dirty just before church, he turned back to Peter. "I don't have anything to give."

Peter smiled softly. "You've always have something, babe. Give Her your songs, hunh? Give Her your prayers. I'm going to sit a ways back and read a book. Do your thing."

With a last smile, he slipped away.

Kevin knelt beneath the statue, crossing himself. Raising his eyes, he studied the abstract Madonna framed in pine branches.

"O most gracious Virgin Mary," he breathed,
"never was it known that anyone who fled to thy protection,
implored thy help, or sought thy intercession
was left unaided.
Inspired with this confidence, I fly to thee,
O Virgin of virgins, my Mother;

to thee do I come;

before thee I stand, sinful and sorrowful.

O Mother of the Word Incarnate,

despise not my petitions,

but in thy mercy hear and answer me.

Heal the soul of the man I love.

Give him of your grace

Give him of your peace

Give him of your blessings

So that he may stand strong in this righteous war

This I pray, Holy Mother

Amen."

He closed his eyes, listening to the cold wind in the trees. But somehow, he still felt more was needed. He had no idea what, but there was something more he could offer. Something he needed to offer.

What had Peter said?

Give Her your song.

Yes. The songs. He could offer the Virgin Her song.

Closing his eyes, he drew a deep breath, and let his voice wind up into the trees.

"Ave Maria

Vergin del ciel

Sovrana di grazie e madre pia

Accogli ognor la fervente preghiera..."

Singing, he poured his love and his fear, his hope and his need into words beseeching a mother who watched over the lost and the wandering.

His voice wound into the songs of the wind in the pines and the chirp of the chickadees, and in his ears they blended, all part of a great living whole.

He poured everything he had into the song, every ounce of emotion and every breath in his body. The mountain wind beat time. The song seemed to have a life of his own.

"Maria, gratia plena

Ave Ave, Dominus..."

When the song was done, the mountain silence rang around him, the pines breathing like a living thing. He panted for air, catching his breath. He felt hollowed out, fragile as an egg shell.

Glancing up, for a heartbeat he thought he saw a smiling face on the statue. Then he blinked, and the carving was abstract smooth again.

On shaky legs, he walked from the sacred circle.

Peter was watching when he came down the path. "Sit down? Catch your breath?" the other man asked. Gladly, Kevin acquiesced.

"Heard your song," Peter whispered, rubbing Kevin's back gently. "You really love this guy, hunh?"

Swamped with emotion, Kevin nodded.

Peter's voice was soft. "Kevin? I'm really glad you found someone as special as that."

All at once, the tears he'd been fighting down for weeks now nearly broke their dam in Kevin's chest. His voice came out choked. "Me too."

Peter's hand was soothing on his back. "I'm calling on the Lady for him to get better," Peter murmured.

Kevin swallowed convulsively. "Me too."

Peter pulled him into a gentle hug. "He's going to be okay, Kev. He will. You'll see."

And that was when the carefully maintained dam inside Kevin broke. Tension draining from his muscles, he wept out his terror for the man he loved and the future he feared in the arms of a man he trusted.

Event File 28
Event Tag: Alternative Medicine
Timestamp: 18:30-3-22-2157/ 8:50-3-23-2157

The fire crackled in the darkness, spiraling up from the tripod of logs and sticks that Barley had spent the last of the daylight preparing. Aidan shivered as the cold worked its way under the robe he was wearing, and asked himself for the hundredth time what the hell he was doing out here.

He did his best to steady his breathing as he watched Brendan bring another few buckets of water from the well, setting them beside a big metal tub near the fire. The flickering light painted the boulder on the far side of the clearing, bringing out carvings in it and the lines of the three siblings' faces.

At his side, Brandi squeezed his shoulder and smiled. "Hey," she whispered, "whatever happens, remember: it's good. You're safe here."

"Thanks," he whispered. He knew what was coming, roughly. Silver and Barley had spent half of yesterday talking him through all of it, and he'd been drinking some awful herb tea and working on wood carving for the last three days as part of getting ready for this.

But it was one thing to talk about a psychologically effective re-enactment event in a warm modern room, with decent lighting. It was a hell of a lot different to stand in front of a blazing fire in a white robe, and realize you were actually standing here, your body aching with cold and strain. Realize you were actually going through with pretending to be a god in some old story, repeating what the god had done in order to beat the same kind of demons.

Brandi nodded, giving him a quick, tight smile, patting his shoulder.

"Bran?"

Brandi looked up at her sibling's voice. Barley nodded, shoving their curls back as they stood. "It's time."

"Yeah." Brandi agreed. Kneeling, she reached into the satchel she'd brought. Carefully, she laid three wrapped bundles at Barley's feet, giving her sibling a quick squeeze of the shoulder before she stepped back. Barley gave their sister a thankful smile as they knelt in front of the red bundle, the white, and the black.

They spread the white bundle open, unwrapping the nine smaller bags inside and laying out eight little piles of dried plants and, of all things, an apple. Next, they untied the red bundle, and laid out a knife as gently as if it were a sleeping puppy. Then they undid the black bundle, and laid out a coil of rope and a mask. The thing was an image of a human face in pain. Once Silver had found out Aidan could carve, they'd handed him a piece of wood and told him to make it for himself. Carve it in the image of what you want to be rid of, Silver had said. Carve your pain into the wood.

Looking at it, he wondered if he'd done the job too well. The thing looked the way he felt right now. He hadn't bothered to put any paint or polish on it; it was bare wood, only colored with a single spot of his blood between the eyes.

Barley stood, walking to Aidan's side. They looked him in the eye, holding out the mask.

With fingers that felt like they didn't belong to him, Aidan took the mask, tying it to his face with the cords hung from either side. Behind it, his breathing sounded too loud.

Away somewhere in the trees, a drum beat like a heart. It came closer, drawing in. Aidan's pulse picked up with it. Never mind the cold, he was starting to sweat now.

With slow grace, Silver walked down the path between the trees. They were dressed in robes of green and black, their white hair unbound and flowing. Behind them, a handful of people kept step with the drum Brendan played. There was the nurse from the medical bay, and both the doctors who'd been checking on him, and a couple of the elders. Mother Marta was in black and white this time, and it looked weirdly solemn.

The group spread out in a circle, but the damn mask was wrecking Aidan's peripheral vision. He could only see right in front of him, and with this many people around that was freaky as hell.

The drum picked up a new, faster rhythm for a minute. Then it went still, and the quiet shivered in Aidan's ears.

Silver spread their arms. "By the fire in our hearts," they called. Aidan jumped when the entire group replied in a swell of words.

"We light a fire in the dark!"

"This place is made whole and holy!" Silver called, and the entire circle returned the words ten times louder.

"Comes to us the wounded. Comes to us the bound," Silver intoned, their voice slow and full of resonance, "Comes to us the weary, long suffering. Ground down."

Goddamn, described like that I sound like a stray dog, Aidan thought behind the mask. Silver glanced his way, and for a split second Aidan could have *sworn* they smiled wryly, as if they'd heard him thinking. Then they lifted a little bottle and a box from the sleeves of their robes.

They tossed what was in the bottle into the fire, and it flared high.

"Silver Tongue, Far Traveler, Fire in the Head, we call you. Sky Treader, Story Smith, we call you. Loki of the Bright Burning, we call you. Be welcome at this fire."

From the box, Silver pulled a little cloth bag, and tossed it. When whatever was in the bag burned, the air smelled weird, musty and sharp. It was a little like the smell of disinfectant, a little like the stinging-clean smell of a medical bay.

"Physician of the Gods," Silver murmured, "we call you. Merciful One, we call you. Healer of Open Hand, Friend to the Fighter, we call you. Eir of the Steady Hand, we call you. Be welcome at this fire."

The last thing that went into the fire gave off smoke like the stuff the guys had gotten together last Christmas, spicy and sweet.

"Rejuvenating One," Barley called this time, their voice high and sweet, "Lady of Youth, Lady of Blessing, we call you. Lady of Gifts, She who is Generous, we call you. Idunn of the Apples, we call you. Be welcome at this fire."

"The gods are with us," Silver called, and the crowd echoed it back.

The eerie way the group spoke in unison, the cold, the flickering of the fire and the sheer weirdness of the moment were closing in on Aidan. Stomach cramping, he felt his breathing growing shallow. Damn, this was exactly like some crap horror movie where the poor dumb sap got his throat cut or his heart ripped out at the finish. What was he *doing* here? He didn't belong here. These weren't his people, and they weren't his gods. He shouldn't *be* here.

He nearly jumped out of his skin when Barley gently touched his arm. The chubby little person's smile was gentle, but their touch was firm.

This was the part Aidan had been wishing he didn't have to go through. But he'd agreed. He'd said he'd try, and this was no time to back down.

As Barley led him to the stone, Silver spoke in time with the drum.

"When a gull circled and shrieked, or scree shifted on the mountain, or wind whistled in his walls, the Trickster felt fear. Fearful he was, hunted and in hiding. And Loki was seized.

"They led the Trickster into a twilit cave, a dismal cavern belonging to bats, and there he was bound."

Silver's voice filled the air as Barley and Brendan used the rope to tie Aidan to the stone. His heart ached in his chest. Every injury on his body prickled. It was like his skin was expecting a new set of wounds, anticipating it with a sick dread. The ropes were nowhere near as tight as the damn cuffs that had left their marks on his wrists, but they were tight enough.

"They trussed Loki's shoulders to one slab, twisting the gut round his body under his armpits; they strapped Loki's loins to one slab, winding the gut round and round his hips; they clamped Loki's kneecaps to one slab, tying the gut round his legs." Silver intoned, and their voice was low and tight, as if they knew how it felt to be tied.

It felt like hell. Aidan tried to be still, but his heart was racing, his body tightening into knots of dread. Being held down like this hit way too close to his memories. Way, way too close.

Breathe, he ordered himself. *It's part of this. It's part of getting past this. Just breathe.*

"For all his wiles and wit, there was nothing Loki could do. He lay still; he looked at nobody and said nothing," Silver murmured. "Above him, the serpent dripped its venom."

Remembering the cue he'd been warned about, Aidan closed his eyes.

"Loki is left unguarded; he screws up his eyes. The snake does not wait. Its venom splashes on to Loki's face and in torment he shudders and writhes."

Something stinging and sharp dripped through his hair, sliding under the mask and down his skin. Fuck, they hadn't told him about this. Nobody had said there would be real pain!

Terror gripped his guts, and his chest tightened in on itself as the stinging drops stung his cheeks. The sharp smell was something he knew, something that wasn't that bad. Some part of his brain was trying to figure it out, but it was drowned in the panic. Pain and bindings. Pain and helplessness. He was right back where he started, and this time he knew he couldn't survive.

He gasped for air, and inhaled stinging drops of...vinegar?

That's what the stuff was, vinegar. Cooking vinegar. The taste mixed with the salt of tears. Shit, when had he started crying? Great, now he was crying in front of all these people. God, he was pathetic.

His body was starting to shake, a sure sign he was on the way to a panic attack. There wasn't enough air in the clearing. All he could breathe was wood smoke and vinegar.

And then the air seemed to loosen in his lungs, and cool water washed down his face. The smell of sharp, clean plants filled his nose; he didn't know them, but they reminded him of mint and pepper, a little bit.

"But what can hold the Shifter of Shapes against his will?" Silver called, and the entire community answered, "Nothing!"

"Loki Bright Burning, and he singes away his bonds," Silver's voice mixed into the sounds of ropes being cut, and Aidan's hands and legs were free. The sheer relief of it was like a bolt of electricity through his system. Gasping in deep lungfuls of air, he pushed himself away from the rock, helped up by Barley and one of his doctors. "Loki, Sky Treader, in all his wiles and wit, he leaves behind his bonds!" Silver's voice rose triumphant as Aidan was led to the fire, legs trembling and knees feeling like jelly.

"Loki, Far Traveler, come into this circle. Be welcome beside our fire. Be cleansed of your wounds. Be cleansed by the nine herbs of healing."

Barley's gentle hands helped Aidan out of his robe and guided him into the big tin tub beside the fire. Standing naked in front of all these strangers really didn't help him calm down much, but the robe was wet already, and he was about to get a lot more wet. At this point he'd take it; anything to wash off the cold sweat and the vinegar.

The first bucket of water sluiced over his head, and Aidan felt the warmth of it tingle against his skin, easing his muscles. Barley took over the speaking as more buckets washed sweat, stinging vinegar and fear from Aidan's body.

"Una your name is, oldest of herbs,

Of might against three, and against thirty.

Of might against the vile foe."

The water was filled, Aidan realized, with bits of herbs. That explained the sweet, clean smell. Of course, bits of leaf kept getting stuck between his skin and the mask he was wearing. Man, he was getting sick of the thing.

"Stithe it is called, it withstands poison," Brandi continued, chanting the names of plants in their sweet singsong, "It stands up against poison, it stands against pain, it ends the wrathful, it casts out the illness."

As Barley went on naming plants and the ways they ended pain, Aidan's doctors helped him wash himself down. Between the cold air and the water he should have been miserable, but the heat of the bath and the heat of the fire made a contrast with the cold that, weirdly, made him feel more awake than he had in a week.

Soft fabric wrapped around him again, and he stepped carefully out of the bath. His feet didn't hurt nearly as much as he'd thought they would when he stepped onto the hard-packed soil beside the fire, facing Silver.

The older person held out an apple and a knife, the metal of the blade flashing in the firelight. Carefully, they split the apple widthwise, showing the two halves with their matching stars inside.

"Far Traveler, do you come here in search of rejuvenation?"

Aidan swallowed. He did his best to raise his voice as he spoke. "I do."

"What do you offer?" Silver asked. Feeling like a kid in a lesson, Aidan held out both of his hands.

Gently, Silver laid half of the apple in his right hand, and pushed up the sleeve of the robe on his left arm. They laid the blade against the crook of his elbow, holding his eyes. "Do you offer this?"

"Yeah," Aidan agreed. "I mean, yes. I do."

The quick, clean sting of the knife drew a little dribble of blood from Aidan's skin, dripping onto the half of the apple still in Silver's hand. Silver waited until the white flesh was spattered in red. Then they held the apple over their head.

"Eir, goddess of healing and compassion, we offer this sacrifice that you may help this man overcome his pains and return to himself."

They tossed the bloody fruit into the fire, where it spat and crackled. Barley stepped forward, their blue eyes glimmering in the firelight. They were holding an honest-to-god cow horn, and it was hollow, filled with liquid. Barley tipped the horn, and a long golden stream fell to splash in the dirt. Aidan smelled apples and honey.

"Idunn, goddess of youth and immortality, this man tastes your fruit in deference, and asks that you help him find the constant soul within."

Barley poured more of the liquor onto the apple half that Aidan held, then gave him a nod. "Eat."

The flesh of the apple was crisp and clean between Aidan's teeth, and the booze it had been doused with brought the flavor out, deepening it. Aidan had been worried that he wouldn't be able to finish this, when they'd told him he'd need to eat the offering in the ceremony. He'd been having so much trouble eating lately. But this taste was something he couldn't get enough of. The apple was gone before he knew it, even with the damn mask getting in the way.

Silver nodded, smiling. Stepping in, they held Aidan's eyes. "Loki, God of the Fire and the Story, help this man shed the shape others have forced him into. He removes the face others have forced upon him. He sheds the skin of a prisoner that chafes his spirit. He removes the mask of wrongdoing that hides his truth. He removes the mask of shame that inhibits his sight. He reveals his true face."

With a rush of relief that bordered on joy, Aidan reached behind his head and untied the goddamn mask. It felt so *good* to feel the night air and the firelight against his skin.

"What is the story your enemies told you?" Silver asked, their voice low. "What net of words did they use to bind your spirit?"

Aidan swallowed. He really didn't want to talk in front of all these strangers. His voice was hoarse on the words. "They called me an aberration. A freak. A sinner. They called me a perversion. They called me a girl. They told me I'd messed up my body." He swallowed. "And they called me a thing. It. They called me "it". They told me I was alone." He swallowed hard. "They told me I'd die in that place, and my life was wasted. They said nobody would come to help me. They said I was fighting for a stupid cause. That we'd lose. And they told me that everyone I...everyone I love was going to get killed because of me."

The words stung more than the vinegar in his eyes. They turned like knives in his gut.

Silver smiled, bright eyes glinting. They nodded at the mask. "That mask is the name others have put upon you. That mask is 'prisoner'. That mask is 'sinner'. That mask is 'she' and 'it'. That mask is 'aberrant' and 'perversion'. These are the stories others try to force you into playing a part in. What will you do with those words?"

In the firelight, Aidan stared into the shadowed recess of the mask, feeling a slow anger simmer up his gut. They'd tried to break him. They'd called him an aberration. A sinner. Worthless. Helpless. They'd tried to turn him into their toy. Worse, they'd wanted to turn him into a traitor.

And he'd almost let them turn him into a victim. Into a headcase. He'd nearly been broken. He'd almost let them win.

Almost.

He tested the strength of the wood. The mask flexed in his hands. His fingers found the weak places, remembering the faults he'd found in carving. Placing his fingers carefully, he put as much strength into his hands as he could.

The mask snapped in his hands.

"That's what I'll do," he stated, and this time his voice was steady.

A little cheer ran around the circle, people whooping and calling 'yeah!'

"Cast the stories others have woven to trap you into the fire. Let the Lord of the Flame burn their deeds away," Silver invited with a smile, and Aidan almost felt like grinning as he tossed the pieces of the mask into the crackling fire.

Stepping forward, Silver put a hand on his shoulder. "Now, tell us your true name. Tell us your true story."

Aidan raised his eyes, studying the people in the circle of firelight: Brandi and Brendan, friends who'd saved his ass a dozen times. Barley, the helpful little person he'd come to like. The elders who'd welcomed him. All these smiling people who lived every day with a vow to keep hope alive, for a tomorrow that might be better.

These people were worth telling the truth.

He raised his voice. "I'm Aidan Headly, Commander of the Wildcards unit," he called, amazed at the strength of his voice. "I'm the man with the best team in the Western Region at my back. I'm the big brother to somebody who kicks ass, and the boyfriend to somebody amazing. I'm the man who has a team that cares about him enough—and is crazy enough—that they break into a max-security Cavanaugh center and rescue me. I'm leading an elite unit of the Democratic State Force. I'm the commander of a unit given the missions nobody thinks anyone can pull off. I'm the leader of the unit who figures out a way, every time. And we are fighting for a country worth living in, for every single one of us. That's who I am!"

The ceremonial circle erupted in cheers. Barley pushed the horn full of booze into Aidan's hand.

"Hail the true story! Hail the Gods!"

"Hail!" the circle cried as Aidan drank deep. The liquor warmed his core, and the taste of apples and honey filled his mouth.

For the first time in weeks, Aidan slept that night without dreams.

It was hunger that woke Aidan in the morning: real, honest-to-god hunger. His stomach ached with emptiness. Damn, how long since he had a decent meal? He carefully sat up and stretched, scrubbing at his eyes as he yawned expansively.

Kevin's arms were around him in a heartbeat. "Hi." he breathed, laying his forehead against Aidan's. Aidan ran his hand over Kevin's hair. "Hey. When did they let you in?"

"Just half an hour ago. Silver's been stonewalling me for bloody days," Kevin grumbled, but his touch was softer than his words. "You alright?"

Aidan smiled and leaned forward for a soft kiss. "Yeah…I think I am. For real, this time."

Kevin drew a shaky breath. He didn't speak for a moment. Then he managed a chuckle. "Well, I suppose it was worth it. I'll have to ask Silver what I should leave Loki, as a thank you."

Aidan laughed. "You? Really?"

Kevin gave a weak little smile, nodding. "When in Rome."

Aidan blinked. "Uh, Kev. This is Colorado."

Kevin snorted. "Ass. It's a turn of phrase." He grinned. "Oh, I have a movie for you about Rome when we get home. 'A Funny Thing Happened on the Way to Forum'. It's a *horrendous* movie. You'll love it."

Aidan chuckled, leaning in for a kiss. "It'll be cool watching movies together again. I miss that. And… Kev, I'm sorry I put you through so much hell recently," he murmured against Kevin's lips. "I love you. And...thank you for standing by me, even when I was freaking the hell out of you."

"Soppy as it sounds, you're worth it, love. And besides, backing you up is what I'm here for, right?" Smiling, Kevin gently pulled at his hands. "Come on. You're cleared for walking now. Let's go get some breakfast, I'm starving."

Aidan smiled his agreement, and stood on wobbly legs. The physical wounds still needed healing, but he felt lighter inside, more convinced the recovery would come. He leaned on Kevin as they left the clinic, and squinted in the morning sun.

After the intensity of last night, the normality in the little village was unreal. Silver was sitting outside a little house with a piece of flatbread and a cup of coffee, and nodded to them as they would nod to any acquaintance as they passed. Only Alice and Topher really reacted; Alice nearly upset her breakfast when she jumped up to stride over to them.

"Wrist." she demanded, taking Aidan's pulse as she yanked out her imaging screen. She peered intently at his face, felt Aidan's brow and practically tried to give him a standing physical, her eyes wide. "Holy....no temperature deviation, no sciatic muscle tremors, no overreaction to stimuli...it's like you're....how do you feel?"

"Good," Aidan smiled weakly as Alice checked him over again. "Still banged up, I mean, but...good."

Alice grinned. Then she forced her face into lines more suitable for a medic. "Come on, I'm giving you a proper checkup for the sake of my sanity."

Kevin caught Aidan's eye, and smirked. "Better do as the doctor orders."

"Damn right." Alice put in with a laugh.

<u>Event File 29</u>
<u>Event Tag: Achieving Connection</u>
<u>Timestamp: 9:00-3-20-2157/ 11:45-3-27-2157</u>

"Incoming!" Dozer called into the bustle of the breakfast canteen, "Got a truck!"

"One of ours?" Liza demanded, shooting to her feet. Dozer gave her a patient smile. "Yeah Liza, it's ours. Relax, okay?"

Liza gave a brittle little smile. "Thanks Dozer. That'll be the last seed shipment, I guess. Only took them forever."

Tweak poked her head out of the book she'd been trying to read, and failing. They'd handed her tons of books and games and junk, everybody had, and it was sweet of them. But she was still going batshit. She needed net like she needed air. She'd been spending every work day since the Net went down linking all the devices she could into a wonky kind of meshnet. She was slowly getting every device that ran Force OS to act as its own node, and she was reaching more devices and more coders who could help her on the work every day.

But it was taking fucking forever, and she had still barely reached Denver and the Sector Command so far. Liza wouldn't let her work on it for more than eight hours at a time, and she hadn't won the argument that she could work longer, yet. The situation was driving her bugnuts. With net, she was a coder. Without it, she was just some freaky little kid. She *hated* being somebody with nothing useful to do. She'd tried helping Janice when she was off work, and gotten kicked out for being too antsy. For now she was filling in for Topher on 3-D print work, and going insane.

For the sake of something to do, she bounced to her feet and trotted after Liza and Dozer. Janice sauntered along behind them, relaxed as ever and hands in her pockets. She caught Tweak's eye and smiled a bit.

"Take it you're bored?"

"Not bored. Bugn-nuts. Going c-crazy," Tweak admitted ruefully. "Thought I could help with g-genes. Till the n-net's back. Think I can learn genome c-code?"

"Knowin' you, I imagine you'll get it without much work," Janice agreed with an easy nod. "You got the brains for it. I can show you what I know; foreman's assistant-grade stuff's all I got taught 'bout plants, plus what I taught myself, but it's a start. Course, it ain't like a bug in the code. You get genomes wrong, you end up with—"

"Yeah, I know." Tweak cut in. "You get me. G-gammas."

Janice shrugged. "Or you get worse. Things ain't wired right, you get death. Aborted embryos. Plants that die in the seed. So we'll need to get you trained up 'fore you dive in. For a real trainin' we'll need somebody better'n me on the plant side of things, but I can get you your ABCs. You up for some study?"

"D-definitely," Tweak agreed, nodding fast. Anything that actually did some *good*.

Janice gave her a genuine smile as they entered the garage. "Alright then, after my work's got started, I'll take a break and get you goin' on the basics. Ain't hard, once you learn the tech for parsing an' recombinin' genomes. Those programs Kev got off AgCo for us a while back do a lot of the grunt work for you. Jus' takes a lot of payin' attention. Let's see what we got in this box; if'n there's monocot seeds that's good; they're a lil' more forgiving."

"What's the M thing?" Tweak asked as a couple of guys helped Dozer heave the crate out of the back of a beat up yellow truck.

"Monocots is stuff that came down outta grasses, basically," Janice replied distractedly, watching Dozer. "Man, you put your back out again an' Damian'll skin you. Lemme take that."

Stepping over, she gently shoulder-checked the big man out of the way and grabbed the box, laying it down. Dozer sighed. "Since when'd he start telling people I was having back problems?"

"Since you weren't listenin' when he told you to lay off usin' that back for a crowbar. You ain't twenty-three no more," Janice replied easily. Dozer cracked a grin. "News flash, neither are you, old lady. Thanks, guys!" he added, nodding at the men in the truck. "Canteen's down the hall on the left, go grab chow."

"Thanks!" the two Dusters who'd brought the shipment replied, heading eagerly into the base while Dozer and Janice lugged the crate down into Janice's office. Yvonne popped her head out as they passed, then trotted along after them. "That the last box? Fuck, that took a long time. I *hate* the net being down; even basic stuff is taking *forever*."

Tweak resisted the instinct to wince. She glanced up at the taller woman, noting the bags under her eyes. Bloodshot eyes. And her hair wasn't as neat as usual.

"You look like shit," she observed. "You sleep?"

Yvonne sighed. "Tweak, sweetie, you still don't get this tact thing, do you?"

"Waste of time," Tweak replied with a shrug. "So, you sleep? Sarah do you too hard?"

Yvonne snorted. "I wish. Tommy's..." she sighed. "He's having bad nightmares, with the guys gone. He keeps dreaming that they're going to...well, that he's going to lose them like he lost Andrea and Laz." Her fingers fiddled with her pale ponytail as they walked. "He keeps waking up crying, and we drag him over to our room till he feels better. Then he's embarrassed because he's twelve and he shouldn't need to come in and sit with us, and we tell him what bull that is, and we stay up and talk for a while. It's happened a couple nights, now." She gave Tweak a rueful smile. "He'll be okay when the guys get home."

Another pang of guilt flashed in Tweak's head. If she was better, they'd *be* home. "Yeah," she agreed quietly.

Inside her office, Janice popped the plastic-sealed lid, giving it a quick shove. The lid slid off, and Janice caught it in the air. "Alright, lessee what they got in...huh." Reaching in, she tugged out a couple folded sheets of paper. Glancing through it, she set down the lid, her eyes widening.

"What?" Dozer asked. Janice looked up at him with an actual grin. "It's Kevin, he wrote this!" Glancing down, she shook her head, laughing. "Dios mio, an actual hardcopy letter. Bet he's havin' fun, goin' back in time an' all." She dropped her eyes to the letter, reading it aloud. "I'm writing to you from the most stupendous...aw fuck a frag grenade, I'm makin' Liza read this, I ain't dealing with his words on top of his handwriting."

Five minutes later, everyone in the base was clustered around Liza as she read out the letter.

"Hello the base!

I'm writing to you from the most stupendous community up in the mountains, they've taken us in for the time being. I won't say more in case this letter is intercepted, but I can't wait to tell everyone about it in person.

I hope you're all keeping yourselves amused during this net shortage. We're mostly in good shape. Aidan is—he crossed out a few words here—doing much better, though the doctors here say he'll need a—and here he did it again, dammit Kev—some time to heal. But I don't want anyone to worry! He's doing fine."

"Lyin' little lily-white brat," Janice grumbled. "If he's crossin' things out it means he started sayin' the truth an' chickened out. Goddamn."

"Janice, quit." Yvonne admonished, cuddling into Sarah's arms. "Go on, Liza. Read the rest."

Liza nodded, running her eyes down the page. "Okay, he says Topher and Alice are fine, and he's fine, and the shipment is our last one, completes everything we wanted. And he says..." She blinked, then glanced up, looking straight at Tweak.

"There's a note for you in here, Tweak."

"Y-yeah?" Tweak asked, shrugging a little deeper into her leather jacket. Liza dropped her eyes, reading. "Please make a special note to mention this to Tweak: I've got a proper reward for our heroine. Tweak, I requested coffee beans that we can use to produce our own coffee tree, possibly. I promised you real coffee when you joined up, remember? Well, I kept my word! Whatever comes off it belongs to you for a year; it's only fitting, given that you saved dozens of lives with your stunts on this mission. I wanted you to know, I'm grateful. We all are."

Tweak's world went still around her as Liza read on. She had asked for coffee, the day she agreed to join up. She'd said it as a challenge and a needle. Nobody under CSS level could land real coffee.

But Kevin had remembered. He'd gotten her a future coffee tree.

Tears pricked hot behind her eyes. Kevin and Aidan were okay. They were going to make it. And they thought she was a hero.

"We'll be home as soon as GPS allows us to navigate safely," Liza finished, "This is Kevin, signing off."

For a moment, the canteen was quiet. Tweak swiped at her stinging eyes.

"Okay. 'Nuff of this. F-fuck this. Done waiting." She pushed herself to her feet.

Liza watched her warily. "Tweak?"

"I'm g-getting us n-net," Tweak stated. "I'm g-getting them home."

It took a week of her hardest work. It was a complete pain in the ass building off their meshnet to allow every Force-OS device to act as its own node. She blew off sleep. She probably would have forgotten to eat, if Billie and Liza hadn't kept after her so much. She had a hell of a headache by Saturday. But she also had a signal.

Fingers trembling, she tapped in Topher's call handle.

"C'mon c'mon c'mon," she whispered.

Two minutes later, Topher's amazed face showed in her screen. "Tweak?!"

Tweak punched the air. "Yes! Yes yes yes!"

"Good God," Topher breathed. "Tweak, stay on the line, please!" He pushed himself back from wherever he was sitting, and took off.

"Guys!" he yelled, his tab joggling all over. He must be running with it in his hand. "Guys! Guys, it's Tweak! She's on my tab!"

A breath later, the holographic image of all her base mates showed up on Tweak's window. She grinned, waving. "Hi, guys."

"Tweak?!" Kevin exclaimed in shock. "How...is the net—"

"Down. Bouncing the signal off all our d-devices. Figured it out. They can't shut down the world." Tweak crossed her arms, grinning. "Dusters the only ones with Net right now. So. Your GPS. You made the Never Summer after all, hunh?"

"Yeah, Tweak," Aidan agreed with a smile, "we made it."

Tweak raked her eyes over him. "You okay? No bullshit."

Aidan shrugged. "No bullshit? I'm still pretty wobbly. But I'm getting better. Is this connection stable?"

"Yep!" Tweak agreed, sure of that at least. Aidan's smile widened. "Have I told you that you're a genius recently, Tweak?"

"Nope. S'okay. I know," Tweak replied, tapping. "Getting your nav back online, pop up inna sec. You need to c-come home."

The compound went practically insane when the jacked up ambulance came in under the slick tarp. Aidan was nearly tugged out of his seat and hugged by about ten people at once, and Dilly and Donny bounced up and down yelling, "you're home you're home you're home you're home!!!"

Kevin grinned as he got hugged by Yvonne and Blake at once. "Hi guys!"

"Hi guys yourself, you little *brat*!" Blake exclaimed with all the drama he could muster, slapping Kevin's shoulder. "We thought you were *dead*! *Never* scare us like that *again*, you *crazy little bastard*!"

"Oh come on Blake, it wasn't—"

"Wasn't anything anybody *sane* would have pulled, I'll tell you *that*!"

While Blake fussed, Damian grabbed Aidan's hand, shaking it and trying to study him at the same time without looking like he was doing anything. He really wasn't as good at faking as he thought he was.

Standing a little bit back from the others, Tweak grinned. Catching sight of her, Aidan walked over and saluted. "Back on base, as ordered."

Tweak couldn't help but giggle. After a second, she got up her guts and stuck her hand out. "Glad you're back. Took long enough."

Aidan gently took her hand, shaking it for so little time that it barely set her skin off at all. Naomi came up behind him and gave her a grin. "Hey kid. We owe you. If you hadn't shut down the Grid, we wouldn't have made it back in one piece."

"Wouldn't have." she retorted, grinning and smug. "I saved your asses."

"Oh sure, rub it in." Janice remarked, then caught her commander in a bear hug. "Good to see you, you crazy 'lil' son of a bitch." Drawing back, she grinned down at Aidan. "You're gonna wanna come in, we got a shit ton done while you were gone." Letting him go, she grabbed Naomi for a hug that made the younger woman squeak.

"I expect a full report," Aidan replied, though his grin wrecked any seriousness he tried for.

"You'll get better'n that, you little shit." Janice laughed as Liza dropped Aidan's badge of office into his hand, then gave him a hug. She opened her mouth to say something, but Dozer's tap on her shoulder distracted her. The wide-set man nodded to one side, and the other two looked over at where Billie had glommed onto Topher and started kissing him. He looked like he couldn't believe it, but he definitely wasn't complaining. In fact, he had his arms around her, and her dark fingers were buried in his black hair. Liza caught Aidan's eyes and grinned, miming a heart shape with both hands. He glanced at the couple and back at Liza, giving her a nod.

Dozer reached out, taking Aidan's arm in one big hand. "Let's get you off your feet, Commander. Damian will wanna look at them."

Aidan gave the doctor a wry smile. "Oh, great."

It was a wild night. Someone had gotten real champagne, and that mixed with all the other booze they'd brewed or pilfered to make things crazy as they celebrated and got stories out of their teammates. They toasted the seeds, toasted Aidan, toasted their new friends in Coomb Olwen and, seriously weirdest of all, toasted Tweak. They all got falling down drunk, and nobody cared. They could afford it until the Grid was up again. For a few nights, they could do anything.

Tweak fell asleep grinning. For once, she was sure the next day would be awesome.

Event File 30
Event Tag: Planting Seeds
Timestamp: 14:00-5-1-2157/ 12:30-5-3-2157

The first of the seeds went into genome reworking a week after they got home. Kevin had rarely had a more nerve-wracking wait than the month it took Janice and Damian to test, synthesize, and print the adjusted genomes into viable embryos. Between waiting to see if all their sacrifice had been worth the cost, debriefing Command on the new situation and his compromised identity, and being remanded to Base until Sector decided whether he could perform the Grid work required of a logistics and requisitions officer any longer, Kevin was ready to climb the walls.

Nobody's life had been made easier by their newly mandated security measures either: a base position change every three months was the new norm. There were new rules about taking circuitous routes back to the base, and new strictures on everyone to maintain their security. Kevin had set a few new rules of his own for the day when—if—he returned to Grid work. The jackals were on his track now, no doubt of that. But he had every intention of leading them on the quintessential wild goose chase.

As the days passed, the seeds sprouted, and the little plants were transplanted from their agar gel in Janice's office to soil in the canteen. Finally, they moved to the amended soil in the mobile planting beds outside.

On the morning Aidan left for his monthly debrief at Sector, Kevin could barely focus on the schedules he was reduced to drawing up for Yvonne and Jim. They took him no time at all to complete. That was the problem.

Moodily, he did a little reading for one of his research projects, but he didn't have the patience for it. He couldn't focus on reading about the past, when the future sat like a lead weight on his mind. Frustrated with himself, he shut his system down and headed for the outer door. Maybe some air would clear his head.

"Where you going?" Yvonne asked, stepping out of her office to fall into step with him. He sighed, shoving his hands in his pockets. "Oh, out to check the plants for pests and kill time. There's not much else I can do at the moment. Restricted to base, and all that."

"Yeah," Yvonne agreed wryly. "I hear you." She glanced up at him. "Got something that'll cheer you up."

"Oh?" Kevin asked, mildly interested. He'd welcome any distraction at the moment. Well, almost any distraction.

"Yep!" Digging in her pocket, Yvonne passed over a small white box. Kevin opened it as they stepped out into their garden area. In their nest of white foam, two golden rings gleamed. He looked up at his foster-sister with a grin. "You got them!" Reaching out, he tugged Yvonne into a hug. She patted his back. "I told you I would." Stepping back, she gave him a beaming smile. "Make sure they fit, okay? Try yours on."

Kevin slipped the larger gold band onto his ring finger. It gleamed in the spring sun. Kevin watched the light play off it, feeling his heart tugged in too many directions at once.

"Hey," Yvonne murmured, "I thought you'd be happy? What's that look for?"

Kevin glanced up. He worked up a smile for her as he slipped the ring off and tucked the box in his pocket. "Oh, I'm happy. It's only...well, it'd be a shame if I present this in time for Aidan to deliver my demotion, if Sector decided I'm too much of a liability on-Grid. The emotional whiplash wouldn't be fun for either one of us."

Yvonne studied his face for a moment, her own smile fading. She pulled him in for a hug. "It'll be okay, Kev baby. They say I have to do your job, I'll threaten to quit. How about that?"

"Worth a try," he murmured, hugging her tight.

Leaning back, she patted his shoulder. "Hey. Seriously. It'll be okay."

He nodded. "From your lips to God's ears. And in all seriousness, thanks, Yve. I appreciate this an awful lot." Clearing his throat, he gave her a look over the rims of his glasses. "You did solemnly swear on your very soul that you wouldn't tell anyone until we announced it. You haven't forgotten that, have you?"

Yvonne rolled her eyes, grinning. "I didn't forget, you giant ball of sap. But don't take forever." Standing on tiptoe, she kissed his brow. "Love you, baby."

"Love you too, my darling girl." he laughed. "Now, do go inside. I want to meet Aidan when he comes in, and I intend to do it unaccompanied. He'll be home any time now. Shoo."

Snorting, Yvonne reached up to ruffle his hair. She pecked his cheek, then headed back in. Irritably, he straightened his hair as he watched her go, wishing he had a mirror.

He was studying a zucchini plant, checking it for spider mites as the reading material he'd been studying had suggested, when Aidan pulled up in his truck. He wandered out of the garage a few minutes later, moving carefully. Kevin watched the way he walked, and repressed a wince at the other man's careful steps. Aidan would be limping for a long time yet. He stood still beside the Stockbot-based garden bed, studying the leaf between his fingers.

"Is that the part of the plant we eat?" Aidan asked, sounding a little dubious.

Glancing up, Kevin chuckled. "No, love. This is a zucchini; we'll eat the fruit off it, when it's ripe. Don't worry, the fruit tastes far better than the leaf looks."

"You know more about plants than I do," Aidan conceded, glancing up with bright eyes. He smiled, gesturing vaguely at the plants growing all around them. "God, Kev…I still can't believe all this is happening. We'll have a real harvest soon."

"Of all the seeds we've sown." Kevin agreed as he straightened. For a moment, they stood side by side in their makeshift mobile garden, gilded into something like beauty by the afternoon light. The leaves glimmered green and gold in the slick-tarp's dappled shade.

Gold, Kevin's mind murmured silently, fingers fiddling in his pocket. Aidan leaned his weight against his other side.

"So," he asked in the closest thing to a casual tone he could manage, "what did Magnum say about everything?"

Aidan fingered the leaves. "Said that the progress on this plant project is pretty great," he remarked. "He approved us taking on somebody with ag skills when we find them. Other mobile bases are signing up for a waiting list, once the stable Rest and Retirement bases and a couple bases like ours figure out how to make this kind of project run efficiently, and put seed and instruction packets together. I put out the word while I was up there, started looking for the ag-specialist Janice put in for. I'm hoping we get lucky and somebody will pop up real soon."

"I'll check with Tio Berto," Kevin murmured, "see if he might have a lead. Janice will skin you if she has to do this much longer on her own."

Aidan groaned. "Don't remind me, she's already been in my office twice this month saying that I'm taking too long finding a plant guy."

They shared a wry smile. "I think we're going to get top priority for a while," Aidan remarked. "Magnum said that having the GreyNet fully independent of Corporation infrastructure is going to be pretty useful, once Tweak and the other coders get all the kinks worked out of the new meshnet she patched together. Between that and the seeds, we pulled some serious tricks. People up top are impressed."

Kevin nodded, his stomach doing somersaults. "And what did Magnum have to say about my position on this base? I know my identity will be a liability, going forward. Wanted dissident and all that." The words came out brittle.

Aidan was silent. When he couldn't bear the quiet any longer, Kevin raised his eyes. Aidan was watching him quietly.

"Yeah. Your identity is a liability," he agreed. "But your skillset and your contact network's a huge asset, and training or bringing in somebody new would set this unit way back. So Magnum and I talked it over. You know that Tortuga Bay contact you got set up for the Force, to get us indie vids?"

"Yes?" Kevin asked. Aidan tipped his head. "Magnum cleared it. Since we're going to have to hide both your genome and the way you look on Grid runs going forward, he's going to authorize paying them to teach you how to do makeup and character acting. You're going to stay with them for a couple weeks and take a course in disguise."

Slowly, Kevin started to smile. "I...wow. I actually get to take theater classes? For the unit?"

Aidan gave him a lopsided grin. "Yeah."

Kevin felt as if his heart had filled with helium. He laughed. "Well, it's definitely not what I expected, but I'll certainly take it!"

"Thought you'd like it," Aidan murmured, resting his hand over Kevin's. Catching his eye, the blonde man gave him a smirk. "Just don't get near Schultz for a while. I got to watch the Sector Quartermaster and the Sector Commander get into it about this. It was something."

"I'll bear that in mind," Kevin chuckled. Leaning in, he brushed his lips over Aidan's. "Thank you, Aidan my love."

"Hey, saves me doing training and transfer paperwork," Aidan murmured teasingly, returning the kiss.

Kevin laughed, putting his arms around his boyfriend's shoulders and feeling giddy. He was staying with his man and his family. He was going to keep doing the work he loved. In spite of the disasters, Aidan was in his arms, getting stronger every day. He couldn't have asked for a better outcome.

The box in his pocket bumped against his hip, reminding him of its presence. He wasn't sure if now was the proper time. He wished he could set something up, mark this with the ceremony it deserved. But he wouldn't have the chance to take Aidan on a romantic getaway any time soon, would he? Not bloody likely, given how their last fun getaway turned out.

And he'd already been too close to losing Aidan this year. Neither of them knew how much time they had.

He squared his shoulders. *All right. No time like the present. Carpe diem.*

Kevin cleared his throat, leaning back. "Aidan?" he murmured. "Er...you know I'm a sap..."

"Yeah, I know you're a sap," Aidan agreed with a soft chuckle, his hair gleaming like summer wheat. "Why're you reminding me this time?"

Kevin stared at his feet for a moment. Then he pulled off his glasses, polishing them industriously. "Um...I was wondering..." he held his glasses up to the light, giving himself a moment to compose himself. It had sounded so *smooth* in his head.

"Yeah?" Aidan asked, leaning in to rest his head on Kevin's shoulder.

Kevin replaced his glasses and tipped his head to the sun, eyes closed. "If I happened to get ahold of a pair of rings, any chance you'd like to wear one?"

Aidan laughed and pulled away, gently bringing Kevin's face down to meet his. Heart in his mouth, Kevin met his bright blue eyes.

"Are you asking me to marry you, Kev?" Aidan asked, eyes dancing.

"Er..." Kevin swallowed. "Yes?"

Aidan chuckled, pulling him into a kiss. "I think I'm supposed to say that. Because the answer is hell yes."

Kevin breathed again, smiling as relief and a touch of embarrassment washed through him. "I know it's merely a formality, really, but...well." he glanced down, digging in his pocket, and held out two golden rings. They caught the diffuse light beneath the slick tarp, glowing like fire made solid.

Aidan held out his hand. When he spoke, his voice was a murmur. "They're beautiful. I'm surprised you didn't want to try for the whole ceremony, you being the sap you are."

"I didn't want to put you through the torment." Kevin replied softly, taking Aidan's hand and slipping on the ring. "I've got the Force forms ready; we can sit down and fill them out, mark ourselves as an official partnership. That's enough for me; you hate pomp and circumstance, and I already know who I belong to. So unless you really want to make Naomi wear a dress and Billie bake a cake...I belong with you, and I always will. I think that covers it."

He raised his eyes from the ring on Aidan's finger to the light shining in his eyes, drinking in the moment. There had been so many times this year when he thought he'd never be graced with the chance to make this promise. But he hadn't lost Aidan. Not to death, not to treachery, not to fear or sickness. He was here.

Aidan grinned and leaned in for another kiss. He gently took Kevin's ring and slipped it on his finger. The color gleamed richly in the light. "I could handle some cake. Been a while since we had decent sweets. But I can skip forcing Naomi into a dress," his fiance chuckled.

Kevin grinned. "Alright, it's a deal. But *you* tell the rampant mob. Liza's going to cry during the ceremony, you know. And so is Yvonne. They always do."

Aidan pulled a face. "Maybe let's skip it after all..."

Kevin smirked, pulling some semblance of composure back around his shoulders. "Your choice, love. I suppose it's a nice excuse for a party; the crew can always use one."

"I feel like the last month has been one big party," Aidan replied with a chuckle. After a moment of studying the ring on his finger, he glanced up, and there was love and laughter in his eyes. "How about we skip the ceremony and just go right to the reception?"

"I think that sounds admirable." Kevin agreed, kissing Aidan under the sun.

They didn't get out of ceremonial proceedings completely, of course. With a bucket on his head and a plunger in one hand, using a blanket for a cloak, Blake pretended to be a bishop and oversee the wedding a few days later. Kevin practically choked on his glass of whiskey when he turned around and saw the spectacle, torn between laughter and horror at the sight.

"Aidan, you may now kiss the bride!" Blake trilled.

"I am not the bride, Blake you vulgarian plebeian twit. And neither is Aidan," Kevin groaned, to much applause and a round of whoops.

"Oh, shut up and kiss me," Aidan laughed, pulling Kevin in for a deep kiss he couldn't avoid, and didn't particularly want to. Out of the corner of his eye, he watched Naomi shake her head, trying not to grin. As she'd promised, she hit the play button on a media set she'd brought, and the sweetly burning notes of Social Distortion poured out. Mike Ness's rough and wonderful voice cut the air.

I don't care about what they say

I wanna marry you some day!

Around him, his family groaned and rolled their eyes, grinning, as Kevin pulled Aidan in for a kiss.

They cut the cake together, Billie passed the slices out, and their friends laughed. There was music in their little garden. Billie and Topher got the dancing started, and soon they were all at it.

Kevin laughed as Aidan pulled him onto the makeshift dance floor. Clouds were on the horizon, he was sure of it. He had no idea when the storm would break. But they had today. For today, they could dance in the sun.

<u>Acknowledgements</u>

I want to take a few lines to say thanks to Jess, Gene, Martha, Alex and Michael. Without you guys, this series would be more lead balloon than Led Zeppelin. I'm grateful for everything you've done. A shout out to V: thanks for your faith. And, as always, a shout out to my partner. We're doing some damn fine things, my friend.

A Wildcards Playlist, Part 4

- Paul Freeman, 'Against The Ropes', The Lost & Found EP 2005

- The Who, 'Sound Round', Endless Wire, UMPG Publishing 2006

- Journey, 'Keep On Runnin'', Escape, Columbia Records 1981

- The Who, 'Mirror Door', Wire And Glass, Polydor Ltd. (UK) 2006

- American Authors, 'What We Live For', What We Live For, Island Records 2016

- Rusted Root, 'Send Me On My Way', Cruel Sun, Island Mercury Records 1994. Mentioned Chapter 6

- John Parr, 'St. Elmos Fire (Man in Motion)', Saint Elmo's Fire, Atlantic Records 1985. Quoted Chapter 6

- Rick Springfield, 'Walk Like a Man', Tao, 1985 RCA Records

- Arcade Fire, 'Sprawl II (Mountains Beyond Mountains)', The Suburbs Deluxe, Merge Records 2011

- Billy Joel, 'Prelude / Angry Young Man', Turnstiles, Columbia Records 1976

- Social Distortion, 'Winners and Losers', Sex, Love and Rock 'n' Roll, Nitro Records 2004

- Blue Oyster Cult, 'Dancin' In The Ruins', Columbia Records 1986
- Neil Young, 'Rockin' In The Free World (Fahrenheit 9/11 Mix)', Rockin' In The Free World (U.S. CD Single), WMG 2012
- Rising Appalachia, 'Make Magic', Leylines, Rising Appalachia 2019
- Las Cafeteras, 'La Bamba Rebelde', Mediamuv, Coral Music 2012
- Sturgill Simpson, 'Ronin', SOUND & FURY Album, Atlantic Records 2019
- Seo Linn, 'Buy Me Time', Buy Me Time / Bain an Glas, Seo Linn 2018
- Warren Zevon, 'Lawyers, Guns and Money', Excitable Boy, Elektra 1978
- Tom Petty and the Heartbreakers,'Running Man's Bible', Mojo, Reprise Records 2010
- Sturgill Simpson, 'Remember to Breathe', SOUND & FURY Album, Atlantic Records 2019
- Playing For Change, 'All Along The Watchtower', SONGS AROUND THE WORLD 10TH ANNIVERSARY, Playing for Change Foundation 2010
- The Gaslight Anthem, 'Antonia Jane (Acoustic)', The B-Sides, SideOneDummy Records 2014
- The Gaslight Anthem, 'I Coul'da Been A Contender', Sink or Swim, XOXO Records 2012
- The Gaslight Anthem, 'We're Getting A Divorce, You Keep The Diner', Sink or Swim, XOXO Records 2012
- Sturgill Simpson, 'Fastest Horse In Town', SOUND & FURY Album, Atlantic Records 2019
- Social Distortion, 'Reach For The Sky', Greatest Hits, The Bicycle Music Company 2007

- Five Finger Death Punch, 'Wrong Side of Heaven', The Wrong Side Of Heaven And The Righteous Side Of Hell, Volume 1, Eleven Seven Music Group 2014

- Styx, 'Renegade', Come Sail Away – The Styx Anthology, A&M Records 2004

- Four Fists, 'Please Go', MMMMMHMMMMM, Doomtree Records 2014

- Five Finger Death Punch, 'I Refuse', And Justice for None, Eleven Seven Music Group 2017

- Jon Bon Jovi, 'Blaze Of Glory', Blaze of Glory, Vertigo 1990

- Nuttin But Stringz, 'Broken Sorrow', Struggle from the Subway to the Charts, eOne Music International Classics 2006

- Placebo, 'Running Up That Hill', A Place for Us to Dream, Rise Records 2016

- The Gaslight Anthem, 'Get Hurt', Get Hurt, Island Records 2014

- Melodicka Bros, 'Country Roads', https://www.youtube.com/watch?v=u1_dy1EmV6w&list=PL8HyB52xsG8X8qRO0pW6Q10Qcgu25Nw5E&index=34. 2019

- The Goo Goo Dolls, 'Long Way Down', Long Way Down (2015 Remaster), Warner Records Label 2015

- The Brilliance, 'All Is Not Lost', All Is Not Lost, Integrity Music 2017

- Rising Appalachia, 'Speak Out (feat. Ani Difranco)', Leylines, Rising Appalachia 2019

- Lindsey Stirling, 'Shadows', Lindsey Stirling, 2012

- 'Ave Maria', Essential Pavarotti II, Luciano Pavarotti, Decca Records 1991

- Laboratorium Pieśni, 'Lecieli Żurauli', Rosna, Laboratorium Pieśni 2016

- Rising Appalachia, 'Medicine', Wider Circles, Rising Appalachia 2015

- S.J. Tucker, 'Trickster Prayer', Traveling Songs, copyright S.J. Tucker 2015.
- Jack Johnson, 'My Own Two Hands', Sing-A-Longs and Lullabies for the Film Curious George, BMG Rights Management 2006
- Bhi Bhiman, 'Have a Little Faith!', Rhythm and Reason, Boocoo Music 2015
- Indigo Girls, 'Closer to Fine', Indigo Girls, Epic Records 1989
- The Interrupters,'By My Side', Say It Out Loud, Interrupters Music Publishing 1993
- RENT Movie Cast, 'I'll Cover You', RENT: the Soundtrack, Universal Music Corp 1996. Quoted Chapter 26
- Social Distortion, 'Angel's Wings', Sex, Love and Rock 'n' Roll, Universal Music 2004. Quoted Chapter 30
- The Piano Guys, 'It's Gonna Be OKAY', Okay, ATV Music Publishing 2016
- Nimo feat. Daniel Nahmod, 'Planting Seeds: A Song to Live By', Water, Empty Hands Music 2006

<u>A Note From the Logistics Officer:</u>

If you're searching, there are resources.
You don't need to make your journey alone.

Hello folks, Kevin here. Sometimes it seems difficult to find the resources you need. If that's the case, here's a few things that may help.

Cheers

<u>National Suicide Prevention Lifeline</u>

We can all help prevent suicide. The Lifeline provides 24/7, free and confidential support for people in distress, prevention and crisis resources for you or your loved ones, and best practices for professionals.

1-800-273-8255

<u>Crisis Text Line</u>

In a dark place right now? Text HOME to 741741 (in the USA) to connect with a Crisis Counselor. 686868 Canada. 85258 UK.

<u>TTY</u>

Also known as the Treatment Referral Routing Service, this helpline provides 24-hour free and confidential treatment referral and information about mental and/or substance use disorders, prevention, and recovery in English and Spanish.

1-800-487-4889

Website: www.samhsa.gov/find-help/national-helpline

The Daring Way

The Daring Way provides this Referral Network as a public service for those interested in working with helping professionals to improve their mental health.

https://daring.memberclicks.net/search

Point Of Pride

Point of Pride works to benefit trans people in need through gender-affirming support programs that empower them to live more authentically.

https://pointofpride.org/

Trans Lifeline

Trans Lifeline is a trans-led organization that connects trans people to the community, support, and resources they need to survive and thrive.

https://www.translifeline.org/
Hotline: 877-565-8860

Believe Out Loud

Believe Out Loud was created in 2008 to encourage Christian clergy to voice their affirmation for LGBT people. As a program of Intersections International – a non-profit organization and the global social justice ministry of the Collegiate Church of New York, Believe Out Loud has grown into a community of thousands of LGBT people of faith and allies who together create space – literally and spiritually – for all of us to live full, authentic and free lives like we believe all humans should be able to.

http://www.believeoutloud.com

Dignity USA

DignityUSA works for respect and justice for people of all sexual orientations, genders, and gender identities—especially gay, lesbian, bisexual, and transgender persons—in the Catholic Church and the world through education, advocacy, and support.

http://www.dignityusa.org/content/what-dignity

Inside Out Youth Services

The mission of Inside Out is to empower, educate and advocate for lesbian, gay, bisexual, transgender, questioning, queer, intersex, and a spectrum (LGBTQ+) youth from Southern Colorado, primarily El Paso and Teller counties. Inside Out does this by creating safe space, support systems and teaching life skills to all youth in our community and work to make our community safer and more accepting of gender and sexual orientation diversity.

https://www.insideoutys.org/

Lambda Legal

Lambda Legal, a 501(c)(3) nonprofit, is a national organization committed to achieving full recognition of the civil rights of lesbians, gay men, bisexuals, transgender people and everyone living with HIV through impact litigation, education and public policy work.

https://www.lambdalegal.org/

interACT

This group uses innovative strategies to advocate for the human rights of children born with intersex traits.

https://interactadvocates.org/

Transgender American Veterans Association

Founded in 2003, the Transgender American Veterans Association (TAVA) is a 501 (c) 3 organization that acts proactively with other concerned gay, lesbian, bisexual and transgender (GLBT) organizations to ensure that transgender veterans will receive appropriate care for their medical conditions in accordance with the Veterans Health Administration's Customer Service Standards promise to "treat you with courtesy and dignity . . . as the first class citizen that you are." Further, TAVA will help in educating the Department of Veterans Affairs (VA) and the Department of Defense (DoD) on issues regarding fair and equal treatment of transgender and transsexual individuals.

http://transveteran.org/

<u>On the Tightrope: A Loki Devotional</u>

For those of you who found the idea of calling on the god Loki affirming or interesting, I've included this book. On the Tightrope is a collection of poetry, prayer, and prose celebrating and honoring Loki, agent of change and freedom. Written by a Lokean of over a decade, this little collection includes pieces for both general devotees and consorts, as well as beautiful illustrations. Pieces include a prayer to help one feel comfortable in their own skin, a love poem that uses different pronouns for Loki throughout, and more.

https://www.wanderingjotun.com/nonfiction-and-poetry.html

Mutual Aid Disaster Relief

Mutual Aid Disaster Relief is a grassroots disaster relief network based on the principles of solidarity, mutual aid, and autonomous direct action. Semi-autonomous working groups exist within the Mutual Aid Disaster Relief network to help drive certain aspects of their work forward. Some working groups are temporary and are formed around specific needs such as campaign research or location specific organizing. Other working groups are more permanent, such as supplies distribution, medical, animal rescue, environmental, permaculture, and media, communications. Working groups communicate via conference calls, emails, listservs, and/or on the ground and are a point of access where anyone in the network can become more involved in shaping the direction of Mutual Aid Disaster Relief. To get involved with a working group, or to start a new one, contact them at mutualaiddisasterrelief@gmail.com. Read more at https://mutualaiddisasterrelief.org/about/

Seed Savers Exchange

For the last four years, Seed Savers Exchange, in partnership with Seed Matters, has distributed toolkits to over 700 community groups across the United States. These toolkits contained valuable resources that empowered gardeners and community leaders to save seeds, and to share both the seeds and seed saving knowledge with their communities. These community groups hosted seed swaps, started seed libraries, and led educational workshops. They donated seeds to food banks, organized community gardens, and worked with schools to introduce gardening to young students. These passionate gardeners and seed enthusiasts have had a huge impact on their communities, and they are instrumental in spreading the importance of saving and sharing seeds.

https://www.seedsavers.org/csrp

Growing Gardens

Growing Gardens manages more than 535 individual community garden plots across eleven locations in Boulder County. Through this program gardeners have the opportunity to grow their own fresh organic produce. Each garden is managed in partnership with a resident Garden Leader (or multiple Garden Leaders) who serve as valuable resources for the individual gardeners as they navigate the dynamic Colorado growing season.

https://www.growinggardens.org/the-community-garden-program

<u>Other Books by O. E. Tearmann</u>

Aces High, Jokers Wild Novels

The Hands We're Given
Call The Bluff
Raise The Stakes
Aces and Eights
*Draw Dead**

Wildcard Shorts

"Bad Hand"

"Betting Stakes" (*Neon Dreams and Nightmares*)

Other Short Fiction

"Title" (*The Boys of Summer Have Gone*)

*forthcoming

About The Author

O.E. Tearmann lives in the shadow of the Rocky Mountains, in what may become the Co-Wy Grid. They share the house with a brat in fur, a husband and a great many books. Their search engine history may garner them a call from the FBI one day. When they're not living on base 1407, they advocate for a more equitable society and more sustainable agricultural practices, participate in sundry geekdom and do their best to walk their characters' talk.

Read more and download an exclusive free short story at

aceshighjokerswild.com/read-for-free